SIDNEY SHELDON is the author of *The Other Side of Midnight*, *A Stranger in the Mirror*, *Bloodline*, *Rage of Angels*, *Master of the Game*, *If Tomorrow Comes*, *Windmills of the Gods*, *The Sands of Time*, *Memories of Midnight*, *The Doomsday Conspiracy*, *The Stars Shine Down*, *Nothing Lasts Forever* and *Morning, Noon and Night*, all Number One international best-sellers. His first book, *The Naked Face*, was acclaimed by the *New York Times* as 'the best first mystery novel of the year'. Mr Sheldon has won a Tony award for Broadway's *Redhead* and an Academy Award for *The Bachelor and the Bobby Soxer*. *Rage of Angels*, *Master of the Game*, *Windmills of the Gods* and *Memories of Midnight* have been made into highly successful television miniseries.

He has written the screenplays for twenty-three motion pictures, including *Easter Parade* (with Judy Garland) and *Annie Get Your Gun*. He also created four long-running television series, including *Hart to Hart* and *I Dream of Jeannie*, which he produced and directed. Sidney Sheldon lives in southern California.

For more about Sidney Sheldon, see his website at http://www.sidneysheldon.com

SIDNEY SHELDON

NOTHING LASTS FOREVER

MORNING, NOON AND NIGHT

HarperCollins*Publishers*

This omnibus edition published in 1999 by
HarperCollins*Publishers*

HarperCollins*Publishers*
77-85 Fulham Palace Road,
Hammersmith, London W6 8JB

Morning, Noon and Night copyright © The
Sydney Sheldon Family Limited Partnership 1995

Nothing Lasts Forever copyright © Sidney Sheldon 1994

The Author asserts the moral right to
be identified as the author of this work

ISBN 0 261 67259 2

Printed and bound in Great Britain by
Creative Print and Design (Wales), Ebbw Vale

To Anastasia and Roderick Mann,
with love

The author wishes to express his deep appreciation
to the many doctors, nurses, and medical technicians
who were generous enough
to share their expertise with him.

What cannot be cured with medicaments is cured
by the knife, what the knife cannot cure
is cured with the searing iron, and whatever
this cannot cure must be considered incurable.

HIPPOCRATES, 5th century B.C.

There are three classes of human beings: men,
women, and women physicians.   SIR WILLIAM OSLER

PROLOGUE

San Francisco
Spring, 1995

District Attorney Carl Andrews was in a fury. 'What the hell is going on here?' he demanded. 'We have three doctors living together and working at the same hospital. One of them almost gets an entire hospital closed down, the second one kills a patient for a million dollars, and the third one is murdered.'

Andrews stopped to take a deep breath. 'And they're all women! Three goddam women doctors! The media is treating them like celebrities. They're all over the tube. *60 Minutes* did a segment on them. Barbara Walters did a special on them. I can't pick up a newspaper or magazine without seeing their pictures, or reading about them. Two to one, Hollywood is going to make a movie about them, and they'll turn the bitches into some kind of heroines! I wouldn't be surprised if the government put their faces on postage stamps, like Presley. Well, by God, I won't have it!' He slammed a fist down against the photograph of a woman on the cover of *Time* magazine. The caption read: *Dr Paige Taylor— Angel of Mercy or the Devil's Disciple?*

'Dr Paige Taylor.' The district attorney's voice was filled with disgust. He turned to Gus Venable, his chief prosecuting attorney. 'I'm handing this trial over to you, Gus. I want a conviction. Murder One. The gas chamber.'

'Don't worry,' Gus Venable said quietly. 'I'll see to it.'

Sitting in the courtroom watching Dr Paige Taylor, Gus Venable thought: *She's jury-proof.* Then he smiled to himself. *No one is jury-proof.* She was tall and slender, with eyes that were a startling dark brown in her pale face. A disinterested observer would have dismissed her as an attractive woman. A more observant one would have noticed something else—that all the different phases of her life coexisted in her. There was the happy excitement of the child, superimposed onto the shy uncertainty of the adolescent and the wisdom and pain of the woman. There was a look of innocence about her. *She's the kind of girl*, Gus Venable thought cynically, *a man would be proud to take home to his mother. If his mother had a taste for cold-blooded killers.*

There was an almost eerie sense of remoteness in her eyes, a look that said that Dr Paige Taylor had retreated deep inside herself to a different place, a different time, far from the cold, sterile courtroom where she was trapped.

The trial was taking place in the venerable old San Francisco Hall of Justice on Bryant Street. The building, which housed the Superior Court and County

Jail, was a forbidding-looking edifice, seven stories high, made of square gray stone. Visitors arriving at the courthouse were funneled through electronic security checkpoints. Upstairs, on the third floor, was the Superior Court. In Courtroom 121, where murder trials were held, the judge's bench stood against the rear wall, with an American flag behind it. To the left of the bench was the jury box, and in the center were two tables separated by an aisle, one for the prosecuting attorney, the other for the defense attorney.

The courtroom was packed with reporters and the type of spectators attracted to fatal highway accidents and murder trials. As murder trials went, this one was spectacular. Gus Venable, the prosecuting attorney, was a show in himself. He was a burly man, larger than life, with a mane of gray hair, a goatee, and the courtly manner of a Southern plantation owner. He had never been to the South. He had an air of vague bewilderment and the brain of a computer. His trademark, summer and winter, was a white suit, with an old-fashioned stiff-collar shirt.

Paige Taylor's attorney, Alan Penn, was Venable's opposite, a compact, energetic shark, who had built a reputation for racking up acquittals for his clients.

The two men had faced each other before, and their relationship was one of grudging respect and total mistrust. To Venable's surprise, Alan Penn had come to see him the week before the trial was to begin.

'I came here to do you a favor, Gus.'

Beware of defense attorneys bearing gifts. 'What did you have in mind, Alan?'

3

'Now understand—I haven't discussed this with my client yet, but suppose—just suppose—I could persuade her to plead guilty to a reduced charge and save the State the cost of a trial?'

'Are you asking me to plea-bargain?'

'Yes.'

Gus Venable reached down to his desk, searching for something. 'I can't find my damn calendar. Do you know what the date is?'

'June first. Why?'

'For a minute there, I thought it must be Christmas already, or you wouldn't be asking for a present like that.'

'Gus . . .'

Venable leaned forward in his chair. 'You know, Alan, ordinarily, I'd be inclined to go along with you. Tell you the truth, I'd like to be in Alaska fishing right now. But the answer is no. You're defending a cold-blooded killer who murdered a helpless patient for his money. I'm demanding the death penalty.'

'I think she's innocent, and I—'

Venable gave a short, explosive laugh. 'No, you don't. And neither does anyone else. It's an open-and-shut case. Your client is as guilty as Cain.'

'Not until the jury says so, Gus.'

'They will.' He paused. 'They will.'

After Alan Penn left, Gus Venable sat there thinking about their conversation. Penn's coming to him was a sign of weakness. Penn knew there was no chance he could win the trial. Gus Venable thought about the irrefutable evidence he had, and the witnesses he was going to call, and he was satisfied.

4

There was no question about it. Dr Paige Taylor was going to the gas chamber.

It had not been easy to impanel a jury. The case had occupied the headlines for months. The cold-bloodedness of the murder had created a tidal wave of anger.

The presiding judge was Vanessa Young, a tough, brilliant black jurist rumored to be the next nominee for the United States Supreme Court. She was not known for being patient with lawyers, and she had a quick temper. There was an adage among San Francisco trial lawyers: *If your client is guilty, and you're looking for mercy, stay away from Judge Young's courtroom.*

The day before the start of the trial, Judge Young had summoned the two attorneys to her chambers.

'We're going to set some ground rules, gentlemen. Because of the serious nature of this trial, I'm willing to make certain allowances to make sure that the defendant gets a fair trial. But I'm warning both of you not to try to take advantage of that. Is that clear?'

'Yes, your honor.'

'Yes, your honor.'

Gus Venable was finishing his opening statement. 'And so ladies and gentlemen of the jury, the State will prove—yes, prove beyond a reasonable doubt—that Dr Paige Taylor killed her patient, John Cronin. And not only did she commit murder,

5

she did it for money . . . a lot of money. She killed John Cronin for one million dollars.

'Believe me, after you've heard all the evidence, you will have no trouble in finding Dr Paige Taylor guilty of murder in the first degree. Thank you.'

The jury sat in silence, unmoved but expectant.

Gus Venable turned to the judge. 'If it please your honor I would like to call Gary Williams as the State's first witness.'

When the witness was sworn in, Gus Venable said, 'You're an orderly at Embarcadero County Hospital?'

'Yes, that's right.'

'Were you working in Ward Three when John Cronin was brought in last year?'

'Yes.'

'Can you tell us who the doctor in charge of his case was?'

'Dr Taylor.'

'How would you characterize the relationship between Dr Taylor and John Cronin?'

'Objection!' Alan Penn was on his feet. 'He's calling for a conclusion from the witness.'

'Sustained.'

'Let me phrase it another way. Did you ever hear any conversations between Dr Taylor and John Cronin?'

'Oh, sure. I couldn't help it. I worked that ward all the time.'

'Would you describe those conversations as friendly?'

'No, sir.'

'Really? Why do you say that?'

'Well, I remember the first day Mr Cronin was brought in, and Dr Taylor started to examine him, he said to keep her . . .' He hesitated. 'I don't know if I can repeat his language.'

'Go ahead, Mr Williams. I don't think there are any children in this courtroom.'

'Well, he told her to keep her fucking hands off him.'

'He said *that* to Dr Taylor?'

'Yes, sir.'

'Please tell the court what else you may have seen or heard.'

'Well, he always called her "that bitch." He didn't want her to go near him. Whenever she came into his room, he would say things like "Here comes that bitch again!" and "Tell that bitch to leave me alone" and "Why don't they get me a *real* doctor?"'

Gus Venable paused to look over to where Dr Taylor was seated. The jurors' eyes followed him. Venable shook his head, as though saddened, then turned back to the witness. 'Did Mr Cronin seem to you to be a man who wanted to give a million dollars to Dr Taylor?'

Alan Penn was on his feet again. 'Objection! He's calling for an opinion again.'

Judge Young said, 'Overruled. The witness may answer the question.'

Alan Penn looked at Paige Taylor and sank back in his seat.

'Hell, no. He hated her guts.'

* * *

7

Dr Arthur Kane was in the witness box.

Gus Venable said, 'Dr Kane, you were the staff doctor in charge when it was discovered that John Cronin was mur—' He looked at Judge Young. '. . . killed by insulin being introduced into his IV. Is that correct?'

'It is.'

'And you subsequently discovered that Dr Taylor was responsible.'

'That's correct.'

'Dr Kane, I'm going to show you the official hospital death form signed by Dr Taylor.' He picked up a paper and handed it to Kane. 'Would you read it aloud, please?'

Kane began to read. '"John Cronin. Cause of Death: Respiratory arrest occurred as a complication of myocardial infarction occurring as a complication of pulmonary embolus."'

'And in layman's language?'

'The report says that the patient died of a heart attack.'

'And that paper is signed by Dr Taylor?'

'Yes.'

'Dr Kane, was that the true cause of John Cronin's death?'

'No. The insulin injection caused his death.'

'So, Dr Taylor administered a fatal dose of insulin and then falsified the report?'

'Yes.'

'And you reported it to Dr Wallace, the hospital administrator, who then reported it to the authorities.'

'Yes. I felt it was my duty.' His voice rang with righteous indignation. 'I'm a doctor. I don't believe in taking the life of another human being under any circumstances.'

The next witness called was John Cronin's widow. Hazel Cronin was in her late thirties, with flaming red hair, and a voluptuous figure that her plain black dress failed to conceal.

Gus Venable said, 'I know how painful this is for you, Mrs Cronin, but I must ask you to describe to the jury your relationship with your late husband.'

The widow Cronin dabbed at her eyes with a large lace handkerchief. 'John and I had a loving marriage. He was a wonderful man. He often told me I had brought him the only real happiness he had ever known.'

'How long were you married to John Cronin?'

'Two years, but John always said it was like two years in heaven.'

'Mrs Cronin, did your husband ever discuss Dr Taylor with you? Tell you what a great doctor he thought she was? Or how helpful she had been to him? Or how much he liked her?'

'He never mentioned her.'

'Never?'

'Never.'

'Did John ever discuss cutting you and your brothers out of his will?'

'Absolutely not. He was the most generous man in the world. He always told me that there was nothing I couldn't have, and that when he died . . .' her voice broke, '. . . that when he died, I would be a wealthy woman, and . . .' She could not go on.

Judge Young said, 'We'll have a fifteen-minute recess.'

Seated in the back of the courtroom, Jason Curtis was filled with anger. He could not believe what the witnesses were saying about Paige. *This is the woman I love*, he thought. *The woman I'm going to marry.*

Immediately after Paige's arrest, Jason Curtis had gone to visit her in jail.

'We'll fight this,' he assured her. 'I'll get you the best criminal lawyer in the country.' A name immediately sprang to mind. *Alan Penn.* Jason had gone to see him.

'I've been following the case in the papers,' Penn said. 'The press has already tried and convicted her of murdering John Cronin for a bundle. What's more she admits she killed him.'

'I know her,' Jason Curtis told him. 'Believe me, there's no way Paige could have done what she did, for money.'

'Since she admits she killed him,' Penn said, 'what we're dealing with here then is euthanasia. Mercy killings are against the law in California, as in most states, but there are a lot of mixed feelings about them. I can make a pretty good case for Florence Nightingale listening to a Higher Voice and all that shit, but the problem is that your lady love killed a patient who left her a million dollars in his will. Which came first, the chicken or the egg? Did she know about the million before she killed him, or after?'

'Paige didn't know a thing about the money,' Jason said firmly.

Penn's tone was noncommittal. 'Right. It was just a happy coincidence. The DA is calling for Murder One, and he wants the death penalty.'

'Will you take the case?'

Penn hesitated. It was obvious that Jason Curtis believed in Dr Taylor. *The way Samson believed in Delilah.* He looked at Jason and thought: *I wonder if the poor son of a bitch had a haircut and doesn't know it.*

Jason was waiting for an answer.

'I'll take the case, as long as you know it's all uphill. It's going to be a tough one to win.'

Alan Penn's statement turned out to be over-optimistic.

When the trial resumed the following morning, Gus Venable called a string of new witnesses.

A nurse was on the stand. 'I heard John Cronin say "I know I'll die on the operating table. You're going to kill me. I hope they get you for murder."'

An attorney, Roderick Pelham, was on the stand. Gus Venable said, 'When you told Dr Taylor about the million dollars from John Cronin's estate, what did she say?'

'She said something like "It seems unethical. He was my patient."'

'She admitted it was unethical?'

'Yes.'

'But she agreed to take the money?'

'Oh yes. Absolutely.'

*   *   *

Alan Penn was cross-examining.

'Mr Pelham, was Dr Taylor expecting your visit?'

'Why, no, I . . .'

'You didn't call her and say, "John Cronin left you one million dollars"?'

'No, I . . .'

'So when you told her, you were actually face to face with her?'

'Yes.'

'In a position to see her reaction to the news.'

'Yes.'

'And when you told her about the money, how did she react?'

'Well—she—she seemed surprised, but . . .'

'Thank you Mr Pelham. That's all.'

The trial was now in its fourth week. The spectators and press had found the prosecuting attorney and defense attorney fascinating to watch. Gus Venable was dressed in white and Alan Penn in black, and the two of them had moved around the courtroom like players in a deadly, choreographed game of chess, with Paige Taylor the sacrificial pawn.

Gus Venable was tying up the loose ends.

'If the court please, I would like to call Alma Rogers to the witness stand.'

When his witness was sworn in, Venable said, 'Mrs Rogers, what is your occupation?'

'It's *Miss* Rogers.'

'I do beg your pardon.'

'I work at the Corniche Travel Agency.'

'Your agency books tours to various countries and

makes hotel reservations and handles other accommodations for your clients?'

'Yes, sir.'

'I want you to take a look at the defendant. Have you ever seen her before?'

'Oh, yes. She came into our travel agency two or three years ago.'

'And what did she want?'

'She said she was interested in a trip to London and Paris, and, I believe, Venice.'

'Did she ask about package tours?'

'Oh, no. She said she wanted everything first-class—plane, hotel. And I believe she was interested in chartering a yacht.'

The courtroom was hushed. Gus Venable walked over to the prosecutor's table and held up some folders. 'The police found these brochures in Dr Taylor's apartment. These are travel itineraries to Paris and London and Venice, brochures for expensive hotels and airlines, and one listing the cost of chartering a private yacht.'

There was a loud murmur from the courtroom.

The prosecutor had opened one of the brochures.

'Here are some of the yachts listed for charter.' He read aloud. 'The *Christina O* . . . twenty-six thousand dollars a week plus ship's expenses . . . the *Resolute Time*, twenty-four thousand five hundred dollars a week . . . the *Lucky Dream*, twenty-seven thousand three hundred dollars a week.' He looked up. 'There's a check mark after the *Lucky Dream*. Paige Taylor had already selected the twenty-seven thousand three hundred a week yacht. She just hadn't selected her victim yet.'

'We'd like to have these marked Exhibit A.' Venable turned to Alan Penn and smiled. Alan Penn looked at Paige. She was staring down at the table, her face pale. 'Your witness.'

Penn rose to his feet, stalling, thinking fast.

'How is the travel business these days, Miss Rogers?'

'I beg your pardon?'

'I asked how business was. Is Corniche a large travel agency?'

'It's quite large, yes.'

'I imagine a lot of people come in to inquire about trips.'

'Oh, yes.'

'Would you say five or six people a day?'

'Oh, no!' Her voice was indignant. 'We talk to as many as fifty people a day about travel arrangements.'

'Fifty people a day?' He sounded impressed. 'And the day we're talking about was two or three years ago. If you multiply fifty by nine hundred days, that's roughly forty-five thousand people.'

'I suppose so.'

'And yet, out of all those people, you remembered Dr Taylor. Why is that?'

'Well, she and her two friends were so excited about taking a trip to Europe. I thought it was lovely. They were like schoolgirls. Oh, yes. I remember them very clearly, particularly because they didn't look like they could afford a yacht.'

'I see. I suppose everyone who comes in and asks for a brochure goes away on a trip?'

'Well, of course not. But —'

'Dr Taylor didn't actually *book* a trip, did she?'

14

'Well, no. Not with us. She—'

'Nor with anyone else. She merely asked to see some brochures.'

'Yes. She—'

'That's not the same as *going* to Paris or London, is it?'

'Well, no, but—'

'Thank you. You may step down.'

Venable turned to Judge Young. 'I would like to call Dr Benjamin Wallace to the stand . . .'

'Dr Wallace, you're in charge of administration at Embarcadero County Hospital?'

'Yes.'

'So, of course, you're familiar with Dr Taylor and her work?'

'Yes, I am.'

'Were you surprised to learn that Dr Taylor was indicted for murder?'

Penn was on his feet, 'Objection your honor. Dr Wallace's answer would be irrelevant.'

'If I may explain,' interrupted Venable. 'It could be very relevant if you'll just let me . . .'

'Well, let's see what develops,' said Judge Young. 'But no nonsense, Mr Venable.'

'Let me approach the question differently,' continued Venable. 'Dr Wallace, every physician is required to take the Hippocratic oath, is that not so?'

'Yes.'

'And part of that oath is . . . ,' the prosecutor read

from a paper in his hand, '"That I shall abstain from every act of mischief or corruption"?'

'Yes.'

'Was there anything Dr Taylor did in the past that made you believe she was capable of breaking her Hippocratic oath?'

'Objection.'

'Overruled.'

'Yes, there was.'

'Please explain what it was.'

'We had a patient who Dr Taylor decided needed a blood transfusion. His family refused to grant permission.'

'And what happened?'

'Dr Taylor went ahead and gave the patient the transfusion anyway.'

'Is that legal?'

'Absolutely not. Not without a court order.'

'And then what did Dr Taylor do?'

'She obtained the court order afterward, and changed the date on it.'

'So she performed an illegal act, and falsified the hospital records to cover it up?'

'That is correct.'

Alan Penn glanced over at Paige, furious. *What the hell else has she kept from me?* he wondered.

If the spectators were searching for any tell-tale sign of emotion on Paige Taylor's face, they were disappointed.

Cold as ice, the foreman of the jury was thinking.

Gus Venable turned to the bench. 'Your honor, as you know, one of the witnesses I had hoped to call is a Dr Lawrence Barker. Unfortunately he is still suffering from the effects of a stroke and is unable to be in this courtroom to testify. Instead I will now question some of the hospital staff who have worked with Dr Barker.'

Penn stood up. 'I object. I don't see the relevance. Dr Barker is not here, nor is Dr Barker on trial here. If . . .'

Venable interrupted. 'Your honor, I assure you that my line of questioning is very relevant to the testimony we have just heard. It also has to do with the defendant's competency as a doctor.'

Judge Young said skeptically, 'We'll see. This is a courtroom, not a river. I won't stand for any fishing expeditions. You may call your witnesses.'

'Thank you.'

Gus Venable turned to the bailiff. 'I would like to call Dr Mathew Peterson.'

An elegant-looking man in his sixties approached the witness box. He was sworn in, and when he took his seat, Gus Venable said, 'Dr Peterson, how long have you worked at Embarcadero County Hospital?'

'Eight years.'

'And what is your specialty?'

'I'm a cardiac surgeon.'

'And during the years you've been at Embarcadero County Hospital, did you ever have occasion to work with Dr Lawrence Barker?'

'Oh, yes. Many times.'

'What was your opinion of him?'

'The same as everyone else's. Aside, possibly, from DeBakey and Cooley, Dr Barker is the best heart surgeon in the world.'

'Were you present in the operating room on the

morning that Dr Taylor operated on a patient named . . .' he pretended to consult a slip of paper. '. . . Lance Kelly?'

The witness's tone changed. 'Yes, I was there.'

'Would you describe what happened that morning?'

Dr Peterson said reluctantly, 'Well, things started to go wrong. We began losing the patient.'

'When you say, "losing the patient . . ."'

'His heart stopped. We were trying to bring him back, and . . .'

'Had Dr Barker been sent for?'

'Yes.'

'And did he come into the operating room while the operation was going on?'

'Toward the end. Yes. But it was too late ιο do anything. We were unable to revive the patienι.'

'And did Dr Barker say anything to Dr Taylor at that time?'

'Well, we were all pretty upset, and . . .'

'I asked you if Dr Barker said anything to Dr Taylor.'

'Yes.'

'And what did Dr Barker say?'

There was a pause, and in the middle of the pause, there was a crack of thunder outside, like the voice of God. A moment later, the storm broke, nailing raindrops to the roof of the courthouse.

'Dr Barker said, "You killed him."'

The spectators were in an uproar. Judge Young slammed her gavel down. 'That's enough! Do you people live in caves? One more outburst like that and you'll all be standing outside in the rain.'

Gus Venable waited for the noise to die down. In

the hushed silence he said, 'Are you sure that's what Dr Barker said to Dr Taylor? "You killed him."'

'Yes.'

'And you have testified that Dr Barker was a man whose medical opinion was valued?'

'Oh, yes.'

'Thank you. That's all, doctor.' He turned to Alan Penn. 'Your witness.'

Penn rose and approached the witness box.

'Dr Peterson, I've never watched an operation, but I imagine there's enormous tension, especially when it's something as serious as a heart operation.'

'There's a great deal of tension.'

'At a time like that, how many people are in the room? Three or four?'

'Oh, no. Always half a dozen or more.'

'Really?'

'Yes. There are usually two surgeons, one assisting, sometimes two anesthesiologists, a scrub nurse, and at least one circulating nurse.'

'I see. Then there must be a lot of noise and excitement going on. People calling out instructions and so on.'

'Yes.'

'And I understand that it's a common practice for music to be playing during an operation.'

'It is.'

'When Dr Barker came in and saw that Lance Kelly was dying, that probably added to the confusion.'

'Well, everybody was pretty busy trying to save the patient.'

'Making a lot of noise?'

'There was plenty of noise, yes.'

'And yet, in all that confusion and noise, and over the music, you could hear Dr Barker say that Dr Taylor had killed the patient. With all that excitement, you could have been wrong, couldn't you?'

'No, sir. I could not be wrong.'

'What makes you so sure?'

Dr Peterson sighed. 'Because I was standing right next to Dr Barker when he said it.'

There was no graceful way out.

'No more questions.'

The case was falling apart, and there was nothing he could do about it. It was about to get worse.

Denise Berry took the witness stand.

'You're a nurse at Embarcadero County Hospital?'

'Yes.'

'How long have you worked there?'

'Five years.'

'During that time, did you ever hear any conversations between Dr Taylor and Dr Barker?'

'Sure. Lots of times.'

'Can you repeat some of them?'

Nurse Berry looked at Dr Taylor and hesitated. 'Well, Dr Barker could be very sharp . . .'

'I didn't ask you that, Nurse Berry. I asked you to tell us some specific things you heard him say to Dr Taylor.'

There was a long pause. 'Well, one time he said she was incompetent, and . . .'

Gus Venable put on a show of surprise. 'You heard Dr Barker say that Dr Taylor was incompetent?'

'Yes, sir. But he was always . . .'

'What other comments did you hear him make about Dr Taylor?'

The witness was reluctant to speak. 'I really can't remember.'

'Miss Berry, you're under oath.'

'Well, once I heard him say . . .' The rest of the sentence was a mumble.

'We can't hear you. Speak up, please. You heard him say what?'

'He said he . . . he wouldn't let Dr Taylor operate on his dog.'

There was a collective gasp from the courtroom.

'But I'm sure he only meant . . .'

'I think we can all assume that Dr Barker meant what he said.'

All eyes were fixed on Paige Taylor.

The prosecutor's case against Paige seemed overwhelming. Yet Alan Penn had the reputation of being a master magician in the courtroom. Now it was his turn to present the defendant's case. Could he pull another rabbit out of his hat?

Paige Taylor was on the witness stand, being questioned by Alan Penn. This was the moment everyone had been waiting for.

'John Cronin was a patient of yours, Dr Taylor?'

'Yes, he was.'

'And what were your feelings toward him?'

'I liked him. He knew how ill he was, but he was

21

very courageous. He had surgery for a cardiac tumor.'

'You performed the heart surgery?'

'Yes.'

'And what did you find during the operation?'

'When we opened up his chest, we found that he had melanoma that had metastasized.'

'In other words, cancer that had spread throughout his body.'

'Yes. It had metastasized throughout the lymph glands.'

'Meaning that there was no hope for him? No heroic measures that could bring him back to health?'

'None.'

'John Cronin was put on life-support systems?'

'That's correct.'

'Dr Taylor, did you deliberately administer a fatal dose of insulin to end John Cronin's life?'

'I did.'

There was a sudden buzz in the courtroom.

She's really a cool one, Gus Venable thought. *She makes it sound as though she gave him a cup of tea.*

'Would you tell the jury why you ended John Cronin's life?'

'Because he asked me to. He begged me to. He sent for me in the middle of the night, in terrible pain. The medications we were giving him were no longer working.' Her voice was steady. 'He said he didn't want to suffer anymore. His death was only a few days away. He pleaded with me to end it for him. I did.'

'Doctor, did you have any reluctance to let him die? Any feelings of guilt?'

22

Dr Paige Taylor shook her head. 'No. If you could have seen . . . There was simply no point to letting him go on suffering.'

'How did you administer the insulin?'

'I injected it into his IV.'

'And did that cause him any additional pain?'

'No. He simply drifted off to sleep.'

Gus Venable was on his feet. 'Objection! I think the defendant means he drifted off to his death! I —'

Judge Young slammed down her gavel. 'Mr Venable, you're out of order. You'll have your chance to cross-examine the witness. Sit down.'

The prosecutor looked over at the jury, shook his head, and took his seat.

'Dr Taylor, when you administered the insulin to John Cronin, were you aware that he had put you in his will for one million dollars?'

'No. I was stunned when I learned about it.'

Her nose should be growing, Gus Venable thought.

'You never discussed money or gifts at any time, or asked John Cronin for anything?'

A faint flush came to her cheeks. 'Never!'

'But you were on friendly terms with him?'

'Yes. When a patient is that ill, the doctor-patient relationship changes. We discussed his business problems and his family problems.'

'But you had no reason to expect anything from him?'

'No.'

'He left that money to you because he had grown to respect you and trust you. Thank you, Dr Taylor.' Penn turned to Gus Venable. 'Your witness.'

23

As Penn returned to the defense table, Paige Taylor glanced toward the back of the courtroom. Jason was seated there, trying to look encouraging. Next to him was Honey. A stranger was sitting next to Honey in the seat that Kat should have occupied. *If she were still alive. But Kat was dead*, Paige thought. *I killed her, too.*

Gus Venable rose and slowly shuffled over to the witness box. He glanced at the rows of press. Every seat was filled, and the reporters were all busily scribbling. *I'm going to give you something to write about*, Venable thought.

He stood in front of the defendant for a long moment, studying her. Then he said casually, 'Dr Taylor . . . was John Cronin the first patient you murdered at Embarcadero County Hospital?'

Alan Penn was on his feet, furious. 'Your honor, I—'

Judge Young had already slammed her gavel down. 'Objection sustained!' She turned to the two attorneys. 'There will be a fifteen-minute recess. I want to see counsel in my chambers.'

When the two attorneys were in her chambers, Judge Young turned to Gus Venable. 'You *did* go to law school, didn't you, Gus?'

'I'm sorry, your honor. I—'

'Did you see a tent out there?'

'I beg your pardon?'

Her voice was a whiplash. 'My courtroom is not a circus, and I don't intend to let you turn it into one. How dare you ask an inflammatory question like that!'

24

'I apologize, your honor. I'll rephrase the question and—'

'You'll do more than that!' Judge Young snapped. 'You'll rephrase your attitude. I'm warning you, you pull one more stunt like that and I'll declare a mistrial.'

'Yes, your honor.'

When they returned to the courtroom, Judge Young said to the jury, 'The jury will completely disregard the prosecutor's last question.' She turned to the prosecutor. 'You may go on.'

Gus Venable walked back to the witness box. 'Dr Taylor, you must have been very surprised when you were informed that the man you murdered left you one million dollars.'

Alan Penn was on his feet. 'Objection!'

'Sustained.' Judge Young turned to Venable. 'You're trying my patience.'

'I apologize, your honor.' He turned back to the witness. 'You must have been on *very* friendly terms with your patient. I mean, it isn't every day that an almost complete stranger leaves us a million dollars, is it?'

Paige Taylor flushed slightly. 'Our friendship was in the context of a doctor-patient relationship.'

'Wasn't it a little more than that? A man doesn't cut his beloved wife and family out of his will and leave a million dollars to a stranger without some kind of persuasion. Those talks you claimed to have had with him about his business problems . . .'

Judge Young leaned forward and said warningly, 'Mr Venable . . .' The prosecutor raised his hands

25

in a gesture of surrender. He turned back to the defendant. 'So you and John Cronin had a friendly chat. He told you personal things about himself, and he liked you and respected you. Would you say that's a fair summation, doctor?'

'Yes.'

'And for doing that he gave you a million dollars?'

Paige looked out at the courtroom. She said nothing. She had no answer.

Venable started to walk back toward the prosecutor's table, then suddenly turned to face the defendant again.

'Dr Taylor, you testified earlier that you had no idea that John Cronin was going to leave you any money, or that he was going to cut his family out of his will.'

'That's correct.'

'How much does a resident doctor make at Embarcadero County Hospital?'

Alan Penn was on his feet. 'Objection! I don't see —'

'It's a proper question. The witness may answer.'

'Thirty-eight thousand dollars a year.'

Venable said sympathetically, 'That's not very much these days, is it? And out of that, there are deductions and taxes and living expenses. That wouldn't leave enough to take a luxury vacation trip, say, to London or Paris or Venice, would it?'

'I suppose not.'

'No. So you didn't plan to take a vacation like that, because you knew you couldn't afford it.'

'That's correct.'

Alan Penn was on his feet again. 'Your honor . . .'

Judge Young turned to the prosecutor. 'Where is this leading, Mr Venable?'

'I just want to establish that the defendant could not plan a luxury trip without getting the money from someone.'

'She's already answered the question.'

Alan Penn knew he had to do something. His heart wasn't in it, but he approached the witness box with all the good cheer of a man who had just won the lottery.

'Dr Taylor, do you remember picking up these travel brochures?'

'Yes.'

'Were you planning to go to Europe or to charter a yacht?'

'Of course not. It was all sort of a joke, an impossible dream. My friends and I thought it would lift our spirits. We were very tired, and . . . it seemed like a good idea at the time.' Her voice trailed off.

Alan Penn glanced covertly at the jury. Their faces registered pure disbelief.

Gus Venable was questioning the defendant on re-examination. 'Dr Taylor, are you acquainted with Dr Lawrence Barker?'

She had a sudden memory flash. *I'm going to kill Lawrence Barker. I'll do it slowly. I'll let him suffer first . . . then I'll kill him.* 'Yes. I know Dr Barker.'

'In what connection?'

'Dr Barker and I have often worked together during the past two years.'

'Would you say that he's a competent doctor?'

Alan Penn jumped up from his chair. 'I object, your honor. The witness . . .'

But before he could finish or Judge Young could rule, Paige answered, 'He's more than competent. He's brilliant.'

Penn sank back in his chair, too stunned to speak.

'Would you care to elaborate on that?'

'Dr Barker is one of the most renowned cardio-vascular surgeons in the world. He had a large private practice, but he donated three days a week to Embarcadero County Hospital.'

'So you have a high regard for his judgement in medical matters?'

'Yes.'

'And do you feel he would be capable of judging another doctor's competence?'

Penn willed Paige to say, *I don't know.*

She hesitated. 'Yes.'

Gus Venable turned to the jury. 'You've heard the defendant testify that she had a high regard for Dr Barker's medical judgement. I hope she listened carefully to Dr Barker's judgement about her competence . . . Or the lack of it.'

Alan Penn was on his feet, furious. 'Objection!'

'Sustained.'

But it was too late. The damage had been done.

During the next recess, Alan Penn pulled Jason into the men's room.

'What the hell have you gotten me into?' Penn demanded angrily. 'John Cronin hated her, Barker hated her. I insist on my clients telling me the truth, and the whole truth. That's the only way I can help them. Well, I can't help *her*. Your lady friend has given me a snow job so deep I need skis. Every time she opens her mouth she puts a nail in her coffin. The fucking case is in free fall!'

That afternoon, Jason Curtis went to see Paige.

'You have a visitor, Dr Taylor.'

Jason walked into Paige's cell.

'Paige . . .'

She turned to him, and she was fighting back tears. 'It looks pretty bad, doesn't it?'

Jason forced a smile. 'You know what the man said—It's not over till it's over.'

'Jason, you don't believe that I killed John Cronin for his money, do you? What I did, I did only to help him.'

'I believe you,' Jason said quietly. 'I love you.'

He took her into his arms. *I don't want to lose her*, Jason thought. *I can't. She's the best thing in my life.* 'Everything is going to be all right. I promised you we would be together forever.'

Paige held him close and thought, *Nothing lasts forever. Nothing. How could everything have gone so wrong . . . so wrong . . . so wrong . . .*

Book One

1

San Francisco
July, 1990

'Hunter, Kate.'
  'Here.'
'Taft, Betty Lou.'
'I'm here.'
'Taylor, Paige.'
  'Here.'
They were the only women among the big group of incoming first-year residents gathered in the large, drab auditorium at Embarcadero County Hospital.

Embarcadero County was the oldest hospital in San Francisco, and one of the oldest in the country. During the earthquake of 1989, God had played a joke on the residents of San Francisco and left the hospital standing. It was an ugly complex, occupying more than three square blocks, with buildings of brick and stone, gray with years of accumulated grime.

Inside the front entrance of the main building was a large waiting room, with hard wooden benches for patients and visitors. The walls were flaking from too many decades of coats of paint, and the corridors were worn and uneven from too many thousands of patients in wheelchairs and on crutches and walkers. The entire complex was coated with the stale patina of time.

Embarcadero County Hospital was a city within a city. There were over nine thousand people employed at the hospital, including four hundred staff physicians, one hundred and fifty part-time voluntary physicians, eight hundred residents, and three thousand nurses, plus the technicians, unit aides, and other technical personnel. The upper floors contained a complex of twelve operating rooms, central supply, a bone bank, central scheduling, three emergency wards, an AIDS ward, and over two thousand beds.

Now, on the first day of the arrival of the new residents in July, Dr Benjamin Wallace, the hospital administrator, rose to address them. Wallace was the quintessential politician, a tall, impressive-looking man with small skills and enough charm to have ingratiated his way up to his present position.

'I want to welcome all of you new resident doctors this morning. For the first two years of medical school, you worked with cadavers. In the last two years, you have worked with hospital patients under the supervision of senior doctors. Now, it's *you* who are going to be responsible for your patients. It's an awesome responsibility, and it takes dedication and skill.'

His eyes scanned the auditorium. 'Some of you are planning to go into surgery. Others of you will be going into internal medicine. Each group will be assigned to a senior resident who will explain the daily routine to you. From now on, everything you do could be a matter of life or death.'

They were listening intently, hanging on every word.

'Embarcadero is a county hospital. That means we admit anyone who comes to our door. Most of the patients are indigent. They come here because they can't afford a private hospital. Our emergency rooms are busy twenty-four hours a day. You're going to be overworked and underpaid. In a private hospital, your first year would consist of routine scut work. In the second year, you would be allowed to hand a scalpel to the surgeon, and in your third year, you would be permitted to do some supervised minor surgery. Well, you can forget all that. Our motto here is "Watch one, do one, teach one."

'We're badly understaffed, and the quicker we can get you into the operating rooms, the better. Are there any questions?'

There were a million questions the new residents wanted to ask.

'None? Good. Your first day officially begins tomorrow. You will report to the main reception desk at five-thirty tomorrow morning. Good luck!'

The briefing was over. There was a general exodus toward the doors and the low buzz of excited conversations. The three women found themselves standing together.

'Where are all the other women?'

'I think we're it.'

'It's a lot like medical school, huh? The boys' club. I have a feeling this place belongs to the Dark Ages.'

The person talking was a flawlessly beautiful black woman, nearly six feet tall, large-boned, but

35

intensely graceful. Everything about her, her walk, her carriage, the cool, quizzical look she carried in her eyes, sent out a message of aloofness. 'I'm Kate Hunter. They call me Kat.'

'Paige Taylor.' Young and friendly, intelligent-looking, self-assured.

They turned to the third woman.

'Betty Lou Taft. They call me Honey.' She spoke with a soft Southern accent. She had an open, guile-less face, soft gray eyes, and a warm smile.

'Where are you from?' Kat asked.

'Memphis, Tennessee.'

They looked at Paige. She decided to give them the simple answer. 'Boston.'

'Minneapolis,' Kat said. *That's close enough*, she thought.

Paige said, 'It looks like we're all a long way from home. Where are you staying?'

'I'm at a fleabag hotel,' Kat said. 'I haven't had a chance to look for a place to live.'

Honey said, 'Neither have I.'

Paige brightened. 'I looked at some apartments this morning. One of them was terrific, but I can't afford it. It has three bedrooms . . .'

They stared at one another.

'If the three of us shared . . .' Kat said.

The apartment was in the Marina district, on Filbert Street. It was perfect for them. 3Br/2Ba, nu cpts, lndry, prkg, utils pd. It was furnished in early Sears Roebuck, but it was neat and clean.

When the three women were through inspecting it, Honey said, 'I think it's lovely.'

'So do I!' Kat agreed.

They looked at Paige.

'Let's take it.'

They moved into the apartment that afternoon. The janitor helped them carry their luggage upstairs.

'So you're gonna work at the hospital,' he said. 'Nurses, huh?'

'Doctors,' Kat corrected him.

He looked at her skeptically. 'Doctors? You mean, like *real* doctors?'

'Yes, like real doctors,' Paige told him.

He grunted. 'Tell you the truth, if I needed medical attention, I don't think I'd want a woman examining my body.'

'We'll keep that in mind.'

'Where's the television set?' Kat asked. 'I don't see one.'

'If you want one, you'll have to buy it. Enjoy the apartment, ladies—er, doctors.' He chuckled.

They watched him leave.

Kat said, imitating his voice, 'Nurses, eh?' She snorted. 'Male chauvinist. Well, let's pick out our bedrooms.'

'Any one of them is fine with me,' Honey said softly.

They examined the three bedrooms. The master bedroom was larger than the other two.

Kat said, 'Why don't you take it, Paige? You found this place.'

Paige nodded. 'All right.'

They went to their respective rooms and began to unpack. From her suitcase, Paige carefully removed a framed photograph of a man in his early thirties. He was attractive, wearing black-framed glasses that

37

gave him a scholarly look. Paige put the photograph at her bedside, next to a bundle of letters.

Kat and Honey wandered in. 'How about going out and getting some dinner?'

'I'm ready,' Paige said.

Kat saw the photograph. 'Who's that?'

Paige smiled. 'That's the man I'm going to marry. He's a doctor who works for the World Health Organization. His name is Alfred Turner. He's working in Africa right now, but he's coming to San Francisco so we can be together.'

'Lucky you,' Honey said wistfully. 'He looks nice.'

Paige looked at her. 'Are you involved with anyone?'

'No. I'm afraid I don't have much luck with men.'

Kat said, 'Maybe your luck will change at Embarcadero.'

The three of them had dinner at Tarantino's, not far from their apartment building. During dinner they chatted about their backgrounds and lives, but there was a restraint to their conversation, a holding back. They were three strangers, probing, cautiously getting to know one another.

Honey spoke very little. *There's a shyness about her*, Paige thought. *She's vulnerable. Some man in Memphis probably broke her heart.*

Paige looked at Kat. *Self-confident. Great dignity. I like the way she speaks. You can tell she came from a good family.*

Meanwhile, Kat was studying Paige. *A rich girl who never had to work for anything in her life. She's gotten by on her looks.*

Honey was looking at the two of them. *They're so confident, so sure of themselves. They're going to have an easy time of it.*

They were all mistaken.

When they returned to their apartment, Paige was too excited to sleep. She lay in bed, thinking about the future. Outside her window, in the street, there was the sound of a car crash, and then people shouting, and in Paige's mind it dissolved into the memory of African natives yelling and chanting, and guns being fired. She was transported back in time, to the small jungle village in East Africa, caught in the middle of a deadly tribal war.

Paige was terrified. 'They're going to kill us!'

Her father took her in his arms. 'They won't harm us, darling. We're here to help them. They know we're their friends.'

And without warning, the chief of one of the tribes had burst into their hut . . .

Honey lay in bed thinking, *This is sure a long way from Memphis, Tennessee, Betty Lou. I guess I can never go back there. Never again.* She could hear the sheriff's voice saying to her, 'Out of respect for his family, we're going to list the death of the Reverend Douglas Lipton as a "suicide for reasons unknown," but I would suggest that you get the fuck out of this town fast, and stay out . . .'

*　　　*　　　*

39

Kat was staring out the window of her bedroom, listening to the sounds of the city. A voice inside her head whispered, *You made it . . . you made it . . . I showed them all they were wrong. You want to be a doctor? A black woman doctor? And the rejections from medical schools. 'Thank you for sending us your application. Unfortunately our enrollment is complete at this time.'*

'In view of your background, perhaps we might suggest that you would be happier at a smaller university.'

She had top grades, but out of twenty-five schools she had applied to, only one had accepted her. The dean of the school had said, 'In these days, it's nice to see someone who comes from a normal, decent background.'

If he had only known the terrible truth.

2

At five-thirty the following morning, when the new residents checked in, members of the hospital staff were standing by to guide them to their various assignments. Even at that early hour, the bedlam had begun.

The patients had been coming in all night, arriving in ambulances, and police cars, and on foot. The staff called them the 'F and J's'—the flotsam and jetsam that streamed into the emergency rooms, broken and bleeding, victims of shootings and stabbings and automobile accidents, the wounded in flesh and spirit, the homeless and the unwanted, the ebb and flow of humanity that streamed through the dark sewers of every large city.

There was a pervasive feeling of organized chaos, frenetic movements and shrill sounds and dozens of unexpected crises that all had to be attended to at once.

The new residents stood in a protective huddle, getting attuned to their new environment, listening to the arcane sounds around them.

Paige, Kat, and Honey were waiting in the corridor when a senior resident approached them. 'Which one of you is Dr Taft?'

Honey looked up and said, 'I am.'

The resident smiled and held out his hand. 'It's an honor to meet you. I've been asked to look out for you. Our chief of staff says that you have the highest medical school grades this hospital has ever seen. We're delighted to have you here.'

Honey smiled, embarrassed. 'Thank you.'

Kat and Paige looked at Honey in astonishment. *I wouldn't have guessed she was that brilliant*, Paige thought.

'You're planning to go into internal medicine, Dr Taft?'

'Yes.'

The resident turned to Kat. 'Dr Hunter?'

'Yes.'

'You're interested in neurosurgery.'

'I am.'

He consulted a list. 'You'll be assigned to Dr Lewis.'

The resident looked over at Paige. 'Dr Taylor?'

'Yes.'

'You're going into cardiac surgery.'

'That's right.'

'Fine. We'll assign you and Dr Hunter to surgical rounds. You can report to the head nurse's office. Margaret Spencer. Down the hall.'

'Thank you.'

Paige looked at the others and took a deep breath. 'Here I go! I wish us all luck!'

Margaret Spencer was more a battleship than a woman, heavyset and stern-looking, with a brusque manner. She was busy behind the nurses' station when Paige approached.

'Excuse me . . .'

Nurse Spencer looked up. 'Yes?'

'I was told to report here. I'm Dr Taylor.'

Nurse Spencer consulted a sheet. 'Just a moment.' She walked through a door and returned a minute later with some scrubs and a white coat.

'Here you are. The scrubs are to wear in the operating theater, and on rounds. And when you're doing rounds you put a white coat over the scrubs.'

'Thanks.'

'Oh. And here.' She reached down and handed Paige a metal tag that read 'Paige Taylor, M.D.' 'Here's your name tag, doctor.'

Paige held it in her hand and looked at it for a long time. *Paige Taylor, M.D.* She felt as though she had been handed the Medal of Honor. All the long hard years of work and study were summed up in those brief words. *Paige Taylor, M.D.*

Nurse Spencer was watching her. 'Are you all right?'

'I'm fine.' Paige smiled. 'I'm just fine, thank you. Where do I . . . ?'

'Doctors' dressing room is down the corridor to the left. You'll be making rounds, so you'll want to change.'

'Thank you.'

Paige walked down the corridor, amazed at the amount of activity around her. The corridor was crowded with doctors, nurses, technicians, and patients, hurrying to various destinations. The insistent chatter of the public address system added to the din.

'Dr Keenan . . . OR Three . . . Dr Keenan . . . OR Three.'

'Dr Talbot . . . Emergency Room One. Stat . . . Dr Talbot . . . Emergency Room One. Stat.'

'Dr Engel . . . Room 212 . . . Dr Engel . . . Room 212.'

Paige approached a door marked DOCTORS' DRESS-ING ROOM and opened it. Inside there were a dozen male doctors in various stages of undress. Two of them were totally naked. They turned to stare at Paige as the door opened.

'Oh! I . . . I'm sorry,' Paige mumbled, and quickly closed the door. She stood there, uncertain about what to do. A few feet down the corridor, she saw a door marked NURSES' DRESSING ROOM. Paige walked over to it and opened the door. Inside, several nurses were changing into their uniforms.

One of them looked up. 'Hello. Are you one of the new nurses?'

'No,' Paige said tightly. 'I'm not.' She closed the door and walked back to the doctors' dressing room. She stood there a moment, then took a deep breath and entered. The conversation came to a stop.

One of the men said, 'Sorry, honey. This room is for doctors.'

'I'm a doctor,' Paige said.

They turned to look at one another. 'Oh? Well, er . . . welcome.'

'Thank you.' She hesitated a moment, then walked over to an empty locker. The men watched as she put her hospital clothes into the locker. She looked at the men for a moment, then slowly started to unbutton her blouse.

The doctors stood there, not sure what to do. One of them said, 'Maybe we should—er—give the little lady some privacy, gentlemen.'

The little lady! 'Thank you,' Paige said. She stood there, waiting, as the doctors finished dressing and left the room. *Am I going to have to go through this every day?* she wondered.

In hospital rounds, there is a traditional formation that never varies. The attending physician is always in the lead, followed by the senior resident, then the other residents, and one or two medical students. The attending physician Paige had been assigned to was Dr William Radnor. Paige and five other residents were gathered in the hallway, waiting to meet him.

In the group was a young Chinese doctor. He held out his hand. 'Tom Chang,' he said. 'I hope you're all as nervous as I am.'

Paige liked him immediately.

A man was approaching the group. 'Good morning,' he said. 'I'm Dr Radnor.' He was soft-spoken, with sparkling blue eyes. Each resident introduced himself.

'This is your first day of rounds. I want you to pay close attention to everything you see and hear, but at the same time, it's important to appear relaxed.'

Paige made a mental note. *Pay close attention, but appear to be relaxed.*

'If the patients see that you're tense, *they're* going to be tense, and they'll probably think they're dying of some disease you aren't telling them about.'

Don't make patients tense.

'Remember, from now on, you're going to be responsible for the lives of other human beings.'

Now responsible for other lives. Oh, my God!

The longer Dr Radnor talked, the more nervous Paige became, and by the time he was finished, her self-confidence had completely vanished. *I'm not ready for this!* she thought. *I don't know what I'm doing. Who ever said I could be a doctor? What if I kill somebody?*

Dr Radnor was going on, 'I will expect detailed notes on each one of your patients — lab work, blood, electrolytes, everything. Is that clear?'

There were murmurs of 'Yes, doctor.'

'There are always thirty to forty surgical patients here at one time. It's your job to make sure that everything is properly organized for them. We'll start the morning rounds now. In the afternoon, we'll make the same rounds again.'

It had all seemed so easy at medical school. Paige thought about the four years she had spent there. There had been one hundred and fifty students, and only fifteen women. She would never forget the first day of Gross Anatomy class. The students had walked into a large white tiled room with twenty tables lined up in rows, each table covered with a yellow sheet. Five students were assigned to each table.

The professor had said, 'All right, pull back the sheets.' And there, in front of Paige, was her first cadaver. She had been afraid that she would faint or be sick, but she felt strangely calm. The cadaver had been preserved, which somehow removed it one step from humanity.

In the beginning the students had been hushed and

respectful in the anatomy laboratory. But, incredibly to Paige, within a week, they were eating sandwiches during the dissections, and making rude jokes. It was a form of self-defense, a denial of their own mortality. They gave the corpses names, and treated them like old friends. Paige tried to force herself to act as casually as the other students, but she found it difficult. She looked at the cadaver she was working on, and thought: *Here was a man with a home and a family. He went to an office every day, and once a year he took a vacation with his wife and children. He probably loved sports and enjoyed movies and plays, and he laughed and cried, and he watched his children grow up and he shared their joys and their sorrows, and he had big, wonderful dreams. I hope they all came true* . . . A bittersweet sadness engulfed her because he was dead and *she* was alive.

In time, even to Paige, the dissections became routine. *Open the chest, examine the ribs, lungs, pericardial sac covering the heart, the veins, arteries, and nerves.*

Much of the first two years of medical school was spent memorizing long lists that the students referred to as the Organ Recital. First the cranial nerves: olfactory, optic, oculomotor, trochlear, trigeminal, abducens, facial, auditory, glossopharyngeal, vagus, spinal, and hypoglossal.

The students used mnemonics to help them remember. The classic one was '*O*n *o*ld *O*lympus's *t*owering *t*ops, *a* *F*rench *a*nd *G*erman *v*ended *s*ome *h*ops.' The modern male version was '*O*h, *o*h, *o*h, *t*o *t*ouch *a*nd *f*eel *a* girl's *v*agina—*s*uch *h*eaven.'

The last two years of medical school were more

interesting, with courses in internal medicine, surgery, pediatrics, and obstetrics, and they worked at the local hospital. *I remember the time* . . . Paige was thinking.

'Dr Taylor . . .' The senior resident was staring at her.

Paige came to with a start. The others were already halfway down the corridor.

'Coming,' she said hastily.

The first stop was at a large, rectangular ward, with rows of beds on both sides of the room, with a small stand next to each bed. Paige had expected to see curtains separating the beds, but here there was no privacy.

The first patient was an elderly man with a sallow complexion. He was sound asleep, breathing heavily. Dr Radnor walked over to the foot of the bed, studied the chart there, then went to the patient's side and gently touched his shoulder. 'Mr Potter?'

The patient opened his eyes. 'Huh?'

'Good morning. I'm Dr Radnor. I'm just checking to see how you're doing. Did you have a comfortable night?'

'It was okay.'

'Do you have any pain?'

'Yeah. My chest hurts.'

'Let me take a look at it.'

When he finished the examination, he said, 'You're doing fine. I'll have the nurse give you something for the pain.'

'Thanks, doctor.'

'We'll be back to see you this afternoon.'

They moved away from the bed. Dr Radnor turned to the residents. 'Always try to ask questions that have a yes or no answer so the patient doesn't tire himself out. And reassure him about his progress. I want you to study his chart and make notes. We'll come back here this afternoon to see how he's doing. Keep a running record of every patient's chief complaint, present illness, past illnesses, family history, and social history. Does he drink, smoke, etc.? When we make the rounds again, I'll expect a report on the progress of each patient.'

They moved on to the bed of the next patient, a man in his forties.

'Good morning, Mr Rawlings.'

'Good morning, doctor.'

'Are you feeling better this morning?'

'Not so good. I was up a lot last night. My stomach's hurting.'

Dr Radnor turned to the senior resident. 'What did the proctoscopy show?'

'No sign of any problem.'

'Give him a barium enema and an upper GI, stat.'

The senior resident made a note.

The resident standing next to Paige whispered in her ear, 'I guess you know what stat stands for. "Shake that ass, tootsie!"'

Dr Radnor heard. '"Stat" comes from the Latin, *statim*. Immediately.'

In the years ahead, Paige was to hear it often.

The next patient was an elderly woman who had had a by-pass operation.

'Good morning, Mrs Turkel.'

'How long are you going to keep me in here?'

'Not very long. The procedure was a success. You'll be going home soon.'

And they moved on to the next patient.

The routine was repeated over and over, and the morning went by swiftly. They saw thirty patients. After each patient, the residents frantically scribbled notes, praying that they would be able to decipher them later.

One patient was a puzzle to Paige. She seemed to be in perfect health.

When they had moved away from her, Paige asked, 'What's her problem, doctor?'

Dr Radnor sighed. 'She has no problem. She's a gomer. And for those of you who forgot what you were taught in medical school, gomer is an acronym for "Get out of my emergency room!" Gomers are people who *enjoy* poor health. That's their hobby. I've admitted her six times in the last year.'

They moved on to the last patient, an old woman on a respirator, who was in a coma.

'She's had a massive heart attack,' Dr Radnor explained to the residents. 'She's been in a coma for six weeks. Her vital signs are failing. There's nothing more we can do for her. We'll pull the plug this afternoon.'

Paige looked at him in shock. 'Pull the plug?'

Dr Radnor said gently, 'The hospital ethics committee made the decision this morning. She's a vegetable. She's eighty-seven years old, and she's brain-dead. It's cruel to keep her alive, and it's breaking her family financially. I'll see you all at rounds this afternoon.'

They watched him walk away. Paige turned to look

at the patient again. She was alive. *In a few hours she will be dead. We'll pull the plug this afternoon. That's murder!* Paige thought.

3

That afternoon, when the rounds were finished, the new residents gathered in the small upstairs lounge. The room held eight tables, an ancient black-and-white television set, and two vending machines that dispensed stale sandwiches and bitter coffee.

The conversations at each table were almost identical.

One of the residents said, 'Take a look at my throat, will you? Does it look raw to you?'

'I think I have a fever. I feel lousy.'

'My abdomen is swollen and tender. I know I have appendicitis.'

'I've got this crushing pain in my chest. I hope to God I'm not having a heart attack!'

Kat sat down at a table with Paige and Honey. 'How did it go?' she asked.

Honey said, 'I think it went all right.'

They both looked at Paige. 'I was tense, but I was relaxed. I was nervous, but I stayed calm.' She sighed. 'It's been a long day. I'll be glad to get out of here and have some fun tonight.'

'Me, too,' Kat agreed. 'Why don't we have dinner and then go see a movie?'

'Sounds great.'

An orderly approached their table. 'Dr Taylor?'

Paige looked up. 'I'm Dr Taylor.'

'Dr Wallace would like to see you in his office.'

The hospital administrator! *What have I done?* Paige wondered.

The orderly was waiting. 'Dr Taylor . . .'

'I'm coming.' She took a deep breath and got to her feet. 'I'll see you later.'

'This way, doctor.'

Paige followed the orderly into an elevator and rode up to the fifth floor, where Dr Wallace's office was located.

Benjamin Wallace was seated behind his desk. He glanced up as Paige walked in. 'Good afternoon, Dr Taylor.'

'Good afternoon.'

Wallace cleared his throat. 'Well! Your first day and you've already made quite an impression!'

Paige looked at him, puzzled. 'I . . . I don't understand.'

'I hear you had a little problem in the doctors' dressing room this morning.'

'Oh.' *So, that's what this is all about!*

Wallace looked at her and smiled. 'I suppose I'll have to make some arrangements for you and the other girls.'

'We're . . .' *We're not girls*, Paige started to say. 'We would appreciate that.'

'Meanwhile, if you don't want to dress with the nurses . . .'

'I'm not a nurse,' Paige said firmly. 'I'm a doctor.'

'Of course, of course. Well, we'll do something about accommodations for you, doctor.'

'Thank you.'

He handed Paige a sheet of paper. 'Meanwhile, this is your schedule. You'll be on call for the next twenty-four hours, starting at six o'clock.' He looked at his watch. 'That's thirty minutes from now.'

Paige was looking at him in astonishment. Her day had started at five-thirty that morning. *'Twenty-four hours?'*

'Well, thirty-six, actually. Because you'll be starting rounds again in the morning.'

Thirty-six hours! I wonder if I can handle this.

She was soon to find out.

Paige went to look for Kat and Honey.

'I'm going to have to forget about dinner and a movie,' Paige said. 'I'm on a thirty-six-hour call.'

Kat nodded. 'We just got our bad news. I go on it tomorrow, and Honey goes on Wednesday.'

'It won't be so bad,' Paige said cheerfully. 'I understand there's an on-call room to sleep in. I'm going to enjoy this.'

She was wrong.

An orderly was leading Paige down a long corridor.

'Dr Wallace told me that I'll be on call for thirty-six hours,' Paige said. 'Do all the residents work those hours?'

'Only for the first three years,' the orderly assured her.

Great!

'But you'll have plenty of chance to rest, doctor.'

'I will?'

'In here. This is the on-call room.' He opened the door, and Paige stepped inside. The room resembled a monk's cell in some poverty-stricken monastery. It contained nothing but a cot with a lumpy mattress, a cracked washbasin, and a bedside stand with a telephone on it. 'You can sleep here between calls.'

'Thanks.'

The calls began as Paige was in the coffee shop, just starting to have her dinner.

'Dr Taylor . . . ER Three . . . Dr Taylor . . . ER Three.'

And all the time she was pursued by nurses.

'We have a patient with a fractured rib . . .'

'Mr Henegan is complaining of chest pains . . .'

'The patient in Ward Two has a headache. Is it all right to give him an acetaminophen . . . ?'

At midnight, Paige had just managed to fall asleep when she was awakened by the telephone.

'Report to ER One.' It was a knife wound, and by the time Paige had taken care of it, it was one-thirty in the morning. At two-fifteen she was awakened again.

'Dr Taylor . . . Emergency Room Two. Stat.'

Paige said, groggily, 'Right.' *What did he say it meant? Shake that ass, tootsie.* She forced herself up and moved down the corridor to the emergency room. A patient had been brought in with a broken leg. He was screaming with pain.

'Get an X-ray,' Paige ordered. 'And give him Demerol, 50 milligrams.' She put her hand on the patient's arm. 'You're going to be fine. Try to relax.'

Over the PA system, a metallic disembodied voice said, 'Dr Taylor . . . Ward Three. Stat.'

Paige looked at the moaning patient, reluctant to leave him.

55

The voice came on again, 'Dr Taylor . . . Ward Three. Stat.'

'Coming,' Paige mumbled. She hurried out the door and down the corridor to Ward Three. A patient had vomited, aspirated, and was choking.

'He can't breathe,' the nurse said.

'Suction him,' Paige ordered. As she watched the patient begin to catch his breath, she heard her name again on the PA system. 'Dr Taylor . . . Ward Four. Ward Four.' Paige shook her head and ran down to Ward Four, to a screaming patient with abdominal spasms. Paige gave him a quick examination. 'It could be intestinal dysfunction. Get an ultrasound,' Paige said.

By the time she returned to the patient with the broken leg, the pain reliever had taken effect. She had him moved to the operating room and set the leg. As she was finishing, she heard her name again. 'Dr Taylor, report to Emergency Room Two. Stat.'

'The stomach ulcer in Ward Four is having a pain . . .'

At 3:30 A.M.: 'Dr Taylor, the patient in Room 310 is hemorrhaging . . .'

There was a heart attack in one of the wards, and Paige was nervously listening to the patient's heartbeat when she heard her name called over the PA system: 'Dr Taylor . . . ER Two. Stat . . . Dr Taylor . . . ER Two. Stat.'

I must not panic, Paige thought. *I've got to remain calm and cool.* She panicked. Who was more important, the patient she was examining, or the next patient? 'You stay here,' she said inanely. 'I'll be right back.'

56

As Paige hurried toward ER Two, she heard her name called again. 'Dr Taylor . . . ER One. Stat . . . Dr Taylor . . . ER One. Stat.'

Oh, my God! Paige thought. She felt as though she were caught up in the middle of some endless terrifying nightmare.

During what was left of the night, Paige was awakened to attend to a case of food poisoning, a broken arm, a hiatal hernia, and a fractured rib. By the time she stumbled back into the on-call room, she was so exhausted that she could hardly move. She crawled onto the little cot and had just started to doze off when the telephone rang.

She reached out for it with her eyes closed. 'H'lo . . .'

'Dr Taylor, we're waiting for you.'

'Wha'?' She lay there, trying to remember where she was.

'Your rounds are starting, doctor.'

'My rounds?' *This is some kind of bad joke*, Paige thought. *It's inhuman. They can't work anyone like this!* But they were waiting for her.

Ten minutes later, Paige was making the rounds again, half asleep. She stumbled against Dr Radnor. 'Excuse me,' she mumbled, 'but I haven't had any sleep . . .'

He patted her on the shoulder sympathetically. 'You'll get used to it.'

When Paige finally got off duty, she slept for fourteen straight hours.

*　　　*　　　*

The intense pressure and punishing hours proved to be too much for some of the residents, and they simply disappeared from the hospital. *That's not going to happen to me*, Paige vowed.

The pressure was unrelenting. At the end of one of Paige's shifts, thirty-six grueling hours, she was so exhausted that she had no idea where she was. She stumbled to the elevator and stood there, her mind numb.

Tom Chang came up to her. 'Are you all right?'

'Fine,' Paige mumbled.

He grinned. 'You look like hell.'

'Thanks. Why do they do this to us?' Paige asked.

Chang shrugged. 'The theory is that it keeps us in touch with our patients. If we go home and leave them, we don't know what's happening to them while we're gone.'

Paige nodded. 'That makes sense.' It made no sense at all. 'How can we take care of them if we're asleep on our feet?'

Chang shrugged again. 'I don't make the rules. It's the way all hospitals operate.' He looked at Paige more closely. 'Are you going to be able to make it home?'

Paige looked at him and said haughtily, 'Of course.'

'Take care.' Chang disappeared down the corridor.

Paige waited for the elevator to arrive. When it finally came, she was standing there, sound asleep.

Two days later, Paige was having breakfast with Kat.

'Do you want to hear a terrible confession?' Paige

58

asked. 'Sometimes when they wake me up at four o'clock in the morning to give somebody an aspirin, and I'm stumbling down the hall, half conscious, and I pass the rooms where all the patients are tucked in and having a good night's sleep, I feel like banging on all the doors and yelling, "Everybody wake up!"'

Kat held out her hand. 'Join the club.'

The patients came in all shapes, sizes, ages, and colors. They were frightened, brave, gentle, arrogant, demanding, considerate. They were human beings in pain.

Most of the doctors were dedicated people. As in any profession, there were good doctors and bad doctors. They were young and old, clumsy and adept, pleasant and nasty. A few of them, at one time or another, made sexual advances to Paige. Some were subtle and some were crude.

'Don't you ever feel lonely at night? I know that I do. I was wondering . . .'

'These hours are murder, aren't they? Do you know what I find gives me energy? Good sex. Why don't we . . . ?'

'My wife is out of town for a few days. I have a cabin near Carmel. This weekend we could . . .'

And the patients.

'So you're my doctor, eh? You know what would cure me . . . ?'

'Come closer to the bed, baby. I want to see if those are real . . .'

Paige gritted her teeth and ignored them all. *When Alfred and I are married, this will stop.* And just the

59

thought of Alfred gave her a glow. He would be returning from Africa soon. *Soon*.

One morning before rounds, Paige and Kat talked about the sexual harassment they were experiencing.

'Most of the doctors behave like perfect gentlemen, but a few of them seem to think we're perks that go with the territory, and that we're there to service them,' Kat said. 'I don't think a week goes by but what one of the doctors hits on me. "Why don't you come over to my place for a drink? I've got some great CDs." Or in the OR, when I'm assisting, the surgeon will brush his arm across my breast. One moron said to me, "You know, whenever I order chicken, I like the dark meat." '

Paige sighed. 'They think they're flattering us by treating us as sex objects. I'd rather they treated us as doctors.'

'A lot of them don't even want us around. They either want to fuck us or they want to fuck us. You know, it's not fair. Women are judged inferior until we prove ourselves, and men are judged superior until they prove what assholes they are.'

'It's the old boys' network,' Paige said. 'If there were more of us, we could start a new girls' network.'

Paige had heard of Arthur Kane. He was the subject of constant gossip around the hospital. His nickname was Dr 007—licensed to kill. His solution to every problem was to operate, and he had a higher rate of operations than any other doctor at the hospital. He also had a higher mortality rate.

He was bald, short, hawk-nosed, with tobacco-stained teeth, and was grossly overweight. Incredibly, he fancied himself a ladies' man. He liked to refer to the new nurses and female residents as 'fresh meat'.

Paige Taylor was fresh meat. He saw her in the upstairs lounge and sat down at her table, uninvited.

'I've been keeping an eye on you.'

Paige looked up, startled. 'I beg your pardon?'

'I'm Dr Kane. My friends call me Arthur.' There was a leer in his voice.

Paige wondered how many friends he had.

'How are you getting along here?'

The question caught Paige off guard. 'I . . . all right, I think.'

He leaned forward. 'This is a big hospital. It's easy to get lost here. Do you know what I mean?'

Paige said warily, 'Not exactly.'

'You're too pretty to be just another face in the crowd. If you want to get somewhere here, you need someone to help you. Someone who knows the ropes.'

The conversation was getting more unpleasant by the minute.

'And you'd like to help me.'

'Right.' He bared his tobacco-stained teeth. 'Why don't we discuss it at dinner?'

'There's nothing to discuss, Dr Kane,' Paige said. 'I'm not interested.'

Arthur Kane watched Paige get up and walk away, and there was a baleful expression on his face.

*   *   *

First-year surgical residents were on a two-month rotation schedule, alternating among obstetrics, orthopedics, urology, and surgery.

Paige learned that it was dangerous to go into a training hospital in the summer for any serious illness, because many of the staff doctors were on vacation and the patients were at the mercy of the inexperienced young residents.

Nearly all surgeons liked to have music in the operating room. One of the doctors was nicknamed Mozart and another Axl Rose because of their tastes in music.

For some reason, operations always seemed to make everyone hungry. They constantly discussed food. A surgeon would be in the middle of removing a gangrenous gallbladder from a patient and say, 'I had a great dinner last night at Bardelli's. Best Italian food in all of San Francisco.'

'Have you eaten the crab cakes at the Cypress Club?'

'If you like good beef, try the House of Prime Rib over on Van Ness.'

And meanwhile, a nurse would be mopping up the patient's blood.

When they weren't talking about food, the doctors talked about baseball or football scores.

'Did you see the 49ers play last Sunday? I bet they miss Joe Montana. He always came through for them in the last two minutes of a game.'

And out would come a ruptured appendix.

Kafka, Paige thought. *Kafka would have loved this*.

*   *   *

At three in the morning when Paige was asleep in the on-call room, she was awakened by the telephone.

A raspy voice said, 'Dr Taylor—Room 419—a heart attack patient. You'll have to hurry!' The line went dead.

Paige sat on the edge of the bed, fighting sleep, and stumbled to her feet. *You have to hurry!* She went into the corridor, but there was no time to wait for an elevator. She rushed up the stairs and ran down the fourth-floor corridor to Room 419, her heart pounding. She flung open the door and stood there, staring.

Room 419 was a storage room.

Kat Hunter was making her rounds with Dr Richard Hutton. He was in his forties, brusque and fast. He spent no more than two or three minutes with each patient, scanning their charts, then snapping out orders to the surgical residents in a machine-gun, staccato fashion.

'Check her hemoglobin and schedule surgery for tomorrow . . .'

'Keep a close eye on his temperature chart . . .'

'Cross-match four units of blood . . .'

'Remove these stitches . . .'

'Get some chest films . . .'

Kat and the other residents were busily making notes on everything, trying hard to keep up with him.

They approached a patient who had been in the hospital a week and had had a battery of tests for a high fever, with no results.

When they were out in the corridor, Kat asked, 'What's the matter with him?'

'It's a GOK,' a resident said. 'A God only knows. We've done X-rays, CAT scans, MRIs, spinal taps, liver biopsy. Everything. We don't know what's wrong with him.'

They moved into a ward where a young patient, his head bandaged after an operation, was sleeping. As Dr Hutton started to unwrap the head dressing, the patient woke up, startled. 'What . . . what's going on?'

'Sit up,' Dr Hutton said curtly. The young man was trembling.

I'll never treat my patients that way, Kat vowed.

The next patient was a healthy-looking man in his seventies. As soon as Dr Hutton approached the bed, the patient yelled, '*Gonzo!* I'm going to sue you, you dirty son of a bitch.'

'Now, Mr Sparolini . . .'

'Don't Mr Sparolini me! You turned me into a fucking eunuch.'

That's an oxymoron, Kat thought.

'Mr Sparolini, you agreed to have the vasectomy, and—'

'It was my wife's idea. Damn bitch! Just wait till I get home.'

They left him muttering to himself.

'What's his problem?' one of the residents asked.

'His problem is that he's a horny old goat. His young wife has six kids and she doesn't want any more.'

Next was a little girl, ten years old. Dr Hutton looked at her chart. 'We're going to give you a shot to make the bad bugs go away.'

A nurse filled a syringe and moved toward the little girl.

'No!' she screamed. 'You're going to hurt me!'

'This won't hurt, baby,' the nurse assured her.

The words were a dark echo in Kat's mind.

This won't hurt, baby . . . It was the voice of her stepfather whispering to her in the scary dark.

'This will feel good. Spread your legs. Come on, you little bitch!' And he had pushed her legs apart and forced his male hardness into her and put his hand over her mouth to keep her from screaming with the pain. She was thirteen years old. After that, his visits became a terrifying nightly ritual. 'You're lucky you got a man like me to teach you how to fuck,' he would tell her. 'Do you know what a Kat is? A little pussy. And I want some.' And he would fall on top of her and grab her, and no amount of crying or pleading would make him stop.

Kat had never known her father. Her mother was a cleaning woman who worked nights at an office building near their tiny apartment in Gary, Indiana. Kat's stepfather was a huge man who had been injured in an accident at a steel mill, and he stayed home most of the time, drinking. At night, when Kat's mother left for work, he would go into Kat's room. 'You say anything to your mother or brother, and I'll kill him,' he told Kat. *I can't let him hurt Mike*, Kat thought. Her brother was five years younger than she, and Kat adored him. She mothered him and protected him and fought his battles for him. He was the only bright spot in Kat's life.

One morning, terrified as Kat was by her step-father's threats, she decided she had to tell her mother what was happening. Her mother would put a stop to it, would protect her.

'Mama, your husband comes to my bed at night when you're away, and forces himself on me.'

Her mother stared at her a moment, then slapped Kat hard across the face.

'Don't you dare make up lies like that, you little slut!'

Kat never discussed it again. The only reason she stayed at home was Mike. *He'd be lost without me*, Kat thought. But the day she learned she was pregnant, she ran away to live with an aunt in Minneapolis. From then, her life completely changed.

'You don't have to tell me what happened,' her Aunt Sophie had said. 'You know that song they sing on *Sesame Street*? "It's Not Easy Being Green"? Well, honey, it's not easy being black, either. You have two choices. You can keep running and hiding and blaming the world for your problems, or you can stand up for yourself and decide to be somebody important.'

'How do I do that?'

'By *knowing* that you're important. First, you get an image in your mind of who you want to be, child, and what you want to be. And then you go to work, *becoming* that person.'

'I'm not going to have his baby,' Kat decided. 'I want an abortion.'

It was arranged quietly, during a weekend, and it was performed by a midwife who was a friend of Kat's aunt. When it was over, Kat thought fiercely,

*I'm never going to let a man touch me again.
Never!*

Minneapolis was a fairyland for Kat. Within a few
blocks of almost every home were lakes and streams
and rivers. And there were over eight thousand acres
of landscaped parks. She went sailing on the city
lakes and took boat rides on the Mississippi.

She visited the Great Zoo with Aunt Sophie and
spent Sundays at the Valleyfair Amusement Park.
She went on the hay rides at Cedar Creek Farm, and
watched knights in armor jousting at the Shakopee
Renaissance Festival.

Aunt Sophie watched Kat and thought, *The girl
has never had a childhood.*

Kat was learning to enjoy herself, but Aunt Sophie
sensed that deep inside her niece was a place that
no one could reach, a barrier she had set up to keep
her from being hurt again.

She made friends at school. But never with boys.
Her girlfriends were all dating, but Kat was a loner,
and too proud to tell anyone why. She looked up to
her aunt, whom she loved very much.

Kat had taken little interest in school, or in reading
books, but Aunt Sophie changed all that. Her home
was filled with books, and Sophie's excitement about
them was contagious.

'There are wonderful worlds in there,' she told the
young girl. 'Read, and you'll learn where you came
from and where you're going. I've got a feeling that
you're going to be famous one day, baby. But you
have to get an education first. This is America. You
can become anybody you want to be. You may be

black and poor, but so were some of our con-
gresswomen, and movie stars, and scientists, and
sports legends. One day we're going to have a black
president. You can be anything you want to be. It's
up to you.'

It was the beginning.

Kat became the top student in her class. She was
an avid reader. In the school library one day, she
happened to pick up a copy of Sinclair Lewis's
Arrowsmith, and she was fascinated by the story of
the dedicated young doctor. She read Agnes
Cooper's *Promises to Keep*, and *Woman Surgeon* by
Dr Else Roe, and it opened up a whole new world
for her. She discovered that there were people on
this earth who devoted themselves to helping others,
to saving lives. When Kat came home from school
one day, she said to Aunt Sophie, 'I'm going to be
a doctor. A famous one.'

4

On Monday morning, three of Paige's patients'
charts were missing, and Paige was blamed.

On Wednesday, Paige was awakened at 4:00 A.M.
in the on-call room. Sleepily, she picked up the telephone. 'Dr Taylor.'

Silence.

'Hello . . . hello.'

She could hear breathing at the other end of the
line. And then there was a click.

Paige lay awake for the rest of the night.

In the morning, Paige said to Kat, 'I'm either
becoming paranoid or someone hates me.' She told
Kat what had happened.

'Patients sometimes get grudges against doctors,'
Kat said. 'Can you think of anyone who . . . ?'

Paige sighed. 'Dozens.'

'I'm sure there's nothing to worry about.'

Paige wished that she could believe it.

In late summer the magic telegram arrived. It was
waiting for Paige when she returned to the apartment
late at night. It read: 'Arriving San Francisco noon
Sunday. Can't wait to see you. Love, Alfred.'

He was finally on his way back to her! Paige
read the telegram again and again, her excitement

growing each time. *Alfred!* His name conjured up a tumbling kaleidoscope of exciting memories . . .

Paige and Alfred had grown up together. Their fathers were part of a medical cadre of WHO that traveled to Third World countries, fighting exotic and virulent diseases. Paige and her mother accompanied Dr Taylor, who headed the team.

Paige and Alfred had had a fantasy childhood. In India, Paige learned to speak Hindi. At the age of two, she knew that the name for the bamboo hut they lived in was *basha*. Her father was *gorashaib*, a white man, and she was *nani*, a little sister. They addressed Paige's father as *abadhan*, the leader, or *baba*, father.

When Paige's parents were not around, she drank *bhanga*, an intoxicating drink made with hashish leaves, and ate *chapati* with *ghi*.

And then they were on their way to Africa. Off to another adventure!

Paige and Alfred became used to swimming and bathing in rivers that had crocodiles and hippopotamuses. Their pets were baby zebras and cheetahs and snakes. They grew up in windowless round huts made of wattle and daub, with packed dirt floors and conical thatched roofs. *Someday*, Paige vowed to herself, *I'm going to live in a real house, a beautiful cottage with a green lawn and a white picket fence*.

To the doctors and nurses, it was a difficult, frustrating life. But to the two children, it was a constant adventure, living in the land of lions, giraffes, and elephants. They went to primitive cinder-block

70

schoolhouses, and when none was available, they had tutors.

Paige was a bright child, and her mind was a sponge, absorbing everything. Alfred adored her.

'I'm going to marry you one day, Paige,' he said when she was twelve, he fourteen.

'I'm going to marry you, too, Alfred.'

They were two serious children, determined to spend the rest of their lives together.

The doctors from WHO were selfless, dedicated men and women who devoted their lives to their work. They often worked under nearly impossible circumstances. In Africa, they had to compete with *wogesha*—the native medical practitioners whose primitive remedies were passed on from father to son, and often had deadly effects. The Masai's traditional remedy for flesh wounds was *olkilorite*, a mixture of cattle blood, raw meat, and essence of a mysterious root.

The Kikuyu remedy for smallpox was to have children drive out the sickness with sticks.

'You must stop that,' Dr Taylor would tell them. 'It doesn't help.'

'Better than having you stick sharp needles in our skin,' they would reply.

The dispensaries were tables lined up under the trees, for surgery. The doctors saw hundreds of patients a day, and there was always a long line, waiting to see them—lepers, natives with tubercular lungs, whooping cough, smallpox, dysentery.

Paige and Alfred were inseparable. As they grew older, they would walk to the market together, to a village miles away. And they would talk about their plans for the future.

Medicine was a part of Paige's early life. She learned to care for patients, to give shots and dispense medications, and she anticipated ways to help her father.

Paige loved her father. Curt Taylor was the most caring, selfless man she had ever known. He genuinely liked people, dedicating his life to helping those who needed him, and he instilled that passion in Paige. In spite of the long hours he worked, he managed to find time to spend with his daughter. He made the discomfort of the primitive places they lived in fun.

Paige's relationship with her mother was something else. Her mother was a beauty from a wealthy social background. Her cool aloofness kept Paige at a distance. Marrying a doctor who was going to work in far-off exotic places had seemed romantic to her, but the harsh reality had embittered her. She was not a warm, loving woman, and she seemed to Paige always to be complaining.

'Why did we ever have to come to this godforsaken place, Curt?'

'The people here live like animals. We're going to catch some of their awful diseases.'

'Why can't you practice medicine in the United States and make money like other doctors?'

And on and on it went.

The more her mother criticized him, the more Paige adored her father.

When Paige was fifteen years old, her mother disappeared with the owner of a large cocoa plantation in Brazil.

'She's not coming back, is she?' Paige asked.

'No, darling. I'm sorry.'

'I'm glad!' She had not meant to say that. She was hurt that her mother had cared so little for her and her father that she had abandoned them.

The experience made Paige draw even closer to Alfred Turner. They played games together and went on expeditions together, and shared their dreams.

'I'm going to be a doctor, too, when I grow up,' Alfred confided. 'We'll get married, and we'll work together.'

'And we'll have lots of children!'

'Sure. If you like.'

On the night of Paige's sixteenth birthday, their lifelong emotional intimacy exploded into a new dimension. At a little village in East Africa, the doctors had been called away on an emergency, because of an epidemic, and Paige, Alfred, and a cook were the only ones left in camp.

They had had dinner and gone to bed. But in the middle of the night Paige had been awakened in her tent by the faraway thunder of stampeding animals. She lay there, and as the minutes went by and the sound of the stampede came closer, she began to grow afraid. Her breath quickened. There was no telling when her father and the others would return.

She got up. Alfred's tent was only a few feet away. Terrified, Paige got up, raised the flap of the tent, and ran to Alfred's tent.

He was asleep.

'Alfred!'

He sat up, instantly awake. 'Paige? Is anything wrong?'

'I'm frightened. Could I get into bed with you for a while?'

'Sure.' They lay there, listening to the animals charging through the brush.

In a few minutes, the sounds began to die away.

Alfred became conscious of Paige's warm body lying next to him.

'Paige, I think you'd better go back to your tent.'

Paige could feel his male hardness pressing against her.

All the physical needs that had been building up within them came boiling to the surface.

'Alfred.'

'Yes?' His voice was husky.

'We're getting married, aren't we?'

'Yes.'

'Then it's all right.'

And the sounds of the jungle around them disappeared, and they began to explore and discover a world no one had ever possessed but themselves. They were the first lovers in the world, and they gloried in the wonderful miracle of it.

At dawn, Paige crept back to her tent and she thought, happily, *I'm a woman now*.

From time to time, Curt Taylor suggested to Paige that she return to the United States to live with his brother in his beautiful home in Deerfield, north of Chicago.

'Why?' Paige would ask.

'So that you can grow up to be a proper young lady.'

'I *am* a proper young lady.'

'Proper young ladies don't tease wild monkeys and try to ride baby zebras.'

Her answer was always the same. 'I won't leave you.'

When Paige was seventeen, the WHO team went to a jungle village in South Africa to fight a typhoid epidemic. Making the situation even more perilous was the fact that shortly after the doctors arrived, war broke out between two local tribes. Curt Taylor was warned to leave.

'I can't, for God's sake. I have patients who will die if I desert them.'

Four days later, the village came under attack. Paige and her father huddled in their little hut, listening to the yelling and the sounds of gunfire outside.

Paige was terrified. 'They're going to kill us!'

Her father had taken her in his arms. 'They won't harm us, darling. We're here to help them. They know we're their friends.'

And he had been right.

The chief of one of the tribes had burst into the hut with some of his warriors. 'Do not worry. We guard you.' And they had.

The fighting and shooting finally stopped, but in the morning Curt Taylor made a decision.

He sent a message to his brother. *Sending Paige out on next plane. Will wire details. Please meet her at airport.*

Paige was furious when she heard the news. She was taken, sobbing wildly, to the dusty little airport where a Piper Cub was waiting to fly her to a town where she could catch a plane to Johannesburg.

'You're sending me away because you want to get rid of me!' she cried.

Her father held her close in his arms. 'I love you more than anything in the world, baby. I'll miss you every minute. But I'll be going back to the States soon, and we'll be together again.'

'Promise?'

'Promise.'

Alfred was there to see Paige off.

'Don't worry,' Alfred told Paige. 'I'll come and get you as soon as I can. Will you wait for me?'

It was a pretty silly question, after all those years.

'Of course I will.'

Three days later, when Paige's plane arrived at O'Hare Airport in Chicago, Paige's Uncle Richard was there to greet her. Paige had never met him. All she knew about him was that he was a very wealthy businessman whose wife had died several years earlier. 'He's the successful one in the family,' Paige's father always said.

Paige's uncle's first words stunned her. 'I'm sorry to tell you this, Paige, but I just received word that your father was killed in a native uprising.'

Her whole world had been shattered in an instant. The ache was so strong that she did not think she could bear it. *I won't let my uncle see me cry*, Paige vowed. *I won't. I never should have left. I'm going back there*.

Driving from the airport, Paige stared out the window, looking at the heavy traffic.

'I hate Chicago.'

'Why, Paige?'
'It's a jungle.'

Richard would not permit Paige to return to Africa and her father's funeral, and that infuriated her.

He tried to reason with her. 'Paige, they've already buried your father. There's no point in your going back.'

But there was a point: *Alfred was there.*

A few days after Paige arrived, her uncle sat down with her to discuss her future.

'There's nothing to discuss,' Paige informed him. 'I'm going to be a doctor.'

At twenty-one, when Paige finished college, she applied to ten medical schools and was accepted by all of them. She chose a school in Boston.

It took two days to reach Alfred by telephone in Zaire, where he was working part-time with a WHO unit.

When Paige told him the news, he said, 'That's wonderful, darling. I'm nearly finished with my medical courses. I'll stay with WHO for a while, but in a few years we'll be practicing together.'

Together. The magical word.

'Paige, I'm desperate to see you. If I can get out for a few days, could you meet me in Hawaii?'

There wasn't the slightest hesitation. 'Yes.'

And they had both managed it. Later, Paige could only imagine how difficult it must have been for Alfred to make the long journey, but he never mentioned it.

They spent three incredible days at a small hotel in Hawaii, called Sunny Cove, and it was as though they had never been apart. Paige wanted so much to ask Alfred to go back to Boston with her, but she knew how selfish that would have been. The work that he was doing was far more important.

On their last day together, as they were getting dressed, Paige asked, 'Where will they be sending you, Alfred?'

'Gambia, or maybe Bangladesh.'

To save lives, to help those who so desperately need him. She held him tightly and closed her eyes. She never wanted to let him go.

As though reading her thoughts, he said, 'I'll never let you get away.'

Paige started medical school, and she and Alfred corresponded regularly. No matter in what part of the world he was, Alfred managed to telephone Paige on her birthday and at Christmas. Just before New Year's Eve, when Paige was in her second year of school, Alfred telephoned.

'Paige?'

'Darling! Where are you?'

'I'm in Senegal. I figured out it's only eighty-eight hundred miles from the Sunny Cove hotel.'

It took a minute for it to sink in.

'Do you mean . . . ?'

'Can you meet me in Hawaii for New Year's Eve?'

'Oh, yes! Yes!'

Alfred traveled nearly halfway round the world to meet her, and this time the magic was even stronger. Time had stood still for both of them.

'Next year I'll be in charge of my own cadre at WHO,' Alfred said. 'When you finish school, I want us to get married . . .'

They were able to get together once more, and when they weren't able to meet, their letters spanned time and space.

All those years he had worked as a doctor in Third World countries, like his father and Paige's father, doing the wonderful work that they did. And now, at last, he was coming home to her.

As Paige read Alfred's telegram for the fifth time, she thought, *He's coming to San Francisco!*

Kat and Honey were in their bedrooms, asleep. Paige shook them awake. 'Alfred's coming! He's coming! He'll be here Sunday!'

'Wonderful,' Kat mumbled. 'Why don't you wake me up Sunday? I just got to bed.'

Honey was more responsive. She sat up and said, 'That's great! I'm dying to meet him. How long since you've seen him?'

'Two years,' Paige said, 'but we've always stayed in touch.'

'You're a lucky girl,' Kat sighed. 'Well, we're all awake now. I'll put on some coffee.'

The three of them sat around the kitchen table.

'Why don't we give Alfred a party?' Honey suggested. 'Kind of a "Welcome to the Groom" party.'

'That's a good idea,' Kat agreed.

'We'll make it a real celebration—a cake, balloons—the works!'

'We'll cook dinner for him here,' Honey said.

Kat shook her head. 'I've tasted your cooking. Let's send out for food.'

Sunday was four days away, and they spent all their spare time discussing Alfred's arrival. By some miracle, the three of them were off duty on Sunday.

Saturday, Paige managed to get to a beauty salon. She went shopping and splurged on a new dress.

'Do I look all right? Do you think he'll like it?'

'You look sensational!' Honey assured her. 'I hope he deserves you.'

Paige smiled. 'I hope I deserve *him*. You'll love him. He's fantastic!'

On The Sunday, an elaborate lunch they had ordered was laid out on the dining-room table, with a bottle of iced champagne. The women stood around, nervously waiting for Alfred's arrival.

At two o'clock, the doorbell rang, and Paige ran to the door to open it. There was Alfred. A bit tired-looking, a little thinner. But he was her Alfred. Standing next to him was a brunette who appeared to be in her thirties.

'Paige!' Alfred exclaimed.

Paige threw her arms around him. Then she turned to Honey and Kat and said proudly, 'This is Alfred Turner. Alfred, these are my roommates, Honey Taft and Kat Hunter.'

'Pleased to meet you,' Alfred said. He turned to the woman at his side. 'And this is Karen Turner. My wife.'

The three women stood there, frozen.

Paige said slowly, 'Your wife?'

'Yes.' He frowned. 'Didn't . . . didn't you get my letter?'

'Letter?'

'Yes. I sent it several weeks ago.'

'No . . .'

'Oh. I . . . I'm terribly sorry. I explained it all in my . . . but of course, if you didn't get the . . .' His voice trailed off. 'I'm really sorry, Paige. You and I have been apart so long, that I . . . and then I met Karen . . . and you know how it is . . .'

'I know how it is,' Paige said numbly. She turned to Karen and forced a smile. 'I . . . I hope you and Alfred will be very happy.'

'Thank you.'

There was an awkward silence.

Karen said, 'I think we had better go, darling.'

'Yes. I think you had,' Kat said.

Alfred ran his fingers through his hair. 'I'm really sorry, Paige. I . . . well . . . goodbye.'

'Goodbye, Alfred.'

The three women stood there, watching the departing newlyweds.

'That bastard!' Kat said. 'What a lousy thing to do.'

Paige's eyes were brimming with tears. 'I . . . he didn't mean to . . . I mean . . . he must have explained everything in his letter.'

Honey put her arms around Paige. 'There ought to be a law that all men should be castrated.'

'I'll drink to that,' Kat said.

'Excuse me,' Paige said. She hurried to her bedroom and closed the door behind her.

She did not come out for the rest of the day.

81

5

During the next few months, Paige saw very little of Kat and Honey. They would have a hurried breakfast in the cafeteria and occasionally pass one another in the corridors. They communicated mainly by leaving notes in the apartment.

'Dinner is in the fridge.'

'The microwave is out.'

'Sorry, I didn't have time to clean up.'

'What about the three of us having dinner out Saturday night?'

The impossible hours continued to be a punishment, testing the limits of endurance for all the residents.

Paige welcomed the pressure. It gave her no time to think about Alfred and the wonderful future they had planned together. And yet, she could not get him out of her mind. What he had done filled her with a deep pain that refused to go away. She tortured herself with the futile game of 'what if?'

What if I had stayed with Alfred in Africa?

What if he had come to Chicago with me?

What if he had not met Karen?

What if . . . ?

*   *   *

82

On a Friday when Paige went into the change room to put on her scrubs, the word 'bitch' had been written on them with a black marker pen.

The following day when Paige went to look for her scut book, it was gone. All her notes had disappeared. *Maybe I misplaced it*, Paige thought.
But she couldn't make herself believe it.

The world outside the hospital ceased to exist. Paige was aware that Iraq was pillaging Kuwait, and that was overshadowed by the needs of a fifteen-year-old patient who was dying of leukemia. The day East and West Germany became united, Paige was busy trying to save the life of a diabetic patient. Margaret Thatcher resigned as prime minister of Great Britain, but more important, the patient in 214 was able to walk again.

What made it bearable were the doctors Paige worked with. With few exceptions, they had dedicated themselves to healing others, relieving pain, and saving lives. Paige watched the miracles they performed every day, and it filled her with a sense of pride.

The greatest stress was working in the ER. The emergency room was constantly overcrowded with people suffering every form of trauma imaginable.

The long hours at the hospital and the pressures placed an enormous strain on the doctors and nurses who worked there. The divorce rate among the doctors was extraordinarily high, and extramarital affairs were common.

Tom Chang was one of those having a problem. He told Paige about it over coffee.

'I can handle the hours,' Chang confided, 'but my wife can't. She complains that she never sees me anymore and that I'm a stranger to our little girl. She's right. I don't know what to do about it.'

'Has your wife visited the hospital?'

'No.'

'Why don't you invite her here for lunch, Tom? Let her see what you're doing here and how important it is.'

Chang brightened. 'That's a good idea. Thanks, Paige. I will. I would like you to meet her. Will you join us for lunch?'

'I'd love to.'

Chang's wife, Sye, turned out to be a lovely young woman with a classic, timeless beauty. Chang showed her around the hospital, and afterward they had lunch in the cafeteria with Paige.

Chang had told Paige that Sye had been born and raised in Hong Kong.

'How do you like San Francisco?' Paige asked.

There was a small silence. 'It's an interesting city,' Sye said politely, 'but I feel as though I am a stranger here. It is too big, too noisy.'

'But I understand Hong Kong is also big and noisy.'

'I come from a small village an hour away from Hong Kong. There, there is no noise and no automobiles, and everyone knows his neighbors.' She looked at her husband. 'Tom and I and our little daughter were very happy there. It is very beautiful on the island of Lamma. It has white beaches and small farms, and nearby is a little fishing village, Sak Kwu Wan. It is so peaceful.'

Her voice was filled with a wistful nostalgia. 'My husband and I were together much of the time, as a family should be. Here, I never see him.'

Paige said, 'Mrs Chang, I know it's difficult for you right now, but in a few years, Tom will be able to set up his own practice, and then his hours will be much easier.'

Tom Chang took his wife's hand. 'You see? Everything will be fine, Sye. You must be patient.'

'I understand,' she said. There was no conviction in her voice.

As they talked, a man walked into the cafeteria, and as he stood at the door, Paige could see only the back of his head. Her heart started to race. He turned around. It was a complete stranger.

Chang was watching Paige. 'Are you all right?'

'Yes,' Paige lied. *I've got to forget him. It's over.* And yet, the memories of all those wonderful years, the fun, the excitement, the love they had for each other . . . *How do I forget all that? I wonder if I could persuade any of the doctors here to do a lobotomy on me.*

Paige ran into Honey in the corridor. Honey was out of breath and looked worried.

'Is everything all right?' Paige asked.

Honey smiled uneasily. 'Yes. Fine.' She hurried on.

Honey had recently been assigned to an attending

physician named Charles Isler, who was known around the hospital as a martinet.

On Honey's first day of rounds, he had said, 'I've been looking forward to working with you, Dr Taft. Dr Wallace has told me about your outstanding record at medical school. I understand you're going to practice internal medicine.'

'Yes.'

'Good. So, we'll have you here for three more years.'

They began their rounds.

The first patient was a young Mexican boy. Dr Isler ignored the other residents and turned to Honey. 'I think you'll find this an interesting case, Dr Taft. The patient has all the classic signs and symptoms: anorexia, weight loss, metallic taste, fatigue, anemia, hyperirritability, and unco-ordination. How would you diagnose it?' He smiled expectantly.

Honey looked at him for a moment. 'Well, it could be several things, couldn't it?'

Dr Isler was watching her, puzzled. 'It's a clear-cut case of —'

One of the other residents broke in, 'Lead poisoning?'

'That's right,' Dr Isler said.

Honey smiled. 'Of course. Lead poisoning.'

Dr Isler turned to Honey again. 'How would you treat it?'

Honey said evasively, 'Well, there are several different methods of treatment, aren't there?'

A second resident spoke up. 'If the patient has had long-term exposure, he should be treated as a potential case of encephalopathy.'

Dr Isler nodded. 'Right. That's what we're doing. We're correcting the dehydration and electrolyte disturbances, and giving him chelation therapy.'

He looked at Honey. She nodded in agreement.

The next patient was a man in his eighties. His eyes were red and his eyelids were nearly stuck together.

'We'll have your eyes taken care of in a moment,' Dr Isler assured him. 'How are you feeling?'

'Oh, not too bad for an old man.'

Dr Isler pulled aside the blanket to reveal the patient's swollen knee and ankle. There were lesions on the soles of his feet.

Dr Isler turned to the residents. 'The swelling is caused by arthritis.' He looked at Honey. 'Combined with the lesions and the conjunctivitis, I'm sure you know what the diagnosis is.'

Honey said slowly, 'Well, it could be . . . you know . . .'

'It's Reiter's syndrome,' one of the residents spoke up. 'The cause is unknown. It's usually accompanied by low-grade fever.'

Dr Isler nodded. 'That's right.' He looked at Honey. 'What is the prognosis?'

'The prognosis?'

The resident replied. 'The prognosis is unclear. It can be treated with anti-inflammation drugs.'

'Very good,' Dr Isler said.

They made the rounds of a dozen more patients, and when they were finished, Honey said to Dr Isler, 'Could I see you for a moment alone. Dr Isler?'

'Yes. Come into my office.'

When they were seated in his office, Honey said, 'I know you're disappointed in me.'

'I must admit that I was a little surprised that you —'

Honey interrupted. 'I know, Dr Isler. I didn't close my eyes last night. To tell you the truth, I was so excited about working with you that I . . . I just couldn't sleep.'

He looked at her in surprise. 'Oh. I see. I knew there had to be a reason for . . . I mean, your medical school record was so fantastic. What made you decide to become a doctor?'

Honey looked down for a moment, then said softly, 'I had a younger brother who was injured in an accident. The doctors did everything they could to try to save him . . . but I watched him die. It took a long time, and I felt so helpless. I decided then that I was going to spend my life helping other people get well.' Her eyes welled up with tears.

She's so vulnerable, Isler thought. 'I'm glad we had this little talk.'

Honey looked at him and thought, *He believed me*.

6

Across town, in another part of the city, reporters and TV crews were waiting in the street for Lou Dinetto as he left the courtroom, smiling and waving, the greeting of royalty to the peasants. There were two bodyguards at his side, a tall, thin man known as the Shadow, and a heavyset man called Rhino. Lou Dinetto was, as always, dressed elegantly and expensively, in a gray silk suit with a white shirt, blue tie, and alligator shoes. His clothes had to be carefully tailored to make him look trim, because he was short and stout, with bandy legs. He always had a smile and a ready quip for the press, and they enjoyed quoting him. Dinetto had been indicted and tried three times on charges ranging from arson to racketeering to murder, and each time he had gone free.

Now as he left the courtroom, one of the reporters yelled out, 'Did you know you were going to be acquitted, Mr Dinetto?'

Dinetto laughed. 'Of course I did. I'm an innocent businessman. The government has got nothing better to do than to persecute me. That's one of the reasons our taxes are so high.'

A TV camera was aimed at him. Lou Dinetto stopped to smile into it.

'Mr Dinetto, can you explain why two witnesses

who were scheduled to testify against you in your murder trial failed to appear?'

'Certainly I can explain it,' Dinetto said. 'They were honest citizens who decided not to perjure themselves.'

'The government claims that you're the head of the West Coast mob, and that it was you who arranged for —'

'The only thing I arrange for is where people sit at my restaurant. I want everybody to be comfortable.' He grinned at the milling crowd of reporters. 'By the way, you're all invited to the restaurant tonight for a free dinner and drinks.'

He was moving toward the curb, where a black stretch limousine was waiting for him.

'Mr Dinetto . . .'

'Mr Dinetto . . .'

'Mr Dinetto . . .'

'I'll see you at my restaurant tonight, boys and girls. You all know where it is.'

And Lou Dinetto was in the car, waving and smiling. Rhino closed the door of the limousine and got into the front seat. The Shadow slipped behind the wheel.

'That was great, boss!' Rhino said. 'You sure know how to handle them bums.'

'Where to?' the Shadow asked.

'Home. I can use a hot bath and a good steak.'

The car started off.

'I don't like that question about the witnesses,' Dinetto said. 'You sure they'll never . . . ?'

'Not unless they can talk underwater, boss.'

Dinetto nodded. 'Good.'

The car was speeding along Fillmore Street.

Dinetto said, 'Did you see the look on the DA's face when the judge dismissed . . . ?'

A small dog appeared out of nowhere, directly in front of the limousine. The Shadow swung the wheel hard to avoid hitting it and jammed on the brakes. The car jumped the curb and crashed into a lamp-post. Rhino's head flew forward into the windshield.

'What the *fuck* are you doing?' Dinetto screamed. 'You trying to kill me?'

The Shadow was trembling. 'Sorry, boss. A dog ran in front of the car . . .'

'And you decided his life was more important than mine? You stupid asshole!'

Rhino was moaning. He turned around, and Dinetto saw blood pouring from a large cut in his forehead.

'For Christ's sake!' Dinetto screamed. 'Look what you've done!'

'I'm all right,' Rhino mumbled.

'The hell you are!' Dinetto turned to the Shadow. 'Get him to a hospital.'

The Shadow backed the limousine off the curb.

'The Embarcadero is only a couple of blocks down. We'll take him to the emergency ward there.'

'Right, boss.'

Dinetto sank back in his seat. 'A dog,' he said disgustedly. 'Jesus!'

Kat was in the emergency ward when Dinetto, the Shadow, and Rhino walked in. Rhino was bleeding heavily.

Dinetto called out to Kat, 'Hey, you!'

Kat looked up. 'Are you talking to me?'

'Who the hell do you think I'm talking to? This man is bleeding. Get him fixed up right away.'

'There are half a dozen others ahead of him,' Kat said quietly. 'He'll have to wait his turn.'

'He's not waiting for anything,' Dinetto told her. 'You'll take care of him now.'

Kat stepped over to Rhino and examined him. She took a piece of cotton and pressed it against the cut. 'Hold it there. I'll be back.'

'I said to take care of him *now*,' Dinetto snapped.

Kat turned to Dinetto. 'This is an emergency hospital ward. I'm the doctor in charge. So either keep quiet or get out.'

The Shadow said, 'Lady, you don't know who you're talking to. You better do what the man says. This is Mr Lou Dinetto.'

'Now that the introductions are over,' Dinetto said impatiently, 'take care of my man.'

'You have a hearing problem,' Kat said. 'I'll tell you once more. Keep quiet or get out of here. I have work to do.'

Rhino said, 'You can't talk to—'

Dinetto turned to him. 'Shut up!' He looked at Kat again, and his tone changed. 'I would appreciate it if you could get to him as soon as possible.'

'I'll do my best.' Kat sat Rhino down on a cot. 'Lie down. I'll be back in a few minutes.' She looked at Dinetto. 'There are some chairs over there in the corner.'

Dinetto and the Shadow watched her walk to the other end of the ward to take care of the waiting patients.

'Jesus,' the Shadow said. 'She has no idea who you are.'

'I don't think it would make any difference. She's got balls.'

Fifteen minutes later, Kat returned to Rhino and examined him. 'No concussion,' she announced. 'You're lucky. That's a nasty cut.'

Dinetto stood watching as Kat skillfully put stitches in Rhino's forehead.

When Kat was finished, she said, 'That should heal nicely. Come back in five days, and I'll take out the stitches.'

Dinetto walked over and examined Rhino's forehead. 'That's a damn good job.'

'Thanks,' Kat said. 'Now, if you'll excuse me . . .'

'Wait a minute,' Dinetto called. He turned to the Shadow. 'Give her a C-note.'

The Shadow took a hundred-dollar bill out of his pocket. 'Here.'

'The cashier's office is outside.'

'This isn't for the hospital. It's for you.'

'No, thanks.'

Dinetto stared as Kat walked away and began working on another patient.

The Shadow said, 'Maybe it wasn't enough, boss.'

Dinetto shook his head. 'She's an independent broad. I like that.' He was silent for a moment. 'Doc Evans is retiring, right?'

'Yeah.'

'Okay. I want you to find out everything you can about this doctor.'

'What for?'

'Leverage. I think she might come in very handy.'

7

Hospitals are run by nurses. Margaret Spencer, the chief nurse, had worked at Embarcadero County Hospital for twenty years and knew where all the bodies—literally and figuratively—were buried. Nurse Spencer was in charge of the hospital, and doctors who did not recognize it were in trouble. She knew which doctors were on drugs or addicted to alcohol, which doctors were incompetent, and which doctors deserved her support. In her charge were all the student nurses, registered nurses, and operating room nurses. It was Margaret Spencer who decided which of them would be assigned to the various surgeries, and since the nurses ranged from indispensable to incompetent, it paid the doctors to get along with her. She had the power to assign an inept scrub nurse to assist on a complicated kidney removal, or, if she liked the doctor, to send her most competent nurse to help him with a simple tonsillectomy. Among Margaret Spencer's many prejudices was an antipathy to woman doctors and to blacks.

Kat Hunter was a black woman doctor.

Kat was having a hard time. Nothing was overtly said or done, and yet prejudice was at work in ways too subtle to pin down. The nurses she asked for were unavailable, those assigned to her were close to incompetent. Kat found herself frequently being sent to examine male clinic patients with venereal diseases. She accepted the first few cases as routine, but when she was given half a dozen to examine in one day, she became suspicious.

At a lunch break she said to Paige, 'Have you examined many men with venereal disease?'

Paige thought for a moment. 'One last week. An orderly.'

I'm going to have to do something about this, Kat thought.

Nurse Spencer had planned to get rid of Dr Hunter by making her life so miserable that she would be forced to quit, but she had not counted on Kat's dedication or her ability. Little by little, Kat was winning over the people she worked with. She had a natural skill that impressed her fellow workers as well as her patients. But the real breakthrough happened because of what came to be known around the hospital as the famous pig blood caper.

On morning rounds one day, Kat was working with a senior resident named Dundas. They were at the bedside of a patient who was unconscious.

'Mr Levy was in an automobile accident,' Dundas informed the younger residents. 'He's lost a great deal of blood, and he needs an immediate transfusion. The hospital is short of blood right now. This man has a family, and they refuse to donate any blood to him. It's infuriating.'

Kat asked, 'Where is his family?'

'In the visitors' waiting room,' Dr Dundas said.

'Do you mind if I talk to them?' Kat asked.

'It won't do any good. I've already spoken to them. They've made up their minds.'

When the rounds were over, Kat went into the visitors' waiting room. The man's wife and grown son and daughter were there. The son wore a yarmulke and ritual tallis.

'Mrs Levy?' Kat asked the woman.

She stood up. 'How is my husband? Is the doctor going to operate?'

'Yes,' Kat said.

'Well, don't ask us to give any of our blood. It's much too dangerous these days, with AIDS and all.'

'Mrs Levy,' Kat said, 'you can't get AIDS by donating blood. It's not poss—'

'Don't tell me! I read the papers. I know what's what.'

Kat studied her a moment. 'I can see that. Well, it's all right, Mrs Levy. The hospital is short of blood right now, but we've solved the problem.'

'Good.'

'We're going to give your husband pig's blood.'

The mother and son were staring at Kat, shocked. *'What?'*

'Pig's blood,' Kat said cheerfully. 'It probably won't do him any harm.' She turned to leave.

'Wait a minute!' Mrs Levy cried.

Kat stopped. 'Yes?'

'I, uh . . . just give us a minute, will you?'

'Certainly.'

Fifteen minutes later, Kat went up to Dr Dundas. 'You don't have to worry about Mr Levy's family anymore. They're all happy to make a blood donation.'

The story became an instant legend around the hospital. Doctors and nurses who had ignored Kat before made a point of speaking to her.

A few days later, Kat went into the private room of Tom Leonard, an ulcer patient. He was eating an enormous lunch that he had had brought in from a nearby delicatessen.

Kat walked up to his bed. 'What are you doing?'

He looked up and smiled. 'Having a decent lunch for a change. Want to join me? There's plenty here.'

Kat rang for a nurse.

'Yes, doctor?'

'Get this food out of here. Mr Leonard is on a strict hospital diet. Didn't you read his chart?'

'Yes, but he insisted on —'

'Remove it, please.'

'Hey! Wait a minute!' Leonard protested. 'I can't eat the pap this hospital is giving me!'

'You'll eat it if you want to get rid of your ulcer.' Kat looked at the nurse. 'Take it out.'

Thirty minutes later, Kat was summoned to the office of the administrator.

'You wanted to see me, Dr Wallace?'

'Yes. Sit down. Tom Leonard is one of your patients, isn't he?'

'That's right. I found him eating a hot pastrami sandwich with pickles and potato salad for lunch today, full of spices and —'

'And you took it away from him.'

'Of course.'

Wallace leaned forward in his chair. 'Doctor, you probably were not aware that Tom Leonard is on

97

the hospital's supervisory board. We want to keep him happy. Do you get my meaning?'

Kat looked at him and said stubbornly, 'No, sir.'

He blinked. 'What?'

'It seems to me that the way to keep Tom Leonard happy is to get him healthy. He's not going to be cured if he tears his stomach apart.'

Benjamin Wallace forced a smile. 'Why don't we let him make that decision?'

Kat stood up. 'Because *I'm* his doctor. Is there anything else?'

'I . . . er . . . no. That's all.'

Kat walked out of the office.

Benjamin Wallace sat there stunned. *Woman doctors!*

Kat was on night duty when she received a call. 'Dr Hunter, I think you had better come up to 320.'

'Right away.'

The patient in Room 320 was Mrs Molloy, a cancer patient in her eighties, with a poor prognosis. As Kat neared the door she heard voices inside, raised in argument. Kat stepped inside the room.

Mrs Molloy was in bed, heavily sedated, but conscious. Her son and two daughters were in the room.

The son was saying, 'I say we split the estate up three ways.'

'No!' one of the daughters said. 'Laurie and I are the ones who have been taking care of Mama. Who's been doing the cooking and cleaning for her? We have! Well, we're entitled to her money and —'

'I'm as much her flesh and blood as you are!' the man yelled.

Mrs Molloy lay in bed, helpless, listening.

Kat was furious. 'Excuse me,' she said.

One of the women glanced at her. 'Come back later, nurse. We're busy.'

Kat said angrily, 'This is my patient. I'm giving you all ten seconds to get out of this room. You can wait in the visitors' waiting room. Now get out before I call security and have you thrown out.'

The man started to say something, but the look in Kat's eyes stopped him. He turned to his sisters and shrugged. 'We can talk outside.'

Kat watched the three of them leave the room. She turned to Mrs Molloy in bed and stroked her head. 'They didn't mean anything by it,' Kat said softly. She sat at the bedside, holding the old woman's hand, and watched her drop off to sleep.

We're all dying, Kat thought. *Forget what Dylan Thomas said. The real trick is to go gentle into that good night.*

Kat was in the middle of treating a patient when an orderly came into the ward. 'There's an urgent call for you at the desk, doctor.'

Kat frowned. 'Thank you.' She turned to the patient, who was in a full body cast, with his legs suspended on a pulley. 'I'll be right back.'

In the corridor, at the nurses' station, Kat picked up the desk telephone. 'Hello?'

'Hi, sis.'

'Mike!' She was excited to hear from him, but her excitement immediately turned to concern. 'Mike, I told you never to call me here. You have the number at the apartment if —'

'Hey, I'm sorry. This couldn't wait. I have a little problem.'

Kat knew what was coming.

'I borrowed some money from a fellow to invest in a business . . .'

Kat didn't bother asking what kind of business. 'And it failed.'

'Yeah. And now he wants his money.'

'How much, Mike?'

'Well, if you could send five thousand . . .'

'What?'

The desk nurse was looking at Kat curiously.

Five thousand dollars. Kat lowered her voice. 'I don't have that much. I . . . I can send you half now and the rest in a few weeks. Will that be all right?'

'I guess so. I hate to bother you, sis, but you know how it is.'

Kat knew exactly how it was. Her brother was twenty-two years old and was always involved in mysterious deals. He ran with gangs, and God only knew what they were up to, but Kat felt a deep responsibility toward him. *It's all my fault*, Kat thought. *If I hadn't run away from home and deserted him* . . . 'Stay out of trouble, Mike. I love you.'

'I love you, too, Kat.'

I'll have to get that money, somehow, Kat thought. *Mike's all I have in the world.*

Dr Isler had been looking forward to working with Honey Taft again. He had forgiven her inept performance and, in fact, was flattered that she was in such awe of him. But now, on rounds with her once more. Honey stayed behind the other residents and never volunteered an answer to his questions.

Thirty minutes after rounds, Dr Isler was seated in Benjamin Wallace's office.

'What's the problem?' Wallace asked.

'It's Dr Taft.'

Wallace looked at him in genuine surprise. 'Dr Taft? She has the best recommendations I've ever seen.'

'That's what puzzles me,' Dr Isler said. 'I've been getting reports from some of the other residents. She's misdiagnosing cases and making serious mistakes. I'd like to know what the hell is going on.'

'I don't understand. She went to a fine medical school.'

'Maybe you should give the dean of the school a call,' Dr Isler suggested.

'That's Jim Pearson. He's a good man. I'll call him.'

A few minutes later, Wallace had Jim Pearson on the telephone. They exchanged pleasantries, and then Wallace said, 'I'm calling about Betty Lou Taft.'

There was a brief silence. 'Yes?'

'We seem to be having a few problems with her, Jim. She was admitted here with your wonderful recommendation.'

'Right.'

'In fact, I have your report in front of me. It says she was one of the brightest students you ever had.'

'That's right.'

'And that she was going to be a credit to the medical profession.'

'Yes.'

'Was there any doubt about . . . ?'

'None,' Dr Pearson said firmly. 'None at all. She's probably a little nervous. She's high-strung, but if you just give her a chance, I'm sure she'll be fine.'

'Well, I appreciate your telling me. We'll certainly give her every chance. Thank you.'

'Not at all.' The line went dead.

Jim Pearson sat there, hating himself for what he had done.

But my wife and children come first.

8

Honey Taft had the bad fortune to have been born into a family of overachievers. Her handsome father was the founder and president of a large computer company in Memphis, Tennessee, her lovely mother was a genetic scientist, and Honey's older twin sisters were as attractive, as brainy, and as ambitious as their parents. The Tafts were among the most prominent families in Memphis.

Honey had inconveniently come along when her sisters were six years old.

'Honey was our little accident,' her mother would tell their friends. 'I wanted to have an abortion, but Fred was against it. Now he's sorry.'

Where Honey's sisters were stunning, Honey was plain. Where they were brilliant, Honey was average. Her sisters had started talking at nine months. Honey had not uttered a word until she was almost two.

'We call her "the dummy",' her father would laugh. 'Honey is the ugly duckling of the Taft family. Only I don't think she's going to turn into a swan.'

It was not that Honey was ugly, but neither was she pretty. She was ordinary-looking, with a thin, pinched face, mousy blond hair, and an unenviable figure. What Honey *did* have was an extraordinarily sweet, sunny disposition, a quality not particularly prized in a family of competitive overachievers.

From the earliest time Honey could remember, her greatest desire was to please her parents and sisters and make them love her. It was a futile effort. Her parents were busy with their careers, and her sisters were busy winning beauty contests and scholarships. To add to Honey's misery, she was inordinately shy. Consciously or unconsciously, her family had implanted in her a feeling of deep inferiority.

In high school, Honey was known as the Wallflower. She attended school dances and parties by herself, and smiled and tried not to show how miserable she was, because she did not want to spoil anyone's fun. She would watch her sisters picked up at the house by the most popular boys at school, and then she would go up to her lonely room to struggle with her homework.

And try not to cry.

On weekends and during the summer holidays, Honey made pocket money by baby-sitting. She loved taking care of children, and the children adored her.

When Honey was not working, she would go off and explore Memphis by herself. She visited Graceland, where Elvis Presley had lived, and walked down Beale Street, where the blues started. She wandered through the Pink Palace Museum, and the Planetarium, with its roaring, stomping dinosaur. She went to the aquarium.

And Honey was always alone.

She was unaware that her life was about to change drastically.

*　　*　　*

Honey knew that many of her classmates were having love affairs. They discussed it constantly at school.

'Have you gone to bed with Ricky yet? He's the best . . . !'

'Joe is really into orgasms . . .'

'I was out with Tony last night. I'm exhausted. What an animal! I'm seeing him again tonight . . .'

Honey stood there listening to their conversations and she was filled with a bittersweet envy, and a feeling that she would never know what sex was like. *Who would want me?* Honey wondered.

One Friday night, there was a school prom. Honey had no intention of going, but her father said, 'You know, I'm concerned. Your sisters tell me that you're a wallflower, and that you're not going to the prom because you can't get a date.'

Honey blushed. 'That's not true,' she said. 'I do have a date, and I *am* going.' *Don't let him ask who my date is*, Honey prayed.

He didn't.

Now Honey found herself at the prom, seated in her usual corner, watching the others dancing and having a wonderful time.

And that was when the miracle occurred.

Roger Merton, the captain of the football team and the most popular boy at school, was on the dance floor, having a fight with his girlfriend. He had been drinking.

'You're a no-good, selfish bastard!' she said.

'And you're a dumb bitch!'

'You can go screw yourself.'

'I don't have to screw myself, Sally. I can screw somebody else. Anyone I want to.'

'Go ahead!' She stormed off the dance floor.

Honey could not help but overhear.

Merton saw her looking at him. 'What the hell are you staring at?' He was slurring his words.

'Nothing,' Honey said.

'I'll show the bitch! You think I won't show her?'

'I . . . yes.'

'Damn right. Let's have a li'l drink.'

Honey hesitated. Merton was obviously drunk. 'Well, I don't . . .'

'Great. I have a bottle in the car.'

'I really don't think I . . .'

And he had Honey's arm and was steering her out of the room. She went along because she did not want to make a scene and embarrass him.

Outside, Honey tried to pull away. 'Roger, I don't think this is a good idea. I . . .'

'What the hell are you—chicken?'

'No, I . . .'

'Okay, then. Come on.'

He led her to his car and opened the door. Honey stood there a moment.

'Get in.'

'I can only stay a moment,' Honey said.

She got in the car because she did not want to upset Roger. He climbed in beside her.

'We're going to show that dumb broad, aren't we?' He held out a bottle of bourbon. 'Here.'

Honey had had only one drink of alcohol before

and she had hated it. But she did not want to hurt Roger's feelings. She looked at him and reluctantly took a small sip.

'You're okay,' he said. 'You're new at school, huh?'

Honey was in three of his classes. 'No,' Honey said. 'I . . .'

He leaned over and began to play with her breasts.

Startled, Honey pulled away.

'Hey! Come on. Don't you want to please me?' he said.

And that was the magic phrase. Honey wanted to please everybody, and if this was the way to do it . . .

In the uncomfortable backseat of Merton's car, Honey had sex for the first time, and it opened an incredible new world to her. She did not particularly enjoy the sex, but that was not important. The important thing was that Merton enjoyed it. In fact, Honey was amazed by how *much* he enjoyed it. It seemed to make him ecstatic. She had never seen anyone enjoy anything so much. *So this is how to please a man*, Honey thought.

It was an epiphany.

Honey was unable to get the miracle of what had occurred out of her mind. She lay in bed, remembering Merton's hard maleness inside her, thrusting faster and faster, and then his moans, 'Oh, yes, yes . . . Jesus, you're fantastic, Sally . . .'

And Honey had not even minded that. She had pleased the captain of the football team! The most popular boy in school! *And I really didn't even know what I was doing*, Honey thought. *If I truly learned how to please a man . . .*

And that was when Honey had her second epiphany.

The following morning, Honey went to the Pleasure Chest, a porno bookstore on Poplar Street, and bought half a dozen books on eroticism. She smuggled them home and read them in the privacy of her room. She was astounded by what she was reading.

She raced through the pages of *The Perfumed Garden* and the *Kama Sutra*, the *Tibetan Arts of Love*, the *Alchemy of Ecstasy*, and then went back for more. She read the words of Gedun Chopel and the arcane accounts by Kanchinatha.

She studied the exciting photographs of the thirty-seven positions of lovemaking, and she learned the meaning of the Half Moon and the Circle, the Lotus Petal, and the Pieces of Cloud, and the way of churning.

Honey became an expert on the eight types of oral sex, and the paths of the sixteen pleasures, and the ecstasy of the string of marbles. She knew how to teach a man to perform *karuna*, to intensify his pleasure. In theory, at least.

Honey felt she was now ready to put her knowledge into practice.

The *Kama Sutra* had several chapters on aphrodisiacs to arouse a man, but since Honey had no idea where she could obtain *Hedysarum gangeticum*, the *kshirika* plant, or the *Xanthochymus pictorius*, she figured out her own substitutes.

When Honey saw Roger Merton in class the following week, she walked up to him and said, 'I really enjoyed the other night. Can we do it again?'

It took him a moment to remember who Honey was. 'Oh. Sure. Why not? My folks are out tonight. Why don't you come by about eight o'clock?'

When Honey arrived at Merton's house that night, she had a small jar of maple syrup with her.

'What's that for?' Merton said.

'I'm going to show you,' Honey said.

She showed him.

The next day, Merton was telling his buddies at school about Honey.

'She's incredible,' he said. 'You wouldn't believe what she can do with a little warm syrup!'

That afternoon, half a dozen boys were asking Honey for dates. From that time on, she started going out every night. The boys were very happy, and that made Honey very happy.

Honey's parents were delighted by their daughter's sudden popularity.

'It took our girl a little while to bloom,' her father said proudly, 'but now she's turned into a real Taft!'

Honey had always had poor grades in mathematics, and she knew she had failed badly on her final test. Her mathematics teacher, Mr Janson, was a bachelor and lived near the school. Honey paid him a visit one evening. He opened the door and looked at her in surprise.

'Honey! What are you doing here?'

'I need your help,' Honey said. 'My father will kill me if I fail your course. I brought some math problems, and I wonder if you would mind going over them with me.'

He hesitated a moment. 'This is unusual, but . . . very well.'

Mr Janson liked Honey. She was not like the other girls in his class. They were raucous and indifferent, while Honey was sensitive and caring, always eager to please. He wished that she had more of an aptitude for mathematics.

Mr Janson sat next to Honey on the couch and began to explain the arcane intricacies of logarithms.

Honey was not interested in logarithms. As Mr Janson talked, Honey moved closer and closer to him. She started breathing on his neck and into his ear, and before he knew what was happening, Mr Janson found that his pants were unzipped.

He was looking at Honey in astonishment. 'What are you doing?'

'I've wanted you since the first time I saw you,' Honey said. She opened her purse and took out a small can of whipped cream.

'What's that?'

'Let me show you . . .'

Honey received an A in math.

It was not only the accessories Honey used that made her so popular. It was the knowledge she had gleaned from all the ancient books on erotica she had read. She delighted her partners with techniques they had never dreamed of, that were thousands of years old, and long forgotten. She brought a new meaning to the word 'ecstasy'.

Honey's grades improved dramatically, and she

was suddenly even more popular than her sisters had been in their high school days. Honey was dined at the Private Eye and the Bombay Bicycle Club, and taken to the Ice Capades at the Memphis Mall. The boys took her skiing at Cedar Cliff and sky diving at Landis Airport.

Honey's years at college were just as successful socially. At dinner one evening, her father said, 'You'll be graduating soon. It's time to think about your future. Do you know what you want to do with your life?'

She answered immediately. 'I want to be a nurse.'

Her father's face reddened. 'You mean a doctor.'

'No, Father. I—'

'You're a Taft. If you want to go into medicine, you'll be a doctor. Is that understood?'

'Yes, Father.'

Honey had meant it when she told her father she wanted to be a nurse. She loved taking care of people, helping them and nurturing them. She was terrified by the idea of becoming a doctor, and being responsible for people's lives, but she knew that she must not disappoint her father. *You're a Taft.*

Honey's college grades were not good enough to get her into medical school, but her father's influence was. He was a heavy contributor to a medical school in Knoxville, Tennessee. He met with Dr Jim Pearson, the dean.

'You're asking for a big favor,' Pearson said, 'but I'll tell you what I'll do. I'll admit Honey on a pro-bationary basis. If at the end of six months we feel she's not qualified to continue, we'll have to let her go.'

'Fair enough. She's going to surprise you.'

He was right.

Honey's father had made arrangements for her to stay in Knoxville with a cousin of his, the Reverend Douglas Lipton.

Douglas Lipton was the minister of the Baptist Church. He was in his sixties, married to a woman ten years older.

The minister was delighted to have Honey in the house.

'She's like a breath of fresh air,' he told his wife.

He had never seen anyone so eager to please.

Honey did fairly well in medical school, but she lacked dedication. She was there only to please her father.

Honey's teachers liked her. There was a genuine niceness about her that made her professors want her to succeed.

Ironically, she was particularly weak in anatomy. During the eighth week, her anatomy teacher sent for her. 'I'm afraid I'm going to have to fail you,' he said unhappily.

I can't fail, Honey thought. *I can't let my father down. What would Boccaccio have advised?*

Honey moved closer to the professor. 'I came to this school because of you. I have heard so much about you.' She moved closer to him. 'I want to be like you.' And closer. 'Being a doctor means everything to me.' And closer. 'Please help me . . .'

One hour later, when Honey left his office, she had the answers to the next examination.

Before Honey was finished with medical school, she had seduced several of her professors. There was a helplessness about her that they were unable to resist. They were all under the impression that it was *they* who were seducing *her*, and they felt guilty about taking advantage of her innocence.

Dr Jim Pearson was the last to succumb to Honey. He was intrigued by all the reports he had heard about her. There were rumors of her extraordinary sexual skills. He sent for Honey one day to discuss her grades. She brought a small box of powdered sugar with her, and before the afternoon was over, Dr Pearson was as hooked as all the others. Honey made him feel young and insatiable. She made him feel that he was a king who had subjugated her and made her his slave.

He tried not to think of his wife and children.

Honey was genuinely fond of the Reverend Douglas Lipton, and it upset her that his wife was a cold, frigid woman who was always criticizing him. Honey felt sorry for the minister. *He doesn't deserve that,* Honey thought. *He needs comforting.*

In the middle of the night, when Mrs Lipton was out of town visiting a sister, Honey walked into the minister's bedroom. She was naked. 'Douglas . . .'

His eyes flew open. 'Honey? Are you all right?'

'No,' she said. 'Can I talk to you?'

'Of course.' He reached for the lamp.

'Don't turn on the light.' She crept into bed beside him.

'What's the matter? Aren't you feeling well?'

'I'm worried.'

'About what?'

'You. You deserve to be loved. I want to make love to you.'

He was wide awake. 'My God!' he said. 'You're just a child. You can't be serious.'

'I am. Your wife's not giving you any love . . .'

'Honey, this is impossible! You'd better get back to your room now, and . . .'

He could feel her naked body pressing against his. 'Honey, we can't do this. I'm . . .'

Her lips were on his, and her body was on top of him, and he was completely swept away. She spent the night in his bed.

At six o'clock in the morning, the door to the bedroom opened and Mrs Lipton walked in. She stood there, staring at the two of them, then walked out without a word.

Two hours later, the Reverend Douglas Lipton committed suicide in his garage.

When Honey heard the news, she was devastated, unable to believe what had happened.

The sheriff arrived at the house and had a talk with Mrs Lipton.

When he was through, he went to find Honey. 'Out of respect for his family, we're going to list the death of the Reverend Douglas Lipton as a "suicide for reasons unknown," but I would suggest that you get the fuck out of this town fast, and stay out.'

Honey had gone to Embarcadero County Hospital in San Francisco.

With a glowing recommendation from Dr Jim Pearson.

9

Time had lost all meaning for Paige. There was no beginning and no end, and the days and nights flowed into one another in a seamless rhythm. The hospital had become her whole life. The outside world was a foreign, faraway planet.

Christmas came and went, and a new year began. In the world outside, US troops liberated Kuwait from Iraq.

There was no word from Alfred. *He'll find out he made a mistake*, Paige thought. *He'll come back to me.*

The early morning crank telephone calls had stopped as suddenly as they had started. Paige was relieved that no new mysterious or threatening incidents had befallen her. It was almost as if they had all been a bad dream . . . except, of course, they hadn't been.

The routine continued to be frantic. There was no time to know patients. They were simply gallbladders and ruptured livers, fractured femurs and broken backs.

The hospital was a jungle filled with mechanical demons—respirators, heart rate monitors, CAT scan equipment, X-ray machines. And each had its own peculiar sound. There were whistles, and buzzers, and the constant chatter on the PA system, and they all blended into a loud, insane cacophony.

The second year of residency was a rite of passage. The residents moved up to more demanding duties and watched the new group come in, feeling a mixture of scorn and arrogance toward them.

'Those poor devils,' Kat said to Paige. 'They have no idea what they're in for.'

'They'll find out soon enough.'

Paige and Honey were becoming worried about Kat. She was losing weight, and seemed depressed. In the middle of conversations, they would find Kat looking off into space, her mind preoccupied. From time to time, she would receive a mysterious phone call, and after each one her depression seemed to worsen.

Paige and Honey sat down to have a talk with her.

'Is everything all right?' Paige asked. 'You know we love you, and if there's a problem, we'd like to help.'

'Thanks. I appreciate it, but there's nothing you can do. It's a money problem.'

Honey looked at her in surprise. 'What do you need money for? We never go anyplace. We haven't any time to buy anything. We—'

'It's not for me. It's for my brother.' Kat had not mentioned her brother before.

'I didn't know you had a brother,' Paige said.

'Does he live in San Francisco?' Honey asked.

Kat was hesitant. 'No. He lives back East. In Detroit. You'll have to meet him one day.'

'We'd like to. What does he do?'

'He's kind of an entrepreneur,' Kat said vaguely. 'He's a little down on his luck right now, but Mike will bounce back. He always does.' *I hope to God I'm right*, Kat thought.

Harry Bowman had transferred from a residency program in Iowa. He was a good-humored, happy-go-lucky fellow who went out of his way to be pleasant to everyone.

One day, he said to Paige, 'I'm giving a little party tomorrow night. If you and Dr Hunter and Dr Taft are free, why don't you come? I think you'll have a good time.'

'Fine,' Paige said. 'What shall we bring?'

Bowman laughed. 'Don't bring anything.'

'Are you sure?' Paige asked. 'A bottle of wine, or . . .'

'Forget it! It's going to be at my little apartment.'

Bowman's little apartment turned out to be a ten-room penthouse, filled with antique furniture.

The three women walked in and stared in amazement.

'My God!' Kat said. 'Where did all this come from?'

'I was smart enough to have a clever father,' Bowman said. 'He left all his money to me.'

'And you're working?' Kat marveled.

Bowman smiled. 'I like being a doctor.'

The buffet consisted of Beluga Malossol caviar, *pâté de campagne*, smoked Scottish salmon, oysters on the half shell, backfin lump crabmeat, *crudités* with a shallot vinaigrette dressing, and Cristal champagne.

Bowman had been right. The three of them did have a wonderful time.

'I can't thank you enough,' Paige told Bowman at the end of the evening when they were leaving.

'Are you free Saturday?' he asked.

'Yes.'

'I have a little motorboat. I'll take you out for a spin.'

'Sounds great.'

At four o'clock in the morning, Kat was awakened out of a deep sleep in the on-call room. 'Dr Hunter, Emergency Room Three . . . Dr Hunter, Emergency Three.'

Kat got out of bed, fighting exhaustion. Rubbing sleep from her eyes, she took the elevator down to the ER.

An orderly greeted her at the door. 'He's over on the gurney in the corner. He's in a lot of pain.'

Kat walked over to him. 'I'm Dr Hunter,' she said sleepily.

He groaned. 'Jesus, doc. You've got to do somethin'. My back is killin' me.'

Kat stifled a yawn. 'How long have you been in pain?'

'About two weeks.'

Kat was looking at him, puzzled. 'Two weeks? Why didn't you come in sooner?'

He tried to move, and winced. 'To tell you the truth, I hate hospitals.'

'Then why are you coming in now?'

He brightened. 'There's a big golf tournament coming up, and if you don't fix my back, I won't be able to enjoy it.'

Kat took a deep breath. 'A golf tournament.'

'Yeah.'

She was fighting to control herself. 'I'll tell you what. Go home. Take two aspirins, and if you aren't feeling better in the morning, give me a call.' She turned and stormed out of the room, leaving him gaping after her.

Harry Bowman's little motorboat was a sleek fifty-foot motor cruiser.

'Welcome aboard!' he said as he greeted Paige, Kat, and Honey at the dock.

The women looked at the boat admiringly.

'It's beautiful,' Paige said.

They cruised around the bay for three hours, enjoying the warm, sunny day. It was the first time any of them had relaxed in weeks.

While they were anchored off Angel Island, eating a delicious lunch, Kat said, 'This is the life. Let's not go back to shore.'

'Good thinking,' Honey said.

All in all, it was a heavenly day.

When they returned to the dock, Paige said, 'I can't tell you how much I've enjoyed this.'

'It's been my pleasure.' Bowman patted her arm. 'We'll do it again. Anytime. You three are always welcome.'

What a lovely man, Paige thought.

Honey liked working in obstetrics. It was a ward filled with new life and new hope, in a timeless, joyful ritual.

120

The first-time mothers were eager and apprehensive. The veterans could not wait to get it over with.

One of the women who was about to deliver said to Honey, 'Thank God! I'll be able to see my toes again.'

If Paige had kept a diary, she would have marked the fifteenth of August as a red-letter day. That was the day Jimmy Ford came into her life.

Jimmy was a hospital orderly, with the brightest smile and the sunniest disposition Paige had ever seen. He was small and thin, and looked seventeen. He was twenty-five, and moved around the hospital corridors like a cheerful tornado. Nothing was too much trouble for him.

He was constantly running errands for everyone. He had absolutely no sense of status and treated doctors, nurses, and janitors alike.

Jimmy Ford loved to tell jokes.

'Did you hear about the patient in a body cast? The fellow in the bed next to him asked him what he did for a living.

'He said, "I was a window washer at the Empire State Building."

'The other fellow said, "When did you quit?"

'"Halfway down."'

And Jimmy would grin and hurry off to help somebody.

He adored Paige. 'I'm going to be a doctor one day. I want to be like you.'

He would bring her little presents—candy bars, and stuffed toys. A joke went with each gift.

'In Houston, a man stopped a pedestrian and asked, "What's the quickest way to the hospital?"

The other man said, "Say something bad about Texas." '

The jokes were terrible, but Jimmy made them sound funny.

He would arrive at the hospital the same time as Paige, and he would race up to her on his motorcycle.

'The patient asked, "Will my operation be dangerous?" And the surgeon said, "No. You can't get a dangerous operation for two hundred dollars." '

And he would be gone.

Whenever Paige, Kat, and Honey were free on the same day, they went out exploring San Francisco. They visited the Dutch Mill and the Japanese Tea Garden. They went to Fisherman's Wharf and rode the cable car. They went to see plays at the Curran Theater, and had dinner at the Maharani on Post Street. All the waiters were Indian, and to the astonishment of Kat and Honey, Paige addressed them in Hindi.

'*Hum Hindustani baht bahut ocho bolta hi.*' And from that moment, the restaurant was theirs.

'Where in the world did you learn to talk Indian?' Honey asked.

'Hindi,' Paige said. She hesitated. 'We . . . I lived in India for a while.' It was still so vivid. She and Alfred were at Agra, staring at the Taj Mahal. *Shah Jahan built that in memory of his wife. It took twenty years, Alfred.*

I'm going to build you a Taj Mahal. I don't care how long it takes!

This is Karen Turner. My wife.

She heard her name called, and turned.

122

'Paige . . .' There was a look of concern on Kat's face. 'Are you all right?'

'Fine. I'm fine.'

The impossible hours continued. Another New Year's Eve came and went, and the second year slid into the third, and nothing had changed. The hospital was untouched by the outside world. The wars and famines and disasters of far-off countries paled by comparison with the life-and-death crises they coped with twenty-four hours a day.

Whenever Kat and Paige met in the hospital corridors, Kat would grin and say, 'Having a good time?'

'When did you sleep last?' Paige asked.

Kat sighed. 'Who can remember?'

They stumbled through the long days and nights, trying to keep up with the incessant, demanding pressure, grabbing sandwiches when they had time, and drinking cold coffee out of paper cups.

The sexual harassment seemed to have become a part of Kat's life. There were the constant innuendos not only from the doctors, but also from patients who tried to get her into bed. They got the same response as the doctors. *There's not a man in the world I'll let touch me.*

And she really believed it.

In the middle of a busy morning, there was another telephone call from Mike.

'Hi, sis.'

And Kat knew what was coming. She had sent him all the money she could spare, but deep down inside, she knew that whatever she sent would never be enough.

'I hate like hell to bother you, Kat. I really do. But I got into a small jam.' His voice sounded strained.

'Mike . . . are you all right?'

'Oh, yeah. It's nothing serious. It's just that I owe somebody who needs his money back right away, and I was wondering . . .'

'I'll see what I can do,' Kat said wearily.

'Thanks. I can always count on you, can't I, sis? I love you.'

'I love you, too, Mike.'

One day, Kat said to Paige and Honey, 'Do you know what we all need?'

'A month's sleep?'

'A vacation. That's where we should be, strolling down the Champs-Elysées, looking in all those expensive shop windows.'

'Right. First-class all the way!' Paige giggled. 'We'll sleep all day and play all night.'

Honey laughed. 'Sounds good.'

'We have some vacation time coming up in a few months,' Paige observed. 'Why don't we make some plans for the three of us to go away somewhere?'

'That's a great idea,' Kat said enthusiastically. 'Saturday, let's stop in at a travel agency.'

They spent the next three days excitedly making plans.

'I'm dying to see London. Maybe we'll run into the queen.'

'Paris is where I want to go. It's supposed to be the most romantic city in the world.'

'I want to ride a gondola in the moonlight in Venice.'

Maybe we'll go to Venice on our honeymoon, Paige, Alfred had said. *Would you like that?*

Oh, yes!

She wondered if Alfred had taken Karen to Venice on their honeymoon.

Saturday morning the three of them stopped in at the Corniche Travel Agency on Powell Street.

The woman behind the counter was polite. 'What kind of trip are you interested in?'

'We'd like to go to Europe — London, Paris, Venice . . .'

'Lovely. We have some economical package tours that —'

'No, no, no.' Paige looked at Honey and grinned. 'First-class.'

'Right. First-class air travel,' Kat chimed in.

'First-class hotels,' Honey added.

'Well, I can recommend the Ritz in London, the Crillon in Paris, the Cipriani in Venice, and —'

Paige said, 'Why don't we just take some brochures with us? We can study them and make up our minds.'

'That will be fine,' the travel agent said.

Paige was looking at a brochure. 'You arrange yacht charters, too?'

'Yes.'

'Good. We may be chartering one.'

'Excellent.' The travel agent collected a handful of brochures and handed them to Paige. 'Whenever you're ready, just let me know and I'll be happy to make your reservations.'

125

'You'll hear from us,' Honey promised.

When they got outside, Kat laughed and said, 'Nothing like dreaming big, is there?'

'Don't worry,' Paige assured her. 'One day we'll be able to go to all those places.'

10

Seymour Wilson, the chief of medicine at Embarcadero County Hospital, was a frustrated man with an impossible job. There were too many patients, too few doctors and nurses, and too few hours in a day. He felt like the captain of a sinking ship, running around vainly trying to plug up the holes.

At the moment, Dr Wilson's immediate concern was Honey Taft. While some doctors seemed to like her a great deal, reliable residents and nurses kept reporting that Dr Taft was incapable of doing her job.

Wilson finally went to see Ben Wallace. 'I want to get rid of one of our doctors,' he said. 'The residents she makes rounds with tell me she's incompetent.'

Wallace remembered Honey. She was the one who had the extraordinarily high grades and glowing recommendation. 'I don't understand it,' he said. 'There must be some mistake.' He was thoughtful for a moment. 'I'll tell you what we'll do, Seymour. Who's the meanest son of a bitch on your staff?'.

'Ted Allison.'

'All right. Tomorrow morning, send Honey Taft out on rounds with Dr Allison. Have him give you a report on her. If he says she's incompetent, I'll get rid of her.'

'Fair enough,' Dr Wilson said. 'Thanks, Ben.'

*   *   *

At lunch, Honey told Paige that she had been assigned to make the rounds with Dr Allison the following morning.

'I know him,' Paige said. 'He has a miserable reputation.'

'That's what I hear,' Honey said thoughtfully.

At that moment, in another part of the hospital, Seymour Wilson was talking to Ted Allison. Allison was a hard-bitten veteran of twenty-five years. He had served as a medical officer in the navy, and he still took pride in 'kicking ass'.

Seymour Wilson was saying, 'I want you to keep a close eye on Dr Taft. If she can't cut it, she's out. Understood?'

'Understood.'

He was looking forward to this. Like Seymour Wilson, Ted Allison despised incompetent doctors. In addition, he had a strong conviction that if women wanted to be in the medical profession, they should be nurses. If it was good enough for Florence Nightingale, it was good enough for the rest of them.

At six o'clock the following morning, the residents gathered in the corridor to begin their rounds. The group consisted of Dr Allison, Tom Benson, who was his chief assistant, and five residents, including Honey Taft.

Now, as Allison looked at Honey, he thought, *Okay, sister, let's see what you've got.* He turned to the group. 'Let's go.'

The first patient in Ward One was a teenage girl lying in bed, covered with heavy blankets. She was asleep when the group approached her.

'All right,' Dr Allison said. 'I want you all to take a look at her chart.'

The residents began to study the patient's chart. Dr Allison turned to Honey. 'This patient has fever, chills, general malaise, and anorexia. She has a temperature, a cough, and pneumonia. What's your diagnosis, Dr Taft?'

Honey stood there, frowning, silent.

'*Well?*'

'Well,' Honey said thoughtfully, 'I would say she probably has psittacosis—parrot fever.'

Dr Allison was looking at her in surprise. 'What . . . what makes you say that?'

'Her symptoms are typical of psittacosis, and I noticed that she works part-time as a clerk in a pet shop. Psittacosis is transmitted by infected parrots.'

Allison nodded slowly. 'That's . . . that's very good. Do you know what the treatment is?'

'Yes. Tetracycline for ten days, strict bed rest, and plenty of fluids.'

Dr Allison turned to the group, 'Did you all hear that? Dr Taft is absolutely right.'

They moved on to the next patient.

Dr Allison said, 'If you'll examine his chart, you'll find that he has mesothelial tumors, bloody effusion, and fatigue. What's the diagnosis?'

One of the residents said, hopefully, 'It sounds like some form of pneumonia.'

A second resident spoke up, 'It could be cancer.'

Dr Allison turned to Honey. 'What is your diagnosis, doctor?'

Honey looked thoughtful. 'Offhand, I'd say it was fibrous pneumoconiosis, a form of asbestos poisoning. His chart shows that he works in a carpet mill.'

Ted Allison could not conceal his admiration. 'Excellent! Excellent! Do you happen to know what the therapy is?'

'Unfortunately, no specific therapy is available yet.'

It became even more impressive. In the next two hours, Honey diagnosed a rare case of Reiter's syndrome, osteitis deformans polycythemia, and malaria.

When the rounds were over, Dr Allison shook Honey's hand. 'I'm not easily impressed, doctor, but I want to tell you that you have a tremendous future!'

Honey blushed. 'Thank you, Dr Allison.'

'And I intend to tell Ben Wallace so,' he said as he walked away.

Tom Benson, Allison's senior assistant, looked at Honey and smiled. 'I'll meet you in half an hour, baby.'

Paige tried to stay out of the way of Dr Arthur Kane—007. But at every opportunity, Kane asked for Paige to assist him with operations. And each time, he would become more offensive.

'What do you mean, you won't go out with me? You must be getting it from someone else.'

And, 'I may be short, honey, but not everywhere. You know what I mean?'

She came to dread the occasions she had to work with him. Time after time, Paige watched Kane perform unnecessary surgery and take out organs that were healthy.

One day, as Paige and Kane were walking toward

the operating room, Paige asked, 'What are we going to operate on, doctor?'

'His wallet!' He saw the look on Paige's face. 'Just kidding, honey.'

'He should be working in a butcher shop,' Paige later said angrily to Kat. 'He has no right to be operating on people.'

After a particularly inept liver operation, Dr Kane turned to Paige and shook his head. 'Too bad. I don't know if he's going to make it.'

It was all Paige could do to contain her anger. She decided to have a talk with Tom Chang.

'Someone should report Dr Kane,' Paige said. 'He's murdering his patients!'

'Take it easy.'

'I can't! It's not right that they let a man like that operate. It's criminal. He should be brought up before the credentials committee.'

'What good would it do? You'd have to get other doctors to testify against him, and no one would be willing to do that. This is a close community, and we all have to live in it, Paige. It's almost impossible to get one doctor to testify against another. We're all vulnerable and we need each other too much. Calm down. I'll take you out and buy you lunch.'

Paige sighed. 'All right, but it's a lousy system.'

At lunch, Paige asked, 'How are you and Sye doing?'

He took a moment to answer. 'I . . . we're having problems. My work is destroying our marriage. I don't know what to do.'

'I'm sure it will work out,' Paige said.

Chang said fiercely, 'It had better.'

Paige looked up at him.

'I would kill myself if she left me.'

The following morning, Arthur Kane was scheduled to perform a kidney operation. The chief of surgery said to Paige, 'Dr Kane asked for you to assist him in OR Four.'

Paige's mouth was suddenly dry. She hated the thought of being near him.

Paige said, 'Couldn't you get someone else to . . . ?'

'He's waiting for you, doctor.'

Paige sighed. 'Right.'

By the time Paige had scrubbed up, the operation was already in progress.

'Give me a hand here, darling,' Kane said to Paige.

The patient's abdomen had been painted with an iodine solution and an incision had been made in the right upper quadrant of the abdomen, just below the rib cage. *So far, so good*, Paige thought.

'Scalpel!'

The scrub nurse handed Dr Kane a scalpel.

He looked up. 'Put some music on.'

A moment later a CD began to play.

Dr Kane kept cutting. 'Let's have something a little peppier.' He looked over at Paige. 'Start the bovie, sweetheart.'

Sweetheart. Paige gritted her teeth and picked up a bovie — an electric cautery tool. She began to cauterize the arteries to reduce the amount of blood in the abdomen. The operation was going well.

Thank God, Paige thought.

'Sponge.'

132

The scrub nurse handed Kane a sponge.

'Good. Let's have some suction.' He cut around the kidney until it was exposed. 'There's the little devil,' Dr Kane said. 'More suction.' He lifted up the kidney with forceps. 'Right. Let's sew him back up.'

For once, everything had gone well, yet something was bothering Paige. She took a closer look at the kidney. It looked healthy. She frowned, wondering if . . .

As Dr Kane began sewing up the patient, Paige hurried over to the X-ray in the lighted wall frame. She studied it for a moment and said softly, 'Oh, my God!'

The X-ray had been put up backward. Dr Kane had removed the wrong kidney.

Thirty minutes later, Paige was in Ben Wallace's office.

'He took out a healthy kidney and left in a diseased one!' Paige's voice was trembling. 'The man should be put in jail!'

Benjamin Wallace said soothingly, 'Paige, I agree with you that it's regrettable. But it certainly wasn't intentional. It was a mistake, and—'

'A *mistake*? That patient is going to have to live on dialysis for the rest of his life. Someone should pay for that!'

'Believe me, we're going to have a peer review evaluation.'

Paige knew what that meant: a group of physicians would review what had happened, but it would be done in confidence. The information would be withheld from the public and the patient.

'Dr Wallace . . .'

'You're part of our team, Paige. You've got to be a team player.'

'He has no business working in this hospital. Or any other hospital.'

'You've got to look at the whole picture. If he were removed, there would be bad publicity and the reputation of the hospital would be hurt. We'd probably face a lot of malpractice suits.'

'What about the patients?'

'We'll keep a closer eye on Dr Kane.' He leaned forward in his chair. 'I'm going to give you some advice. When you get into private practice, you're going to need the goodwill of other doctors for referrals. Without that, you'll go nowhere, and if you get the reputation of being a maverick and blowing the whistle on your fellow doctors, you won't get any referrals. I can promise you that.'

Paige rose. 'So you aren't going to do anything?'

'I told you, we're going to do a peer review evaluation.'

'And that's it?'

'That's it.'

'It's not fair,' Paige said. She was in the cafeteria having lunch with Kat and Honey.

Kat shook her head. 'Nobody said life has to be fair.'

Paige looked around the antiseptic white-tiled room. 'This whole place depresses me. Everybody is sick.'

'Or they wouldn't be here,' Kat pointed out.

'Why don't we give a party?' Honey suggested.

'A party? What are you talking about?'

Honey's voice was suddenly filled with enthusiasm. 'We could order up some decent food and liquor, and have a celebration! I think we could all use a little cheering up.'

Paige thought for a second. 'You know,' she said, 'that's not a bad idea. Let's do it!'

'It's a deal. I'll organize things,' Honey told them. 'We'll do it tomorrow after rounds.'

Arthur Kane approached Paige in the corridor. There was ice in his voice. 'You've been a naughty girl. Someone should teach you to keep your mouth shut!' And he walked away.

Paige looked after him in disbelief. *Wallace told him what I said. He shouldn't have done that. 'If you get the reputation of being a maverick and blowing the whistle on your fellow doctors . . .' Would I do it again?* Paige pondered. *Darned right I would!*

News of the forthcoming party spread rapidly. All the residents chipped in. A lavish menu was ordered from Ernie's restaurant, and liquor was delivered from a nearby store. The party was set for five o'clock in the doctors' lounge. The food and drinks arrived at four-thirty. There was a feast: seafood platters with lobster and shrimp, a variety of pâtés, Swedish meatballs, hot pasta, fruit, and desserts. When Paige, Kat, and Honey walked into the lounge at five-fifteen, it was already crowded with eager residents, interns, and nurses, eating and having a wonderful time.

Paige turned to Honey. 'This was a great idea!'
Honey smiled. 'Thank you.'

An announcement came over the loudspeaker. 'Dr Finley and Dr Ketler to the ER. Stat.' And the two doctors, in the middle of downing shrimp, looked at each other, sighed, and hurriedly left the room.

Tom Chang came up to Paige. 'We ought to do this every week,' he said.

'Right. It's —'

The loudspeaker came on again. 'Dr Chang . . . Room 317 . . . Dr Chang . . . Room 317.'

And a minute later, 'Dr Smythe . . . ER Two . . . Dr Smythe to ER Two.'

The loudspeaker never stopped. Within thirty minutes, almost every doctor and nurse had been called away on some emergency. Honey heard her name called, and then Paige's, and Kat's.

'I can't believe what's happening,' Kat said. 'You know how people talk about having a guardian angel? Well, I think the three of us are under the spell of a guardian devil.'

Her words proved to be prophetic.

The next Monday morning, when Paige got off duty and went to get into her car, two of the tires had been slashed. She stared at them in disbelief. *Someone should teach you to keep your mouth shut!*

When she got back to the apartment she said to Kat and Honey, 'Watch out for Arthur Kane. He's crazy.'

11

Kat was awakened by the ring of the telephone. Without opening her eyes, she reached out for it and put the receiver to her ear.

'H'lo?'

'Kat? It's Mike.'

She sat up, her heart suddenly pounding. 'Mike, are you all right?' She heard him laugh.

'Never better, sis. Thanks to you and your friend.'

'My friend?'

'Mr Dinetto.'

'Who?' Kat tried to concentrate, groggy with sleep.

'Mr Dinetto. He really saved my life.'

Kat had no idea what he was talking about. 'Mike . . .'

'You know the fellows I owed money to? Mr Dinetto got them off my back. He's a real gentleman. And he thinks the world of you. Kat.'

Kat had forgotten the incident with Dinetto, but now it suddenly flashed into her mind: *Lady, you don't know who you're talking to. You better do what the man says. This is Mr Lou Dinetto.*

Mike was going on. 'I'm sending you some cash, Kat. Your friend arranged for me to get a job. It pays real good money.'

Your friend. Kat was nervous. 'Mike, listen to me. I want you to be careful.'

She heard him laugh again.

'Don't worry about me. Didn't I tell you everything would be coming up roses? Well, I was right.'

'Take care of yourself, Mike. Don't —'

The connection was broken.

Kat was unable to go back to sleep. *Dinetto! How did he find out about Mike, and why is he helping him?*

The following night, when Kat left the hospital, a black limousine was waiting for her at the curb. The Shadow and Rhino were standing beside it.

As Kat started to pass, Rhino said, 'Get in, doctor. Mr Dinetto wants to see you.'

She studied the man for a moment. Rhino was ominous-looking, but it was the Shadow who frightened Kat. There was something deadly about his stillness. Under other circumstances, Kat would never have gotten into the car, but Mike's telephone call had puzzled her. And worried her.

She was driven to a small apartment on the outskirts of the city, and when she arrived, Dinetto was waiting for her.

'Thanks for coming, Dr Hunter,' he said. 'I appreciate it. A friend of mine had a little accident. I want you to take a look at him.'

'What are you doing with Mike?' Kat demanded.

'Nothing,' he said innocently. 'I heard he was in a little trouble, and I got it taken care of.'

'How did . . . how did you find out about him? I mean, that he was my brother and . . .'

Dinetto smiled. 'In my business, we're all friends. We help each other. Mike got mixed up with some bad boys, so I helped him out. You should be grateful.'

'I am,' Kat said. 'I really am.'

'Good! You know the saying "One hand washes the other"?'

Kat shook her head. 'I won't do anything illegal.'

'Illegal?' Dinetto said. He seemed hurt. 'I wouldn't ask you to do anything like that. This friend of mine was in a little accident and he hates hospitals. Would you take a look at him?'

What am I letting myself in for? Kat wondered. 'Very well.'

'He's in the bedroom.'

Dinetto's friend had been badly beaten up. He was lying in bed, unconscious.

'What happened to him?' Kat asked.

Dinetto looked at her and said, 'He fell down a flight of stairs.'

'He should be in a hospital.'

'I told you, he doesn't like hospitals. I can get whatever hospital equipment you need. I had another doctor who took care of my friends, but he had an accident.'

The words sent a chill through Kat. She wanted nothing more than to run out of the place and go home, and never hear Dinetto's name again, but nothing in life was free. *Quid pro quo.* Kat took off her coat and went to work.

By the beginning of her fourth year of residency, Paige had assisted in hundreds of operations. They had become second nature to her. She knew the surgery procedures for the gallbladder, spleen, liver, appendix, and, most exciting, the heart. But Paige was frustrated because she was not doing the operations herself. *Whatever happened to 'Watch one, do one, teach one'?* she wondered.

The answer came when George Englund, chief of surgery, sent for her.

'Paige, there's a hernia operation scheduled for tomorrow in OR Three, seven-thirty A.M.'

She made a note. 'Right. Who's doing the operation?'

'You are.'

'Right. I . . .' The words suddenly sank in. '*I* am?'

'Yes. Any problem with that?'

Paige's grin lit up the room. 'No, sir! I . . . thanks!'

'You're ready for it. I think the patient's lucky to have you. His name is Walter Herzog. He's in 314.'

'Herzog. Room 314. Right.'

And Paige was out the door.

Paige had never been so excited. *I'm going to do my first operation! I'm going to hold a human being's life in my hands. What if I'm not ready? What if I make a mistake? Things can go wrong. It's Murphy's Law.* By the time Paige was through arguing with herself, she was in a state of panic.

She went into the cafeteria and sat down to have a cup of black coffee. *It's going to be all right,* she told herself. *I've assisted in dozens of hernia operations. There's nothing to it. He's lucky to have me.* By the time she finished her coffee, she was calm enough to face her first patient.

Walter Herzog was in his sixties, thin, bald, and very nervous. He was in bed, clutching his groin, when Paige walked in, carrying a bouquet of flowers. Herzog looked up.

'Nurse . . . I want to see a doctor.'

Paige walked over to the bed and handed him the flowers. 'I'm the doctor. I'm going to operate on you.'

He looked at the flowers, and looked at her. 'You're *what*?'

'Don't worry,' Paige said reassuringly. 'You're in good hands.' She picked up his chart at the foot of the bed and studied it.

'What does it say?' the man asked anxiously. *Why did she bring me flowers?*

'It says you're going to be just fine.'

He swallowed. 'Are you really going to do the operation?'

'Yes.'

'You seem awfully . . . awfully young.'

Paige patted his arm. 'I haven't lost a patient yet.' She looked around the room. 'Are you comfortable?

Can I get you anything to read? A book or magazine?'

He was listening, nervously. 'No, I'm okay.' *Why was she being so nice to him? Was there something she wasn't telling him?*

'Well, then, I'll see you in the morning,' Paige said cheerfully. She wrote something on a piece of paper and handed it to him. 'Here's my home number. You call me if you need me tonight. I'll stay right by the phone.'

By the time Paige left, Walter Herzog was a nervous wreck.

A few minutes later, Jimmy found Paige in the lounge. He walked up to her with his wide grin. 'Congratulations! I hear you're going to do a procedure.'

Word gets around fast, Paige thought. 'Yes.'

'Whoever he is, he's lucky,' Jimmy said. 'If anything ever happened to me, you're the only one I'd let operate on me.'

'Thanks, Jimmy.'

And, of course, with Jimmy, there was always a joke.

'Did you hear the one about the man who had a strange pain in his ankles? He was too cheap to go to a doctor, so when his friend told him he had exactly the same pain, he said, "You'd better get to a doctor right away. And tell me exactly what he says."

'The next day, he learns his friend is dead. He rushes to a hospital and has five thousand dollars' worth of tests. They can't find anything wrong. He

142

calls his friend's widow, and says, "Was Chester in a lot of pain before he died?"

'"No," she says. "He didn't even see the truck that hit him!"'

And Jimmy was gone.

Paige was too excited to eat dinner. She spent the evening practicing tying surgical knots on table legs and lamps. *I'm going to get a good night's sleep*, Paige decided, *so I'll be nice and fresh in the morning*.

She was awake all night, going over the operation again and again in her mind.

There are three types of hernias: reducible hernia, where it's possible to push the intestines back into the abdomen; irreducible hernia, where adhesions prevent returning the contents to the abdomen; and the most dangerous, strangulated hernia, where the blood flow through the hernia is shut off, damaging the intestines. Walter Herzog's was a reducible hernia.

At six o'clock in the morning, Paige drove to the hospital parking lot. A new red Ferrari was next to her parking space. Idly, Paige wondered who owned it. Whoever it was had to be rich.

At seven o'clock, Paige was helping Walter Herzog change from pajamas to a blue hospital gown. The nurse had already given him a sedative to relax him while they waited for the gurney that would take him to the operating room.

'This is my first operation,' Walter Herzog said.

Mine, too, Paige thought.

The gurney arrived and Walter Herzog was on his way to OR Three. Paige walked down the corridor beside him, and her heart was pounding so loudly that she was afraid he could hear it.

OR Three was one of the larger operating rooms, able to accommodate a heart monitor, a heart-lung machine, and an array of other technical parapher-nalia. When Paige walked into the room, the staff were already there, preparing the equipment. There was an attending physician, the anesthesiologist, two residents, a scrub nurse, and two circulating nurses.

The staff were watching her expectantly, eager to see how she would handle her first operation.

Paige walked up to the operating table. Walter Herzog had had his groin shaved and scrubbed with an antiseptic solution. Sterile drapes had been placed around the operating area.

Herzog looked up at Paige and said drowsily, 'You're not going to let me die, are you?'

Paige smiled. 'What? And spoil my perfect record?'

She looked over at the anesthesiologist, who would give the patient an epidural anesthesia, a saddle block. Paige took a deep breath and nodded.

The operation began.

'Scalpel.'

As Paige was about to make the first cut through the skin, the circulating nurse said something.

'What?'

'Would you like some music, doctor?'

It was the first time she had been asked that question. Paige smiled. 'Right. Let's have some Jimmy Buffett.'

The moment Paige made the first incision, her nervousness vanished. It was as though she had done this all her life. Skillfully, she cut through the first layers of fat and muscle, to the site of the hernia. All the while, she was aware of the familiar litany that was echoing through the room.

'Sponge . . .'

'Give me a bovie . . .'

'There it is . . .'

'Looks like we got there just in time . . .'

'Clamp . . .'

'Suction, please . . .'

Paige's mind was totally focused on what she was doing. Locate the hernial sac . . . free it . . . place the contents back into the abdominal cavity . . . tie off the base of the sac . . . cut off the remainder . . . inguinal ring . . . suture it . . .

One hour and twenty minutes after the first incision, the operation was finished.

Paige should have felt drained, but instead she felt wildly exhilarated.

When Walter Herzog had been sewn up, the scrub nurse turned to Paige. 'Dr Taylor . . .'

Paige looked up. 'Yes?'

The nurse grinned. 'That was beautiful, doctor.'

It was Sunday and the three women had the day off.

'What should we do today?' Kat asked.

Paige had an idea. 'It's such a lovely day, why

don't we drive out to Tree Park? We can pack a picnic lunch and eat outdoors.'

'That sounds lovely,' Honey said.

'Let's do it!' Kat agreed.

The telephone rang. The three of them stared at it.

'Jesus!' Kat said. 'I thought Lincoln freed us. Don't answer it. It's our day off.'

'We *have* no days off,' Paige reminded her.

Kat walked over to the telephone and picked it up. 'Dr Hunter.' She listened for a moment and handed the telephone to Paige. 'It's for you, Dr Taylor.'

Paige said resignedly, 'Right.' She picked up the receiver. 'Dr Taylor . . . Hello, Tom . . . What? . . . No, I was just going out . . . I see . . . All right. I'll be there in fifteen minutes.' She replaced the receiver. *So much for the picnic*, she thought.

'Is it bad?' Honey asked.

'Yes, we're about to lose a patient. I'll try to be back for dinner tonight.'

When Paige arrived at the hospital, she drove into the doctors' parking lot and parked next to the new bright red Ferrari. *I wonder how many operations it took to pay for that?*

Twenty minutes later, Paige was walking into the visitors' waiting room. A man in a dark suit was seated in a chair, staring out the window.

'Mr Newton?'

He rose to his feet. 'Yes.'

'I'm Dr Taylor. I was just in to see your little

boy. He was brought in suffering abdominal pains.'

'Yes. I'm going to take him home.'

'I'm afraid not. Peter has a ruptured spleen. He needs an immediate transfusion and an operation, or he'll die.'

Mr Newton shook his head. 'We are Jehovah's Witnesses. The Lord will not let him die, and I will not let him be tainted with someone else's blood. It was my wife who brought him here. She will be punished for that.'

'Mr Newton, I don't think you understand how serious the situation is. If we don't operate right away, your son is going to die.'

The man looked at her and smiled. 'You don't know God's ways, do you?'

Paige was angry. 'I may not know a lot about God's ways, but I do know a lot about a ruptured spleen.' She took out a piece of paper. 'He's a minor, so you'll have to sign this consent form for him.' She held it out.

'And if I don't sign it?'

'Why . . . then we can't operate.'

He nodded. 'Do you think your powers are stronger than the Lord's?'

Paige was staring at him. 'You're not going to sign, are you?'

'No. A higher power than yours will help my son. You will see.'

When Paige returned to the ward, six-year-old Peter Newton had lapsed into unconsciousness.

'He's not going to make it,' Chang said. 'He's lost too much blood. What do you want to do?'

Paige made her decision. 'Get him into OR One. Stat.'

Chang looked at her in surprise. 'His father changed his mind?'

Paige nodded. 'Yes. He changed his mind. Let's move it.'

'Good for you! I talked to him for an hour and I couldn't budge him. He said God would take care of it.'

'God is taking care of it,' Paige assured him.

Two hours and four pints of blood later, the operation was successfully completed. All the boy's vital signs were strong.

Paige gently stroked his forehead. 'He's going to be fine.'

An orderly hurried into the operating room. 'Dr Taylor? Dr Wallace wants to see you right away.'

Benjamin Wallace was so angry his voice was cracking. 'How could you do such an outrageous thing? You gave him a blood transfusion and operated without permission? You broke the law!'

'I saved the boy's life!'

Wallace took a deep breath. 'You should have gotten a court order.'

'There was no time,' Paige said. 'Ten minutes more and he would have been dead. God was busy elsewhere.'

Wallace was pacing back and forth. 'What are we going to do now?'

'Get a court order.'

'What for? You've already *done* the operation.'

'I'll backdate the court order one day. No one will ever know the difference.'

Wallace looked at her and began to hyperventilate. 'Jesus!' He mopped his brow. 'This could cost me my job.'

Paige looked at him for a long moment. Then she turned and started toward the door.

'Paige . . . ?'

She stopped. 'Yes?'

'You'll never do anything like this again, will you?'

'Only if I have to,' Paige assured him.

13

All hospitals have problems with drug theft. By law, each narcotic that is taken from the dispensary must be signed for, but no matter how controlled the security is, drug addicts almost invariably find a way to circumvent it.

Embarcadero County Hospital was having a major problem. Margaret Spencer went to see Ben Wallace.

'I don't know what to do, doctor. Our fentanyl keeps disappearing.'

Fentanyl is a highly addictive narcotic and anesthetic drug.

'How much is missing?'

'A great deal. If it were just a few bottles, there could be an innocent explanation for it, but it's happening now on a regular basis. More than a dozen bottles a week are disappearing.'

'Do you have any idea who might be taking it?'

'No, sir. I've talked to security. They're at a loss.'

'Who has access to the dispensary?'

'That's the problem. Most of the anesthetists have pretty free access to it, and most of the nurses and surgeons.'

Wallace was thoughtful. 'Thank you for coming to me. I'll take care of it.'

'Thank you, doctor.' Nurse Spencer left.

I don't need this right now, Wallace thought

angrily. A hospital board meeting was coming up, and there were already enough problems to be dealt with. Ben Wallace was well aware of the statistics. More than 10 percent of the doctors in the United States became addicted, at one time or another, to either drugs or alcohol. The easy accessibility of the drugs made them a temptation. It was simple for a doctor to open a cabinet, take out the drug he wanted, and use a tourniquet and syringe to inject it. An addict could need a fix as often as every two hours.

Now it was happening at his hospital. Something had to be done about it before the board meeting. *It would look bad on my record.*

Ben Wallace was not sure whom he could trust to help him find the culprit. He had to be careful. He was certain that neither Dr Taylor nor Dr Hunter was involved, and after a great deal of thought, he decided to use them.

He sent for the two of them. 'I have a favor to ask of you,' he told them. He explained about the missing fentanyl. 'I want you to keep your eyes open. If any of the doctors you work with has to step out of the OR for a moment, in the middle of an operation, or shows any other signs of addiction, I want you to let me know. Look for any changes in personality — depression or mood swings — or tardiness, or missed appointments. I would appreciate it if you would keep this strictly confidential.'

When they left the office, Kat said, 'This is a big hospital. We're going to need Sherlock Holmes.'

'No, we won't,' Paige said unhappily. 'I know who it is.'

*   *   *

Mitch Campbell was one of Paige's favorite doctors. Dr Campbell was a likable gray-haired man in his fifties, always good-humored, and one of the hospital's best surgeons. Paige had noticed lately that he was always a few minutes late for an operation, and that he had developed a noticeable tremor. He used Paige to assist him as often as possible, and he usually let her do a major part of the surgery. In the middle of an operation, his hands would begin to shake and he would hand the scalpel to Paige.

'I'm not feeling well,' he would mumble. 'Would you take over?'

And he would leave the operating room.

Paige had been concerned about what could be wrong with him. Now she knew. She debated what to do. She was aware that if she brought her information to Wallace, Dr Campbell would be fired, or worse, his career would be destroyed. On the other hand, if she did nothing, she would be putting patients' lives in danger. *Perhaps I could talk to him*, Paige thought. *Tell him what I know, and insist that he get treatment.* She discussed it with Kat.

'It's a problem,' Kat agreed. 'He's a nice guy, and a good doctor. If you blow the whistle, he's finished, but if you don't, you have to think about the harm he might do. What do you think will happen if you confront him?'

'He'll probably deny it, Kat. That's the usual pattern.'

'Yeah. It's a tough call.'

*   *   *

152

The following day, Paige had an operation scheduled with Dr Campbell. *I hope I'm wrong*, Paige prayed. *Don't let him be late, and don't let him leave during the operation.*

Campbell was fifteen minutes late, and in the middle of the operation, he said, 'Take over, will you, Paige? I'll be right back.'

I must talk to him, Paige decided. *I can't destroy his career.*

The following morning, as Paige and Honey drove into the doctors' parking lot, Harry Bowman pulled up next to them in the red Ferrari.

'That's a beautiful car,' Honey said. 'How much does one of those cost?'

Bowman laughed. 'If you have to ask, you can't afford it.'

But Paige wasn't listening. She was staring at the car, and thinking about the penthouse, the lavish parties, and the boat. *I was smart enough to have a clever father. He left all his money to me.* And yet Bowman worked at a county hospital. Why?

Ten minutes later, Paige was in the personnel office, talking to Karen, the secretary in charge of records.

'Do me a favor, will you, Karen? Just between us, Harry Bowman has asked me to go out with him and I have a feeling he's married. Would you let me have a peek at his personnel file?'

'Sure. Those horny bastards. They never get enough, do they? You're darn right I'll let you look at his file.' She went over to a cabinet and found what she was looking for. She brought some papers back to Paige.

Paige glanced through them quickly. Dr Harry Bowman's application showed that he had come from a small university in the Midwest and, according to the records, had worked his way through medical school. He was an anesthesiologist.

His father was a barber.

Honey Taft was an enigma to most of the doctors at Embarcadero County Hospital. During the morning rounds, she appeared to be unsure of herself. But on the afternoon rounds, she seemed like a different person. She was surprisingly knowledgeable about each patient, and crisp and efficient in her diagnoses.

One of the senior residents was discussing her with a colleague.

'I'll be damned if I understand it,' he said. 'In the morning, the complaints about Dr Taft keep piling up. She keeps making mistakes. You know the joke about the nurse who gets everything wrong? A doctor is complaining that he told her to give the patient in Room 4 three pills, and she gave the patient in Room 3 four pills, and just as he's talking about her, he sees her chasing a naked patient down the hall, holding a pan of boiling water. The doctor says, "Look at that! I told her to prick his boil!"'

His colleague laughed.

'Well, that's Dr Taft. But in the afternoon she's absolutely brilliant. Her diagnoses are correct, her notes are wonderful, and she's as sharp as hell. She must be taking some kind of miracle pill that only works afternoons.' He scratched his head. 'It beats the hell out of me.'

Dr Nathan Ritter was a pedant, a man who lived and worked by the book. While he lacked the spark of brilliance, he was capable and dedicated, and he expected the same qualities from those who worked with him.

Honey had the misfortune to be assigned to his team.

Their first stop was a ward containing a dozen patients. One of them was just finishing breakfast. Ritter looked at the chart at the foot of the bed. 'Dr Taft, the chart says this is your patient.'

Honey nodded. 'Yes.'

'He's having a bronchoscopy this morning.'

Honey nodded. 'That's right.'

'And you're allowing him to *eat*?' Dr Ritter snapped. '*Before* a bronchoscopy?'

Honey said, 'The poor man hasn't had anything to eat since —'

Nathan Ritter turned to his assistant. 'Postpone the procedure.' He started to say something to Honey, then controlled himself. 'Let's move on.'

The next patient was a Puerto Rican who was coughing badly. Dr Ritter examined him. 'Whose patient is this?'

'Mine,' Honey said.

He frowned. 'His infection should have cleared up before now.' He took a look at the chart. 'You're giving him fifty milligrams of ampicillin four times a day?'

'That's right.'

'That's *not* right. It's *wrong*! That's supposed to be *five hundred* milligrams four times a day. You left off a zero.'

'I'm sorry, I . . .'

'No wonder the patient's not getting any better! I want it changed immediately.'

'Yes, doctor.'

When they came to another patient of Honey's, Dr Ritter said impatiently, 'He's scheduled for a colonoscopy. Where is the radiology report?'

'The radiology report? Oh. I'm afraid I forgot to order one.'

Ritter gave Honey a long speculative look.

The morning went downhill from there.

The next patient they saw was moaning tearfully. 'I'm in such pain. What's wrong with me?'

'We don't know,' Honey said.

Dr Ritter glared at her. 'Dr Taft, may I see you outside for a moment?'

In the corridor, he said, 'Never, *never* tell a patient that you don't know. You're the one they're looking to for help! And if you don't know the answer, make one up. Do you understand?'

'It doesn't seem right to . . .'

'I didn't ask you whether it seemed right. Just do as you're told.'

They examined a hiatal hernia, a hepatitis patient, a patient with Alzheimer's disease, and two dozen others. The minute the rounds were over, Dr Ritter went to Benjamin Wallace's office.

'We have a problem,' Ritter said.

'What is it, Nathan?'

'It's one of the residents here. Honey Taft.'

156

Again! 'What about her?'

'She's a disaster.'

'But she had such a wonderful recommendation.'

'Ben, you'd better get rid of her before the hospital gets in real trouble, before she kills a patient or two.'

Wallace thought about it for a moment, then made his decision. 'Right. She'll be out of here.'

Paige was busy in surgery most of the morning. As soon as she was free, she went to see Dr Wallace, to tell him of her suspicions about Harry Bowman.

'Bowman? Are you sure? I mean . . . I've seen no signs of any addiction.'

'He doesn't use it,' Paige explained. 'He sells it. He's living like a millionaire on a resident's salary.'

Ben Wallace nodded. 'Very well. I'll check it out. Thank you, Paige.'

Wallace sent for Bruce Anderson, head of security. 'We may have identified the drug thief,' Wallace told him. 'I want you to keep a close watch on Dr Harry Bowman.'

'Bowman?' Anderson tried to conceal his surprise. Dr Bowman was constantly giving the guards Cuban cigars and other little gifts. They all loved him.

'If he goes into the dispensary, search him when he comes out.'

'Yes, sir.'

Harry Bowman was headed for the dispensary. He had orders to fill. A *lot* of orders. It had started as a lucky accident. He had been working in a small hospital in Ames, Iowa, struggling to get by on a resident's salary. He had champagne taste and a beer pocketbook, and then Fate had smiled on him.

One of his patients who had been discharged from the hospital telephoned him one morning.

'Doctor, I'm in terrible pain. You have to give me something for it.'

'Do you want to check back in?'

'I don't want to leave the house. Couldn't you bring something here for me?'

Bowman thought about it. 'All right. I'll drop by on my way home.'

When he visited the patient, he brought with him a bottle of fentanyl.

The patient grabbed it. 'That's wonderful!' he said. He pulled out a handful of bills. 'Here.'

Bowman looked at him, surprised. 'You don't have to pay me for that.'

'Are you kidding? This stuff is like gold. I have a lot of friends who will pay you a fortune if you bring them this stuff.'

That was how it had begun. Within two months, Harry Bowman was making more money than he had ever dreamed possible. Unfortunately, the head of the hospital got wind of what was going on. Fearing a public scandal, he told Bowman that if he left quietly, nothing would appear on his record.

I'm glad I left, Bowman thought. *San Francisco has a much bigger market.*

He reached the dispensary. Bruce Anderson was standing outside. Bowman nodded to him. 'Hi, Bruce.'

'Good afternoon, Dr Bowman.'

Five minutes later when Bowman came out of the dispensary, Anderson said, 'Excuse me. I'm going to have to search you.'

158

Harry Bowman stared at him. 'Search me? What are you talking about, Bruce?'

'I'm sorry, doctor. We have orders to search everyone who uses the dispensary,' Anderson lied.

Bowman was indignant. 'I've never heard of such a thing. I absolutely refuse!'

'Then I'll have to ask you to come along with me to Dr Wallace's office.'

'Fine! He's going to be furious when he hears about this.'

Bowman stormed into Wallace's office. 'What's going on, Ben? This man wanted to search me, for God's sake!'

'And did you refuse to be searched?'

'Absolutely.'

'All right.' Wallace reached for the telephone. 'I'll let the San Francisco police do it, if you prefer.' He began to dial.

Bowman panicked. 'Wait a minute! That's not necessary.' His face suddenly cleared. 'Oh! I know what this is all about!' He reached in his pocket and took out a bottle of fentanyl. 'I was taking these to use for an operation, and . . .'

Wallace said quietly, 'Empty your pockets.'

A look of desperation came over Bowman's face. 'There's no reason to . . .'

'Empty your pockets.'

Two hours later, the San Francisco office of the Drug Enforcement Agency had a signed confession and the names of the people to whom Bowman had been selling drugs.

*   *   *

159

When Paige heard the news, she went to see Mitch Campbell. He was sitting in an office, resting. His hands were on the desk when Paige walked in, and she could see the tremor in them.

Campbell quickly moved his hands to his lap. 'Hello, Paige. How're you doing?'

'Fine, Mitch. I wanted to talk to you.'

'Sit down.'

She took a seat opposite him. 'How long have you had Parkinson's?'

He turned a shade whiter. 'What?'

'That's it, isn't it? You've been trying to cover it up.'

There was a heavy silence. 'I . . . I . . . yes. But I . . . I can't give up being a doctor. I . . . I just can't give it up. It's my whole life.'

Paige leaned forward and said earnestly, 'You don't have to give up being a doctor, but you shouldn't be operating.'

He looked suddenly old. 'I know. I was going to quit last year.' He smiled wanly. 'I guess I'll have to quit now, won't I? You're going to tell Dr Wallace.'

'No,' Paige said gently. '*You're* going to tell Dr Wallace.'

Paige was having lunch in the cafeteria when Tom Chang joined her.

'I heard what happened,' he said. 'Bowman! Unbelievable. Nice work.'

She shook her head. 'I almost had the wrong man.'

Chang sat there, silent.

'Are you all right, Tom?'

160

'Do you want the "I'm fine", or do you want the truth?'

'We're friends. I want the truth.'

'My marriage has gone to hell.' His eyes suddenly filled with tears. 'Sye has left. She's gone back home.'

'I'm so sorry.'

'It's not her fault. We didn't have a marriage anymore. She said I'm married to the hospital, and she's right. I'm spending my whole life here, taking care of strangers, instead of being with the people I love.'

'She'll come back. It will work out,' Paige said soothingly.

'No. Not this time.'

'Have you thought about counseling, or . . . ?'

'She refuses.'

'I'm sorry, Tom. If there's anything I . . .' She heard her name on the loudspeaker.

'Dr Taylor, Room 410 . . .'

Paige felt a sudden pang of alarm. 'I have to go,' she said. Room 410. That was Sam Bernstein's room. He was one of her favorite patients, a gentle man in his seventies who had been brought in with inoperable stomach cancer. Many of the patients at the hospital were constantly complaining, but Sam Bernstein was an exception. Paige admired his courage and his dignity. He had a wife and two grown sons who visited him regularly, and Paige had grown fond of them, too.

He had been put on life-support systems with a note, DNR—Do Not Resuscitate—if his heart stopped.

When Paige walked into his room, a nurse was at the bedside. She looked up as Paige entered. 'He's

161

gone, doctor. I didn't start emergency procedures, because . . .' Her voice trailed off.

'You were right not to,' Paige said slowly. 'Thank you.'

'Is there anything I . . . ?'

'No. I'll make the arrangements.' Paige stood by the bedside and looked down at the body of what had been a living, laughing human being, a man who had a family and friends, someone who had spent his life working hard, taking care of the ones he loved. And now . . .

She walked over to the drawer where he kept his possessions. There was an inexpensive watch, a set of keys, fifteen dollars in cash, dentures, and a letter to his wife. All that remained of a man's life.

Paige was unable to shake the feeling of depression that hung over her. 'He was such a dear man. Why . . . ?'

Kat said, 'Paige, you can't let yourself get emotionally involved with your patients. It will tear you apart.'

'I know. You're right, Kat. It's just that . . . it's over so quickly, isn't it? This morning he and I were talking. Tomorrow is his funeral.'

'You're not thinking of going to it?'

'No.'

The funeral took place at the Hills of Eternity Cemetery.

In the Jewish religion, burial must take place as soon as possible following the death, and the service usually takes place the next day.

The body of Sam Bernstein was dressed in a *takhri-*

162

khim, a white robe, and wrapped in a *talit*. The family was gathered around the graveside. The rabbi was intoning, '*Hamakom y'nathaim etkhem b'tokh sh'ar availai tziyon veeyerushalayim.*'

A man standing next to Paige saw the puzzled expression on her face, and he translated for her. '"May the Lord comfort you with all the mourners of Zion and Jerusalem."'

To Paige's astonishment, the members of the family began tearing at the clothes they were wearing as they chanted, '*Baruch ata adonai elohainu melech haolam dayan ha-emet.*'

'What . . . ?'

'That's to show respect,' the man whispered. '"From dust you are and to dust you have returned, but the spirit returns to God who gave it."'

The ceremony was over.

The following morning, Kat ran into Honey in the corridor. Honey looked nervous.

'Anything wrong?' Kat asked.

'Dr Wallace sent for me. He asked me to be in his office at two o'clock.'

'Do you know why?'

'I think I messed up at rounds the other day. Dr Ritter is a monster.'

'He can be,' Kat said. 'But I'm sure everything will be all right.'

'I hope so. I just have a bad feeling.'

Promptly at two o'clock, she arrived at Benjamin Wallace's office, carrying a small jar of honey in her purse. The receptionist was at lunch. Dr Wallace's door was open. 'Come in, Dr Taft,' he called.

Honey walked into his office.

'Close the door behind you, please.'

Honey closed the door.

'Take a seat.'

Honey sat down across from him. She was almost trembling.

Benjamin Wallace had been putting this off as long as he could. He looked across at her and thought, *It's like kicking a puppy. But what has to be done has to be done.* 'I'm afraid I have some unfortunate news for you,' he said.

One hour later, Honey met Kat in the solarium. Honey sank into a chair next to her, smiling.

'Did you see Dr Wallace?' Kat asked.

'Oh, yes. We had a long talk. Did you know that his wife left him last September? They were married for fifteen years. He has two grown children from an earlier marriage, but he hardly ever sees them. The poor darling is so lonely.'

Book Two

14

It was New Year's Eve again, and Paige, Kat and Honey ushered in 1994 at Embarcadero County Hospital. It seemed to them that nothing in their lives had changed except the names of their patients.

As Paige walked through the parking lot, she was reminded of Harry Bowman and his red Ferrari. *How many lives were destroyed by the poison Harry Bowman was selling?* she wondered. Drugs were so seductive. And, in the end, so deadly.

Jimmy Ford showed up with a small bouquet of flowers for Paige.

'What's this for, Jimmy?'

He blushed. 'I just wanted you to have it. Did you know I'm getting married?'

'No! That's wonderful. Who's the lucky girl?'

'Her name is Betsy. She works at a dress shop. We're going to have half a dozen kids. The first girl is going to be named Paige. I hope you don't mind.'

'Mind? I'm flattered.'

He was embarrassed. 'Did you hear the one about the doctor who gave a patient two weeks to live? "I can't pay you right now," the man said. "All right, I'll give you another two weeks." '

And Jimmy was gone.

Paige was worried about Tom Chang. He was having violent mood swings from euphoria to deep depression.

One morning during a talk with Paige, he said, 'Do you realize that most of the people in here would die without us? We have the power to heal their bodies and make them whole again.'

And the next morning: 'We're all kidding ourselves, Paige. Our patients would get better faster without us. We're hypocrites, pretending that we have all the answers. Well, we don't.'

Paige studied him a moment. 'What do you hear from Sye?'

'I talked to her yesterday. She won't come back here. She's going ahead with the divorce.'

Paige put her hand on his arm. 'I'm so sorry, Tom.'

He shrugged. 'Why? It doesn't bother me. Not anymore. I'll find another woman.' He grinned. 'And have another child. You'll see.'

There was something unreal about the conversation.

That night Paige said to Kat, 'I'm worried about Tom Chang. Have you talked to him lately?'

'Yes.'

'Did he seem normal to you?'

'No man seems normal to me,' Kat said.

Paige was still concerned. 'Let's invite him out for dinner tomorrow night.'

'All right.'

The next morning when Paige reported to the hospital, she was greeted with the news that a janitor had found Tom Chang's body in a basement equipment room. He had died of an overdose of sleeping pills.

Paige was near hysteria. 'I could have saved him,' she cried. 'All this time he was calling out for help, and I didn't hear him.'

Kat said firmly, 'There's no way you could have helped him, Paige. You were not the problem, and you were not the solution. He didn't want to live without his wife and child. It's as simple as that.'

Paige wiped the tears from her eyes. 'Damn this place!' she said. 'If it weren't for the pressure and the hours, his wife never would have left him.'

'But she did,' Kat said gently. 'It's over.'

Paige had never been to a Chinese funeral before. It was an incredible spectacle. It began at the Green Street Mortuary in Chinatown early in the morning, where a crowd started gathering outside. A parade was assembled, with a large brass marching band, and at the head of the parade, mourners carried a huge blowup of a photograph of Tom Chang.

The march began with the band loudly playing, winding through the streets of San Francisco, with a hearse at the end of the procession. Most of the mourners were on foot, but the more elderly rode in cars.

To Paige, the parade seemed to be moving around the city at random. She was puzzled. 'Where are they going?' she asked one of the mourners.

He bowed slightly and said, 'It is our custom to

169

take the departed past some of the places that have meaning in his life — restaurants where he ate, shops that he used, places he visited . . .'

'I see.'

The parade ended in front of Embarcadero County Hospital.

The mourner turned to Paige and said, 'This is where Tom Chang worked. This is where he found his happiness.'

Wrong, Paige thought. *This is where he lost his happiness.*

Walking down Market Street one morning, Paige saw Alfred Turner. Her heart started pounding. She had not been able to get him out of her mind. He was starting to cross the street as the light was changing. When Paige got to the corner, the light had turned to red. She ignored it and ran out into the street, oblivious to the honking horns and the outraged cries of motorists.

Paige reached the other side and hurried to catch up with him. She grabbed his sleeve. 'Alfred . . .'

The man turned. 'I beg your pardon?'

It was a total stranger.

Now that Paige and Kat were fourth-year residents, they were performing operations on a regular basis.

Kat was working with doctors in neurosurgery, and she never ceased to be amazed at the miracle of the hundred billion complex digital computers called neurons that lived in the skull. The work was exciting.

Kat had enormous respect for most of the doctors she worked with. They were brilliant, skilled surgeons. There were a few doctors who gave her a hard time. They tried to date her, and the more Kat refused to go out with them, the more of a challenge she became.

She heard one doctor mutter, 'Here comes old ironpants.'

She was assisting Dr Kibler at a brain operation. A tiny incision was made in the cortex, and Dr Kibler pushed the rubber cannula into the left lateral ventricle, the cavity in the center of the left half of the brain, while Kat held the incision open with a small retractor. Her entire concentration was focused on what was happening in front of her.

Dr Kibler glanced at her and, as he worked, said, 'Did you hear about the wino who staggered into a bar and said, "Give me a drink, quick!" "I can't do that," the bartender said. "You're already drunk."'

The burr was cutting in deeper.

'"If you don't give me a drink, I'll kill myself."'

Cerebral spinal fluid flowed out of the cannula from the ventricle.

'"I'll tell you what I'll do," the bartender said. "There are three things I want. You do them for me, and I'll give you a bottle."'

As he went on talking, fifteen milliliters of air were injected into the ventricle, and X-rays were taken of the anterior-posterior view and the lateral view.

'"See that football player sitting in the corner? I can't get him out of here. I want you to throw him out. Next, I have a pet crocodile in my office with a bad tooth. He's so mean I can't get a vet to go near

171

him. Lastly, there's a lady doctor from the Department of Health who's trying to close up this place. You fuck her, and you get the bottle."'

A scrub nurse was using suction to reduce the amount of blood in the field.

'The wino throws out the football player, and goes into the office where the crocodile is. He comes out fifteen minutes later, all bloody, and his clothes torn, and he says, "Where's the lady doctor with the bad tooth?"'

Dr Kibler roared with laughter. 'Do you get it? He fucked the crocodile instead of the doctor. It was probably a better experience!'

Kat stood there, furious, wanting to slap him.

When the operation was over, Kat went to the on-call room to try to get over her anger. *I'm not going to let the bastards beat me down. I'm not.*

From time to time, Paige went out with doctors from the hospital, but she refused to get romantically involved with any of them. Alfred Turner had hurt her too deeply, and she was determined never to go through that again.

Most of her days and nights were spent at the hospital. The schedule was grueling, but Paige was doing general surgery and she enjoyed it.

One morning, George Englund, the chief of surgery, sent for her.

'You're starting your specialty this year. Cardiovascular surgery.'

She nodded. 'That's right.'

'Well, I have a treat for you. Have you heard of Dr Barker?'

172

Paige looked at him in surprise. 'Dr *Lawrence* Barker?'

'Yes.'

'Of course.'

Everyone had heard of Lawrence Barker. He was one of the most famous cardiovascular surgeons in the world.

'Well, he returned last week from Saudi Arabia, where he operated on the king. Dr Barker's an old friend of mine, and he's agreed to give us three days a week here. *Pro bono.*'

'That's fantastic!' Paige exclaimed.

'I'm putting you on his team.'

For a moment, Paige was speechless. 'I . . . I don't know what to say. I'm very grateful.'

'It's a wonderful opportunity for you. You can learn a lot from him.'

'I'm sure I can. Thank you, George. I really appreciate this.'

'You'll start your rounds with him tomorrow morning at six o'clock.'

'I'm looking forward to it.'

'Looking forward to it' was an understatement. It had been Paige's dream to work with someone like Dr Lawrence Barker. *What do I mean, 'someone like Dr Lawrence Barker'? There's only one Dr Lawrence Barker.*

She had never seen a photograph of him, but she could visualize what he looked like. He would be tall and handsome, with silver-gray hair, and slender, sensitive hands. A warm and gentle man. *We'll be working closely together*, Paige thought, *and I'm*

173

going to make myself absolutely indispensable. I wonder if he's married?

That night, Paige had an erotic dream about Dr Barker. They were performing an operation in the nude. In the middle of it, Dr Barker said, 'I want you.' A nurse moved the patient off the operating table and Dr Barker picked Paige up and put her on the table, and made love to her.

When Paige woke up, she was falling off the bed.

At six o'clock the following morning, Paige was nervously waiting in the second-floor corridor with Joel Philips, the senior resident, and five other residents, when a short, sour-faced man stormed toward them. He leaned forward as he walked, as though battling a stiff wind.

He approached the group. 'What the hell are you all standing around for? Let's go!'

It took Paige a moment to regain her composure. She hurried along to catch up with the rest of the group. As they moved along the corridor, Dr Barker snapped, 'You'll have between thirty and thirty-five patients to care for every day. I'll expect you to make detailed notes on each one of them. Clear?'

There were murmurs of 'Yes, sir.'

They had reached the first ward. Dr Barker walked over to the bed of a patient, a man in his forties. Barker's gruff and forbidding manner went through an instant change. He touched the patient gently on the shoulder and smiled. 'Good morning. I'm Dr Barker.'

'Good morning, doctor.'

'How are you feeling this morning?'

'My chest hurts.'

Dr Barker studied the chart at the foot of the bed, then turned to Dr Philips. 'What do his X-rays show?'

'No change. He's healing nicely.'

'Let's do another CBC.'

Dr Philips made a note.

Dr Barker patted the man on the arm and smiled. 'It's looking good. We'll have you out of here in a week.' He turned to the residents and snapped, 'Move it! We have a lot of patients to see.'

My God! Paige thought. *Talk about Dr Jekyll and Mr Hyde!*

The next patient was an obese woman who had had a pacemaker put in. Dr Barker studied her chart. 'Good morning, Mrs Shelby.' His voice was soothing. 'I'm Dr Barker.'

'How long are you going to keep me in this place?'

'Well, you're so charming, I'd like to keep you here forever, but I have a wife.'

Mrs Shelby giggled. 'She's a lucky woman.'

Barker was examining her chart again. 'I'd say you're just about ready to go home.'

'Wonderful.'

'I'll stop by to see you this afternoon.'

Lawrence Barker turned to the residents. 'Move on.'

They obediently trailed behind the doctor to a semiprivate room where a young Guatemalan boy lay in bed, surrounded by his anxious family.

'Good morning,' Dr Barker said warmly. He scanned the patient's chart. 'How are you feeling this morning?'

'I am feeling good, doctor.'

175

Dr Barker turned to Philips. 'Any change in the electrolytes?'

'No, doctor.'

'That's good news.' He patted the boy's arm. 'You hang in there, Juan.'

The mother asked anxiously, 'Is my son going to be all right?'

Dr Barker smiled. 'We're going to do everything we can for him.'

'Thank you, doctor.'

Dr Barker stepped out into the corridor, the others trailing behind him. He stopped. 'The patient has myocardiopathy, irregular fever tremors, headaches, and localized edema. Can any of you geniuses tell me what the most common cause of it is?'

There was a silence. Paige said hesitantly, 'I believe it's congenital . . . hereditary.'

Dr Barker looked at her and nodded encouragingly.

Pleased, Paige went on. 'It skips . . . wait . . .' She was struggling to remember. 'It skips a generation and is passed along by the genes of the mother.' She stopped, flushed, proud of herself.

Dr Barker stared at her a moment. 'Horseshit! It's Chagas' disease. It affects people from Latin American countries.' He looked at Paige with disgust. 'Jesus! Who told you you were a doctor?'

Paige's face was flaming red.

The rest of the rounds was a blur to her. They saw twenty-four patients and it seemed to Paige that Dr Barker spent the morning trying to humiliate her. She was always the one Barker addressed his questions to, testing, probing. When she was right, he never complimented her. When she was wrong, he

176

yelled at her. At one point, when Paige made a mistake, Barker roared, 'I wouldn't let you operate on my dog!'

When the rounds were finally over, Dr Philips, the senior resident, said, 'We'll start rounds again at two o'clock. Get your scut books, make notes on each patient, and don't leave anything out.'

He looked at Paige pityingly, started to say something, then turned away to join Dr Barker.

Paige thought, *I never want to see that bastard again.*

The following night, Paige was on call. She ran from one crisis to the next, frantically trying to stem the tide of disasters that flooded the emergency rooms.

At 1:00 A.M., she finally fell asleep. She did not hear the sound of a siren screaming out its warning as an ambulance roared to a stop in front of the emergency entrance of the hospital. Two paramedics swung open the ambulance door, transferred the unconscious patient from his stretcher to a gurney, and ran it through the entrance doors of ER One.

The staff had been alerted by radiophone. A nurse ran alongside the patient, while a second nurse waited at the top of the ramp. Sixty seconds later, the patient was transferred from the gurney to the examination table.

He was a young man, and he was covered with so much blood that it was difficult to tell what he looked like.

A nurse went to work, cutting his torn clothes off with large shears.

'It looks like everything's broken.'

177

'He's bleeding like a stuck pig.'

'I'm not getting a pulse.'

'Who's on call?'

'Dr Taylor.'

'Get her. If she hurries, he may still be alive.'

Paige was awakened by the ringing of the telephone.

'H'lo . . .'

'We have an emergency in ER One, doctor. I don't think he's going to make it.'

Paige sat up on the cot. 'Right. I'm coming.'

She looked at her wristwatch. 1:30 A.M. She stumbled out of bed and made her way to the elevator.

A minute later, she was walking into ER One. In the middle of the room, on the examining table, was the blood-covered patient.

'What do we have here?' Paige asked.

'Motorcycle accident. He was hit by a bus. He wasn't wearing a helmet.'

Paige moved toward the unconscious figure, and even before she saw his face, she somehow knew.

She was suddenly wide awake. 'Get three IV lines in him!' Paige ordered. 'Get him on oxygen. I want some blood sent down, stat. Call Records to get his blood type.'

The nurse looked at her in surprise. 'You know him?'

'Yes.' She had to force herself to say the words. 'His name is Jimmy Ford.'

Paige ran her fingers over his scalp. 'There's heavy edema. I want a head scan and X-rays. We're going to push the envelope on this one. I want him alive!'

'Yes, doctor.'

Paige spent the next two hours making sure that everything possible was being done for Jimmy Ford. The X-rays showed a fractured skull, a brain contusion, a broken humerus, and multiple lacerations. But everything would have to wait until he was stabilized.

At 3:30 A.M., Paige decided there was nothing more she could do for the present. He was breathing better, and his pulse was stronger. She looked down at the unconscious figure. *We're going to have half a dozen kids. The first girl is going to be named Paige. I hope you don't mind.*

'Call me if there's any change at all,' Paige said.

'Don't worry, doctor,' one of the nurses said. 'We'll take good care of him.'

Paige made her way back to the on-call room. She was exhausted, but she was too concerned about Jimmy to go back to sleep.

The telephone rang again. She barely had the energy to pick it up. 'H'lo.'

'Doctor, you'd better come up to the third floor. Stat. I think one of Dr Barker's patients is having a heart attack.'

'Coming,' Paige said. *One of Dr Barker's patients.* Paige took a deep breath, staggered out of bed, threw cold water on her face, and hurried to the third floor.

A nurse was waiting outside a private room. 'It's Mrs Hearns. It looks like she's having another heart seizure.'

Paige went into the room.

Mrs Hearns was a woman in her fifties. Her face

179

still held the remnants of a onetime beauty, but her body was fat and bloated. She was holding her chest and moaning. 'I'm dying,' she said. 'I'm dying. I can't breathe.'

'You're going to be all right,' Paige said reassuringly. She turned to the nurse. 'Did you do an EKG?'

'She won't let me touch her. She said she's too nervous.'

'We must do an EKG,' Paige told the patient.

'No! I don't want to die. Please don't let me die . . .'

Paige said to the nurse, 'Call Dr Barker. Ask him to get down here right away.'

The nurse hurried off.

Paige put a stethoscope to Mrs Hearns's chest. She listened. The heartbeat seemed normal, but Paige could not afford to take any chances.

'Dr Barker will be here in a few minutes,' she told Mrs Hearns. 'Try to relax.'

'I've never felt this bad. My chest feels so heavy. Please don't leave me.'

'I'm not going to leave you,' Paige promised her.

While she was waiting for Dr Barker to arrive, Paige telephoned the intensive care unit. There was no change in Jimmy Ford's condition. He was still in a coma.

Thirty minutes later, Dr Barker appeared. He had obviously dressed in haste. 'What's going on?' he demanded.

Paige said, 'I think Mrs Hearns is having another heart attack.'

Dr Barker moved over to the bedside. 'Did you do an EKG?'

'She wouldn't let us.'

180

'Pulse?'

'Normal. No fever.'

Dr Barker put a stethoscope against Mrs Hearns's back. 'Take a deep breath.'

She obliged.

'Again.'

Mrs Hearns let out a loud belch. 'Excuse me.' She smiled. 'Oh. That's better.'

He studied her a moment. 'What did you have for dinner, Mrs Hearns?'

'I had a hamburger.'

'Just a hamburger? That's all? One?'

'Two.'

'Anything else?'

'Well, you know . . . onions and french fries.'

'And to drink?'

'A chocolate milk shake.'

Dr Barker looked down at the patient. 'Your heart is fine. It's your appetite we have to worry about.' He turned to Paige. 'What you're seeing here is a case of heartburn. I'd like to see you outside, doctor.'

When they were in the corridor, he roared, 'What the hell did they teach you in medical school? Don't you even know the difference between heartburn and a heart attack?'

'I thought . . .'

'The problem is, you *didn't*! If you ever wake me up again in the middle of the night for a heartburn case, I'll have your ass. You understand that?'

Paige stood there stiffly, her face grim.

'Give her some antacid, *doctor*,' Lawrence Barker said sarcastically, 'and you'll find that she's cured. I'll see you at six o'clock for rounds.'

181

Paige watched him storm out.

When Paige stumbled back to her cot in the on-call room, she thought, *I'm going to kill Lawrence Barker. I'll do it slowly. He'll be very ill. He'll have a dozen tubes in his body. He'll beg me to put him out of his misery, but I won't. I'll let him suffer, and then when he feels better . . . that's when I'll kill him!*

15

Paige was on morning rounds with the Beast, as she secretly referred to Dr Barker. She had assisted him in three cardiothoracic surgeries, and in spite of her bitter feelings toward him, she could not help but admire his incredible skill. She watched in awe as he opened up a patient, deftly replaced the old heart with a donor heart, and sewed him up. The operation took less than five hours.

Within a few weeks, Paige thought, *that patient will be able to return to a normal life. No wonder surgeons think they're gods. They bring the dead back to life.*

Time after time, Paige watched a heart stop and turn to an inert piece of flesh. And then the miracle would occur, and a lifeless organ would begin to pulsate again and send blood through a body that had been dying.

One morning, a patient was scheduled for a procedure to insert an intra-aortic balloon. Paige was in the operating room assisting Dr Barker. As they were about to begin, Dr Barker snapped, 'Do it!'

Paige looked at him. 'I beg your pardon?'

'It's a simple procedure. Do you think you can handle it?' There was contempt in his voice.

'Yes,' Paige said tightly.

'Well, then, get on with it!'

He was infuriating.

Barker watched as Paige expertly inserted a hollow tube into the patient's artery and threaded it up into the heart. It was done flawlessly. Barker stood there, without saying a word.

To hell with him, Paige thought. *Nothing I could ever do would please him.*

Paige injected a radiopaque dye through the tube. They watched the monitor as the dye flowed into the coronary arteries. Images appeared on a fluoroscopy screen and showed the degree of blockage and its location in the artery, while an automatic motion-picture camera recorded the X-rays for a permanent record.

The senior resident looked at Paige and smiled. 'Nice job.'

'Thank you.' Paige turned to Dr Barker.

'Too damned slow,' he growled.

And he walked out.

Paige was grateful for the days that Dr Barker was away from the hospital, working at his private practice. She said to Kat, 'Being away from him for a day is like a week in the country.'

'You really hate him, don't you?'

'He's a brilliant doctor, but he's a miserable human being. Have you ever noticed how some people fit their names? If Dr Barker doesn't stop barking at people, he's going to have a stroke.'

'You should see some of the beauties I have to put up with.' Kat laughed. 'They all think they're

184

God's gift to pussies. Wouldn't it be great if there were no men in the world!'

Paige looked at her, but said nothing.

Paige and Kat went to check on Jimmy Ford. He was still in a coma. There was nothing they could do.

Kat sighed. 'Dammit. Why does it happen to the good guys?'

'I wish I knew.'

'Do you think he'll make it?'

Paige hesitated. 'We've done everything we can. Now it's up to God.'

'Funny. I thought *we* were God.'

The following day when Paige was in charge of afternoon rounds, Kaplan, a senior resident, stopped her in the corridor. 'This is your lucky day.' He grinned. 'You're getting a new medical school student to take around.'

'Really?'

'Yeah, the IN.'

'IN?'

'Idiot nephew. Dr Wallace's wife has a nephew who wants to be a doctor. They threw him out of his last two schools. We've all had to put up with him. Today it's your turn.'

Paige groaned. 'I don't have time for this. I'm up to my . . .'

'It's not an option. Be a good girl and Dr Wallace will give you brownie points.' Kaplan moved off.

Paige sighed and walked over to where the new residents were waiting to start the rounds. *Where's the IN?* She looked at her watch. He was already three minutes late. *I'll give him one more minute*, Paige decided, *and then to hell with him.* She saw him then, a tall, lean-looking man, hurrying toward her, down the hall.

He walked up to Paige, out of breath, and said, 'Excuse me. Dr Wallace asked me to —'

'You're late,' Paige said curtly.

'I know. I'm sorry. I was held up at —'

'Never mind. What's your name?'

'Jason. Jason Curtis.' He was wearing a sport jacket.

'Where's your white coat?'

'My white coat?'

'Didn't anyone tell you to wear a white coat on rounds?'

He looked flustered. 'No. I'm afraid I . . .'

Paige said irritably, 'Go back to the head nurse's office and tell her to give you a white coat. And you don't have a scut book.'

'No.'

'Idiot nephew' doesn't begin to describe him. 'Meet us in Ward One.'

'Are you sure? I . . .'

'Just do it!' Paige and the others started off, leaving Jason Curtis staring after them.

They were examining their third patient when Jason Curtis came hurrying up. He was wearing a white coat. Paige was saying, '. . . tumors of the heart can be primary, which is rare, or secondary, which is much more common.'

She turned to Curtis. 'Can you name the three types of tumors?'

He stared at her. 'I'm afraid I . . . I can't.'

186

Of course not. 'Epicardial. Myocardial. Endo-cardial.'

He looked at Paige and smiled. 'That's really inter-esting.'

My God! Paige thought. *Dr Wallace or no Dr Wallace, I'm going to get rid of him fast.*

They moved on to the next patient, and when Paige was through examining him, she took the group into the corridor, out of earshot. 'We're deal-ing here with a thyroid storm, with fever and extreme tachycardia. It came on after surgery.' She turned to Jason Curtis. 'How would you treat him for that?'

He stood there, thoughtful for a moment. Then he said, 'Gently?'

Paige fought for self-control. 'You're not his mother, you're his doctor! He needs continuous IV fluids to combat dehydration, along with IV iodine and antithyroid drugs and sedatives for convulsions.'

Jason nodded. 'That sounds about right.'

The rounds got no better. When they were over, Paige called Jason Curtis aside. 'Do you mind my being frank with you?'

'No. Not at all,' he said agreeably. 'I'd appreciate it.'

'Look for another profession.'

He stood there, frowning. 'You don't think I'm cut out for this?'

'Quite honestly, no. You don't enjoy this, do you?'

'Not really.'

'Then why did you choose to go into this?'

'To tell you the truth, I was pushed into it.'

'Well, you tell Dr Wallace that he's making a mis-take. I think you should find something else to do with your life.'

'I really appreciate your telling me this,' Jason

187

Curtis said earnestly. 'I wonder if we could discuss this further. If you aren't doing anything for dinner tonight . . . ?'

'We have nothing further to discuss,' Paige said curtly. 'You can tell your uncle . . .'

At that moment Dr Wallace came into view. 'Jason!' he called. 'I've been looking all over for you.' He turned to Paige. 'I see you two have met.'

'Yes, we've met,' Paige said grimly.

'Good. Jason is the architect in charge of designing the new wing we're building.'

Paige stood there, motionless. 'He's . . . *what*?'

'Yes. Didn't he tell you?'

She felt her face getting red. *Didn't anyone tell you to wear a white coat on rounds? Why did you go into this? To tell you the truth, I was pushed into it. By me!*

Paige wanted to crawl into a hole. He had made a complete fool of her. She turned to Jason. 'Why didn't you tell me who you were?'

He was watching her, amused. 'Well, you really didn't give me a chance.'

'She didn't give you a chance to what?' Dr Wallace asked.

'If you'll excuse me . . .' Paige said tightly.

'What about dinner tonight?'

'I don't eat. And I'm busy.' And Paige was gone.

Jason looked after her, admiringly. 'That's quite a woman.'

'She is, isn't she? Shall we go to my office and talk about the new designs?'

'Fine.' But his thoughts were on Paige.

*   *   *

It was July, time for the ritual that took place every twelve months at hospitals all over the United States, as new residents came in to begin their journey toward becoming real doctors.

The nurses had been looking forward to the new crop of residents, staking out claims on the ones they thought would make good lovers or husbands. On this particular day, as the new residents appeared, nearly every female eye was fixed on Dr Ken Mallory.

No one knew why Ken Mallory had transferred from an exclusive private hospital in Washington, DC, to Embarcadero County Hospital in San Francisco. He was a fifth-year resident, and a general surgeon. There were rumors that he had had to leave Washington in a hurry because of an affair with a congressman's wife. There was another rumor that a nurse had committed suicide because of him and he had been asked to leave. The only thing the nurses were sure of was that Ken Mallory was, without doubt, the best-looking man they had ever seen. He had a tall, athletic body, wavy blond hair, and a face that would have looked great on a movie screen.

Mallory blended into the hospital routine as though he had been there forever. He was a charmer, and almost from the beginning, the nurses were fighting for his attention. Night after night, the other doctors would watch Mallory disappear into an empty on-call room with a different nurse. His reputation as a stud was becoming legendary around the hospital.

Paige, Kat, and Honey were discussing him.

'Can you believe all those nurses throwing

themselves at him?' Kat laughed. 'They're actually fighting to be the flavor of the week!'

'You have to admit, he *is* attractive,' Honey pointed out.

Kat shook her head. 'No. I don't.'

One morning, half a dozen residents were in the doctors' dressing room when Mallory walked in.

'We were just talking about you,' one of them said. 'You must be exhausted.'

Mallory grinned. 'It was not a bad night.' He had spent the night with two nurses.

Grundy, one of the residents, said, 'You're making the rest of us look like eunuchs, Ken. Isn't there anyone in this hospital you can't lay?'

Mallory laughed. 'I doubt it.'

Grundy was thoughtful for a moment. 'I'll bet I can name someone.'

'Really? Who's that?'

'One of the senior residents here. Her name is Kat Hunter.'

Mallory nodded. 'The black doll. I've seen her. She's very attractive. What makes you think I can't take her to bed?'

'Because we've all struck out. I don't think she likes men.'

'Or maybe she just hasn't met the right one,' Mallory suggested.

Grundy shook his head. 'No. You wouldn't have a chance.'

It was a challenge. 'I'll bet you're wrong.'

One of the other residents spoke up. 'You mean you're willing to bet on it?'

Mallory smiled. 'Sure. Why not?'

'All right.' The group began to crowd around Mallory. 'I'll bet you five hundred dollars you can't lay her.'

'You're on.'

'I'll bet you three hundred.'

Another one spoke up. 'Let me in on it. I'll bet you six hundred.'

In the end, five thousand dollars was bet.

'What's the time limit?' Mallory asked.

Grundy thought for a moment. 'Let's say thirty days. Is that fair?'

'More than fair. I won't need that much time.'

Grundy said, 'But you have to prove it. She has to admit that she went to bed with you.'

'No problem.' Mallory looked around the group and grinned. 'Suckers!'

Fifteen minutes later, Grundy was in the cafeteria where Kat, Paige, and Honey were having breakfast. He walked over to their table. 'Can I join you ladies—you doctors—for a moment?'

Paige looked up. 'Sure.'

Grundy sat down. He looked at Kat and said apologetically, 'I hate to tell you this, but I'm really mad, and I think it's only fair that you should know . . .'

Kat was looking at him, puzzled. 'Know what?'

Grundy sighed. 'That new senior resident who came in—Ken Mallory?'

'Yes. What about him?'

Grundy said, 'Well, I . . . God, this is embarrassing. He bet some of the doctors five thousand dollars that he could get you into bed in the next thirty days.'

Kat's face was grim. 'He did, did he?'

Grundy said piously, 'I don't blame you for being angry. It made me sick when I heard about it. Well, I just wanted to warn you. He'll be asking you out, and I thought it was only right that you should know why he was doing it.'

'Thanks,' Kat said. 'I appreciate your telling me.'

'It was the least I could do.'

They watched Grundy leave.

In the corridor outside the cafeteria, the other residents were waiting for him.

'How did it go?' they asked.

Grundy laughed. 'Perfect. She's as mad as hell. The son of a bitch is dead meat!'

At the table, Honey was saying, 'I think that's just terrible.'

Kat nodded. 'Someone should give him a dickotomy. They'll be ice skating in hell before I go out with that bastard.'

Paige sat there thinking. After a moment, she said, 'You know something, Kat? It might be interesting if you *did* go out with him.'

Kat looked at her in surprise. *'What?'*

There was a glint in Paige's eye. 'Why not? If he wants to play games, let's help him — only he'll play *our* game.'

Kat leaned forward. 'Go on.'

'He has thirty days, right? When he asks you out, you'll be warm and loving and affectionate. I mean, you'll be absolutely *crazy* about the man. You'll drive him out of his mind. The only thing you *won't*

192

do, bless your heart, is to go to bed with him. We'll teach him a five-thousand-dollar lesson.'

Kat thought of her stepfather. It was a way of getting revenge. 'I like it,' she said.

'You mean you're going to do it?' Honey said.

'I am.'

And Kat had no idea that with those words, she had signed her death warrant.

16

Jason Curtis had been unable to get Paige Taylor out of his mind. He telephoned Ben Wallace's secretary. 'Hi. This is Jason Curtis. I need a home telephone number for Dr Paige Taylor.'

'Certainly, Mr Curtis. Just a moment.' She gave him the number.

Honey answered the telephone. 'Dr Taft.'

'This is Jason Curtis. Is Dr Taylor there?'

'No, she's not. She's on call at the hospital.'

'Oh. That's too bad.'

Honey could hear the disappointment in his voice. 'If it's some kind of emergency, I can . . .'

'No, no.'

'I could take a message for her and have her call you.'

'That will be fine.' Jason gave her his telephone number.

'I'll give her the message.'

'Thank you.'

'Jason Curtis called,' Honey said when Paige returned to the apartment. 'He sounded cute. Here's his number.'

'Burn it.'

'Aren't you going to call him back?'

'No. Never.'

'You're still hung up on Alfred, aren't you?'

'Of course not.'

And that was all Honey could get out of her.

Jason waited two days before he called again.

This time Paige answered the telephone. 'Dr Taylor.'

'Hello there!' Jason said. 'This is Dr Curtis.'

'Doctor . . . ?'

'You may not remember me,' Jason said lightly. 'I was on rounds with you the other day, and I asked you to have dinner with me. You said—'

'I said I was busy. I still am. Goodbye, Mr Curtis.' She slammed the receiver down.

'What was that all about?' Honey asked.

'About nothing.'

At six o'clock the following morning, when the residents gathered with Paige for morning rounds, Jason Curtis appeared. He was wearing a white coat.

'I hope I'm not late,' he said cheerfully. 'I had to get a white coat. I know how upset you get when I don't wear one.'

Paige took a deep, angry breath. 'Come in here,' she said. She led Jason into the deserted doctors' dressing room. 'What are you doing here?'

'To tell you the truth, I've been worried about some of the patients we saw the other day,' he said earnestly. 'I came to see if everyone is all right.'

The man was infuriating. 'Why aren't you out building something?'

Jason looked at her and said, quietly, 'I'm trying to.' He pulled out a handful of tickets. 'Look, I don't know what your tastes are, so I got tickets for tonight's Giants game, the theater, the opera, and a concert. Take your choice.'

The man was exasperating. 'Do you always throw your money away like this?'

'Only when I'm in love,' Jason said.

'Wait a min—'

He held the tickets out to her. 'Take your choice.'

Paige reached out and took them all. 'Thank you,' she said sweetly. 'I'll give them to my outpatients. Most of them don't have a chance to go to the theater or opera.'

He smiled. 'Great! I hope they enjoy it. Will you have dinner with me?'

'No.'

'You have to eat, anyway. Won't you change your mind?'

Paige felt a small frisson of guilt about the tickets. 'I'm afraid I wouldn't be very good company. I was on call last night, and . . .'

'We'll make it an early evening. Scout's honor.'

She sighed. 'All right, but . . .'

'Wonderful! Where shall I pick you up?'

'I'll be through here at seven.'

'I'll pick you up here then.' He yawned. 'Now I'm going home and going back to bed. What an ungodly hour to be up! What makes you do it?'

Paige watched him walk away, and she could not help smiling.

*   *   *

At seven o'clock that evening when Jason arrived at the hospital to pick up Paige, the supervising nurse said, 'I think you'll find Dr Taylor in the on-call room.'

'Thanks.' Jason walked down the corridor to the on-call room. The door was closed. He knocked. There was no answer. He knocked again, then opened the door and looked inside. Paige was on the cot, in a deep sleep. Jason walked over to where she lay and stood there for a long time, looking down at her. *I'm going to marry you, lady*, he thought. He tiptoed out of the room and quietly closed the door behind him.

The following morning, Jason was in a meeting when his secretary came in with a small bouquet of flowers. The card read: *I'm sorry. RIP.* Jason laughed. He telephoned Paige at the hospital. 'This is your date calling.'

'I really am sorry about last night,' Paige said. 'I'm embarrassed.'

'Don't be. But I have a question.'

'Yes?'

'Does RIP stand for Rest in Peace or Rip Van Winkle?'

Paige laughed. 'Take your choice.'

'My choice is dinner tonight. Can we try again?'

She hesitated. *I don't want to become involved. You're not still hung up on Alfred, are you?*

'Hello. Are you there?'

'Yes.' *One evening won't do any harm*, Paige decided. 'Yes. We can have dinner.'

'Wonderful.'

*   *   *

197

As Paige was getting dressed that evening, Kat said, 'It looks like you have a heavy date. Who is it?'

'He's a doctor-architect,' Paige said.

'A *what*?'

Paige told her the story.

'He sounds like fun. Are you interested in him?'

'Not really.'

The evening went by pleasantly. Paige found Jason easy to be with. They talked about everything and nothing, and the time seemed to fly.

'Tell me about you,' Jason said. 'Where did you grow up?'

'You won't believe me.'

'I promise I will.'

'All right. The Congo, India, Burma, Nigeria, Kenya . . .'

'I don't believe you.'

'It's true. My father worked for WHO.'

'Who? I give up. Is this going to be an Abbott and Costello rerun?'

'The World Health Organization. He was a doctor. I spent my childhood traveling to most of the Third World countries with him.'

'That must have been difficult for you.'

'It was exciting. The hardest part was that I was never able to stay long enough to make friends.' *We don't need anyone else, Paige. We'll always have each other . . . This is my wife, Karen.* She shook off the memory. 'I learned a lot of strange languages, and exotic customs.'

'For instance?'

'Well, for instance, I . . .' She thought for a

moment. 'In India they believe in life after death, and that the next life depends on how you behaved in this one. If you were bad, you would come back as an animal. I remember that in one village, we had a dog, and I used to wonder who he used to be and what he did that was bad.'

Jason said, 'He probably barked up the wrong tree.'

Paige smiled. 'And then there was the *gherao*.'

'The *gherao*?'

'It's a very powerful form of punishment. A crowd surrounds a man.' She stopped.

'And?'

'That's it.'

'That's it?'

'They don't say anything or do anything. But he can't move, and he can't get away. He's trapped until he gives in to what they want. It can last for many, many hours. He stays inside the circle, but the crowd keeps changing shifts. I saw a man try to escape the *gherao* once. They beat him to death.'

The memory of it made Paige shudder. The normally friendly people had turned into a screaming frenzied mob. 'Let's get away from here,' Alfred had yelled. He had taken her arm and led her to a quiet side street.

'That's terrible,' Jason said.

'My father moved us away the next day.'

'I wish I could have known your father.'

'He was a wonderful doctor. He would have been a big success on Park Avenue, but he wasn't interested in money. His only interest was in helping people.' *Like Alfred*, she thought.

'What happened to him?'

'He was killed in a tribal war.'

'I'm sorry.'

'He loved doing what he did. In the beginning, the natives fought him. They were very superstitious. In the remote Indian villages, everyone has a *jatak*, a horoscope done by the village astrologer, and they live by it.' She smiled. 'I loved having mine done.'

'And did they tell you that you were going to marry a handsome young architect?'

Paige looked at him and said firmly, 'No.' The conversation was getting too personal. 'You're an architect, so you'll appreciate this. I grew up in huts made of wattle, with earthen floors and thatched roofs which mice and bats liked to inhabit. I lived in *tukuls* with grass roofs and no windows. My dream was to live one day in a comfortable two-story house with a veranda and a green lawn and a white picket fence, and . . .' Paige stopped. 'Sorry. I didn't mean to go on like this, but you *did* ask.'

'I'm glad I asked,' Jason said.

Paige looked at her watch. 'I had no idea it was so late.'

'Can we do this again?'

I don't want to lead him on, Paige thought. *Nothing is going to come of this*. She thought of something Kat had said to her. *You're clinging to a ghost. Let go*. She looked at Jason and said, 'Yes.'

Early the following morning, a messenger arrived with a package. Paige opened the door for him.

'I have something for Dr Taylor.'

'I'm Dr Taylor.'

The messenger looked at her in surprise. 'You're a doctor?'

'Yes,' Paige said patiently. 'I'm a doctor. Do you mind?'

He shrugged. 'No, lady. Not at all. Would you sign here, please?'

The package was surprisingly heavy. Curious, Paige carried it to the living-room table and unwrapped it. It was a miniature model of a beautiful white two-story house with a veranda. In front of the house was a little lawn and garden, surrounded by a white picket fence. *He must have stayed up all night, making it.* There was a card that read:

Mine [ ]
Ours [ ]
Please check one.

She sat there looking at it for a long time. It was the right house, but it was the wrong man.

What's the matter with me? Paige asked herself. *He's bright and attractive and charming.* But she knew what the matter was. He was not Alfred.

The telephone rang. It was Jason. 'Did you get your house?' he asked.

'It's beautiful!' Paige said. 'Thank you so much.'

'I'd like to build you the real thing. Did you fill in the box?'

'No.'

'I'm a patient man. Are you free for dinner tonight?'

'Yes, but I have to warn you, I'm going to be operating all day, and by this evening I'll be exhausted.'

201

'We'll make it an early evening. By the way, it's going to be at my parents' home.'

Paige hesitated a moment. 'Oh?'

'I've told them all about you.'

'That's fine,' Paige said. Things were moving too quickly. It made her nervous.

When Paige hung up, she thought: *I really shouldn't be doing this. By tonight I'm going to be too tired to do anything but go to sleep.* She was tempted to telephone Jason back and cancel their date. *It's too late to do that now. We'll make it an early evening.*

As Paige was getting dressed that night, Kat said, 'You look exhausted.'

'I am.'

'Why are you going out? You should be going to bed. Or is that redundant?'

'No. Not tonight.'

'Jason again?'

'Yes. I'm going to meet his parents.'

'Ah.' Kat shook her head.

'It's not like that at all,' Paige said. *It's really not.*

Jason's mother and father lived in a charming old house in the Pacific Heights district. Jason's father was an aristocratic-looking man in his seventies. Jason's mother was a warm, down-to-earth woman. They made Paige feel instantly at home.

'Jason has told us so much about you,' Mrs Curtis said. 'He didn't tell us how beautiful you are.'

'Thank you.'

They went into the library, filled with miniature models of buildings that Jason and his father had designed.

'I guess that between us, Jason, his great-grandfather, and I have done a lot of the landscape of San Francisco,' Jason's father said. 'My son is a genius.'

'That's what I keep telling Paige,' Jason said.

Paige laughed. 'I believe it.' Her eyes were getting heavy and she was fighting to stay awake.

Jason was watching her, concerned. 'Let's go in to dinner,' he suggested.

They went into the large dining room. It was oak-paneled, furnished with attractive antiques and portraits on the wall. A maid began serving.

Jason's father said, 'That painting over there is Jason's great-grandfather. All the buildings he designed were destroyed in the earthquake of 1906. It's too bad. They were priceless. I'll show you some photographs of them after dinner if you . . .'

Paige's head had dropped to the table. She was sound asleep.

'I'm glad I didn't serve soup,' Jason's mother said.

Ken Mallory had a problem. As word of the wager about Kat had spread around the hospital, the bets had quickly increased to ten thousand dollars. Mallory had been so confident of his success that he had bet much more than he could afford to pay off.

If I fail, I'm in a hell of a lot of trouble. But I'm not going to fail. Time for the master to go to work.

Kat was having lunch in the cafeteria with Paige and Honey when Mallory approached the table.

'Mind if I join you doctors?'

Not ladies, not girls. Doctors. The sensitive type, Kat thought cynically. 'Not at all. Sit down,' she said.

Paige and Honey exchanged a look.

'Well, I have to get going,' Paige said.

'Me, too. See you later.'

Mallory watched Paige and Honey leave.

'Busy morning?' Mallory asked. He made it sound as though he really cared.

'Aren't they all?' Kat gave him a warm, promising smile.

Mallory had planned his strategy carefully. *I'm going to let her know I'm interested in her as a person, not just as a woman. They hate the sex-object thing. Discuss medicine with her. I'll take it slow and easy. I have a whole month to get her in the sack.*

'Did you hear about the postmortem on Mrs Turnball?' Mallory began. 'The woman had a Coca-Cola bottle in her stomach! Can you imagine how . . . ?'

Kat leaned forward. 'Are you doing anything Saturday night, Ken?'

Mallory was caught completely off guard. 'What?'

'I thought you might like to take me out to dinner.'

He found himself almost blushing. *My God!* he thought. *Talk about shooting fish in a barrel! This is no lesbian. The guys said that because they couldn't get into her pants. Well, I'm going to. She's actually asking for it!* He tried to remember with whom he had a date on Saturday. *Sally, the little nurse in OR. She can wait.*

'Nothing important,' Mallory said. 'I'd love to take you to dinner.'

Kat put her hand over his. 'Wonderful,' she said softly. 'I'll really be looking forward to it.'

He grinned. 'So will I.' *You have no idea how much, baby. Ten thousand dollars' worth!*

That afternoon, Kat reported back to Paige and Honey.

'His mouth dropped open!' Kat laughed. 'You should have seen the look on his face! He looked like the cat that swallowed the canary.'

Paige said, 'Remember, you're the Kat. He's the canary.'

'What are you going to do Saturday night?' Honey asked.

'Any suggestions?'

'I have,' Paige answered. 'Here's the plan . . .'

Saturday evening, Kat and Ken Mallory had dinner at Emilio's, a restaurant on the bay. She had dressed carefully for him, in a white cotton dress, off the shoulder.

'You look sensational,' Mallory said. He was careful to strike just the right note. *Appreciative, but not pressing. Admiring, but not suggestive.* Mallory had determined to be at his most charming, but it was not necessary. It quickly became obvious to him that Kat was intent on charming *him*.

Over a drink, she said, 'Everyone talks about what a wonderful doctor you are, Ken.'

'Well,' Mallory said modestly, 'I've had fine training, and I care a lot about my patients. They're very important to me.' His voice was filled with sincerity.

Kat put her hand over his. 'I'm sure they are.

Where are you from? I want to know all about you. The *real* you.'

Jesus! Mallory thought. *That's the line I use.* He could not get over how easy this was going to be. He was an expert on the subject of women. His radar knew all the signals they put out. They could say yes with a look, a smile, a tone of voice. Kat's signals were jamming his radar.

She was leaning close to him, and her voice was husky. 'I want to know everything.'

He talked about himself during dinner, and every time he tried to change the subject and bring it around to Kat, she said, 'No, no. I want to hear more. You've had such a fascinating life!'

She's crazy about me, Mallory decided. He wished now that he had taken more bets. *I might even win tonight*, he thought. And he was sure of it when Kat said, as they were having coffee, 'Would you like to come up to my apartment for a nightcap?'

Bingo! Mallory stroked her arm and said softly, 'I'd love to.' *The guys were all crazy*, Mallory decided. *She's the horniest broad I've ever met.* He had a feeling that he was about to be raped.

Thirty minutes later, they were walking into Kat's apartment.

'Nice,' Mallory said, looking around. 'Very nice. Do you live here alone?'

'No. Dr Taylor and Dr Taft live with me.'

'Oh.' She could hear the note of regret in his voice.

Kat gave him a beguiling smile. 'But they won't be home until much later.'

Mallory grinned. 'Good.'

'Would you like a drink?'

206

'Love one. Scotch and soda, please.' He watched as Kat walked over to the little bar and mixed two drinks. *She's got great buns*, Mallory thought. *And she's damned good-looking, and I'm getting ten thousand dollars to lay her*. He laughed aloud.

Kat turned. 'What's so funny?'

'Nothing. I was just thinking how lucky I am to be here alone with you.'

'I'm the lucky one,' Kat said warmly. She handed him his drink.

Mallory raised his glass and started to say, 'Here's to . . .'

Kat beat him to it. 'Here's to us!' she said.

He nodded. 'I'll drink to that.'

He started to say, 'How about a little music?' and as he opened his mouth, Kat said, 'Would you like some music?'

'You're a mind reader.'

Kat put on an old Cole Porter standard. She surreptitiously glanced at her watch, then turned to Mallory. 'Do you like to dance?'

Mallory moved closer to her. 'It depends on whom I'm dancing with. I'd love to dance with you.'

Kat moved into his arms, and they began to dance to the slow and dreamy music. He felt Kat's body pressing hard against his, and he could feel himself getting aroused. He held her tighter, and Kat smiled up at him.

Now is the time to go in for the kill, he thought.

'You're lovely, you know,' Mallory said huskily. 'I've wanted you since the first moment I saw you.'

Kat looked into his eyes. 'I've felt the same way

about you, Ken.' His lips moved toward hers, and he gave her a warm, passionate kiss.

'Let's go into the bedroom,' Mallory said. There was a sudden urgency in him.

'Oh, yes!'

He took her by the arm and she started leading him toward her bedroom. And at that moment, the front door opened and Paige and Honey walked in.

'Hi, there!' Paige called. She looked at Ken Mallory in surprise. 'Oh, Dr Mallory! I didn't expect to see you here.'

'Well, I . . . I . . .'

'We went out to dinner,' Kat said.

Mallory was filled with a dark rage. He fought to control it. He turned to Kat. 'I should go. It's late and I have a big day tomorrow.'

'Oh. I'm sorry you're leaving,' Kat said. There was a world of promise in her eyes.

Mallory said, 'What about tomorrow night?'

'I'd love to . . .'

'Great!'

'. . . but I can't.'

'Oh. Well, what about Friday?'

Kat frowned. 'Oh, dear. I'm afraid Friday isn't good, either.'

Mallory was getting desperate. 'Saturday?'

Kat smiled. 'Saturday would be lovely.'

He nodded, relieved. 'Good. Saturday it is, then.'

He turned to Paige and Honey. 'Good night.'

'Good night.'

Kat walked Mallory to the door. 'Sweet dreams,' she said softly. 'I'm going to dream about you.'

Mallory squeezed her hand. 'I believe in making dreams come true. We'll make up for this Saturday night.'

'I can't wait.'

That night, Kat lay in her bed thinking about Mallory. She hated him. But to her surprise, she had enjoyed the evening. She was sure that Mallory had enjoyed it too, in spite of the fact that he was playing a game. *If only this were real*, Kat thought, *and not a game*. She had no idea how dangerous a game it was.

17

Maybe it's the weather, Paige thought wearily. It was cold and dreary outside, with a heavy fog that depressed the spirits. Her day had begun at six o'clock in the morning, and it was filled with constant problems. The hospital seemed to be full of gomers, all complaining at once. The nurses were surly and careless. They drew blood from the wrong patients, lost X-rays that were urgently needed, and snapped at the patients. In addition, there was a staff shortage because of a flu epidemic. It was that kind of day.

The only bright spot was the telephone call from Jason Curtis.

'Hello,' he said cheerily. 'Just thought I'd check in and see how all our patients are doing.'

'They're surviving.'

'Any chance of our having lunch?'

Paige laughed. 'What's lunch? If I'm lucky, I'll be able to grab a stale sandwich about four o'clock this afternoon. It's pretty hectic around here.'

'All right. I won't keep you. May I call you again?'

'All right.' *No harm in that.*

'Bye.'

Paige worked until midnight without a moment to rest, and when she was finally relieved, she was almost too tired to move. She briefly debated staying at the hospital and sleeping on the cot in the on-call room, but the thought of her warm, cozy bed at home was too tempting. She changed clothes and lurched her way to the elevator.

Dr Peterson came up to her. 'My God!' he said. 'Where's the cat that dragged you in?'

Paige smiled wearily. 'Do I look that bad?'

'Worse.' Peterson grinned. 'You're going home now?'

Paige nodded.

'You're lucky. I'm just starting.'

The elevator arrived. Paige stood there half asleep.

Peterson said gently, 'Paige?'

She shook herself awake. 'Yes?'

'Are you going to be able to drive home?'

'Sure,' Paige mumbled. 'And when I get there, I'm going to sleep for twenty-four hours straight.'

She walked to the parking lot and got into her car. She sat there drained, too tired to turn on the ignition. *I mustn't go to sleep here. I'll sleep at home.*

Paige drove out of the parking lot and headed toward the apartment. She was unaware of how erratically she was driving until a driver yelled at her, 'Hey, get off the road, you drunken broad!'

She forced herself to concentrate. *I must not fall asleep . . . I must not fall asleep.* She snapped the radio on and turned the volume up loudly. When she reached her apartment building, she sat in the car for a long time before she was able to summon enough strength to go upstairs.

Kat and Honey were in their beds, asleep. Paige looked at the clock at her bedside. *One o'clock.* She stumbled into her bedroom and started to get undressed, but the effort was too much for her. She fell into bed with her clothes on, and in an instant was sound asleep.

She was awakened by the shrill ringing of a telephone that seemed to be coming from some far-off planet. Paige fought to stay asleep, but the ringing was like needles penetrating her brain. She sat up groggily and reached for the phone. 'H'lo?'

'Dr Taylor?'

'Yes.' Her voice was a hoarse mumble.

'Dr Barker wants you in OR Four to assist him, stat.'

Paige cleared her throat. 'There must be some mistake,' she mumbled. 'I just got off duty.'

'OR Four. He's waiting.' The line went dead.

Paige sat on the edge of the bed, numb, her mind clouded by sleep. She looked at the clock on the bedside table. Four-fifteen. Why was Dr Barker asking for her in the middle of the night? There was only one answer. Something had happened to one of her patients.

Paige staggered into the bathroom and threw cold water on her face. She looked in the mirror and thought, *My God! I look about eighty*.

Ten minutes later, Paige was making her way back to the hospital. She was still half asleep when she took the elevator to the fourth floor to OR Four. She went into the dressing room and changed, then scrubbed up and stepped into the operating room.

There were three nurses and a resident assisting Dr Barker.

He looked up as Paige entered and yelled, 'For Christ's sake, you're wearing a hospital gown! Didn't anyone ever inform you that you're supposed to wear *scrubs* in an operating room?'

Paige stood there, stunned, jolted wide awake, her eyes blazing. 'You listen to me,' she said, furiously. 'I'm supposed to be off duty. I came in as a favor to you. I don't —'

'Don't argue with me,' Dr Barker said curtly. 'Get over here and hold this retractor.'

Paige walked over to the operating table and looked down. It was not her patient on the table. It was a stranger. *Barker had no reason to call me. He's trying to force me to quit the hospital. Well, I'll be damned if I will!* She gave him a baleful look, picked up the retractor, and went to work.

The operation was an emergency coronary artery bypass graft. The skin incision had already been made down the center of the chest to the breastbone, which had been split with an electric saw. The heart and major blood vessels were exposed.

Paige inserted the metal retractor between the cut sides of the breastbone, forcing the edges apart. She watched as Dr Barker skillfully opened the pericardial sac, exposing the heart.

He indicated the coronary arteries. 'Here's the problem,' Barker said. 'We're going to do some grafting.'

He had already removed a long strip of vein from one leg. He sewed a piece of it into the main artery coming out of the heart. The other end he attached to one of the coronary arteries, beyond the obstructed area, sending the blood through the vein graft, bypassing the obstruction.

Paige was watching a master at work. *If only he weren't such a bastard!*

The operation took three hours. By the time it was over, Paige was only half conscious. When the incision had been closed, Dr Barker turned to the staff and said, 'I want to thank all of you.' He was not looking at Paige.

Paige stumbled out of the room without a word and went upstairs to the office of Dr Benjamin Wallace.

Wallace was just arriving. 'You look exhausted,' he said. 'You should get some rest.'

Paige took a deep breath to control her anger. 'I want to be transferred to another surgical team.'

Wallace studied her a moment. 'You're assigned to Dr Barker, right?'

'Right.'

'What's the problem?'

'Ask *him*. He hates me. He'll be glad to get rid of me. I'll go with anyone else. Anyone.'

'I'll talk to him,' Wallace said.

'Thank you.'

Paige turned and walked out of the office. *They'd better take me away from him. If I see him again, I'll kill him.*

Paige went home and slept for twelve hours. She woke up with a feeling that something wonderful had happened, and then she remembered. *I don't have to see the Beast anymore!* She drove to the hospital, whistling.

As Paige was walking down the corridor, an orderly came up to her. 'Dr Taylor . . .'

'Yes?'

'Dr Wallace would like to see you in his office.'

214

'Thank you,' Paige said. She wondered who the new senior surgeon would be. *Anybody will be an improvement*, Paige thought. She walked into Benjamin Wallace's office.

'Well, you look much better now, Paige.'

'Thanks. I feel much better.' And she did. She felt great, filled with an enormous sense of relief.

'I talked to Dr Barker.'

Paige smiled. 'Thank you. I really appreciate it.'

'He won't let you go.'

Paige's smile faded. *What?*

'He said you're assigned to his team and you'll stay there.'

She could not believe what she was hearing. 'But *why?*' She knew why. The sadistic bastard needed a whipping girl, someone to humiliate. 'I'm not going to stand for it.'

Dr Wallace said ruefully, 'I'm afraid you have no choice. Unless you want to leave the hospital. Would you like to think about it?'

Paige did not have to think about it. 'No.' She was not going to let Barker force her to quit. That was his plan. 'No,' she repeated slowly. 'I'll stay.'

'Good. Then that's settled.'

Not by a long shot, Paige thought. *I'm going to find some way to pay him back.*

In the doctors' dressing room, Ken Mallory was getting ready to make his rounds. Dr Grundy and three other doctors walked in.

'There's our man!' Grundy said. 'How are you doing, Ken?'

'Fine,' Mallory said.

Grundy turned to the others. 'He doesn't look like he just got laid, does he?' He turned back to Mallory. 'I hope you have our money ready. I plan to make a down payment on a little car.'

Another doctor joined in. 'I'm buying a whole new wardrobe.'

Mallory shook his head pityingly. 'I wouldn't count on it, suckers. Get ready to pay me off!'

Grundy was studying him. 'What do you mean?'

'If she's a lesbian, I'm a eunuch. She's the horniest broad I ever met. I practically had to hold her off the other night!'

The men were looking at one another, worried.

'But you didn't get her into the sack?'

'The only reason I didn't, my friends, is because we were interrupted on the way to the bedroom. I have a date with her Saturday night, and it's already over but the shouting.' Mallory finished dressing. 'Now, if you gentlemen will excuse me . . .'

An hour later, Grundy stopped Kat in the corridor.

'I've been looking for you,' he said. He looked angry.

'Is something wrong?'

'It's that bastard Mallory. He's so sure of himself that he's telling everyone that he's going to get you into bed by Saturday night.'

'Don't worry,' Kat said grimly. 'He's going to lose.'

When Ken Mallory picked Kat up Saturday night, she had on a low-cut dress that accentuated her voluptuous figure.

'You look gorgeous,' he said admiringly.

She put her arms around him. 'I want to look good for you.' She was clinging to him.

God, she really wants it! When Mallory spoke, his voice was husky. 'Look, I have an idea, Kat. Before we go out to dinner, why don't we slip into the bedroom and . . .'

She was stroking his face. 'Oh, darling, I wish we could. Paige is home.' Paige was actually at the hospital, working.

'Oh.'

'But after dinner . . .' She let the suggestion hang in the air.

'Yes?'

'We could go to your place.'

Mallory put his arms around her and kissed her. 'That's a wonderful idea!'

He took her to the Iron Horse, and they had a delicious dinner. In spite of herself, Kat was having a wonderful time. He was charming and amusing, and incredibly attractive. He seemed genuinely interested in knowing everything about her. She knew he was flattering her, but the look in his eye made the compliments seem real.

If I didn't know better . . .

Mallory had hardly tasted his food. All he could think was, *In two hours I will be making ten thousand dollars . . . In one hour, I will be making ten thousand dollars . . . In thirty minutes . . .*

They finished their coffee.

'Are you ready?' Mallory asked.

Kat put her hand over his. 'You have no idea how ready, darling. Let's go.'

They took a taxi to Mallory's apartment. 'I'm

absolutely crazy about you,' Mallory murmured. 'I've never known anyone like you.'

And she could hear Grundy's voice: *He's so sure of himself that he says he's going to get you into bed by Saturday night.*

When they arrived at the apartment, Mallory paid the taxi driver and led Kat into the elevator. It seemed to Mallory to take forever to get up to his apartment. He opened the door and said eagerly, 'Here it is.'

Kat stepped inside.

It was an ordinary little bachelor's apartment that desperately needed a woman's touch.

'Oh, it's lovely,' Kat breathed. She turned to Mallory. 'It's *you.*'

He grinned. 'Let me show you *our* room. I'll put some music on.'

As he went over to the tape deck, Kat glanced at her watch. The voice of Barbra Streisand filled the room.

Mallory took her hand. 'Let's go, honey.'

'Wait a minute,' Kat said softly.

He was looking at her, puzzled. 'What for?'

'I just want to enjoy this moment with you. You know, before we . . .'

'Why don't we enjoy it in the bedroom?'

'I'd love a drink.'

'A drink?' He tried to hide his impatience. 'Fine. What would you like?'

'A vodka and tonic, please.'

He smiled. 'I think we can handle that.' He went over to the little bar and hurriedly mixed two drinks.

Kat looked at her watch again.

Mallory returned with the drinks and handed one to Kat. 'Here you are, baby.' He raised his glass. 'To togetherness.'

'To togetherness,' Kat said. She took a sip of the drink. 'Oh, my God!'

He looked at her, startled. 'What's the matter?'

'This is vodka!'

'That's what you asked for.'

'Did I? I'm sorry. I hate vodka!' She stroked his face. 'May I have a scotch and soda?'

'Sure.' He swallowed his impatience and went back to the bar to mix another drink.

Kat glanced at her watch again.

Ken Mallory returned. 'Here you are.'

'Thank you, darling.'

She took two sips of her drink. Mallory took the glass from her and set it on a table. He put his arms around Kat and held her close, and she could feel that he was aroused.

'Now,' Ken said softly, 'let's make history.'

'Oh, yes!' Kat said. 'Yes!'

She let him lead her into the bedroom.

I've done it! Mallory exulted. *I've done it! Here go the walls of Jericho!* He turned to Kat. 'Get undressed, baby.'

'You first, darling. I want to watch you get undressed. It excites me.'

'Oh? Well, sure.'

As Kat stood there watching, Mallory slowly took his clothes off. First his jacket, then his shirt and tie, then his shoes and stockings, and then his trousers. He had the firm figure of an athlete.

'Does this excite you, baby?'

'Oh, yes. Now take off your shorts.'

Slowly Mallory let his shorts fall to the floor. He had a turgid erection.

'That's beautiful,' Kat said.

'Now it's your turn.'

'Right.'

And at that moment, Kat's beeper went off.

Mallory was startled. 'What the hell . . . ?'

'They're calling me,' Kat said. 'May I use your telephone?'

'*Now?*'

'Yes. It must be an emergency.'

'*Now?* Can't it wait?'

'Darling, you know the rules.'

'But . . .'

As Mallory watched, Kat walked over to the tele- phone and dialed a number. 'Dr Hunter.' She listened. 'Really? Of course. I'll be right there.'

Mallory was staring at her, stupefied. 'What's going on?'

'I have to get back to the hospital, angel.'

'*Now?*'

'Yes. One of my patients is dying.'

'Can't he wait until . . . ?'

'I'm sorry. We'll do this another night.'

Ken Mallory stood there, buck naked, watching Kat walk out of his apartment, and as the door closed behind her, he picked up her drink and slammed it into the wall. *Bitch . . bitch . . . bitch . . .*

When Kat got back to the apartment, Paige and Honey were eagerly waiting for her.

'How did it go?' Paige asked. 'Was I on time?'

Kat laughed. 'Your timing was perfect.'

220

She began to describe the evening. When she came to the part about Mallory standing in the bedroom naked, with an erection, they laughed until tears came to their eyes.

Kat was tempted to tell them how enjoyable she really found Ken Mallory, but she felt foolish. After all, he was seeing her only so he could win a bet.

Somehow, Paige seemed to sense how Kat felt. 'Be careful of him, Kat.'

Kat smiled. 'Don't worry. But I will admit that if I didn't know about that bet . . . He's a snake, but he gives good snake oil.'

'When are you going to see him again?' Honey asked.

'I'm going to give him a week to cool off.'

Paige was studying her. 'Him or you?'

Dinetto's black limousine was waiting for Kat outside the hospital. This time, the Shadow was alone. Kat wished that Rhino were there. There was something about the Shadow that petrified her. He never smiled and seldom spoke, but he exuded menace.

'Get in,' he said as Kat approached the car.

'Look,' Kat said indignantly, 'you tell Mr Dinetto that he can't order me around. I don't work for him. Just because I did him a favor once . . .'

'Get in. You can tell him yourself.'

Kat hesitated. It would be easy to walk away and not get involved any further, but how would it affect Mike? Kat got into the car.

*   *   *

221

The victim this time had been badly beaten, whipped with a chain. Lou Dinetto was there with him.

Kat took one look at the patient and said, 'You've got to get him to a hospital right away.'

'Kat,' Dinetto said, 'you have to treat him here.'

'Why?' Kat demanded. But she knew the answer, and it terrified her.

18

It was one of those clear days in San Francisco when there was a magic in the air. The night wind had swept away the rainclouds, producing a crisp, sunny Sunday morning.

Jason had arranged to pick up Paige at the apartment. When he arrived, she was surprised at how pleased she was to see him.

'Good morning,' Jason said. 'You look beautiful.'

'Thank you.'

'What would you like to do today?'

Paige said, 'It's your town. You lead, I'll follow.'

'Fair enough.'

'If you don't mind,' Paige said, 'I'd like to make a quick stop at the hospital.'

'I thought this was your day off.'

'It is, but there's a patient I'm concerned about.'

'No problem.' Jason drove her to the hospital.

'I won't be long,' Paige promised as she got out of the car.

'I'll wait for you here.'

Paige went up to the third floor and into Jimmy Ford's room. He was still in a coma, attached to an array of tubes feeding him intravenously.

A nurse was in the room. She looked up as Paige entered. 'Good morning, Dr Taylor.'

'Good morning.' Paige walked over to the boy's bedside. 'Has there been any change?'

'I'm afraid not.'

Paige felt Jimmy's pulse and listened to his heartbeat.

'It's been several weeks now,' the nurse said. 'It doesn't look good, does it?'

'He's going to come out of it,' Paige said firmly. She turned to the unconscious figure on the bed and raised her voice. 'Do you hear me? You're going to get well!' There was no reaction. She closed her eyes a moment and said a silent prayer. 'Have them beep me at once if there's any change.'

'Yes, doctor.'

He's not going to die, Paige thought. *I'm not going to let him die . . .*

Jason got out of the car as Paige approached. 'Is everything all right?'

There was no point in burdening him with her problems. 'Everything's fine,' Paige said.

'Let's play real tourists today,' Jason said. 'There's a state law that all tours have to start at Fisherman's Wharf.'

Paige smiled. 'We mustn't break the law.'

Fisherman's Wharf was like an outdoor carnival. The street entertainers were out in full force. There were mimes, clowns, dancers and musicians. Vendors were selling steaming caldrons of Dungeness crabs and clam chowder with fresh sourdough bread.

'There's no place like this in the world,' Jason said warmly.

Paige was touched by his enthusiasm. She had seen Fisherman's Wharf before and most of the other tourist sites of San Francisco, but she did not want to spoil his fun.

'Have you ridden a cable car yet?' Jason asked.

'No.' *Not since last week.*

'You haven't lived! Come along.'

They walked to Powell Street and boarded a cable car. As they started up the steep grade, Jason said, 'This was known as Hallidie's Folly. He built it in 1873.'

'And I'll bet they said it wouldn't last!'

Jason laughed. 'That's right. When I was going to high school, I used to work weekends as a tour guide.'

'I'm sure you were good.'

'The best. Would you like to hear some of my spiel?'

'I'd love to.'

Jason adopted the nasal tone of a tour guide. 'Ladies and gentlemen, for your information, the oldest street in San Francisco is Grant Avenue, the longest is Mission Street—seven and a half miles long—the widest is Van Ness Avenue at one hundred twenty-five feet, and you'll be surprised to know that the narrowest, DeForest Street, is only four and a half feet. That's right, ladies and gentlemen, four and a half feet. The steepest street we can offer you is Filbert Street, with a thirty-one and a half percent grade.' He looked at Paige and grinned. 'I'm surprised that I still remember all that.'

When they alit from the cable car, Paige looked up at Jason and smiled. 'What's next?'

'We're going to take a carriage ride.'

Ten minutes later, they were seated in a horse-drawn carriage that took them from Fisherman's Wharf to Ghirardelli Square to North Beach. Jason pointed out the places of interest along the way, and Paige was surprised at how much she was enjoying herself. *Don't let yourself get carried away.*

They went up to Coit Tower for a view of the city. As they ascended, Jason asked, 'Are you hungry?'

The fresh air had made Paige very hungry. 'Yes.'

'Good. I'm going to take you to one of the best Chinese restaurants in the world — Tommy Toy's.'

Paige had heard the hospital staff speak of it.

The meal turned out to be a banquet. They started with lobster pot stickers with chili sauce, and hot and sour soup with seafood. That was followed by filet of chicken with snow peas and pecans, veal filet with Szechuan sauce, and four-flavored fried rice. For dessert, they had a peach mousse. The food was wonderful.

'Do you come here often?' Paige asked.

'As often as I can.'

There was a boyish quality about Jason that Paige found very attractive.

'Tell me,' Paige said, 'did you always want to be an architect?'

'I had no choice.' Jason grinned. 'My first toys were Erector sets. It's exciting to dream about something and then watch that dream become concrete and bricks and stone, and soar up into the sky and become a part of the city you live in.'

I'm going to build you a Taj Mahal. I don't care how long it takes!

'I'm one of the lucky ones, Paige, spending my life doing what I love to do. Who was it who said, "Most people live lives of quiet desperation"?'

Sounds like a lot of my patients, Paige thought.

'There's nothing else I would want to do, or any other place I would want to live. This is a fabulous city.' His voice was filled with excitement. 'It has everything anyone could want. I never get tired of it.'

Paige studied him for a moment, enjoying his enthusiasm. 'You've never been married?'

Jason shrugged. 'Once. We were both too young. It didn't work out.'

'I'm sorry.'

'No need to be. She's married to a very wealthy meat packer. Have you been married?'

I'm going to be a doctor, too, when I grow up. We'll get married, and we'll work together.

'No.'

They took a bay cruise under the Golden Gate and Bay Bridge. Jason assumed his tour guide's voice again. 'And there, ladies and gentlemen, is the storied Alcatraz, former home of some of the world's most infamous criminals—Machine Gun Kelly, Al Capone, and Robert Stroud, known as the Birdman! "Alcatraz" means pelican in Spanish. It was originally called Isla de los Alcatraces, after the birds that were its only inhabitants. Do you know why they had hot showers every day for the prisoners here?'

'No.'

'So that they wouldn't get used to the cold bay water when they were trying to escape.'

'Is that true?' Paige asked.

'Have I ever lied to you?'

It was late afternoon when Jason said, 'Have you ever been to Noe Valley?'

Paige shook her head. 'No.'

'I'd like to show it to you. It used to be farms and streams. Now it's filled with brightly colored Victorian homes and gardens. The houses are very old, because it was about the only area spared in the 1906 earthquake.'

'It sounds lovely.'

Jason hesitated. 'My home is there. Would you like to see it?' He saw Paige's reaction. 'Paige, I'm in love with you.'

'We hardly know each other. How could you . . . ?'

'I knew it from the moment you said, "Don't you know you're supposed to wear a white coat on rounds?" That's when I fell in love with you.'

'Jason . . .'

'I'm a firm believer in love at first sight. My grandfather saw my grandmother riding a bicycle in the park and he followed her, and they got married three months later. They were together for fifty years, until he died. My father saw my mother crossing a street, and he knew she was going to be his wife. They've been married for forty-five years. You see, it runs in the family. I want to marry you.'

It was the moment of truth.

Paige looked at Jason and thought, *He's the first man I've been attracted to since Alfred. He's adorable and bright and genuine. He's everything a woman could want in a man. What's the matter with me? I'm holding on to a ghost.* Yet deep inside her, she still had the overpowering feeling that one day Alfred was going to come back to her.

She looked at Jason and made her decision. 'Jason . . .'

And at that moment, Paige's beeper went off.

'Paige . . .'

'I have to get to a telephone.' Two minutes later, she was talking to the hospital.

Jason watched Paige's face turn pale.

She was shouting into the telephone, 'No! Absolutely not! Tell them I'll be right there.' She slammed the phone down.

'What is it?' Jason asked.

She turned to him, and her eyes were filled with tears. 'It's Jimmy Ford, my patient. They're going to take him off the respirator. They're going to let him die.'

When Paige reached Jimmy Ford's room, there were three people there beside the comatose figure in bed: George Englund, Benjamin Wallace, and a lawyer, Silvester Damone.

'What's going on here?' Paige demanded.

Benjamin Wallace said, 'At the hospital ethics committee meeting this morning, it was decided that Jimmy Ford's condition is hopeless. We've decided to remove —'

'No!' Paige said. 'You can't! I'm his doctor. I say

he has a chance to come out of it! We're *not* going to let him die.'

Silvester Damone spoke up. 'It's not your decision to make, doctor.'

Paige looked at him defiantly. 'Who are you?'

'I'm the family's attorney.' He pulled out a document and handed it to Paige. 'This is Jimmy Ford's living will. It specifically states that if he has a life-threatening trauma, he's not to be kept alive by mechanical means.'

'But I've been monitoring his condition,' Paige pleaded. 'He's been stabilized for weeks. He could come out of the coma any moment.'

'Can you guarantee that?' Damone asked.

'No, but . . .'

'Then you'll have to do as you're ordered, doctor.'

Paige looked down at the figure of Jimmy. 'No! You have to wait a little longer.'

The lawyer said smoothly, 'Doctor, I'm sure it benefits the hospital to keep patients here as long as possible, but the family cannot afford the medical expenses any longer. I'm ordering you now to take him off the respirator.'

'Just another day or two,' Paige said desperately, 'and I'm sure . . .'

'No,' Damone said firmly. 'Today.'

George Englund turned to Paige. 'I'm sorry, but I'm afraid we have no choice.'

'Thank you, doctor,' the lawyer said. 'I'll leave it to you to handle it. I'll notify the family that it will be taken care of immediately, so they can begin to make the funeral arrangements.' He turned to Benjamin Wallace. 'Thank you for your cooperation. Good day.'

They watched him walk out of the room.

'We can't do this to Jimmy!' Paige said.

Dr Wallace cleared his throat. 'Paige . . .'

'What if we got him out of here and hid him in another room? There must be something we haven't thought of. Something . . .'

Benjamin Wallace said, 'This isn't a request. It's an order.' He turned to George Englund. 'Do you want to . . . ?'

'No!' Paige said. 'I'll . . . I'll do it.'

'Very well.'

'If you don't mind, I'd like to be alone with him.'

George Englund squeezed her arm. 'I'm sorry, Paige.'

'I know.'

Paige watched the two men leave the room.

She was alone with the unconscious boy. She looked at the respirator that was keeping him alive and the IVs that were feeding his body. It would be so simple to turn the respirator off, to snuff out a life. But he had had so many wonderful dreams, such high hopes.

I'm going to be a doctor one day. I want to be like you.

Did you know I'm getting married? . . . Her name is Betsy . . . We're going to have half a dozen kids. The first girl is going to be named Paige.

He had so very much to live for.

Paige stood there looking down at him, tears blurring the room. 'Damn you!' she said. 'You're a quitter!' She was sobbing now. 'What happened to those dreams of yours? I thought you wanted to become a doctor! Answer me! Do you hear me? Open your eyes!' She looked down at the pale figure.

231

There was no reaction. 'I'm sorry,' Paige said. 'I'm so sorry.' She leaned down to kiss him on the cheek, and as she slowly straightened up, she was looking into his open eyes.

'Jimmy! *Jimmy!*'

He blinked and closed his eyes again. Paige squeezed his hand. She leaned forward and said through her sobs, 'Jimmy, did you hear the one about the patient who was being fed intravenously? He asked the doctor for an extra bottle. He was having a guest for lunch.'

19

Honey was happier than she had ever been in her life. She had a warm relationship with patients that few of the other doctors had. She genuinely cared about them. She worked in geriatrics, in pediatrics, and in various other wards, and Dr Wallace saw to it that she was given assignments that kept her out of harm's way. He wanted to make sure that she stayed at the hospital and was available to him.

Honey envied the nurses. They were able to nurture their patients without worrying about major medical decisions. *I never wanted to be a doctor*, Honey thought. *I always wanted to be a nurse.*

There are no nurses in the Taft family.

In the afternoon when Honey left the hospital, she would go shopping at the Bay Company, and Streetlight Records, and buy gifts for the children in pediatric care.

'I love children,' she told Kat.

'Are you planning to have a large family?'

'Someday,' Honey said wistfully. 'I have to find their father first.'

One of Honey's favorite patients in the geriatric ward was Daniel McGuire, a cheerful man in his nineties who was suffering from a diseased liver condition. He had been a gambler in his youth, and he liked to make bets with Honey.

'I'll bet you fifty cents the orderly is late with my breakfast.'

'I'll bet you a dollar it's going to rain this afternoon.'

'I'll bet you the Giants win.'

Honey always took his bets.

'I'll bet you ten to one I beat this thing,' he said.

'This time I'm not going to bet you,' Honey told him. 'I'm on your side.'

He took her hand. 'I know you are.' He grinned. 'If I were a few months younger . . .'

Honey laughed. 'Never mind. I like older men.'

One morning a letter came for him at the hospital. Honey took it to him in his room.

'Read it to me, would you?' His eyesight had faded.

'Of course,' Honey said. She opened the envelope, looked at it a moment, and let out a cry. 'You've won the lottery! Fifty thousand dollars! Congratulations!'

'How about that?' He yelled. 'I always knew I'd win the lottery one day! Give me a hug.'

Honey leaned down and hugged him.

'You know something, Honey? I'm the luckiest man in the world.'

When Honey came back to visit him that afternoon, he had passed away. He had lost the most important bet of all.

Honey was in the doctors' lounge when Dr Stevens walked in. 'Is there a Virgo here?'

One of the doctors laughed. 'If you mean a virgin, I doubt it.'

'A *Virgo*,' Stevens repeated. 'I need a Virgo.'

'I'm a Virgo,' Honey said. 'What's the problem?'

He walked up to her. 'The problem is that I have a goddam maniac on my hands. She won't let anyone near her but a Virgo.'

Honey got up. 'I'll go see her.'

'Thanks. Her name is Frances Gordon.'

Frances Gordon had just had a hip replacement. The moment Honey walked into the room, the woman looked up and said, 'You're a Virgo. Born on the cusp, right?'

Honey smiled. 'That's right.'

'Those Aquarians and Leos don't know what the hell they're doin'. They treat patients like they're meat.'

'The doctors here are very good,' Honey protested. 'They—'

'Ha! Most of them are in it for the money.' She looked at Honey more closely. 'You're different.'

Honey scanned the chart at the foot of the bed, a surprised look on her face.

'What's the matter? What are you lookin' at?'

Honey blinked. 'It says here that your occupation is a . . . a psychic.'

Frances Gordon nodded. 'That's right. Don't you believe in psychics?'

Honey shook her head. 'I'm afraid not.'

'That's too bad. Sit down a minute.'

Honey took a chair.

'Let me hold your hand.'

Honey shook her head. 'I really don't . . .'

'C'mon, give me your hand.'

Reluctantly, Honey let her take her hand.

Frances Gordon held it for a moment, and closed her eyes. When she opened them, she said, 'You've had a difficult life, haven't you?'

Everyone has had a difficult life, Honey thought. *Next she'll be telling me that I'll be taking a trip across the water.*

'You've used a lot of men, haven't you?'

Honey felt herself stiffen.

'There's been some kind of change in you — just recently — hasn't there?'

Honey could not wait to get out of the room. The woman was making her nervous. She started to pull away.

'You're going to fall in love.'

Honey said, 'I'm afraid I really have to . . .'

'He's an artist.'

'I don't know any artists.'

'You will.' Frances Gordon let go of her hand. 'Come back and see me,' she commanded.

'Sure.'

Honey fled.

Honey stopped in to visit Mrs Owens, a new patient, a thin woman who appeared to be in her late forties. Her chart noted that she was twenty-eight. She had a broken nose and two black eyes, and her face was puffy and bruised.

Honey walked up to the bed. 'I'm Dr Taft.'

The woman looked at her with dull, expressionless eyes. She remained silent.

'What happened to you?'

'I fell down some stairs.' When she opened her mouth, she revealed a gap where two front teeth were missing.

Honey glanced at the chart. 'It says here that you have two broken ribs and a fractured pelvis.'

'Yeah. It was a bad fall.'

'How did you get the black eyes?'

'When I fell.'

'Are you married?'

'Yeah.'

'Any children?'

'Two.'

'What does your husband do?'

'Let's leave my husband out of this, okay?'

'I'm afraid it's not okay,' Honey said. 'Is he the one who beat you up?'

'No one beat me up.'

'I'm going to have to file a police report.'

Mrs Owens was suddenly panicky. 'No! Please don't!'

'Why not?'

'He'll kill me! You don't know him!'

'Has he beaten you up before?'

'Yes, but he . . . he doesn't mean anything by it. He gets drunk and loses his temper.'

'Why haven't you left him?'

Mrs Owens shrugged, and the movement caused her pain. 'The kids and I have nowhere to go.'

Honey was listening, furious. 'You don't have to take this, you know. There are shelters and agencies that will take care of you and protect you and the children.'

The woman shook her head in despair. 'I have no

money. I lost my job as a secretary when he started . . .' She could not go on.

Honey squeezed her hand. 'You're going to be fine. I'll see that you're taken care of.'

Five minutes later Honey marched into Dr Wallace's office. He was delighted to see her. He wondered what she had brought with her this time. At various times, she had used warm honey, hot water, melted chocolate, and—his favorite—maple syrup. Her ingenuity was boundless.

'Lock the door, baby.'

'I can't stay, Ben. I have to get back.'

She told him about her patient.

'You'll have to file a police report,' Wallace said. 'It's the law.'

'The law hasn't protected her before. Look, all she wants to do is get away from her husband. She worked as a secretary. Didn't you say you needed a new file clerk?'

'Well, yes, but . . . wait a minute!'

'Thanks,' Honey said. 'We'll get her on her feet, and find her a place to live, and she'll have a new job!'

Wallace sighed. 'I'll see what I can do.'

'I knew you would,' Honey said.

The next morning, Honey went back to see Mrs Owens.

'How are you feeling today?' Honey asked.

'Better, thanks. When can I go home? My husband doesn't like it when—'

'Your husband is not going to bother you any-more,' Honey said firmly. 'You'll stay here until we

238

find a place for you and the children to live, and when you're well enough, you're going to have a job here at the hospital.'

Mrs Owens stared at her unbelievingly. 'Do . . . do you mean that?'

'Absolutely. You'll have your own apartment with your children. You won't have to put up with the kind of horror you've been living through, and you'll have a decent, respectable job.'

Mrs Owens clutched Honey's hand. 'I don't know how to thank you,' she sobbed. 'You don't know what it has been like.'

'I can imagine,' Honey said. 'You're going to be fine.'

The woman nodded, too choked up to speak.

The following day when Honey returned to see Mrs Owens, the room was empty.

'Where is she?' Honey asked.

'Oh,' the nurse said, 'she left this morning with her husband.'

Her name was on the PA system again. 'Dr Taft . . . Room 215 . . . Dr Taft . . . Room 215.'

In the corridor Honey ran into Kat. 'How's your day going?' Kat asked.

'You wouldn't believe it!' Honey told her.

Dr Ritter was waiting for her in Room 215. In bed was an Indian man in his late twenties.

Dr Ritter said, 'This is your patient?'

'Yes.'

'It says here that he speaks no English. Right?'

'Yes.'

He showed her the chart. 'And this is your writing? Vomiting, cramps, thirst, dehydration . . .'

'That's right,' Honey said.

'. . . absence of peripheral pulse . . .'

'Yes.'

'And what was your diagnosis?'

'Stomach flu.'

'Did you take a stool sample?'

'No. What for?'

'Because your patient has cholera, that's what for!' He was screaming. 'We're going to have to close down the fucking hospital!'

20

'*Cholera?* Are you telling me this hospital has a patient with *cholera?*' Benjamin Wallace yelled.

'I'm afraid so.'

'Are you absolutely *sure?*'

'No question,' Dr Ritter said. 'His stool is swarming with vibrios. He has low arterial pH, with hypotension, tachycardia, and cyanosis.'

By law, all cases of cholera and other infectious diseases must immediately be reported to the state health board and to the Center for Disease Control in Atlanta.

'We're going to have to report it, Ben.'

'They'll close us down!' Wallace stood up and began to pace. 'We can't afford that. I'll be goddamned if I'm going to put every patient in this hospital under quarantine.' He stopped pacing for a moment. 'Does the patient know what he has?'

'No. He doesn't speak English. He's from India.'

'Who has had contact with him?'

'Two nurses and Dr Taft.'

'And Dr Taft diagnosed it as stomach flu?'

'Right. I suppose you're going to dismiss her.'

'Well, no,' Wallace said. 'Anyone can make a mistake. Let's not be hasty. Does the patient's chart read stomach flu?'

'Yes.'

Wallace made his decision. 'Let's leave it that way.

Here's what I want you to do. Start intravenous rehydration — use lactated Ringer's solution. Also give him tetracycline. If we can restore his blood volume and fluid immediately, he could be close to normal in a few hours.'

'We aren't going to report this?' Dr Ritter asked.

Wallace looked him in the eye. 'Report a case of stomach flu?'

'What about the nurses and Dr Taft?'

'Give them tetracycline, too. What's the patient's name?'

'Hari Singh.'

'Put him in quarantine for forty-eight hours. He'll either be cured by then or dead.'

Honey was in a panic. She went to find Paige.

'I need your help.'

'What's the problem?'

Honey told her. 'I wish you would talk to him. He doesn't speak English, and you speak Indian.'

'Hindi.'

'Whatever. Will you talk to him?'

'Of course.'

Ten minutes later, Paige was talking to Hari Singh.

'Aap ki tabyat kaisi hai?'

'Karab hai.'

'Aap jald acha ko hum kardenge.'

'Bhagwan aap ki soney ga.'

'Aap ka ilaj hum jalb shuroo kardenge.'

'Shukria.'

'Dost kiss liay hain?'

*   *   *

242

Paige took Honey outside in the corridor.

'What did he say?'

'He said he feels terrible. I told him he's going to get well. He said to tell it to God. I told him we're going to start treatment immediately. He said he's grateful.'

'So am I.'

'What are friends for?'

Cholera is a disease that can cause death within twenty-four hours from dehydration, or that can be cured within a few hours.

Five hours after his treatment began, Hari Singh was nearly back to normal.

Paige stopped in to see Jimmy Ford.

His face lit up when he saw her. 'Hi.' His voice was weak, but he had improved miraculously.

'How are you feeling?' Paige asked.

'Great. Did you hear about the doctor who said to his patient, "The best thing you can do is give up smoking, stop drinking, and cut down on your sex life"? The patient said, "I don't deserve the best. What's the second best?"'

And Paige knew Jimmy Ford was going to get well.

Ken Mallory was getting off duty and was on his way to meet Kat when he heard his name being paged. He hesitated, debating whether or not simply to slip out. His name was paged once more. Reluctantly, he picked up a telephone. 'Dr Mallory.'

'Doctor, could you come to ER Two, please? We have a patient here who —'

'Sorry,' Mallory said, 'I just checked out. Find someone else.'

'There's no one else available who can handle this. It's a bleeding ulcer, and the patient's condition is critical. I'm afraid we're going to lose him if . . .'

Damn! 'All right. I'll be right there.' *I'll have to call Kat and tell her I'll be late.*

The patient in the emergency room was a man in his sixties. He was semiconscious, ghost-pale, perspiring, and breathing hard, obviously in enormous pain. Mallory took one look at him and said, 'Get him into an OR, stat!'

Fifteen minutes later, Mallory had the patient on an operating table. The anesthesiologist was monitoring his blood pressure. 'It's dropping fast.'

'Pump some more blood into him.'

Ken Mallory began the operation, working against time. It took only a moment to cut through the skin, and after that, the layer of fat, the fascia, the muscle, and finally the smooth, translucent peritoneum, the lining of the abdomen. Blood was pouring into the stomach.

'Bovie!' Mallory said. 'Get me four units of blood from the blood bank.' He began to cauterize the bleeding vessels.

The operation took four hours, and when it was over, Mallory was exhausted. He looked down at the patient and said, 'He's going to live.'

One of the nurses gave Mallory a warm smile. 'It's a good thing you were here, Dr Mallory.'

He looked over at her. She was young and pretty and obviously open to an invitation. *I'll get to you*

244

later, baby, Mallory thought. He turned to a junior resident. 'Close him up and get him into the recovery room. I'll check on him in the morning.'

Mallory debated whether to telephone Kat, but it was midnight. He sent her two dozen roses.

When Mallory checked in at 6:00 A.M., he stopped by the recovery room to see his new patient.

'He's awake,' the nurse said.

Mallory walked over to the bed. 'I'm Dr Mallory. How do you feel?'

'When I think of the alternative, I feel fine,' the patient said weakly. 'They tell me you saved my life. This was the damnedest thing. I was in the car on my way to a dinner party, and I got this sudden pain and I guess I blacked out. Fortunately, we were only a block away from the hospital, and they brought me to the emergency room here.'

'You were lucky. You lost a lot of blood.'

'They told me that in another ten minutes, I would have been gone. I want to thank you, doctor.'

Mallory shrugged. 'I was just doing my job.'

The patient was studying him carefully. 'I'm Alex Harrison.'

The name meant nothing to Mallory. 'Glad to know you, Mr Harrison.' He was checking Harrison's pulse. 'Are you in any pain now?'

'A bit, but I guess they have me pretty well doped up.'

'The anesthetic will wear off,' Mallory assured him. 'So will the pain. You're going to be fine.'

'How long will I have to be in the hospital?'

'We should have you out of here in a few days.'

245

A clerk from the business office came in, carrying some hospital forms. 'Mr Harrison, for our records, the hospital needs to know whether you have medical coverage.'

'You mean you want to know if I can pay my bill.'

'Well, I wouldn't put it like that, sir.'

'You might check with the San Francisco Fidelity Bank,' he said dryly. 'I own it.'

In the afternoon, when Mallory stopped by to see Alex Harrison, there was an attractive woman with him. She was in her early thirties, blond and trim, and elegant-looking. She was wearing an Adolfo dress that Mallory figured must have cost more than his monthly salary.

'Ah! Here's our hero,' Alex Harrison said. 'It's Dr Mallory, isn't it?'

'Yes. Ken Mallory.'

'Dr Mallory, this is my daughter, Lauren.'

She held out a slim, manicured hand. 'Father tells me you saved his life.'

He smiled. 'That's what doctors are for.'

Lauren was looking over him approvingly. 'Not all doctors.'

It was obvious to Mallory that these two did not belong in a county hospital. He said to Alex Harrison, 'You're coming along fine, but perhaps you'd feel more comfortable if you called your own doctor.'

Alex Harrison shook his head. 'That won't be necessary. He didn't save my life. You did. Do you like it here?'

It was a strange question. 'It's interesting, yes. Why?'

Harrison sat up in bed. 'Well, I was just thinking. A good-looking fellow as capable as you are could have a damned bright future. I don't think you have much of a future in a place like this.'

'Well, I . . .'

'Maybe it was fate that brought me here.'

Lauren spoke up. 'I think what my father is trying to say is that he would like to show you his appreciation.'

'Lauren is right. You and I should have a serious talk when I get out of here. I'd like you to come up to the house for dinner.'

Mallory looked at Lauren and said slowly, 'I'd like that.'

And it changed his life.

Ken Mallory was having a surprisingly difficult time getting together with Kat.

'How's Monday night, Kat?'

'Wonderful.'

'Good. I'll pick you up at—'

'Wait! I just remembered. A cousin from New York is coming to town for the night.'

'Well, Tuesday?'

'I'm on call Tuesday.'

'What about Wednesday?'

'I promised Paige and Honey that we'd do something together Wednesday.'

Mallory was getting desperate. His time was running out too fast.

'Thursday?'

'Thursday is fine.'

'Great. Shall I pick you up?'

'No. Why don't we meet at Chez Panisse?'
'Very well. Eight o'clock?'
'Perfect.'

Mallory waited at the restaurant until nine o'clock and then telephoned Kat. There was no answer. He waited another half hour. *Maybe she misunderstood*, he thought. *She wouldn't deliberately break a date with me.*

The following morning, he saw Kat at the hospital. She ran up to him.

'Oh, Ken, I'm so sorry! It was the silliest thing. I decided to take a little nap before our date. I fell asleep and when I woke up it was the middle of the night. Poor darling. Did you wait for me long?'

'No, no. It's all right.' *The stupid woman!* He moved closer to her. 'I want to finish what we started, baby. I go crazy when I think about you.'

'Me, too,' Kat said. 'I can't wait.'

'Maybe next weekend we can . . .'

'Oh, dear. I'm busy over the weekend.'

And so it went.

The clock was running.

Kat was reporting events to Paige when her beeper went off.

'Excuse me.' Kat picked up a telephone. 'Dr Hunter.' She listened a moment. 'Thanks. I'll be right there.' She replaced the receiver. 'I have to go. Emergency.'

Paige sighed. 'What else is new?'

Kat strode down the corridor and took an elevator

248

down to the emergency room. Inside were two dozen cots, all of them occupied. Kat thought of it as the suffering room, filled day and night with victims of automobile accidents, gunshots or knife wounds, and twisted limbs. A kaleidoscope of broken lives. To Kat it was a small corner of hell.

An orderly hurried up to her. 'Dr Hunter . . .'

'What have we got?' Kat asked. They were moving toward a cot at the far end of the room.

'He's unconscious. It looks as though someone beat him up. His face and head are battered, he has a broken nose, a dislocated shoulder blade, at least two different fractures to his right arm, and . . .'

'Why did you call me?'

'The paramedics think there's a head injury. There could be brain damage.'

They had reached the cot where the victim lay. His face was caked with blood, swollen and bruised. He was wearing alligator shoes and . . . Kat's heart skipped a beat. She leaned forward and took a closer look. It was Lou Dinetto.

Kat ran skillful fingers over his scalp and examined his eyes. There was a definite concussion.

She hurried over to a telephone and dialed. 'This is Dr Hunter. I want a head CAT scan done. The patient's name is Dinetto. Lou Dinetto. Send down a gurney, stat.'

Kat replaced the receiver and turned her attention back to Dinetto. She said to the orderly, 'Stay with him. When the gurney arrives, take him to the third floor. I'll be waiting.'

Thirty minutes later on the third floor, Kat was studying the CAT scan she had ordered. 'He has some brain hemorrhaging, he has a high fever, and he's in shock. I want him stabilized for twenty-four hours. I'll decide then when we'll operate.'

Kat wondered whether what had happened to Dinetto might affect Mike.

And how.

Paige stopped by to see Jimmy. He was feeling much better.

'Did you hear about the flasher in the garment district? He walked up to a little old lady and opened up his raincoat. She studied him a moment and said, "You call *that* a lining?"'

Kat was having dinner with Mallory at an intimate little restaurant near the bay. Seated across from Mallory, studying him, Kat felt guilty. *I should never have started this*, she thought. *I know what he is, and yet I'm having a wonderful time. Damn the man! But I can't stop our plan now.*

They had finished their coffee.

Kat leaned forward. 'Can we go to your place, Ken?'

'You bet!' *Finally*, Mallory thought.

Kat shifted in her chair uncomfortably and frowned. 'Uh, oh!'

'Are you all right?' Mallory asked.

'I don't know. Would you excuse me for a moment?'

'Certainly.' He watched her get up and head for the ladies' room.

When she returned, she said, 'It's bad timing, darling. I'm so sorry. You'd better get me home.'

He stared at her, trying to conceal his frustration. The damned fates were conspiring against him.

'Right,' Mallory said curtly. He was ready to explode.

He was going to lose a precious five days.

Five minutes after Kat returned to the apartment, the front doorbell rang. Kat smiled to herself. Mallory had found an excuse to come back, and she hated herself for being so pleased. She walked over to the door and opened it.

'Ken . . .'

Rhino and the Shadow were standing there. Kat felt a sudden sense of fear. The two men pushed past her into the apartment.

Rhino spoke. 'You doin' the operation on Mr Dinetto?'

Kat's throat was dry. 'Yes.'

'We don't want anything to happen to him.'

'Neither do I,' Kat said. 'Now, if you'll excuse me. I'm tired and—'

'Is there a chance he'll die?' the Shadow asked.

Kat hesitated. 'In brain surgery there's always a risk of—'

'You better not let it happen.'

'Believe me, I—'

'Don't let it happen.' He looked at Rhino. 'Let's go.'

Kat watched them start to leave.

At the door, the Shadow turned and said, 'Say hello to Mike for us.'

Kat was suddenly very still. 'Is . . . is this some kind of threat?'

251

'We don't threaten people, doc. We're telling you. If Mr Dinetto dies, you and your fucking family are gonna be wiped out.'

21

In the doctors' dressing room, half a dozen doctors were waiting for Ken Mallory to appear.

When he walked in, Grundy said, 'Hail the conquering hero! We want to hear all the lurid details.' He grinned. 'But the catch is, buddy, we want to hear them from *her*.'

'I ran into a little bad luck.' Mallory smiled. '*But you can all start getting your money ready*.'

Kat and Paige were getting into scrubs.

'Have you ever done a procedure on a doctor?' Kat asked.

'No.'

'You're lucky. They're the worst patients in the world. They know too much.'

'Who are you operating on?'

'Dr Mervyn "Don't Hurt Me" Franklin.'

'Good luck.'

'I'll need it.'

Dr Mervyn Franklin was a man in his sixties, thin, bald, and irascible.

When Kat walked into his room, he snapped, 'It's about time you got here. Did the damned electrolyte reports come back?'

'Yes,' Kat said. 'They're normal.'

'Who says so? I don't trust the damn lab. Half the time they don't know what they're doing. And make sure there's no mix-up on the blood transfusion.'

'I'll make sure,' Kat said patiently.

'Who's doing the operation?'

'Dr Jurgenson and I. Dr Franklin, I promise you, there's nothing for you to worry about.'

'Whose brain are they operating on, yours or mine? All operations are risky. You know why? Because half of the damned surgeons are in the wrong profession. They should have been butchers.'

'Dr Jurgenson is very capable.'

'I know he is, or I wouldn't let him touch me. Who's the anesthesiologist?'

'I believe it's Dr Miller.'

'That quack? I don't want him. Get me someone else.'

'Dr Franklin . . .'

'Get me someone else. See if Haliburton is available.'

'All right.'

'And get me the names of the nurses in the OR. I want to check them out.'

Kat looked him in the eye. 'Would you prefer to do the operation yourself?'

'What?' He stared at her a moment, then smiled sheepishly. 'I guess not.'

Kat said gently, 'Then why don't you let us handle it?'

'Okay. You know something? I like you.'

'I like you, too. Did the nurse give you a sedative?'

'Yes.'

'All right. We'll be ready in a few minutes. Is there anything I can do for you?'

'Yeah. Teach my stupid nurse where my veins are located.'

In OR Four, the brain surgery on Dr Mervyn Franklin was going perfectly. He had complained every step of the way from his room to the operating theater.

'Now mind you,' he said, 'minimal anesthetic. The brain has no feeling, so once you get in there, you won't need much.'

'I'm aware of that,' Kat said patiently.

'And see that the temperature is kept down to forty degrees. That's maximum.'

'Right.'

'Let's have some fast music on during the operation. Keep you all on your toes.'

'Right.'

'And make sure you have a top scrub nurse in there.'

'Right.'

And on and on it went.

When the opening in Dr Franklin's skull was drilled, Kat said, 'I see the clot. It doesn't look too bad.' She went to work.

Three hours later as they were beginning to close the incision, George Englund, the chief of surgery, came into the operating room and went up to Kat.

'Kat, are you almost through here?'

'We're just wrapping it up.'

'Let Dr Jurgenson take over. We need you fast. There's an emergency.'

255

Kat nodded. 'Coming.' She turned to Jurgenson. 'Will you finish up here?'

'No problem.'

Kat walked out with George Englund. 'What's happening?'

'You were scheduled to do an operation later, but your patient has started to hemorrhage. They're taking him to OR Three now. It doesn't look as though he's going to make it. You'll have to operate right away.'

'Who — ?'

'A Mr Dinetto.'

Kat looked at him aghast. *'Dinetto?'* *If Mr Dinetto dies, you and your fucking family are gonna be wiped out.*

Kat hurried down the corridor that led to OR Three. Approaching her were Rhino and the Shadow.

'What's going on?' Rhino demanded.

Kat's mouth was so dry that it was difficult to speak. 'Mr Dinetto started hemorrhaging. We must operate right away.'

The Shadow grabbed her arm. 'Then do it! But remember what we told you. Keep him alive.'

Kat pulled away and hurried into the operating room.

Dr Vance was doing the operation with Kat. He was a good surgeon. Kat began the ritual scrub: a half minute on each arm first, then a half minute on each hand. She repeated it and then scrubbed her nails.

Dr Vance stepped in beside her and started his scrub. 'How are you feeling?'

'Fine,' Kat lied.

Lou Dinetto was wheeled semiconscious into the operating room on a gurney, and carefully transferred to the operating table. His shaven head was scrubbed and painted with Merthiolate solution that gleamed a bright orange under the operating lights. He was as pale as death.

The team was in place: Dr Vance, another resident, an anesthesiologist, two scrub nurses, and a circulating nurse. Kat checked to make sure that everything they might require was there. She glanced at the wall monitors—oxygen saturation, carbon dioxide, temperature, muscle stimulators, precordial stethoscope, EKG, automatic blood pressure, and disconnect alarms. Everything was in order.

The anesthesiologist strapped a blood pressure cuff on Dinetto's right arm, then placed a rubber mask over the patient's face. 'All right, now. Breathe deeply. Take three big breaths.'

Dinetto was asleep before the third breath.

The procedure began.

Kat was reporting aloud. 'There's an area of damage in the middle of the brain, caused by a clot that's broken off the aorta valve. It's blocking a small blood vessel on the right side of the brain and extending slightly into the left half.' She probed deeper. 'It's at the lower edge of the aqueduct of Sylvius. Scalpel.'

A tiny burr hole about the size of a dime was made

257

by an electric drill to expose the dura mater. Next, Kat cut open the dura to expose a segment of the cerebral cortex that lay underneath. 'Forceps!'

The scrub nurse handed her the electric forceps.

The incision was held open by a small retractor which maintained itself in place.

'There's a hell of a lot of bleeding,' Vance said.

Kat picked up the bovie and started to cauterize the bleeders. 'We're going to control it.'

Dr Vance started suction on soft cotton patties that were placed on the dura. The oozing veins on the surface of the dura were identified and coagulated.

'It looks good,' Vance said. 'He's going to make it.'

Kat breathed a sigh of relief.

And at that instant, Lou Dinetto stiffened and his body went into spasm. The anesthesiologist called out, 'Blood pressure's dropping!'

Kat said, 'Get some more blood into him!'

They were all looking at the monitor. The curve was rapidly flattening out. There were two quick heartbeats followed by ventricular fibrillation.

'Shock him!' Kat snapped. She quickly attached the electric pads to his body and turned on the machine.

Dinetto's chest heaved up once and then fell.

'Inject him with epinephrine! Quick!'

'No heartbeat!' the anesthesiologist called out a moment later.

Kat tried again, raising the dial.

Once again, there was a quick convulsive movement.

'No heartbeat!' the anesthesiologist cried. 'Asystole. No rhythm at all.'

Desperately, Kat tried one last time. The body rose higher this time, then fell again. Nothing.
'He's dead,' Dr Vance said.

22

Code Red is an alert that immediately brings all-out medical assistance to try to save the life of a patient. When Lou Dinetto's heart stopped in the middle of his operation, the operating room Code Red team rushed to give aid.

Over the public address system Kat could hear, 'Code Red, OR Three . . . Code Red . . .' *Red rhymes with dead.*

Kat was in a panic. She applied the electroshock again. It was not only his life she was trying to save — it was Mike's and her own. Dinetto's body leaped into the air, then fell back, inert.

'Try once more!' Dr Vance urged.

We don't threaten people, doc. We're telling you. If Mr Dinetto dies, you and your fucking family are gonna be wiped out.

Kat turned on the switch and applied the machine to Dinetto's chest again. Once more his body rose a few inches into the air and then fell back.

'Again!'

It's not going to happen, Kat thought despairingly. *I'm going to die with him.*

The operating room was suddenly filled with doctors and nurses.

'What are you waiting for?' someone asked.

Kat took a deep breath and pressed down once

again. For an instant, nothing happened. Then a faint blip appeared on the monitor. It faltered a moment, then appeared again and faltered, and then began to grow stronger and stronger, until it became a steady, stabilized rhythm.

Kat stared at it unbelievingly.

There was a cheer from the crowded room. 'He's going to make it!' someone yelled.

'Jesus, that was close!'

They have no idea how close, Kat thought.

Two hours later, Lou Dinetto was off the table and on a gurney, on his way back to intensive care. Kat was at his side. Rhino and the Shadow were waiting in the corridor.

'The operation was successful,' Kat said. 'He's going to be fine.'

Ken Mallory was in deep trouble. It was the last day to make good on his bet. The problem had been growing so gradually that he had hardly been aware of it. From almost the first night, he had been positive that he would have no trouble getting Kat into bed. *Trouble? She's eager for it!* Now his time was up, and he was facing disaster.

Mallory thought about all the things that had gone wrong—Kat's roommates coming in just as she was about to go to bed with him, the difficulty of getting together for a date, Kat's being called away by her beeper and leaving him standing naked, her cousin coming to town, her oversleeping, her period. He stopped suddenly and thought, *Wait a minute! They couldn't have all been coincidences!* Kat was doing this to him deliberately! She had somehow gotten wind of the bet, and had decided to make a fool of him, to play a joke on him, a joke that was going to cost him ten thousand dollars that he didn't have. *The bitch!* He was no closer to winning than he had been at the beginning. She had deliberately led him on. *How the hell did I let myself get into this?* He knew there was no way he could come up with the money.

When Mallory walked into the doctors' dressing room, they were waiting for him.

'Payoff day!' Grundy sang out.

Mallory forced a smile. 'I have until midnight, right? Believe me, she's ready, fellows.'

There was a snicker. 'Sure. We'll believe you when we hear it from the lady herself. Just have the cash ready in the morning.'

Mallory laughed. 'You'd better have *yours* ready!'

He *had* to find a way. And suddenly he had the answer.

Ken Mallory found Kat in the lounge. He sat down opposite her. 'I hear you saved a patient's life.'

'And my own.'

'What?'

'Nothing.'

'How would you like to save my life?'

Kat looked at him quizzically.

'Have dinner with me tonight.'

'I'm too tired, Ken.' She was weary of the game she was playing with him. *I've had enough*, Kat thought. *It's time to stop. It's over. I've fallen into my own trap.* She wished he were a different kind of man. If only he had been honest with her. *I really could have cared for him*, Kat thought.

There was no way Mallory was going to let Kat get away. 'We'll make it an early night,' he coaxed. 'You have to have dinner somewhere.'

Reluctantly, Kat nodded. She knew it was going to be the last time. She was going to tell him she knew about the bet. She was going to end the game. 'All right.'

Honey finished her shift at 4:00 P.M. She looked at her watch and decided that she had just enough time to do some quick shopping. She went to the Candelier to buy some candles for the apartment, then to the San Francisco Tea and Coffee Company so there would be some drinkable coffee for breakfast, and on to Chris Kelly for linens.

Loaded down with packages, Honey headed for the apartment. *I'll fix myself some dinner at home*, Honey decided. She knew that Kat had a date with Mallory, and that Paige was on call.

Fumbling with her packages, Honey entered the apartment and closed the door behind her. She switched on the light. A huge black man was coming out of the bathroom, dripping blood on the white carpet. He was pointing a gun at her.

'Make one sound, and I'll blow your fucking head off!'

Honey screamed.

Mallory was seated across from Kat at Schroeder's restaurant on Front Street.

What was going to happen when he couldn't pay the ten thousand dollars? Word would spread quickly around the hospital, and he would become known as a welcher, a sick joke.

Kat was chatting about one of her patients, and Mallory was looking into her eyes, not hearing a word she said. He had more important things on his mind.

Dinner was almost over, and the waiter was serving coffee. Kat looked at her watch. 'I have an early call, Ken. I think we'd better go.'

He sat there, staring down at the table. 'Kat . . .' He looked up. 'There's something I have to tell you.'

'Yes?'

'I have a confession to make.' He took a deep breath. 'This isn't easy for me.'

She watched him, puzzled. 'What is it?'

'I'm embarrassed to tell you.' He was fumbling for words. 'I . . . I made a stupid bet with some of the doctors that . . . that I could take you to bed.'

Kat was staring at him. 'You . . .'

'Please don't say anything yet. I'm so ashamed of what I did. It started out as a kind of joke, but the joke is on me. Something happened that I didn't count on. I fell in love with you.'

'Ken . . .'

'I've never been in love before, Kat. I've known a lot of women, but never felt anything like this. I haven't been able to stop thinking about you.' He took a shaky breath. 'I want to marry you.'

Kat's mind was spinning. Everything was being turned topsy-turvy. 'I . . . I don't know what to . . .'

'You're the only woman I've ever proposed to. Please say yes. Will you marry me, Kat?'

So he had really meant all the lovely things he had said to her! Her heart was pounding. It was like a wonderful dream suddenly come true. All she had wanted from him was honesty. And now he was being honest with her. All this time he had been feeling guilty about what he had done. He was not like other men. He was genuine, and sensitive.

When Kat looked at him, her eyes were glowing. 'Yes, Ken. Oh, yes!'

His grin lit up the room. 'Kat . . .' He leaned over and kissed her. 'I'm so sorry about that stupid bet.' He shook his head in self-derision. 'Ten thousand dollars. We could have used that money for our honeymoon. But it's worth losing it to have you.'

Kat was thinking, *Ten thousand dollars*.

'I was such a fool.'

'When is your deadline up?'

'At midnight tonight, but that's not important any- more. The important thing is us. That we're going to be married. We —'

'Ken?'

'Yes, darling?'

'Let's go to your place.' There was a mischievous

glint in Kat's eyes. 'You still have time to win your bet.'

Kat was a tigress in bed.

My God! This was worth waiting for, Mallory thought. All the feelings that Kat had kept bottled up over the years suddenly exploded. She was the most passionate woman Ken Mallory had ever known. At the end of two hours, he was exhausted. He held Kat in his arms. 'You're incredible,' he said.

She lifted herself up on her elbows and looked down at him. 'So are you, darling. I'm so happy.'

Mallory grinned. 'So am I.' *Ten thousand dollars' worth!* he thought. *And great sex.*

'Promise me it will always be like this, Ken.'

'I promise,' Mallory said in his sincerest voice.

Kat looked at her watch. 'I'd better get dressed.'

'Can't you spend the night here?'

'No, I'm riding to the hospital with Paige in the morning.' She gave him a warm kiss. 'Don't worry. We'll have all our lives to spend together.'

He watched her get dressed.

'I can't wait to collect on that bet. It will buy us a great honeymoon.' He frowned. 'But what if the boys don't believe me? They aren't going to take my word for it.'

Kat was thoughtful for a moment. Finally, she said, 'Don't worry. I'll let them know.'

Mallory grinned. 'Come on back to bed.'

24

The black man with the gun pointed at Honey screamed, 'I told you to shut up!'

'I . . . I'm sorry,' Honey said. She was trembling. 'Wh . . . what do you want?'

He was pressing his hand against his side, trying to stop the flow of blood. 'I want my sister.'

Honey looked at him, puzzled. He was obviously insane. 'Your sister?'

'Kat.' His voice was becoming faint.

'Oh, my God! You're Mike!'

'Yeah.'

The gun dropped, and he slipped to the floor. Honey rushed to him. Blood was pouring out from what looked like a gunshot wound.

'Lie still,' Honey said. She hurried into the bathroom and gathered up some peroxide and a large bath towel. She returned to Mike. 'This is going to hurt,' she warned.

He lay there, too weak to move.

She poured peroxide into the wound and pressed the towel against his side. He bit down on his hand to keep from screaming.

'I'm going to call an ambulance and get you to the hospital,' Honey said.

He grabbed her arm. 'No! No hospitals. No police.' His voice was getting weaker. 'Where's Kat?'

'I don't know,' Honey said helplessly. She knew Kat was out somewhere with Mallory, but she had no idea where. 'Let me call a friend of mine.'

'Paige?' he asked.

Honey nodded. 'Yes.' *So Kat told him about the two of us.*

It took the hospital ten minutes to reach Paige.

'You'd better come home,' Honey said.

'I'm on call, Honey. I'm in the middle of —'

'Kat's brother is here.'

'Oh, well, tell him —'

'He's been shot.'

'He *what*?'

'He's been shot!'

'I'll send the paramedics over and —'

'He says no hospitals and no police. I don't know what to do.'

'How bad is it?'

'Pretty bad.'

There was a pause. 'I'll find someone to cover for me. I'll be there in half an hour.'

Honey replaced the receiver and turned to Mike. 'Paige is coming.'

Two hours later, on her way back to the apartment, Kat was filled with a glorious sense of well-being. She had been nervous about making love, afraid that she would hate it after the terrible experience she had had, but instead, Ken Mallory had turned it into something wonderful. He had unlocked emotions in her that she had never known existed.

Smiling to herself at the thought of how they had outwitted the doctors at the last moment and won the bet, Kat opened the door to the apartment and stood there in shock. Paige and Honey were kneeling beside Mike. He was lying on the floor, a pillow under his head, a towel pressed against his side, his clothes soaked with blood.

Paige and Honey looked up as Kat entered.

'Mike! My God!' She rushed over to Mike and knelt beside him. 'What happened?'

'Hi, sis.' His voice was barely a whisper.

'He's been shot,' Paige said. 'He's hemorrhaging.'

'Let's get him to the hospital,' Kat said.

Mike shook his head. 'No,' he whispered. 'You're a doctor. Fix me up.'

Kat looked over at Paige.

'I've stopped as much of the bleeding as I can, but the bullet is still inside him. We don't have the instruments here to —'

'He's still losing blood,' Kat said. She cradled Mike's head in her arms. 'Listen to me, Mike. If you don't get help, you're going to die.'

'You . . . can't . . . report . . . this . . . I don't want any police.'

Kat asked quietly, 'What are you involved in, Mike?'

'Nothing. I was in a . . . a business deal . . . and it went sour . . . and this guy got mad and shot me.'

It was the kind of story Kat had been listening to for years. Lies. All lies. She had known that then, and she knew it now, but she had tried to keep the truth from herself.

Mike held on to her arm. 'Will you help me, sis?'

'Yes. I'm going to help you, Mike.' Kat leaned down and kissed him on the cheek. Then she rose and went to the telephone. She picked up the receiver and dialed the emergency room at the hospital. 'This is Dr Hunter,' she said in an unsteady voice. 'I need an ambulance right away . . .'

At the hospital, Kat asked Paige to perform the operation to remove the bullet.

'He's lost a lot of blood,' Paige said. She turned to the assisting surgeon. 'Give him another unit.'

It was dawn when the operation was finished. The surgery was successful.

When it was over, Paige called Kat aside. 'How do you want me to report this?' she asked. 'I could list it as an accident, or . . .'

'No,' Kat said. Her voice was filled with pain. 'I should have done this a long time ago. I want you to report it as a gunshot wound.'

Mallory was waiting for Kat outside the operating theater.

'Kat! I heard about your brother and . . .'

Kat nodded wearily.

'I'm so sorry. Is he going to be all right?'

Kat looked at Mallory and said, 'Yes. For the first time in his life, Mike is going to be all right.'

Mallory squeezed Kat's hand. 'I just want you to know how wonderful last night was. You were a miracle. Oh. That reminds me. The doctors I bet with are in the lounge waiting, but I suppose with all that has happened, you wouldn't want to go in and . . .'

'Why not?'

She took his arm and the two of them walked

into the lounge. The doctors watched them as they approached.

Grundy said, 'Hi, Kat. We need to have your word on something. Dr Mallory claims that you and he spent the night together, and it was great.'

'It was better than great,' Kat said. 'It was *fantastic*!' She kissed Mallory on the cheek. 'I'll see you later, lover.'

The men sat there, gaping, as Kat walked away.

In their dressing room, Kat said to Paige and Honey, 'In all the excitement, I haven't had a chance to tell you the news.'

'What news?' Paige asked.

'Ken asked me to marry him.'

There were looks of disbelief on their faces.

'You're joking!' Paige said.

'No. He proposed to me last night. I accepted.'

'But you can't marry him!' Honey exclaimed. 'You know what he's like. I mean, he tried to get you to go to bed on a bet!'

'He succeeded.' Kat grinned.

Paige looked at her. 'I'm confused.'

Kat said, 'We were wrong about him. Completely wrong. Ken told me about that bet himself. All this time, it's been bothering his conscience. Don't you see what happened? I went out with him to punish him, and he went out with me to win some money, and we ended up falling in love with each other. Oh, I can't tell you how happy I am!'

Honey and Paige looked at each other. 'When are you getting married?' Honey asked.

'We haven't discussed it yet, but I'm sure it will

be soon. I want you two to be my bridesmaids.'

'You can count on it,' Paige said. 'We'll be there.' But there was a nagging doubt in the back of her mind. She yawned. 'It's been a long night. I'm going home and get some sleep.'

'I'll stay here with Mike,' Kat said. 'When he wakes up, the police want to talk to him.' She took their hands in hers. 'Thank you for being such good friends.'

On the way home, Paige thought about what had happened that night. She knew how much Kat loved her brother. It had taken a lot of courage to turn him over to the police. *I should have done this a long time ago.*

The telephone was ringing as Paige walked into the apartment. She hurried to pick it up.

It was Jason. 'Hi! I just called to tell you how much I miss you. What's going on in your life?'

Paige was tempted to tell him, to share it with somebody, but it was too personal. It belonged to Kat.

'Nothing,' Paige said. 'Everything is fine.'

'Good. Are you free for dinner tonight?'

Paige was aware that it was more than an invitation to dinner. *If I see him any more, I'm going to get involved*, she thought. She knew that it was one of the most important decisions of her life.

She took a deep breath. 'Jason . . .' The doorbell rang. 'Hold it a minute, will you, Jason?'

Paige put the telephone down and went to the door and opened it.

Alfred Turner was standing there.

25

Paige stood there, frozen.

Alfred smiled. 'May I come in?'

She was flustered. 'Of . . . of course. I'm s . . . sorry.' She watched Alfred walk into the living room, and she was filled with conflicting emotions. She was happy and excited and angry at the same time. *Why am I going on like this?* Paige thought. *He probably dropped by to say hello.*

Alfred turned to her. 'I've left Karen.'

The words were a shock.

Alfred moved closer to her. 'I made a big mistake, Paige. I never should have let you go. Never.'

'Alfred . . .' Paige suddenly remembered. 'Excuse me.'

She hurried to the telephone and picked it up. 'Jason?'

'Yes, Paige. About tonight, we could—'

'I . . . I can't see you.'

'Oh. If tonight is bad, what about tomorrow night?'

'I . . . I'm not sure.'

He sensed the tension in her voice. 'Is anything wrong?'

'No. Everything is fine. I'll call you tomorrow and explain.'

'All right.' He sounded puzzled.

Paige replaced the receiver.

'I've missed you, Paige,' Alfred said. 'Have you missed me?'

No. I just follow strangers on the street and call them Alfred. 'Yes,' Paige admitted.

'Good. We belong together, you know. We always have.'

Have we? Is that why you married Karen? Do you think you can walk in and out of my life anytime you please?

Alfred was standing close to her. 'Haven't we?'

Paige looked at him and said, 'I don't know.' It was all too sudden.

Alfred took her hand in his. 'Of course you do.'

'What happened with Karen?'

Alfred shrugged. 'Karen was a mistake. I kept thinking about you and all the great times we had. We were always good for each other.'

She was watching him, wary, guarded. 'Alfred . . .'

'I'm here to stay, Paige. When I say "here", I don't exactly mean that. We're going to New York.'

'New York?'

'Yes. I'll tell you all about it. I could use a cup of coffee.'

'Of course. I'll make a fresh pot. It will just take a few minutes.'

Alfred followed her into the kitchen, where Paige began to prepare the coffee. She was trying to get her thoughts in order. She had wanted Alfred back so desperately, and now that he was here . . .

Alfred was saying, 'I've learned a lot in the last few years, Paige. I've grown up.'

'Oh?'

'Yes. You know I've been working with WHO all these years.'

'I know.'

'Those countries haven't changed any since we were kids. In fact, some of them are worse. There's more disease down there, more poverty . . .'

'But you were there, helping,' Paige said.

'Yes, and I suddenly woke up.'

'Woke up?'

'I realized I was throwing my life away. I was down there, living in misery, working twenty-four hours a day, helping those ignorant savages, when I could have been making a bundle of money over here.'

Paige was listening in disbelief.

'I met a doctor who has a practice on Park Avenue in New York. Do you know how much he makes a year? Over five hundred thousand dollars! Did you hear me? Five hundred thousand a year!'

Paige was staring at him.

'I said to myself, "Where has that kind of money been all of my life?" He offered me a position as an associate,' Alfred said proudly, 'and I'm going in with him. That's why you and I are going to New York.'

Paige stood there, numbed by what she was hearing.

'I'll be able to afford a penthouse apartment for us, and to get you pretty dresses, and all the things I've always promised you.' He was grinning. 'Well, are you surprised?'

Paige's mouth was dry. 'I . . . I don't know what to say, Alfred.'

He laughed. 'Of course you don't. Five hundred

275

thousand dollars a year is enough to make anyone speechless.'

'I wasn't thinking of the money,' Paige said slowly.

'No?'

She was studying him, as though seeing him for the first time. 'Alfred, when you were working for WHO, didn't you feel you were helping people?'

He shrugged. 'Nothing can help those people. And who the hell really cares? Would you believe that Karen wanted me to stay down there in Bangladesh? I told her no way, so she went back.' He took Paige's hand. 'So here I am . . . You're a little quiet. I guess you're overwhelmed by all this, huh?'

Paige thought of her father. *He would have been a big success on Park Avenue, but he wasn't interested in money. His only interest was in helping people.*

'I've already divorced Karen, so we can get married right away.' He patted her hand. 'What do you think of the idea of living in New York?'

Paige took a deep breath. 'Alfred . . .'

There was an expectant smile on his face. 'Yes?'

'Get out.'

The smile slowly faded. 'What?'

Paige rose. 'I want you to get out of here.'

He was confused. 'Where do you want me to go?'

'I won't tell you,' Paige said. 'It would hurt your feelings.'

After Alfred had gone, Paige sat lost in thought. Kat had been right. She had been clinging to a ghost. *Helping those ignorant savages, when I could have been making a bundle over here . . . Five hundred thousand a year!*

And that's what I've been hanging on to, Paige thought wonderingly. She should have felt depressed, but instead she was filled with a feeling of elation. She suddenly felt free. She knew now what she wanted.

She walked over to the telephone and dialed Jason's number.

'Hello.'

'Jason, it's Paige. Remember telling me about your house in Noe Valley?'

'Yes . . .'

'I'd love to see it. Are you free tonight?'

Jason said quietly, 'Do you want to tell me what's going on, Paige? I'm very confused.'

'*I'm* the one who's confused. I thought I was in love with a man I knew a long time ago, but he's not the same man. I know what I want now.'

'Yes?'

'I want to see your house.'

Noe Valley belonged to another century. It was a colorful oasis in the heart of one of the most cosmopolitan cities in the world.

Jason's house was a reflection of him—comfortable, neat, and charming. He escorted Paige through the house. 'This is the living room, the kitchen, the guest bathroom, the study . . .' He looked at her and said, 'The bedroom is upstairs. Would you like to see it?'

Paige said quietly, 'Very much.'

They went up the stairs into the bedroom. Paige's

heart was pounding wildly. But what was happening seemed inevitable. *I should have known from the beginning*, she thought.

Paige never knew who made the first move, but somehow they were in each other's arms and Jason's lips were on hers, and it seemed the most natural thing in the world. They started to undress each other, and there was a fierce urgency in both of them. And then they were in bed, and he was making love to her.

'God,' he whispered. 'I love you.'

'I know,' Paige teased. 'Ever since I told you to put on the white coat.'

After they made love, Paige said, 'I'd like to spend the night here.'

Jason smiled. 'You won't hate me in the morning?'

'I promise.'

Paige spent the night with Jason, talking . . . making love . . . talking. In the morning, she cooked breakfast for him.

Jason watched her, and said, 'I don't know how I got so lucky, but thank you.'

'I'm the lucky one,' Paige told him.

'You know something? I never got an answer to my proposal.'

'You'll have an answer this afternoon.'

That afternoon, a messenger arrived at Jason's office, with an envelope. Inside was the card that Jason had sent with the model house.

Mine   [ ]
Ours   [x]
Please check one.

The nurse handed Paige a syringe, and Paige injected it into a vein. Paige turned to the nurse. 'Tell the head nurse to get an operating team together, stat. And send for Dr Barker!'

Fifteen minutes later, Kelly was on the operating table. The team consisted of two scrub nurses, a circulating nurse, and two residents. A television monitor was perched high in a corner of the room to display the heart rate, EKG, and blood pressure.

The anesthesiologist walked in, and Paige felt like cursing. Most of the anesthesiologists at the hospital were skilled doctors, but Herman Koch was an exception. Paige had worked with him before and tried to avoid him as much as possible. She did not trust him. Now she had no choice.

Paige watched him secure a tube to the patient's throat, while she unfolded a paper drape with a clear window and placed it over the patient's chest.

'Put a line into the jugular vein,' Paige said.

Koch nodded. 'Right.'

One of the residents asked, 'What's the problem here?'

'Dr Barker replaced the mitral valve yesterday. I think it's ruptured.' Paige looked over at Dr Koch. 'Is he out?'

Koch nodded. 'Sleeping like he's in bed at home.'

I wish you were, Paige thought. 'What are you using?'

'Propofol.'

She nodded. 'All right.'

She watched Kelly being connected to the heart-lung machine so she could perform a cardio-pulmonary bypass. Paige studied the monitors on the wall. Pulse 140 . . . blood oxygen saturation 92

281

percent . . . blood pressure 80 over 60. 'Let's go,' she said.

One of the residents put on music.

Paige stepped up to the operating table under eleven hundred watts of hot white light and turned to the scrub nurse. 'Scalpel, please . . .'

The operation began.

Paige removed all the sternal wires from the operation the day before. She then cut from the base of the neck to the lower end of the sternum, while one of the residents blotted away the blood with gauze pads.

She carefully went through the layers of fat and muscle, and in front of her was the erratically beating heart. 'There's the problem,' Paige said. 'The atrium is perforated. Blood is collecting around the heart and compressing it.' Paige was looking at the monitor on the wall. The pump pressure had dropped dangerously.

'Increase the flow,' Paige ordered.

The door to the operating room opened and Lawrence Barker stepped in. He stood to one side, watching what was happening.

Paige said, 'Dr Barker. Do you want to . . . ?'

'It's your operation.'

Paige took a quick look at what Koch was doing. 'Be careful. You'll overanesthetize him, dammit! Slow it down!'

'But I . . .'

'He's in V-tach! His pressure is dropping!'

'What do you want me to do?' Koch asked helplessly.

He should know, Paige thought angrily. 'Give him lidocaine and epinephrine! *Now!*' She was yelling.

'Right.'

Paige watched as Koch picked up a syringe and injected it into the patient's IV.

A resident looked at the monitor and called out, 'Blood pressure is falling.'

Paige was working frantically to stop the flow of blood. She looked up at Koch. 'Too much flow! I told you to . . .'

The noise of the heartbeat on the monitor suddenly became chaotic.

'My God! Something's gone wrong!'

'Give me the defibrillator!' Paige yelled.

The circulating nurse reached for the defibrillator on the crash cart, opened two sterile paddles, and plugged them in. She turned the buttons up to charge them and ten seconds later handed them to Paige.

She took the paddles and positioned them directly over Kelly's heart. Kelly's body jumped, then fell back.

Paige tried again, *willing* him to come back to life, willing him to breathe again. Nothing. The heart lay still, a dead, useless organ.

Paige was in a fury. Her part of the operation had been successful. Koch had overanesthetized the patient.

As Paige was applying the defibrillator to Lance Kelly's body for the third futile time, Dr Barker stepped up to the operating table and turned to Paige.

'You killed him.'

27

Jason was in the middle of a design meeting when his secretary said, 'Dr Taylor is on the phone for you. Shall I tell her you'll call back?'

'No. I'll take it.' Jason picked up the phone. 'Paige?'

'Jason . . . I need you!' She was sobbing.

'What happened?'

'Can you come to the apartment?'

'Of course. I'll be right there.' He stood up. 'The meeting is over. We'll pick it up in the morning.'

Half an hour later, Jason was at the apartment. Paige opened the door and threw her arms around him. Her eyes were red from crying.

'What happened?' Jason asked.

'It's awful! Dr Barker told me I . . . I killed a patient, and honestly, it . . . it wasn't my fault!' Her voice broke. 'I can't take any more of his . . .'

'Paige,' Jason said gently, 'you've told me how mean he always is. That's the man's character.'

Paige shook her head. 'It's more than that. He's been trying to force me out since the day I started working with him. Jason, if he were a bad doctor and didn't think I was any good, I wouldn't mind so much, but the man is brilliant. I have to respect his opinion. I just don't think I'm good enough.'

'Nonsense,' Jason said angrily. 'Of course you are. Everyone I talk to says you're a wonderful doctor.'

'Not Lawrence Barker.'

'Forget Barker.'

'I'm going to,' Paige said. 'I'm quitting the hospital.'

Jason took her in his arms. 'Paige, I know you love the profession too much to give it up.'

'I won't give it up. I just never want to see that hospital again.'

Jason took out a handkerchief and dried Paige's tears.

'I'm sorry to bother you with all of this,' Paige said.

'That's what husbands-to-be are for, isn't it?'

She managed a smile. 'I like the sound of that. All right.' Paige took a deep breath. 'I feel better now. Thanks for talking to me. I telephoned Dr Wallace and told him I was quitting. I'm going over to the hospital to see him now.'

'I'll see you at dinner tonight.'

Paige walked through the corridors of the hospital, knowing that she was seeing them for the last time. There were the familiar noises and the people hurrying up and down the corridors. It had become more of a home to her than she'd realized. She thought of Jimmy and Chang, and all the wonderful doctors she had worked with. Darling Jason going on rounds with her in his white coat. She passed the cafeteria where she and Honey and Kat had had a hundred breakfasts, and the lounge, where they had tried to have a party. The corridors and rooms were full of so many memories. *I'm going to miss it*, Paige thought, *but I refuse to work under the same roof as that monster.*

She went up to Dr Wallace's office. He was waiting for her.

'Well, I must say, your telephone call surprised me, Paige! Have you definitely made up your mind?'

'Yes.'

Benjamin Wallace sighed. 'Very well. Before you go, Dr Barker would like to see you.'

'I want to see him.' All of Paige's pent-up anger boiled to the surface.

'He's in the lab. Well . . . good luck.'

'Thanks.' Paige headed for the lab.

Dr Barker was examining some slides under a microscope when Paige entered. He looked up. 'I'm told you've decided to quit the hospital.'

'That's right. You finally got your wish.'

'And what was that?' Barker asked.

'You've wanted me out of here from the first moment you saw me. Well, you've won. I can't fight you anymore. When you told me I killed your patient, I . . .' Paige's voice broke. 'I . . . I think you're a sadistic, cold-hearted son of a bitch, and I hate you.'

'Sit down,' Dr Barker said.

'No. I have nothing more to say.'

'Well, I have. Who the hell do you think you . . . ?'

He suddenly stopped and began to gasp.

As Paige watched in horror, he clutched his chest and toppled over in his chair, his face twisted to one side in a horrible rictus.

Paige was at his side instantly. 'Dr Barker!' She

grabbed the telephone and shouted into it, 'Code Red! Code Red!'

Dr Peterson said, 'He's suffered a massive stroke. It's too early to tell whether he's going to come out of it.'

It's my fault, Paige thought. *I wanted him dead*. She felt miserable.

She went back to see Ben Wallace. 'I'm sorry about what happened,' Paige said. 'He was a good doctor.'

'Yes. It's regrettable. Very . . .' Wallace studied her a moment. 'Paige, if Dr Barker can't practice here anymore, would you consider staying on?'

Paige hesitated. 'Yes. Of course.'

His chart read, 'John Cronin, white male, age 70. Diagnosis: Cardiac tumor.'

Paige had not yet met John Cronin. He was scheduled to have heart surgery. She walked into his room, a nurse and staff doctor at her side. She smiled warmly and said, 'Good morning, Mr Cronin.'

They had just extubated him, and there were the marks of adhesive tape around his mouth. IV bottles hung overhead, and the tubing had been inserted in his left arm.

Cronin looked over at Paige. 'Who the hell are you?'

'I'm Dr Taylor. I'm going to examine you and —'

'Like hell you are! Keep your fucking hands off me. Why didn't they send in a *real* doctor?'

Paige's smile died. 'I'm a cardiovascular surgeon. I'm going to do everything I can to get you well again.'

'*You're* going to operate on my heart?'

'That's right. I . . .'

John Cronin looked at the staff doctor and said, 'For Christ's sakes, is this the best this hospital can do?'

'I assure you, Dr Taylor is thoroughly qualified,' the staff doctor said.

'So is my ass.'

Paige said stiffly, 'Would you rather bring in your own surgeon?'

'I don't have one. I can't afford those high-priced quacks. You doctors are all alike. All you're interested in is money. You don't give a damn about people. We're just pieces of meat to you, aren't we?'

Paige was fighting to control her temper. 'I know you're upset right now, but —'

'Upset? Just because you're going to cut my heart out?' He was screaming. 'I know I'll die on the operating table. You're going to kill me, and I hope they get you for murder!'

'That's enough!' Paige said.

He was grinning at her maliciously. 'It wouldn't look good on your record if I died, would it, doctor? Maybe I *will* let you operate on me.'

Paige found that she was hyperventilating. She turned to the nurse. 'I want an EKG and a chemistry panel.' She took one last look at John Cronin, then turned and left the room.

When Paige returned an hour later with the reports on the tests, John Cronin looked up. 'Oh, the bitch is back.'

Paige operated on John Cronin at six o'clock the following morning.

The moment she opened him up, she knew that there was no hope. The major problem was not the heart. Cronin's organs showed signs of melanoma.

A resident said, 'Oh, my God! What are we going to do?'

'We're going to pray that he doesn't have to live with this too long.'

When Paige stepped out of the operating room into the corridor, she found a woman and two men waiting for her. The woman was in her late thirties. She had bright red hair and too much makeup, and she wore a heavy, cheap perfume. She had on a tight dress that accentuated a voluptuous figure. The men were in their forties, and both had red hair. To Paige, they looked like a circus troupe.

The woman said to Paige, 'You Dr Taylor?'

'Yes.'

'I'm Mrs Cronin. These are my brothers. How's my husband?'

Paige hesitated. She said carefully, 'The operation went as well as could be expected.'

'Oh, thank God!' Mrs Cronin said melodramatically, dabbing at her eyes with a lace handkerchief. 'I'd die if anything happened to John!'

Paige felt as if she were watching an actress in a bad play.

'Can I see my darling now?'

'Not yet, Mrs Cronin. He's in the recovery room. I suggest that you come back tomorrow.'

'We'll be back.' She turned to the men. 'Come along, fellas.'

Paige watched as they walked away. *Poor John Cronin*, she thought.

Paige was given the report the next morning. The cancer had metastasized throughout Cronin's body. It was too late for radiation treatment.

The oncologist said to Paige, 'There's nothing to do but try to keep him comfortable. He's going to be in a hell of a lot of pain.'

'How much time does he have?'

'A week or two at the most.'

Paige went to visit John Cronin in intensive care. He was asleep. He was no longer a bitter, vitriolic man, but a human being, fighting desperately for his life. He was on a respirator, and being fed intravenously. Paige sat down at his bedside, watching him. He looked tired and defeated. *He's one of the unlucky ones*, Paige thought. *Even with all the modern medical miracles, there's nothing we can do to save him.* Paige touched his arm gently. After a while, she left.

Later that afternoon, Paige stopped by to see John Cronin again. He was off the respirator now. When he opened his eyes and saw Paige, he said drowsily, 'The operation's over, huh?'

Paige smiled reassuringly. 'Yes. I just came by to make sure that you're comfortable.'

'Comfortable?' he snorted. 'What the hell do you care?'

Paige said, 'Please. Let's not fight.'

Cronin lay there, silently studying her. 'The other doctor told me you did a good job.'

Paige said nothing.

'I have cancer, don't I?'

'Yes.'

'How bad is it?'

The question posed a dilemma that all surgeons

were faced with sooner or later. Paige said, 'It's pretty bad.'

There was a long silence. 'What about radiation or chemotherapy?'

'I'm sorry. It would make you feel worse, and it wouldn't help.'

'I see. Well . . . I've had a good life.'

'I'm sure you have.'

'You may not think so, looking at me now, but I've had a lot of women.'

'I believe it.'

'Yeah. Women . . . thick steaks . . . good cigars . . . You married?'

'No.'

'You ought to be. Everyone should be married. I've been married. Twice. First, for thirty-five years. She was a wonderful lady. She died of a heart attack.'

'I'm sorry.'

'It's okay.' He sighed. 'Then I got sucked into marrying a bimbo. Her and her two hungry brothers. It's my fault for being so horny, I guess. Her red hair turned me on. She's some piece of work.'

'I'm sure she . . .'

'No offense, but do you know why I'm in this cockamamie hospital? My wife put me here. She didn't want to waste money on me for a private hospital. This way there'll be more to leave to her and her brothers.' He looked up at Paige. 'How much time *do* I have left?'

'Do you want it straight?'

'No . . . yes.'

'A week or two.'

'Jesus! The pain is going to get worse, isn't it?'

'I'll try to keep you as comfortable as possible, Mr Cronin.'

'Call me John.'

'John.'

'Life is a bitch, isn't it?'

'You said you've had a good life.'

'I did. It's kinda funny, knowing it's about over. Where do you think we go?'

'I don't know.'

He forced a smile. 'I'll let you know when I get there.'

'Some medication is on the way. Can I do anything to make you more comfortable?'

'Yeah. Come back and talk to me tonight.'

It was Paige's night off, and she was exhausted. 'I'll come back.'

That night when Paige went back to see John Cronin, he was awake.

'How are you feeling?'

He winced. 'Terrible. I was never very good about pain. I guess I've got a low threshold.'

'I understand.'

'You met Hazel, huh?'

'Hazel?'

'My wife. The bimbo. She and her brothers were here to see me. They said they talked to you.'

'Yes.'

'She's something, ain't she? I sure got myself into a bundle of trouble there. They can't wait for me to kick the bucket.'

'Don't say that.'

'It's true. The only reason Hazel married me was

for my money. To tell you the truth, I didn't mind that so much. I really had a good time with her in bed, but then she and her brothers started to get greedy. They always wanted more.'

The two of them sat there in a comfortable silence.

'Did I tell you I used to travel a lot?'

'No.'

'Yeah. I've been to Sweden . . . Denmark . . . Germany. Have you been to Europe?'

She thought about the day at the travel agency. *I'm dying to see London. Paris is where I want to go. I want to ride a gondola in the moonlight in Venice.* 'No. I haven't.'

'You ought to go.'

'Maybe one day I will.'

'I guess you don't make much money working at a hospital like this, huh?'

'I make enough.'

He nodded to himself. 'Yeah. You have to go to Europe. Do me a favor. Go to Paris . . . stay at the Crillon, have dinner at Maxim's, order a big, thick steak and a bottle of champagne, and when you eat that steak and drink that champagne, I want you to think of me. Will you do that?'

Paige said slowly, 'I'll do that one day.'

John Cronin was studying her. 'Good. I'm tired now. Will you come back tomorrow and talk to me again?'

'I'll come back,' Paige said.

John Cronin slept.

Ken Mallory was a great believer in Lady Luck, and after meeting the Harrisons, he believed even more firmly that she was on his side. The odds against a man as wealthy as Alex Harrison being brought to Embarcadero County Hospital were enormous. *And I'm the one who saved his life, and he wants to show his gratitude*, Mallory thought gleefully.

He had asked a friend of his about the Harrisons.

'Rich doesn't even begin to cover it,' his friend had said. 'He's a millionaire a dozen times over. And he has a great-looking daughter. She's been married three or four times. The last time to a count.'

'Have you ever met the Harrisons?'

'No. They don't mingle with the *hoi polloi*.'

On a Saturday morning, Alex Harrison telephoned Ken Mallory. 'Ken, do you think I'll be in shape to give a dinner party a week from now?'

'If you don't overdo it, I don't see why not,' Mallory said.

Alex Harrison smiled. 'Fine. You're the guest of honor.'

Mallory felt a sudden thrill. *The old man really meant what he said.* 'Well . . . thank you.'

'Lauren and I will expect you at seven-thirty next Saturday night.' He gave Mallory an address on Nob Hill.

'I'll be there,' Mallory said. *Will I ever!*

Mallory had promised to take Kat to the theater that evening, but it would be easy to cancel. He had collected his winnings, and he enjoyed having sex with her. Several times a week they had managed to get together in one of the empty on-call rooms, or a deserted hospital room, or at her apartment or his. *Her fires were banked a long time*, Mallory thought happily, *but when the explosion came — wow! Well, one of these days, it will be time to say arrivederci.*

On the day he was to have dinner with the Harrisons, Mallory telephoned Kat. 'Bad news, baby.'

'What's the matter, darling?'

'One of the doctors is sick and they've asked me to cover for him. I'm afraid I'm going to have to break our date.'

She did not want to let him know how disappointed she was, how much she needed to be with him. Kat said lightly, 'Oh well, that's the doctor business, isn't it?'

'Yeah. I'll make it up to you.'

'You don't have to make anything up to me,' she said warmly. 'I love you.'

'I love you, too.'

'Ken, when are we going to talk about us?'

'What do you mean?' He knew exactly what she meant. A commitment. They were all alike. *They use their pussies for bait, hoping to hook a sucker into spending his life with them.* Well, he was too smart for that. When the time came, he would regretfully bow out, as he had done a dozen times before.

Kat was saying, 'Don't you think we should set a date, Ken? I have a lot of plans to make.'

'Oh, sure. We'll do that.'

'I thought maybe June. What do you think?'

You don't want to know what I think. If I play my cards right, there's going to be a wedding, but it won't be with you. 'We'll talk about it, baby. I really have to go now.'

The Harrisons' home was a mansion out of a motion picture, situated on acres of manicured grounds. The house itself seemed to go on forever. There were two dozen guests, and in the huge drawing room a small orchestra was playing. When Mallory walked in, Lauren hurried over to greet him. She was wearing a silky clinging gown. She squeezed Mallory's hand. 'Welcome, guest of honor. I'm so glad you're here.'

'So am I. How is your father?'

'Very much alive, thanks to you. You're quite a hero in this house.'

Mallory smiled modestly. 'I only did my job.'

'I suppose that's what God says every day.' She took his hand and began introducing him to the other guests.

The guest list was blue-ribbon. The governor of California was there, the French ambassador, a justice of the Supreme Court, and a dozen assorted politicians, artists, and business tycoons. Mallory could feel the power in the room, and it thrilled him. *This is where I belong*, he thought. *Right here, with these people.*

The dinner was delicious and elegantly served. At the end of the evening, when the guests started to leave, Harrison said to Mallory, 'Don't rush off, Ken. I'd like to talk to you.'

'I'd be delighted.'

Harrison, Lauren, and Mallory sat in the library. Harrison was seated in a chair next to his daughter.

'When I told you at the hospital that I thought you had a great future before you, I meant it.'

'I really appreciate your confidence, sir.'

'You should be in private practice.'

Mallory laughed self-deprecatingly. 'I'm afraid it's not that easy, Mr Harrison. It takes a long time to build up a practice, and I'm . . .'

'Ordinarily, yes. But you're not an ordinary man.'

'I don't understand.'

'After you finish your residency, Father wants to set you up in your own practice,' Lauren said.

For a moment, Mallory was speechless. It was too easy. He felt as though he were living in some kind of wonderful dream. 'I . . . I don't know what to say.'

'I have a lot of very wealthy friends. I've already spoken to some of them about you. I can promise you that you'll be swamped the minute you put up your shingle.'

'Father, lawyers put up shingles,' Lauren said.

'Whatever. In any case, I'd like to finance you. Are you interested?'

Mallory was finding it difficult to breathe. 'Very much so. But I . . . I don't know when I would be able to repay you.'

'You don't understand. I'm repaying *you*. You won't owe me anything.'

Lauren was looking at Mallory, her eyes warm. 'Please say yes.'

'I'd be stupid to say no, wouldn't I?'

'That's right,' Lauren said softly. 'And I'm sure you're not stupid.'

On his way home, Ken Mallory was in a state of euphoria. *This is as good as it gets*, he thought. But he was wrong. It got better.

Lauren telephoned him. 'I hope you don't mind mixing business with pleasure.'

He smiled to himself. 'Not at all. What did you have in mind?'

'There's a charity ball next Saturday night. Would you like to take me?'

Oh, baby, I'm going to take you all right. 'I'd love to.' He was on duty Saturday night, but he would call in sick and they would have to find someone to take his place.

Mallory was a man who believed in planning ahead, and what was happening to him now went beyond his wildest dreams.

Within a few days he was swept up in Lauren's social circle, and life took on a dizzying pace. He would be out with Lauren dancing half the night, and stumble through his days at the hospital. There were mounting complaints about his work, but he didn't care. *I'll be out of here soon*, he told himself.

The thought of getting away from the dreary county hospital and having his own practice was exciting enough, but Lauren was the bonus that Lady Luck had given him.

Kat was becoming a nuisance. Mallory had to keep finding pretexts to avoid seeing her. When she would press him, he would say, 'Darling, I'm crazy about you . . . of course I want to marry you, but right now, I . . .' and he would go into a litany of excuses.

It was Lauren who suggested that the two of them spend the weekend at the family lodge at Big Sur. Mallory was elated. *Everything is coming up roses*, he thought. *I'm going to own the whole damned world!*

The lodge was spread across pine-covered hills, an enormous structure built of wood and tile and stone, overlooking the Pacific Ocean. It had a master bedroom, eight guest bedrooms, a spacious living room with a stone fireplace, an indoor swimming pool, and a large hot tub. Everything smelled of old money.

When they walked in, Lauren turned to Mallory and said, 'I let the servants go for the weekend.'

Mallory grinned. 'Good thinking.' He put his arms around Lauren and said softly, 'I'm wild about you.'

'Show me,' Lauren said.

They spent the day in bed, and Lauren was almost as insatiable as Kat.

'You're wearing me out!' Mallory laughed.

'Good. I don't want you to be able to make love to anyone else.' She sat up in bed. 'There *is* no one else, is there, Ken?'

'Absolutely not,' Mallory said sincerely. 'There's no one in the world for me but you. I'm in love with you, Lauren.' Now was the time to take the plunge, to wrap his whole future up in one neat package. It would be one thing to be a successful doctor in private practice. It would be something else to be Alex Harrison's son-in-law. 'I want to marry you.'

He held his breath, waiting for her answer.

'Oh, yes, darling,' Lauren said. 'Yes.'

At the apartment, Kat was frantically trying to reach Mallory. She telephoned the hospital.

'I'm sorry, Dr Hunter, Dr Mallory is not on call, and doesn't answer his page.'

'Didn't he leave word where he could be reached?'

'We have no record of it.'

Kat replaced the receiver and turned to Paige. 'Something's happened to him, I know it. He would have called me by now.'

'Kat, there could be a hundred reasons why you haven't heard from him. Perhaps he had to go out of town suddenly, or . . .'

'You're right. I'm sure there's some good excuse.' Kat looked at the phone and *willed* it to ring.

When Mallory returned to San Francisco, he telephoned Kat at the hospital.

'Dr Hunter is off duty,' the receptionist told him.

'Thank you.' Mallory called the apartment. Kat was there.

'Hi, baby!'

'Ken! Where have you been? I've been worried about you. I tried everywhere to reach—'

'I had a family emergency,' he said smoothly. 'I'm sorry. I didn't have a chance to call you. I had to go out of town. May I come over?'

'You know you may. I'm so glad you're all right. I—'

'Half an hour.' He replaced the receiver and

thought happily, *'The time has come,'* *the Walrus* *said,* *'To talk of many things.'* *Kat, baby, it was great* *fun, but it was just one of those things.*

When Mallory arrived at the apartment, Kat threw her arms around him. 'I've missed you!' She could not tell him how desperately worried she had been. Men hated that kind of thing. She stood back. 'Darling, you look absolutely exhausted.'

Mallory sighed. 'I've been up for the last twenty-four hours.' *That part is true,* he thought.

Kat hugged him. 'Poor baby. Can I fix something for you?'

'No, I'm fine. All I really need is a good night's sleep. Let's sit down, Kat. We have to have a talk.' He sat on the couch next to her.

'Is anything wrong?' Kat asked.

Mallory took a deep breath. 'Kat, I've been thinking a lot about us lately.'

She smiled. 'So have I. I have news for you—'

'No, wait. Let me finish. Kat, I think we're rushing into things too fast. I . . . I think I proposed too hastily.'

She paled. 'What . . . what are you saying?'

'I'm saying that I think we should postpone everything.'

She felt as though the room were closing in on her. She was finding it difficult to breathe. 'Ken, we can't postpone anything. I'm having your baby.'

30

Paige got home at midnight, drained. It had been an exhausting day. There had been no time for lunch, and dinner had consisted of a sandwich between operations. She fell into her bed and was asleep instantly. She was awakened by the ringing of the telephone. Groggily, she reached for the instrument and automatically glanced at the bedside clock. It was three in the morning. 'H'lo?'

'Dr Taylor? I'm sorry to disturb you, but one of your patients is insisting on seeing you right away.'

Paige's throat was so dry she could hardly talk. 'I'm off duty,' she mumbled. 'Can't you get someone . . . ?'

'He won't talk to anyone else. He says he needs *you*.'

'Who is it?'

'John Cronin.'

She sat up straighter. 'What's happened?'

'I don't know. He refuses to speak with anyone but you.'

'All right,' she said wearily. 'I'm on my way.'

Thirty minutes later, Paige arrived at the hospital. She went directly to John Cronin's room. He was lying in bed, awake. Tubes were protruding from his nostrils and his arms.

'Thanks for coming.' His voice was weak and hoarse.

Paige sat down in a chair next to the bed. She smiled. 'That's all right, John. I had nothing to do, anyway, but sleep. What can I do for you that no one else here at this great big hospital couldn't have done?'

'I want you to talk to me.'

Paige groaned. 'At this hour? I thought it was some kind of emergency.'

'It is. I want to leave.'

She shook her head. 'That's impossible. You can't go home now. You couldn't get the kind of treatment—'

He interrupted her. 'I don't want to go home. I want to leave.'

She looked at him and said slowly, 'What are you saying?'

'You know what I'm saying. The medication isn't working anymore. I can't stand this pain. I want out.'

Paige leaned over and took his hand. 'John, I can't do that. Let me give you some—'

'No. I'm tired, Paige. I want to go wherever it is I'm going, but I don't want to hang around here like this. Not anymore.'

'John . . .'

'How much time do I have left? A few more days? I told you, I'm not good about pain. I'm lying here like a trapped animal, filled with all these goddam tubes. My body is being eaten away inside. This isn't living—it's dying. For God's sake, help me!'

He was racked by a sudden spasm of pain. When he spoke again, his voice was even weaker. 'Help me . . . please . . .'

Paige knew what she had to do. She had to report John Cronin's request to Dr Benjamin Wallace. He would pass it on to the administration committee. They would assemble a panel of doctors to assess Cronin's condition, and then make a decision. After that, it would have to be approved by . . .

'Paige . . . it's *my* life. Let me do with it as I like.'

She looked over at the helpless figure locked in his pain.

'I'm begging you . . .'

She took his hand and held it for a long time. When she spoke, she said, 'All right, John. I'll do it.'

He managed a trace of a smile. 'I knew I could count on you.'

Paige leaned over and kissed him on the forehead. 'Close your eyes and go to sleep.'

'Good night, Paige.'

'Good night, John.'

John Cronin sighed and closed his eyes, a beatific smile on his face.

Paige sat there watching him, thinking about what she was about to do. She remembered how horrified she had been on her first day of rounds with Dr Radnor. *She's been in a coma for six weeks. Her vital signs are failing. There's nothing more we can do for her. We'll pull the plug this afternoon.* Was it wrong to release a fellow human being from his misery?

Slowly, as though she were moving under water, Paige rose and walked to a cabinet in the corner, where a bottle of insulin was kept for emergency use. She removed the bottle and stood there, staring at it. Then she uncapped the bottle. She filled a syringe with the insulin and walked back to John Cronin's bedside. There was still time to go back. *I'm lying here like a trapped animal . . . This isn't living—it's dying. For God's sake, help me!*

Paige leaned forward and slowly injected the insulin into the IV attached to Cronin's arm.

'Sleep well,' Paige whispered. She was unaware that she was sobbing.

Paige drove home and stayed awake the rest of the night, thinking about what she had done.

At six o'clock in the morning, she received a telephone call from one of the residents at the hospital.

'I'm sorry to give you bad news, Dr Taylor. Your patient John Cronin died of cardiac arrest early this morning.'

The staff doctor in charge that morning was Dr Arthur Kane.

31

The one other time Ken Mallory had gone to an opera, he had fallen asleep. On this night he was watching *Rigoletto* at the San Francisco Opera House and enjoying every minute of it. He was seated in a box with Lauren Harrison and her father. In the lobby of the opera house during intermission, Alex Harrison had introduced him to a large number of friends.

'This is my future son-in-law and a brilliant doctor, Ken Mallory.'

Being Alex Harrison's son-in-law was enough to *make* him a brilliant doctor.

After the performance, the Harrisons and Mallory went to the Fairmont Hotel for supper in the elegant main dining room. Mallory enjoyed the deferential greeting that the maître d' gave to Alex Harrison as he led them to their booth. *From now on, I'll be able to afford places like this*, Mallory thought, *and everyone is going to know who I am*.

After they had ordered, Lauren said, 'Darling, I think we should have a party to announce our engagement.'

'That's a good idea!' her father said. 'We'll make it a big one. What do you say, Ken?'

A warning bell sounded in Mallory's mind. An

engagement party would mean publicity. *I'll have to set Kat straight first. A little money should take care of that.* Mallory cursed the stupid bet he had made. For a mere ten thousand dollars, his whole shining future might now be in jeopardy. He could just imagine what would happen if he tried to explain Kat to the Harrisons.

By the way, I forgot to mention that I'm already engaged to a doctor at the hospital. She's black . . .

Or: *Do you want to hear something funny? I bet the boys at the hospital ten thousand dollars I could fuck this black doctor . . .*

Or: *I already have one wedding planned . . .*

No, he thought, *I'll have to find a way to buy Kat off.*

They were looking at Mallory expectantly.

Mallory smiled. 'A party sounds like a wonderful idea.'

Lauren said enthusiastically, 'Good. I'll get things started. You men have no idea what it takes to give a party.'

Alex Harrison turned to Mallory. 'I've already started the ball rolling for you, Ken.'

'Sir?'

'Gary Gitlin, the head of North Shore Hospital, is an old golf buddy of mine. I talked to him about you, and he doesn't think there will be any problem about having you affiliated with his hospital. That's quite prestigious, you know. And at the same time, I'll get you set up in your own practice.'

Mallory listened, filled with a sense of euphoria. 'That's wonderful.'

'Of course it will take a few years to build up a really lucrative practice, but I think you should be able to make two or three hundred thousand dollars the first year or two.'

Two or three hundred thousand! My God! Mallory thought. *He makes it sound like peanuts.* 'That . . . that would be very nice, sir.'

Alex Harrison smiled. 'Ken, since I'm going to be your father-in-law, let's get off this "sir" business. Call me Alex.'

'Right, Alex.'

'You know, I've never been a June bride,' Lauren said. 'Is June all right with you, darling?'

He could hear Kat's voice saying: *Don't you think we should set a date? I thought maybe June.*

Mallory took Lauren's hand in his. 'That sounds great.' *That will give me plenty of time to handle Kat*, Mallory decided. He smiled to himself. *I'll offer her some of the money I won getting her into bed.*

'We have a yacht in the south of France,' Alex Harrison was saying. 'Would you two like to honeymoon on the French Riviera? You can fly over in our Gulfstream.'

A yacht. The French Riviera. It was like a fantasy come true. Mallory looked at Lauren. 'I'd honeymoon anywhere with Lauren.'

Alex Harrison nodded. 'Well, it looks like everything is settled.' He smiled at his daughter. 'I'm going to miss you, baby.'

'You're not losing me, Father. You're gaining a doctor!'

Alex Harrison nodded. 'And a damn good one. I can never thank you enough for saving my life, Ken.'

Lauren stroked Mallory's hand. 'I'll thank him for you.'

'Ken, why don't we have lunch next week?' Alex

Harrison said. 'We'll pick out some decent office space for you, maybe in the Post Building, and I'll make a date for you to see Gary Gitlin. A lot of my friends are dying to meet you.'

'I think you might rephrase that, Father,' Lauren suggested. She turned to Ken. 'I've been talking to *my* friends about you and they're eager to meet you, too, only I'm not going to let them.'

'I'm not interested in anyone but you,' Mallory said warmly.

When they got into their chauffeur-driven Rolls-Royce, Lauren asked, 'Where can we drop you, darling?'

'The hospital. I've got to check on a few patients.' He had no intention of seeing any patients. Kat was on duty at the hospital.

Lauren stroked his cheek. 'My poor baby. You work much too hard.'

Mallory sighed. 'It doesn't matter. As long as I'm helping people.'

Mallory went quickly to the doctors' dressing room and changed out of his dinner jacket.

He found Kat in the geriatric ward.

'Hi, Kat.'

She was in an angry mood. 'We had a date last night, Ken.'

'I know. I'm sorry. I wasn't able to make it, and—'

'That's the third time in the last week. What's going on?'

310

She was becoming a boring nag. 'Kat, I have to talk to you. Is there an empty room around here?'

She thought for a moment. 'A patient checked out of 315. Let's go in there.'

They started down the corridor. A nurse walked up to them. 'Oh, Dr Mallory! Dr Peterson has been looking for you. He —'

'Tell him I'm busy.' He took Kat by the arm and led her to the elevator.

When they arrived at the third floor, they walked silently down the corridor and went into Room 315. Mallory closed the door behind them. He was hyperventilating. His whole golden future depended on the next few minutes.

He took Kat's hand in his. It was time to be sincere. 'Kat, you know I'm crazy about you. I've never felt about anyone the way I feel about you. But, honey, the idea of having a baby right now . . . well . . . can't you see how wrong it would be? I mean . . . we're both working day and night, we aren't making enough money to . . .'

'But we can manage,' Kat said. 'I love you, Ken, and I —'

'Wait. All I'm asking is that we put everything off for a little while. Let me finish my term at the hospital and get started in private practice somewhere. Maybe we'll go back East. In a few years we'll be able to afford to get married and have a baby.'

'*In a few years?* But I told you, I'm pregnant.'

'I know, darling, but it's been what, now . . . two months? There's still plenty of time to abort it.'

Kat looked at him, shocked. 'No! I won't abort it. I want us to get married right away. Now.'

We have a yacht in the south of France. Would you

two like to honeymoon on the French Riviera? You can fly over in our Gulfstream.

'I've already told Paige and Honey that we're getting married. They're going to be my bridesmaids. And I told them about the baby.'

Mallory felt a cold chill go through him. Things were getting out of hand. If the Harrisons got wind of this, he would be finished. 'You shouldn't have done that.'

'Why not?'

Mallory forced a smile. 'I want to keep our private lives private.' *I'll get you set up in your own practice . . . You should be able to make two or three hundred thousand dollars the first year or two.* 'Kat, I'm going to ask you this for the last time. Will you have an abortion?' He was *willing* her to say yes, trying to keep the desperation out of his voice.

'No.'

'Kat . . .'

'I can't, Ken. I told you how I felt about the abortion I had as a girl. I swore I could never live through such a thing again. Don't ask me again.'

And it was at that moment that Ken Mallory realized he could not take a chance. He had no choice. He was going to have to kill her.

32

Honey looked forward every day to seeing the patient in Room 306. His name was Sean Reilly, and he was a good-looking Irishman, with black hair and black sparkling eyes. Honey guessed that he was in his early forties.

When Honey first met him on her rounds, she had looked at his chart and said, 'I see you're here for a cholecystectomy.'

'I thought they were going to remove my gallbladder.'

Honey smiled. 'Same thing.'

Sean fixed his black eyes on her. 'They can cut out anything they want except my heart. That belongs to you.'

Honey laughed. 'Flattery will get you everywhere.'

'I hope so, darlin'.'

When Honey had a few minutes to spare, she would drop by and chat with Sean. He was charming and amusing.

'It's worth bein' operated on just to have you around, little darlin'.'

'You aren't nervous about the operation, are you?' she asked.

'Not if you're going to operate, love.'

'I'm not a surgeon. I'm an internist.'

'Are internists allowed to have dinner with their patients?'

'No. There's a rule against it.'

'Do internists ever break rules?'

'Never.' Honey was smiling.

'I think you're beautiful,' Sean said.

No one had ever told Honey that before. She found herself blushing. 'Thank you.'

'You're like the fresh mornin' dew in the fields of Killarney.'

'Have you ever been to Ireland?' Honey asked.

He laughed. 'No, but I promise you we'll go there together one day. You'll see.'

It was ridiculous Irish blarney, and yet . . .

That afternoon when Honey went in to see Sean, she said, 'How are you feeling?'

'The better for seeing you. Have you thought about our dinner date?'

'No,' Honey said. She was lying.

'I was hoping after my operation, I could take you out. You're not engaged, or married, or anything silly like that, are you?'

Honey smiled. 'Nothing silly like that.'

'Good! Neither am I. Who would have me?'

A lot of women, Honey thought.

'If you like home cooking, I happen to be a great cook.'

'We'll see.'

When Honey went to Sean's room the following morning, he said, 'I have a little present for you.' He handed her a sheet of drawing paper. On it was a softened, idealized sketch of Honey.

'I love it!' Honey said. 'You're a wonderful artist!' And she suddenly remembered the psychic's words:

You're going to fall in love. He's an artist. She was looking at Sean strangely.

'Is anything wrong?'

'No,' Honey said slowly. 'No.'

Five minutes later, Honey walked into Frances Gordon's room. The psychic was constantly being readmitted for a series of tests.

'Here comes the Virgo!'

Honey said, 'Do you remember telling me that I was going to fall in love with someone—an artist?'

'Yes.'

'Well, I . . . I think I've met him.'

Frances Gordon smiled. 'See? The stars never lie.'

'Could . . . could you tell me a little about him? About us?'

'There are some tarot cards in that drawer over there. Could you give them to me, please?'

As Honey handed her the cards, she thought, *This is ridiculous! I don't believe in this!*

Frances Gordon was laying out the cards. She kept nodding to herself, and nodding and smiling, and suddenly she stopped. Her face went pale. 'Oh, my God!' She looked up at Honey.

'What . . . what's the matter?' Honey asked.

'This artist. You say you've already met him?'

'I think so. Yes.'

Frances Gordon's voice was filled with sadness. 'The poor man.' She looked up at Honey. 'I'm sorry . . . I'm so sorry.'

*   *   *

315

Sean Reilly was scheduled to have his operation the following morning.

8:15 A.M. Dr William Radnor was in OR Two, preparing for the operation.

8:25 A.M. A truck containing a week's supply of bags of blood pulled up at the emergency entrance to Embarcadero County Hospital. The driver carried the bags to the blood bank in the basement. Eric Foster, the resident doctor on duty, was sharing coffee and a danish with a pretty young nurse, Andrea.

'Where do you want these?' the driver asked.

'Just set them down there.' Foster pointed to a corner.

'Right.' The driver put the bags down and pulled out a form. 'I need your John Hancock.'

'Okay.' Foster signed the form. 'Thanks.'

'No sweat.' The driver left.

Foster turned to Andrea. 'Where were we?'

'You were telling me how adorable I am.'

'Right. If you weren't married, I'd really go after you,' the resident said. 'Do you ever fool around?'

'No. My husband is a boxer.'

'Oh. Do you have a sister?'

'As a matter of fact, I do.'

'Is she as pretty as you are?'

'Prettier.'

'What's her name?'

'Marilyn.'

'Why don't we double-date one night?'

316

As they chatted, the fax machine began to click. Foster ignored it.

8:45 A.M. Dr Radnor began the operation on Sean Reilly. The beginning went smoothly. The operating room functioned like a well-oiled machine, run by capable people doing their jobs.

9:05 A.M. Dr Radnor reached the cystic duct. A text-book operation up until then. As he started to excise the gallbladder, his hand slipped and the scalpel nicked an artery. Blood began to pour out.

'Jesus!' He tried to stop the flow.

The anesthesiologist called out, 'His blood pressure just dropped to 95. He's going into shock!'

Radnor turned to the circulating nurse. 'Get some more blood up here, stat!'

'Right away, doctor.'

9:06 A.M. The telephone rang in the blood bank.

'Don't go away,' Foster told Andrea. He walked past the fax machine, which had stopped clicking, and picked up the telephone. 'Blood supply.'

'We need four units of Type O in OR Two, stat.'

'Right.' Foster replaced the receiver and went to the corner where the new blood had been deposited. He pulled out four bags and placed them on the top shelf of the metal cart used for such emergencies. He double-checked the bags. 'Type O,' he said aloud. He rang for an orderly.

'What's going on?' Andrea asked.

317

Foster looked at the schedule in front of him. 'It looks like one of the patients is giving Dr Radnor a bad time.'

9:10 A.M. The orderly came into the blood bank. 'What have we got?'

'Take this to OR Two. They're waiting for it.'

He watched the orderly wheel out the cart, then turned to Andrea. 'Tell me about your sister.'

'She's married, too.'

'Aw . . .'

Andrea smiled. 'But she fools around.'

'Does she really?'

'I'm only kidding. I have to go back to work, Eric. Thanks for the coffee and danish.'

'Anytime.' He watched her leave and thought, *What a great ass!*

9.12 A.M. The orderly was waiting for an elevator to take him to the second floor.

9.13 A.M. Dr Radnor was doing his best to minimize the catastrophe. 'Where's the damned blood?'

9:15 A.M. The orderly pushed at the door to OR Two and the circulating nurse opened it.

'Thanks,' she said. She carried the bags into the room. 'It's here, doctor.'

'Start pumping it into him. Fast!'

*   *   *

In the blood bank, Eric Foster finished his coffee, thinking about Andrea. *All the good-looking ones are married.*

As he started toward his desk, he passed the fax machine. He pulled out the fax. It read:

Recall Warning Alert #687, June 25: Red Blood Cells, Fresh Frozen Plasma. Units CB83711, CB800007. Community Blood Bank of California, Arizona, Washington, Oregon. Blood products testing repeatedly reactive for Antibody HIV Type 1 were distributed.

He stared at it a moment, then walked over to his desk and picked up the invoice he had signed for the bags of blood that had just been delivered. He looked at the number on the invoice. The number on the warning was identical.

'Oh, my God!' he said. He grabbed the telephone. 'Get me OR Two, fast!'

A nurse answered.

'This is the blood bank. I just sent up four units of Type O. Don't use it! I'm sending up some fresh blood immediately.'

The nurse said, 'Sorry, it's too late.'

Dr Radnor broke the news to Sean Reilly.

'It was a mistake,' Radnor said. 'A terrible mistake. I would give anything if it had not happened.'

Sean was staring at him, in shock. 'My God! I'm going to die.'

'We won't know whether you're HIV-positive for six or eight weeks. And even if you are, that does

319

not necessarily mean you will get AIDS. We're going to do everything we can for you.'

'What the hell can you do for me that you haven't already done?' Sean said bitterly. 'I'm a dead man.'

When Honey heard the news, she was devastated. She remembered Frances Gordon's words. *The poor man.*

Sean Reilly was asleep when Honey walked into his room. She sat at his bedside for a long time, watching him.

He opened his eyes and saw Honey. 'I dreamed that I was dreaming, and that I wasn't going to die.'

'Sean . . .'

'Did you come to visit the corpse?'

'Please don't talk that way.'

'How could this happen?' he cried.

'Someone made a mistake, Sean.'

'God, I don't want to die of AIDS!'

'Some people who get HIV may never get AIDS. The Irish are lucky.'

'I wish I could believe you.'

She took his hand in hers. 'You've got to.'

'I'm not a praying man,' Sean said, 'but I sure as hell am going to start now.'

'I'll pray with you,' Honey said.

He smiled wryly. 'I guess we can forget about that dinner, huh?'

'Oh, no. You don't get out of it that easily. I'm looking forward to it.'

He studied her a moment. 'You really mean that, don't you?'

'You bet I do! No matter what happens. Remember, you promised to take me to Ireland.'

33

'Are you all right, Ken?' Lauren asked. 'You seem tense, darling.'

They were alone in the huge Harrison library. A maid and a butler had served a six-course dinner, and during dinner he and Alex Harrison—*Call me Alex*—had chatted about Mallory's brilliant future.

'Why are you tense?'

Because this pregnant black bitch expects me to marry her. Because any minute word is going to leak out about our engagement and she'll hear about it and blow the whistle. Because my whole future could be destroyed.

He took Lauren's hand in his. 'I guess I'm working too hard. My patients aren't just patients to me, Lauren. They're people in trouble, and I can't help worrying about them.'

She stroked his face. 'That's one of the things I love about you, Ken. You're so caring.'

'I guess I was brought up that way.'

'Oh, I forgot to tell you. The society editor of the *Chronicle* and a photographer are coming here Monday to do an interview.'

It was like a blow to the pit of his stomach.

'Is there any chance you could be here with me, darling? They want a picture of you.'

'I . . . I wish I could, but I have a busy day scheduled at the hospital.' His mind was racing. 'Lauren, do you think it's a good idea to do an interview now? I mean, shouldn't we wait until . . . ?'

Lauren laughed. 'You don't know the press, darling. They're like bloodhounds. No, it's much better to get it over with now.'

Monday!

The following morning, Mallory tracked down Kat in a utility room. She looked tired and haggard. She had no makeup on and her hair was uncurled. *Lauren would never let herself go like that*, Mallory thought.

'Hi, honey!'

Kat did not answer.

Mallory took her in his arms. 'I've been thinking a lot about us, Kat. I didn't sleep at all last night. There's no one else for me. You were right, and I was wrong. I guess the news came as kind of a shock to me. I want you to have our baby.' He watched the sudden glow on Kat's face.

'Do you really mean that, Ken?'

'You bet I do.'

She put her arms around him. 'Thank God! Oh, darling. I was so worried. I don't know what I would do without you.'

'You don't have to worry about that. From now on, everything is going to be wonderful.' *You'll never know how wonderful.* 'Look, I have Sunday night off. Are you free?'

She grasped his hand. 'I'll make myself free.'

'Great! We'll have a nice quiet dinner and then

we'll go back to your place for a nightcap. Do you think you can get rid of Paige and Honey? I want us to be alone.'

Kat smiled. 'No problem. You don't know how happy you've made me. Did I ever tell you how much I love you?'

'I love you, too. I'll show you how much Sunday night.'

Thinking it over, Mallory decided it was a foolproof plan. He had worked it out to the smallest detail. There was no way Kat's death could ever be blamed on him.

It was too risky to get what he needed from the hospital pharmacy because security had been tightened after the Bowman affair. Instead, early Sunday morning, Mallory went looking for a pharmacy far away from the neighborhood where he lived. Most of them were closed on Sunday, and he went to half a dozen before he found one that was open.

The pharmacist behind the counter said, 'Morning. Can I help you?'

'Yes. I'm going to see a patient in this area, and I want to take a prescription to him.' He pulled out his prescription pad and wrote on it.

The pharmacist smiled. 'Not many doctors make house calls these days.'

'I know. It's a pity, isn't it? People just don't care anymore.' He handed the slip of paper to the pharmacist.

The pharmacist looked at it and nodded. 'This will only take a few minutes.'

'Thank you.'
Step one.

That afternoon, Mallory made a stop at the hospital. He was there no more than ten minutes, and when he left, he was carrying a small package.
Step two.

Mallory had arranged to meet Kat at Trader Vic's for dinner, and he was waiting for her when she arrived. He watched her walking toward the table and thought, *It's the Last Supper, bitch.*

He rose and gave her a warm smile. 'Hello, doll. You look beautiful.' And he had to admit that she did. She looked sensational. *She could have been a model. And she's great in bed. All she lacks*, Ken thought, *is about twenty million dollars, give or take a few million.*

Kat was aware again of how the other women in the restaurant were eyeing Ken, envying her. But he only had eyes for her. He was the old Ken, warm and attentive.

'How was your day?' he asked.

She sighed. 'Busy. Three operations in the morning and two this afternoon.' She leaned forward. 'I know it's too early, but I swear I could feel the baby kicking when I was getting dressed.'

Mallory smiled. 'Maybe it wants to get out.'

'We should do an ultrasound test and find out if it's a boy or a girl. Then I can start buying clothes for it.'

'Great idea.'

'Ken, can we set a wedding date? I'd like to have our wedding as soon as possible.'

'No problem,' Mallory said easily. 'We can apply for a license next week.'

'That's wonderful!' She had a sudden thought. 'Maybe we could get a few days off and go somewhere on our honeymoon. Somewhere not too far away—up to Oregon or Washington.'

Wrong, baby. I'll be honeymooning in June, on my yacht on the French Riviera.

'That sounds great. I'll talk to Wallace.'

Kat squeezed his hand. 'Thank you,' she said huskily. 'I'm going to make you the best wife in the whole world.'

'I'm sure of it.' Mallory smiled. 'Now eat your vegetables. We want the baby to be healthy, don't we?'

They left the restaurant at 9:00 P.M. As they approached Kat's apartment building, Mallory said, 'Are you sure Paige and Honey won't be home?'

'I made sure,' Kat said. 'Paige is at the hospital, on call, and I told Honey you and I wanted to be alone here.'

Shit!

She saw the expression on his face. 'Is anything wrong?'

'No, baby. I told you, I just like our private times to be private.' *I'll have to be careful*, he thought. *Very careful.* 'Let's hurry.'

His impatience warmed Kat.

*   *   *

Inside the apartment, Mallory said, 'Let's go into the bedroom.'

Kat grinned. 'That sounds like a great idea.'

Mallory watched Kat undress, and he thought, *She still has a great figure. A baby would ruin it.*

'Aren't you going to get undressed, Ken?'

'Of course.' He remembered the time she had gotten him to undress and then walked out on him. Well, now she was going to pay for that.

He took his clothes off slowly. *Can I perform?* he wondered. He was almost trembling with nervousness. *What I'm going to do is her fault. Not mine. I gave her a chance to back out and she was too stupid to take it.*

He slipped into bed beside her and felt her warm body against his. They began to stroke each other, and he felt himself getting aroused. He entered her and she began to moan.

'Oh, darling . . . it feels so wonderful . . .' She began to move faster and faster. 'Yes . . . yes . . . oh, my God! . . . Don't stop . . .' And her body began to jerk spasmodically, and she shuddered and then lay still in his arms.

She turned to him anxiously. 'Did you . . . ?'

'Of course,' Mallory lied. He was much too tense. 'How about a drink?'

'No. I shouldn't. The baby . . .'

'But this is a celebration, honey. One little drink isn't going to hurt.'

Kat hesitated. 'All right. A small one.' Kat started to get up.

Mallory stopped her. 'No, no. You stay in bed, Mama. You have to get used to being pampered.'

Kat watched Mallory as he walked into the living

327

room and she thought, *I'm the luckiest woman in the world!*

Mallory walked over to the little bar and poured scotch into two glasses. He glanced toward the bedroom to make sure he could not be seen, then went over to the couch, where he had placed his jacket. He took a small bottle from his pocket and poured the contents into Kat's drink. He returned to the bar and stirred Kat's drink and smelled it. There was no odor. He took the two glasses back to the bedroom, and handed Kat her drink.

'Let's drink a toast to our baby,' Kat said.

'Right. To our baby.'

Ken watched as Kat took a swallow of her drink.

'We'll find a nice apartment somewhere,' Kat said dreamily. 'I'll fix up a nursery. We're going to spoil our child rotten, aren't we?' She took another sip.

Mallory nodded. 'Absolutely.' He was watching her closely. 'How do you feel?'

'Wonderful. I've been so worried about us, darling, but I'm not, not anymore.'

'That's good,' Mallory said. 'You have nothing to worry about.'

Kat's eyes were getting heavy. 'No,' she said. 'There's nothing to worry about.' Her words were beginning to slur. 'Ken, I feel funny.' She was beginning to sway.

'You should never have gotten pregnant.'

She was staring up at him stupidly. 'What?'

'You spoiled everything, Kat.'

'Spoiled . . . ?' She was having trouble concentrating.

'You got in my way.'

'Wha'?'

328

'No one gets in my way.'

'Ken, I feel dizzy.'

He stood there, watching her.

'Ken . . . help me, Ken . . .' Her head fell back onto the pillow.

Mallory looked at his watch again. There was plenty of time.

34

It was Honey who arrived at the apartment first and stumbled across Kat's mutilated body, lying in a pool of blood on the floor of the bathroom, obscenely sprawled against the cold white tiles. A bloodstained curette lay beside her. She had hemorrhaged from her womb.

Honey stood there in shock. 'Oh, my God!' Her voice was a strangled whisper. She knelt beside the body and placed a trembling finger against the carotid artery. There was no pulse. Honey hurried back into the living room, picked up the telephone and dialed 911.

A male voice said, 'Nine-one-one Emergency.'

Honey stood there paralyzed, unable to speak.

'Nine-one-one Emergency . . . Hello . . . ?'

'H . . . help! I . . . there's . . .' She was choking over her words. 'Sh . . . she's dead.'

'Who is dead, miss?'

'Kat.'

'Your cat is dead?'

'*No!*' Honey screamed. '*Kat's* dead. Get someone over here right away.'

'Lady . . .'

Honey slammed down the receiver. With shaking fingers, she dialed the hospital. 'Dr T . . . Taylor.' Her voice was an agonized whisper.

'One moment, please.'

Honey gripped the telephone and waited two minutes before she heard Paige's voice. 'Dr Taylor.'

'Paige! You . . . you've got to come home right away!'

'Honey? What's happened?'

'Kat's . . . dead.'

'*What?*' Paige's voice was filled with disbelief. 'How?'

'It . . . it looks like she tried to abort herself.'

'Oh, my God! All right. I'll be there as soon as I can.'

By the time Paige arrived at the apartment, there were two policemen, a detective, and a medical examiner there. Honey was in her bedroom, heavily sedated. The medical examiner was leaning over Kat's naked body. The detective looked up as Paige entered the bloody bathroom.

'Who are you?'

Paige was staring at the lifeless body. Her face was pale. 'I'm Dr Taylor. I live here.'

'Maybe *you* can help me. I'm Inspector Burns. I was trying to talk to the other lady who lives here. She's hysterical. The doctor gave her a sedative.'

Paige looked away from the awful sight on the floor. 'What . . . what do you want to know?'

'She lived here?'

'Yes.'

I'm going to have Ken's baby. How good can it get?

'It looks like she tried to get rid of the kid, and messed it up,' the detective said.

331

Paige stood there, her mind spinning. When she spoke, she said, 'I don't believe it.'

Inspector Burns studied her a moment. 'Why don't you believe it, doctor?'

'She wanted that baby.' She was beginning to think clearly again. 'The father didn't want it.'

'The father?'

'Dr Ken Mallory. He works at Embarcadero County Hospital. He didn't want to marry her. Look, Kat is — *was* —' it was so painful to say *was* —'a doctor. If she had wanted to have an abortion, there's no way she would try to do it herself in a bathroom.' Paige shook her head. 'There's something wrong.'

The medical examiner rose from beside the body. 'Maybe she tried it herself because she didn't want anyone else to know about the baby.'

'That's not true. She told us about it.'

Inspector Burns was watching Paige. 'Was she alone here this evening?'

'No. She had a date with Dr Mallory.'

Ken Mallory was in bed, carefully going over the events of the evening. He replayed every step of the way, making sure there were no loose ends. *Perfect*, he decided. He lay in bed, wondering why it was taking the police so long, and even as he was thinking it, the doorbell rang. Mallory let it ring three times, then got up, put on a robe over his pajamas, and went into the living room.

He stood in front of the door. 'Who's there?' He sounded sleepy.

A voice said, 'Dr Mallory?'

332

'Yes.'

'Inspector Burns. San Francisco Police Department.'

'Police Department?' There was just the right note of surprise in his voice. Mallory opened the door.

The man standing in the hall showed his badge. 'May I come in?'

'Yes. What's this all about?'

'Do you know a Dr Hunter?'

'Of course I do.' A look of alarm crossed his face. 'Has something happened to Kat?'

'Were you with her earlier this evening?'

'Yes. My God! Tell me what's happened! Is she all right?'

'I'm afraid I have some bad news. Dr Hunter is dead.'

'*Dead*? I can't believe it. *How?*'

'Apparently she tried to perform an abortion on herself and it went wrong.'

'Oh, my God!' Mallory said. He sank into a chair. 'It's my fault.'

The inspector was watching him closely. 'Your fault?'

'Yes. I . . . Dr Hunter and I were going to be married. I told her I didn't think it was a good idea for her to have a baby now. I wanted to wait, and she agreed. I suggested she go to the hospital and have them take care of it, but she must have decided to . . . I . . . I can't believe it.'

'What time did you leave, Dr Hunter?'

'It must have been about ten o'clock. I dropped her off at her apartment and left.'

'You didn't go into the apartment?'

333

'No.'

'Did Dr Hunter talk about what she planned to do?'

'You mean about the . . . ? No. Not a word.'

Inspector Burns pulled out a card. 'If you think of anything else that might be helpful, doctor, I'd appreciate it if you gave me a call.'

'Certainly. I . . . you have no idea what a shock this is.'

Paige and Honey stayed up all night, talking about what had happened to Kat, going over it and over it, in shocked disbelief.

At nine o'clock, Inspector Burns came by.

'Good morning. I wanted to tell you that I spoke to Dr Mallory last night.'

'And?'

'He said they went out to dinner, and then he dropped her off and went home.'

'He's lying,' Paige said. She was thinking. 'Wait! Did they find any traces of semen in Kat's body?'

'Yes, as a matter of fact.'

'Well, then,' Paige said excitedly, 'that *proves* he's lying. He did take her to bed and—'

'I went to talk to him about that this morning. He says they had sex *before* they went out to dinner.'

'Oh.' She would not give up. 'His fingerprints will be on the curette he used to kill her.' Her voice was eager. 'Did you find fingerprints?'

'Yes, doctor,' he said patiently. 'They were hers.'

'That's imp—Wait! Then he wore gloves, and when he was finished, he put her prints on the curette. How does that sound?'

334

'Like someone's been watching too many *Murder, She Wrote* television programs.'

'You don't believe Kat was murdered, do you?'

'I'm afraid I don't.'

'Have they done an autopsy?'

'Yes.'

'And?'

'The medical examiner is listing it as an accidental death. Dr Mallory told me she decided not to have the baby, so apparently she —'

'Went into the bathroom and butchered herself?' Paige interrupted. 'For God's sakes, inspector! She was a doctor, a surgeon! There's no way in the world she would have done that to herself.'

Inspector Burns said thoughtfully, 'You think Mallory persuaded her to have an abortion, and tried to help her, and then left when it went wrong?'

Paige shook her head. 'No. It couldn't have happened that way. Kat would never have agreed. He deliberately murdered her.' She was thinking out loud. 'Kat was strong. She would have had to be unconscious for him to . . . to do what he did.'

'The autopsy showed no signs of any blows or anything that would have caused her to become unconscious. No bruises on her throat . . .'

'Were there any traces of sleeping pills or . . . ?'

'Nothing.' He saw the expression on Paige's face. 'This doesn't look to me like a murder. I think Dr Hunter made an error in judgement, and . . . I'm sorry.'

She watched him start toward the door. 'Wait!' Paige said, 'You have a motive.'

He turned. 'Not really. Mallory says she agreed to have the abortion. That doesn't leave us much, does it?'

'It leaves you with a murder,' Paige said stubbornly.

'Doctor, what we *don't* have is any evidence. It's his word against the victim's and she's dead. I'm really sorry.'

Paige watched him leave.

I'm not going to let Ken Mallory get away with it, she thought despairingly.

Jason came by to see Paige. 'I heard what happened,' he said. 'I can't believe it! How could she have done that to herself?'

'She didn't,' Paige said. 'She was murdered.' She told Jason about her conversation with Inspector Burns. 'The police aren't going to do anything about it. They think it was an accident. Jason, it's my fault that Kat is dead.'

'Your fault?'

'I'm the one who persuaded her to go out with Mallory in the first place. She didn't want to. It started out as a silly joke, and then she . . . she fell in love with him. Oh, Jason!'

'You can't blame yourself for that,' he said firmly.

Paige looked around in despair. 'I can't live in this apartment anymore. I have to get out of here.'

Jason took her in his arms. 'Let's get married right away.'

'It's too soon. I mean, Kat isn't even . . .'

'I know. We'll wait a week or two.'

'All right.'

'I love you, Paige.'

'I love you, too, darling. Isn't it stupid! I feel guilty because Kat and I both fell in love, and she's dead and I'm alive.'

The photograph appeared on the front page of the *San Francisco Chronicle* on Tuesday. It showed a smiling Ken Mallory with his arm around Lauren Harrison. The caption read: 'Heiress to Wed Doctor.'

Paige stared at it in disbelief. Kat had been dead for only two days, and Ken Mallory was announcing his engagement to another woman! All the time he had been promising to marry Kat, he had been planning to marry someone else. *That's why he killed Kat. To get her out of the way!*

Paige picked up the telephone and dialed police headquarters.

'Inspector Burns, please.'

A moment later, she was talking to the inspector.

'This is Dr Taylor.'

'Yes, doctor.'

'Have you seen the photograph in this morning's *Chronicle*?'

'Yes.'

'Well, there's your motive!' Paige exclaimed. 'Ken Mallory had to shut Kat up before Lauren Harrison found out about her. You've got to arrest Mallory.' She was almost yelling into the telephone.

'Wait a minute. Calm down, doctor. We may have a motive, but I told you, we don't have a shred of

337

evidence. You said yourself that Dr Hunter would have had to be unconscious before Mallory could perform an abortion on her. After I spoke to you, I talked to our forensic pathologist again. There was no sign of any kind of blow that could have caused unconsciousness.'

'Then he must have given her a sedative,' Paige said stubbornly. 'Probably chloral hydrate. It's fast-acting and —'

Inspector Burns said patiently, 'Doctor, there was no trace of chloral hydrate in her body. I'm sorry — I really am — but we can't arrest a man because he's going to get married. Was there anything else?'

Everything else. 'No,' Paige said. She slammed down the receiver and sat there thinking. *Mallory has to have given Kat some kind of drug. The easiest place for him to have gotten it would be the hospital pharmacy.*

Fifteen minutes later, Paige was on her way to Embarcadero County Hospital.

Pete Samuels, the chief pharmacist, was behind the counter. 'Good morning, Dr Taylor. How can I help you?'

'I believe Dr Mallory came by a few days ago and picked up some medication. He told me the name of it, but I can't remember what it was.'

Samuels frowned. 'I don't remember Dr Mallory coming by here for at least a month.'

'Are you sure?'

Samuels nodded. 'Positive. I would have remembered. We always talk football.'

Paige's heart sank. 'Thank you.'

He must have written a prescription at some other

pharmacy. Paige knew that the law required that all prescriptions for narcotics be made out in triplicate—one copy for the patient, one to be sent to the Bureau of Controlled Substances, and the third for the pharmacy's files.

Somewhere, Paige thought, *Ken Mallory had a prescription filled. There are probably two or three hundred pharmacies in San Francisco.* There was no way she could track down the prescription. It was likely that Mallory had gotten it just before he murdered Kat. That would have been on Saturday or Sunday. *If it was Sunday, I might have a chance*, Paige thought. *Very few pharmacies are open on Sunday. That narrows it down.*

She went upstairs to the office where the assignment sheets were kept and looked up the roster for Saturday. Dr Ken Mallory had been on call all day, so the chances were that he had had the prescription filled on Sunday. How many pharmacies were open on Sunday in San Francisco?

Paige picked up the telephone and called the state pharmaceutical board.

'This is Dr Taylor,' Paige said. 'Last Sunday, a friend of mine left a prescription at a pharmacy. She asked me to pick it up for her, but I can't remember the name of the pharmacy. I wonder if you could help me.'

'Well, I don't see how, doctor. If you don't know . . .'

'Most drugstores are closed on Sunday, aren't they?'

'Yes, but . . .'

'I'd appreciate it if you could give me a list of those that were open.'

There was a pause. 'Well, if it's important . . .'
'It's very important,' Paige assured her.
'Hold on, please.'

There were thirty-six stores on the list, spread all over the city. It would have been simple if she could have gone to the police for help, but Inspector Burns did not believe her. *Honey and I are going to have to do this ourselves*, Paige thought. She explained to Honey what she had in mind.

'It's a real long shot, isn't it?' Honey said. 'You don't even know if he filled the prescription on Sunday.'

'It's the only shot we have.' *That Kat has.* 'I'll check out the ones in Richmond, the Marina, North Beach, Upper Market, Mission, and Potrero, and you check out the Excelsior, Ingleside, Lake Merced, Western Addition, and Sunset areas.'

'All right.'

At the first pharmacy Paige went into, she showed her identification and said, 'A colleague of mine, Dr Ken Mallory, was in here Sunday for a prescription. He's out of town, and he asked me to get a refill, but I can't remember the name of it. Would you mind looking it up, please?'

'Dr Ken Mallory? Just a moment.' He came back a few minutes later. 'Sorry, we didn't fill any prescriptions Sunday for a Dr Mallory.'

'Thank you.'

Paige got the same response at the next four pharmacies.

Honey was having no better luck.

'We have thousands of prescriptions here, you know.'

'I know, but this was last Sunday.'

'Well, we have no prescriptions here from a Dr Mallory. Sorry.'

The two of them spent the day going from pharmacy to pharmacy. They were both getting discouraged. It was not until late afternoon, just before closing time, that Paige found what she was looking for in a small pharmacy in the Potrero district.

The pharmacist said, 'Oh, yes, here we are. Dr Ken Mallory. I remember him. He was on his way to make a house call on a patient. I was impressed, because not many doctors do that these days.'

No resident ever makes house calls. 'What's the prescription for?'

Paige found she was holding her breath.

'Chloral hydrate.'

Paige was almost trembling with excitement. 'You're sure?'

'It says so right here.'

'What was the patient's name?'

He looked at the copy of the prescription. 'Spyros Levathes.'

'Would you mind giving me a copy of that prescription?' Paige asked.

'Not at all, doctor.'

One hour later, Paige was in Inspector Burns's office. She laid the prescription on his desk.

'Here's your proof,' Paige said. 'On Sunday, Dr Mallory went to a pharmacy miles away from where he lives, and had this prescription for chloral hydrate filled. He put the chloral hydrate in Kat's drink, and when she was unconscious, he butchered her to make it look like an accident.'

'There's only one problem with that, Dr Taylor. There *was* no chloral hydrate in her body.'

'There has to be. Your pathologist made a mistake. Ask him to check again.'

He was losing his patience. 'Doctor . . .'

'Please! I know I'm right.'

'You're wasting everybody's time.'

Paige sat across from him, her eyes fixed on his face.

He sighed. 'All right. I'll call him again. Maybe he *did* make a mistake.'

Jason picked Paige up for dinner. 'We're having dinner at my house,' he said. 'There's something I want you to see.'

During the drive there, Paige brought Jason up to date on what was happening.

'They'll find the chloral hydrate in her body,' Paige said. 'And Ken Mallory will get what's coming to him.'

'I'm so sorry about all this, Paige.'

'I know.' She pressed his hand against her cheek. 'Thank God for you.'

The car pulled up in front of Jason's home.

Paige looked out of the window and she gasped. Around the green lawn in front of the house was a new white picket fence.

*　　*　　*

She was alone in the dark apartment. Ken Mallory used the key that Kat had given him and moved quietly toward the bedroom. Paige heard his footsteps coming toward her, but before she could move, he had leaped at her, his hands tight around her throat.

'You bitch! You're trying to destroy me. Well, you aren't going to snoop around anymore.' He began squeezing harder. 'I outsmarted all of you, didn't I?' His fingers squeezed tighter. 'No one can ever prove I killed Kat.'

She tried to scream, but it was impossible to breathe. She struggled free, and was suddenly awake. She was alone in her room. Paige sat up in bed trembling.

She stayed awake the rest of the night, waiting for Inspector Burns's phone call. It came at 10:00 A.M.

'Dr Taylor?'

'Yes.' She was holding her breath.

'I just got the *third* report from the forensic pathologist.'

'And?' Her heart was pounding.

'There was no trace of chloral hydrate or any other sedative in Dr Hunter's body. None.'

That was impossible! There had to be. There was no sign of any blow or anything that would have caused her to become unconscious. No bruises on her throat. It didn't make sense. Kat had to have been unconscious when Mallory killed her. The forensic pathologist was wrong.

Paige decided to go talk to him herself.

*   *   *

343

Dr Dolan was in an irritable mood. 'I don't like to be questioned like this,' he said. 'I've checked it three times. I told Inspector Burns that there was no trace of chloral hydrate in any of her organs, and there wasn't.'

'But . . .'

'Is there anything else, doctor?'

Paige looked at him helplessly. Her last hope was gone. Ken Mallory was going to get away with murder. 'I . . . I guess not. If you didn't find any chemicals in her body, then I don't . . .'

'I didn't say I didn't find *any* chemicals.'

She looked at him a moment. 'You found something?'

'Just a trace of trichloroethylene.'

She frowned. 'What would that do?'

He shrugged. 'Nothing. It's an analgesic drug. It wouldn't put anyone to sleep.'

'I see.'

'Sorry I can't help you.'

Paige nodded. 'Thank you.'

She walked down the long, antiseptic corridor of the morgue, depressed, feeling that she was missing something. She had been so sure Kat had been put to sleep with chloral hydrate.

All he found was a trace of trichloroethylene. It wouldn't put anyone to sleep. But why would trichloroethylene be in Kat's body? Kat had not been taking any medications. Paige stopped in the middle of the corridor, her mind working furiously.

When Paige arrived at the hospital, she went directly to the medical library on the fifth floor. It took her less than a minute to find trichloroethylene. The description read: *A colorless, clear, volatile liquid with a specific gravity of 1.47 at 59 degrees F. It is a halogenated hydrocarbon, having the chemical formula $CCl_2, CHCl$.*

And there, on the last line, she found what she was looking for. *When chloral hydrate is metabolized, it produces trichloroethylene as a by-product.*

'Inspector, Dr Taylor is here to see you.'

'Again?' He was tempted to turn her away. She was obsessed with the half-baked theory she had. He was going to have to put a stop to it. 'Send her in.'

When Paige walked into his office, Inspector Burns said, 'Look, doctor, I think this has gone far enough. Dr Dolan called to complain about—'

'I know how Ken Mallory did it!' Her voice was charged with excitement. 'There was trichloroethylene in Kat's body.'

He nodded. 'Dr Dolan told me that. But he said it couldn't have made her unconscious. He—'

'Chloral hydrate turns into trichloroethylene!' Paige said triumphantly. 'Mallory lied when he said he didn't go back into the apartment with Kat. He put chloral hydrate in her drink. It has no taste when you mix it with alcohol, and it only takes a few minutes for it to work. Then when she was unconscious, he killed her and made it look like a bungled abortion.'

'Doctor, if you'll forgive my saying so, that's a hell of a lot of speculation.'

'No, it isn't. He wrote the prescription for a patient named Spyros Levathes, but he never gave it to him.'

'How do you know that?'

'Because he *couldn't* have. I checked on Spyros Levathes. He has erythropoietic porphyria.'

'What's that?'

'It's a genetic metabolic disorder. It causes photo-sensitivity and lesions, hypertension, tachycardia, and a few other unpleasant symptoms. It's the result of a defective gene.'

'I still don't understand.'

'Dr Mallory didn't give his patient chloral hydrate because it would have killed him! Chloral hydrate is contra-indicated for porphyria. It would have caused immediate convulsive seizures.'

For the first time, Inspector Burns was impressed. 'You've really done your homework, haven't you?'

Paige pressed on. 'Why would Ken Mallory go to a remote pharmacy and fill a prescription for a patient he knew he couldn't *give* it to? You've *got* to arrest him.'

His fingers were drumming on his desk. 'It's not that simple.'

'You've got to . . .'

Inspector Burns raised a hand. 'All right. I'll tell you what I'll do. I'll talk to the district attorney's office and see whether they think we have a case.'

Paige knew she had gone as far as she could. 'Thank you, inspector.'

'I'll get back to you.'

After Paige Taylor left, Inspector Burns sat there thinking about their conversation. There was no hard evidence against Dr Mallory, only the suspicions of a persistent woman. He reviewed the few facts that he had. Dr Mallory had been engaged to Kat Hunter. Two days after she died, he was engaged to Alex

Harrison's daughter. Interesting, but not against the law.

Mallory had said that he dropped Dr Hunter off at her front door and did not go into the apartment. Semen was found in her body, but he had a plausible explanation for that.

Then there was the matter of the chloral hydrate. Mallory had written a prescription for a drug that could have killed his patient. Was he guilty of murder? Not guilty?

Burns buzzed his secretary on the intercom. 'Barbara, get me an appointment with the district attorney this afternoon.'

There were four men in the office when Paige walked in: the district attorney, his assistant, a man named Warren, and Inspector Burns.

'Thank you for stopping by, Dr Taylor,' the district attorney said. 'Inspector Burns has been telling me of your interest in the death of Dr Hunter. I can appreciate that. Dr Hunter was your roommate, and you want to see justice done.'

So they're going to arrest Ken Mallory after all!

'Yes,' Paige said. 'There's no doubt about it. Dr Mallory killed her. When you arrest him, he —'

'I'm afraid we can't do that.'

Paige looked at him blankly. 'What?'

'We can't arrest Dr Mallory.'

'But why?'

'We have no case.'

'Of course you have!' Paige exclaimed. 'The trichloroethylene proves that —'

'Doctor, in a court of justice, ignorance of the law is no excuse. But ignorance in medicine *is*.'

'I don't understand.'

'It's simple. It means that Dr Mallory could claim he made a mistake, that he didn't know what effect chloral hydrate would have on a patient with porphyria. No one could prove he was lying. It might prove that he's a lousy doctor, but it wouldn't prove that he's guilty of murder.'

Paige looked at him in frustration. 'You're going to let him get away with this?'

He studied her a moment. 'I'll tell you what I'm prepared to do. I've discussed this with Inspector Burns. With your permission, we're going to send someone to your apartment to pick up the glasses in the bar. If we find any traces of chloral hydrate, we'll take the next step.'

'What if he rinsed them out?'

Inspector Burns said dryly, 'I don't imagine he took the time to use a detergent. If he just rinsed out the glasses, we'll find what we're looking for.'

Two hours later, Inspector Burns was on the phone with Paige.

'We did a chemical analysis of all the glasses in the bar, doctor,' Burns said.

Paige steeled herself for disappointment.

'We found one with traces of chloral hydrate.'

Paige closed her eyes in a silent prayer of thanks.

'And there were fingerprints on that glass. We're going to check them against Dr Mallory's prints.'

Paige felt a surge of excitement.

The inspector went on, 'When he killed her —

if he did kill her—he was wearing gloves, so his fingerprints wouldn't be on the curette. But he couldn't very well have served her a drink while he wore gloves, and he might not have worn them when he put the glass back on the shelf after rinsing it out.'

'No,' Paige said. 'He couldn't, could he?'

'I have to admit that in the beginning, I didn't believe your theory was going anywhere. I think now maybe Dr Mallory could be our man. But proving it is going to be another matter.' He continued, 'The district attorney is right. It would be a tricky business to bring Mallory to trial. He can still say that the prescription was for his patient. There's no law against making a medical mistake. I don't see how we—'

'Wait a minute!' Paige said excitedly. 'I think I know how!'

Ken Mallory was listening to Lauren on the telephone. 'Father and I found some office space that you're going to adore, darling! It's a beautiful suite in the 490 Post Building. I'm going to hire a receptionist for you, someone not too pretty.'

Mallory laughed. 'You don't have to worry about that, baby. There isn't anyone in the world for me but you.'

'I'm dying for you to come see it. Can you get away now?'

'I'm off in a couple of hours.'

'Wonderful! Why don't you pick me up at the house?'

'All right. I'll be there.' Mallory replaced the telephone. *It doesn't get any better than this*, he thought. *There is a God, and She loves me.*

He heard his name called over the PA system, 'Dr Mallory . . . Room 430 . . . Dr Mallory . . . Room 430.' He sat there daydreaming, thinking about the golden future that lay ahead of him. *A beautiful suite in the 490 Post Building, filled with rich old ladies, eager to throw their money at him.* He heard his name called again. 'Dr Mallory . . . Room 430.' He sighed and got to his feet. *I'll be out of this goddam madhouse soon*, he thought. He headed toward Room 430.

A resident was waiting for him in the corridor, outside the room. 'I'm afraid we have a problem here,' he said. 'This is one of Dr Peterson's patients, but Dr Peterson isn't here. I'm having an argument with one of the other doctors.'

They stepped inside. There were three people in the room — a man in bed, a male nurse, and a doctor Mallory had not met before.

The resident said, 'This is Dr Edwards. We need your advice, Dr Mallory.'

'What's the problem?'

The resident explained. 'This patient is suffering from erythropoietic porphyria, and Dr Edwards insists on giving him a sedative.'

'I don't see any problem with that.'

'Thank you,' Dr Edwards said. 'The man hasn't slept in forty-eight hours. I've prescribed chloral hydrate for him so he can get some rest and . . .'

Mallory was looking at him in astonishment. 'Are you out of your mind? That could kill him! He'd have a convulsive seizure, tachycardia, and he'd probably die. Where in hell did you study medicine?'

351

The man looked at Mallory and said quietly, 'I didn't.' He flashed a badge. 'I'm with the San Francisco Police Department, Homicide.' He turned to the man in bed. 'Did you get that?'

The man pulled out a tape recorder from under the pillow. 'I got it.'

Mallory was looking from one to the other, frowning. 'I don't understand. What is this? What's going on?'

The inspector turned to Mallory. 'Dr Mallory, you're under arrest for the murder of Dr Kate Hunter.'

36

The headline in the *San Francisco Chronicle* read, DOCTOR ARRESTED IN LOVE TRIANGLE. The story beneath it went on at length to detail the lurid facts of the case.

Mallory read the newspaper in his cell. He slammed it down.

His cellmate said, 'Looks like they got you cold, pal.'

'Don't you believe it,' Mallory said confidently. 'I've got connections, and they're going to get me the best goddam lawyer in the world. I'll be out of here in twenty-four hours. All I have to do is make one phone call.'

The Harrisons were reading the newspaper at breakfast.

'My God!' Lauren said. 'Ken! I can't believe it!'

A butler approached the breakfast table. 'Excuse me, Miss Harrison. Dr Mallory is on the telephone for you. I believe he's calling from jail.'

'I'll take it.' Lauren started to get up from the table.

'You'll stay here and finish your breakfast,' Alex

Harrison said firmly. He turned to the butler. 'We don't know any Dr Mallory.'

Paige read the newspaper as she was getting dressed. Mallory was going to be punished for the terrible thing he had done, but it gave Paige no satisfaction. Nothing they did to him could ever bring Kat back.

The doorbell rang, and Paige went to answer it. A stranger stood there. He was wearing a dark suit and carried a briefcase.

'Dr Taylor?'

'Yes . . .'

'My name is Roderick Pelham. I'm an attorney with Rothman and Rothman. May I come in?'

Paige studied him, puzzled. 'Yes.'

He entered the apartment.

'What did you want to see me about?'

She watched him open the briefcase and take out some papers.

'You are aware, of course, that you are the principal beneficiary of John Cronin's will?'

Paige looked at him blankly. 'What are you talking about? There must be some mistake.'

'Oh, there's no mistake. Mr Cronin has left you the sum of one million dollars.'

Paige sank into a chair, overwhelmed, remembering.

You have to go to Europe. Do me a favor. Go to Paris . . . stay at the Crillon, have dinner at Maxim's, order a big, thick steak and a bottle of champagne, and when you eat that steak and drink that champagne, I want you to think of me.

'If you'll just sign here, we'll take care of all the necessary paperwork.'

Paige looked up. 'I . . . I don't know what to say. I . . . he had a family.'

'According to the terms of his will, they get only the remainder of his estate, not a large amount.'

'I can't accept this,' Paige told him.

Pelham looked at her in surprise. 'Why not?'

She had no answer. John Cronin had wanted her to have this money. 'I don't know. It . . . it seems unethical, somehow. He was my patient.'

'Well, I'll leave the check here with you. You can decide what you want to do with it. Just sign here.'

Paige signed the paper in a daze.

'Goodbye, doctor.'

She watched him leave and sat there thinking of John Cronin.

The news of Paige's inheritance was the talk of the hospital. Somehow, Paige had hoped it could be kept quiet. She still had not made up her mind about what to do with the money. *It doesn't belong to me*, she thought. *He had a family*.

Paige was not emotionally ready to go back to work, but her patients had to be taken care of. An operation was scheduled for that morning. Arthur Kane was waiting for Paige in the corridor. They had not spoken to each other since the incident of the reversed X-rays. Although Paige had no proof it was Kane, the tire-slashing episode had scared her.

'Hello, Paige. Let's let bygones be bygones. What do you say?'

Paige shrugged. 'Fine.'

'Wasn't that a terrible thing about Ken Mallory?' he asked.

'Yes,' Paige said.

Kane was looking at her slyly. 'Can you imagine a doctor deliberately killing a human being? It's horrible, isn't it?'

'Yes.'

'By the way,' he said, 'congratulations. I hear that you're a millionairess.'

'I can't see . . .'

'I have tickets for the theater tonight, Paige. I thought that the two of us could go.'

'Thanks,' Paige said. 'I'm engaged to someone.'

'Then I suggest you get unengaged.'

She looked at him, surprised. 'I beg your pardon?'

Kane moved closer to her. 'I ordered an autopsy on John Cronin.'

Paige found her heart beginning to beat faster. 'Yes?'

'He didn't die of heart failure. Someone gave him an overdose of insulin. I guess that particular someone never figured on an autopsy.'

Paige's mouth was suddenly dry.

'You were with him when he died, weren't you?'

She hesitated. 'Yes.'

'I'm the only one who knows that, and I'm the only one who has the report.' He patted her arm. 'And my lips are sealed. Now, about those tickets tonight . . .'

Paige pulled away from him. 'No!'

'Are you sure you know what you're doing?'

She took a deep breath. 'Yes. Now, if you'll excuse me . . .' And she walked away. Kane looked after her, and his face hardened. He turned and headed toward Dr Benjamin Wallace's office.

The telephone awakened her at 1:00 A.M. at her apartment.

'You have been a naughty girl again.'

It was the same raspy voice disguised in a breathy whisper, but this time Paige recognized it. *My God*, she thought, *I was right to be scared*.

The following morning, when Paige arrived at the hospital, two men were waiting for her.

'Dr Paige Taylor?'

'Yes.'

'You'll have to come with us. You're under arrest for the murder of John Cronin.'

37

It was the final day of Paige's trial. Alan Penn, the defense attorney, was making his summation to the jury.

'Ladies and gentlemen, you have heard a lot of testimony about Dr Taylor's competence or incompetence. Well, Judge Young will instruct you that's not what this trial is about. I'm sure that for every doctor who did not approve of her work, we could produce a dozen doctors who did. But that is not the issue.

'Paige Taylor is on trial for the death of John Cronin. She has admitted helping him die. She did so because he was in great pain, and he asked her to do so. That is euthanasia, and it's being accepted more and more throughout the world. In the past year, the California Supreme Court has upheld the right of a mentally competent adult to refuse or demand the withdrawal of medical treatment of any form. It is the individual who must live or die with the course of treatment chosen or rejected.'

He looked into the faces of the jurors. 'Euthanasia is a crime of compassion, of mercy, and I daresay it takes place in some form or another in hospitals all over the world. The prosecuting attorney is asking for a death sentence. Don't let him confuse the issue. There has never been a death sentence for euthanasia. Sixty-three percent of Americans believe euthanasia should be legal, and in eighteen states in this country, it *is* legal. The question is, do we have the right to compel helpless patients to live in pain, to force them to stay alive and suffer? The question has become complicated because of the great strides we've made in medical technology. We've turned the care of patients over to machines. Machines have no mercy. If a horse breaks a leg, we put it out of its misery by shooting it. With a human being, we condemn him or her to a half life that is hell.

'Dr Taylor didn't decide when John Cronin would die. John Cronin decided. Make no mistake about it, what Dr Taylor did was an act of mercy. She has taken full responsibility for that. But you can rest assured that she knew nothing about the money that was left to her. What she did, she did in a spirit of compassion. John Cronin was a man with a failing heart and an untreatable, fatal cancer that had spread through his body, causing him agony. Just ask yourself one question. Under those circumstances, would you like to go on living? Thank you.' He turned, walked back to the table, and sat next to Paige.

Gus Venable rose and stood before the jury. '*Compassion? Mercy?*' He looked over at Paige, shook his head, then turned back to the jury. 'Ladies and gentlemen, I have been practicing law in courtrooms for more than twenty years, and I must tell you that in all those years, I have never—never—seen a more clear-cut case of cold-blooded, deliberate murder for profit.'

Paige was hanging on every word, tense and pale.

'The defense talked about euthanasia. Did Dr Taylor do what she did out of a feeling of compassion? I don't think so. Dr Taylor and others have testified that Mr Cronin had only a few more days to live. Why didn't she let him live those few days? Perhaps it was because Dr Taylor was afraid Mrs Cronin might learn about her husband changing his will, and put a stop to it.

'It's a most remarkable coincidence that immediately after Mr Cronin changed his will and left Dr Taylor the sum of one million dollars, she gave him an overdose of insulin and murdered him.

'Again and again, the defendant has convicted herself with her own words. She said that she was on friendly terms with John Cronin, that he liked and respected her. But you have heard witnesses testify that he hated Dr Paige, that he called her "that bitch" and told her "to keep her fucking hands off him".'

Gus Venable glanced at the defendant again. There was a look of despair on Paige's face. He turned back to the jury. 'An attorney has testified that Dr Taylor said, about the million dollars that was left to her, "It's unethical. He was my patient." But she grabbed the money. She needed it. She had a drawerful of travel brochures at home—Paris, London, the Riviera. And bear in mind that she didn't go to the travel agency *after* she got the money. Oh, no. She planned those trips earlier. All she needed was the money and the opportunity, and John Cronin supplied both. A helpless, dying man she could control. She had at her mercy a man who she admitted was in enormous pain—agony, in fact,

360

according to her own admission. When you're in that kind of pain, you can imagine how difficult it must be to think clearly. We don't know *how* Dr Taylor persuaded John Cronin to change his will, to cut out the family he loved and to make her his main beneficiary. What we *do* know is that he summoned her to his bedside on that fatal night. What did they talk about? Could he have offered her a million dollars to put him out of his misery? It's a possibility we must face. In either case, it was cold-blooded murder.

'Ladies and gentlemen, during this trial, do you know who was the most damaging witness of all?' He pointed a dramatic finger at Paige. 'The defendant herself! You've heard her testify that she never violated the sacred Hippocratic oath that she took, but she lied. We've heard testimony that she gave an illegal blood transfusion and then falsified the record. She said that she never killed a patient except John Cronin, but we've heard testimony that Dr Barker, a physician respected by everybody, accused her of killing his patient.

'Unfortunately, ladies and gentlemen, Lawrence Barker suffered a stroke and can't be here with us today to testify against the defendant. But let me remind you of Dr Barker's opinion of the defendant. This is Dr Peterson, testifying about a patient Dr Taylor was operating on.'

He read from the transcript.

'"Dr Barker came into the operating room during the operation?"

'"Yes." And did Dr Barker say anything?'

'Answer: "He turned to Dr Taylor and said, 'You killed him.'"'

'This is from Nurse Berry. "Tell me some specific

things you heard Dr Barker say to Dr Taylor."

'Answer: "He said she was incompetent . . . Another time he said he wouldn't let her operate on his dog." '

Gus Venable looked up. 'Either there is some kind of conspiracy going on, where all these reputable doctors and nurses are lying about the defendant, or Dr Taylor is a liar. Not *just* a liar, but a pathological . . .'

The rear door of the courtroom had opened and an aide hurried in. He paused in the doorway a moment, trying to make a decision. Then he moved down the aisle toward Gus Venable.

'Sir . . .'

Gus Venable turned, furious. 'Can't you see I'm . . . ?'

The aide whispered in his ear.

Gus Venable looked at him, stunned. '*What? That's wonderful!*'

Judge Young leaned forward, her voice ominously quiet. 'Forgive me for interrupting you two, but what exactly do you think you're doing?'

Gus Venable turned to the judge excitedly. 'Your honor, I've just been informed that Dr Lawrence Barker is outside this courtroom. He's in a wheelchair, but he's able to testify. I'd like to call him to the stand.'

There was a loud buzz in the courtroom.

Alan Penn was on his feet. 'Objection!' he yelled. 'The prosecuting attorney is in the middle of his summation. There's no precedent for calling a new witness at this late hour. I —'

Judge Young slammed her gavel down. 'Would counsel please approach the bench.'

362

Penn and Venable moved up to the bench.

'This is highly irregular, your honor. I object . . .'

Judge Young said, 'You're right about its being irregular, Mr Penn, but you're wrong about its being without precedent. I can cite a dozen cases around the country where material witnesses were allowed to testify under special circumstances. In fact, if you're so interested in precedent, you might look up a case that took place in this courtroom five years ago. I happened to be the judge.'

Alan Penn swallowed. 'Does this mean you're going to allow him to testify?'

Judge Young was thoughtful. 'Since Dr Barker is a material witness to this case, and was physically unable to testify earlier, in the interest of justice, I'm going to rule that he be allowed to take the stand.'

'Exception! There is no proof that the witness is competent to testify. I demand a battery of psychiatrists—'

'Mr Penn, in this courtroom, we don't demand. We request.' She turned to Gus Venable. 'You may bring in your witness.'

Alan Penn stood there, deflated. *It's all over*, he thought. *Our case is down the drain.*

Gus Venable turned to his aide. 'Bring Dr Barker in.'

The door opened slowly, and Dr Lawrence Barker entered the courtroom. He was in a wheelchair. His head was tilted, and one side of his face was drawn up in a slight rictus.

Everyone watched the pale and fragile figure being wheeled to the front of the courtroom. As he moved past Paige, he looked over at her.

363

There was no friendliness in his eyes, and Paige remembered his last words: *Who the hell do you think you . . . ?*

When Lawrence Barker was in front of the bench, Judge Young leaned forward and said gently, 'Dr Barker, are you able to testify here today?'

When Barker spoke, his words were slurred. 'I am, your honor.'

'Are you fully aware of what is going on in this courtroom?'

'Yes, your honor.' He looked over to where Paige was seated. 'That woman is being tried for the murder of a patient.'

Paige winced. *That woman!*

Judge Young made her decision. She turned to the bailiff. 'Would you swear the witness in, please?'

When Dr Barker had been sworn in, Judge Young said, 'You may stay in the chair, Dr Barker. The prosecutor will proceed, and I will allow the defense to cross-examine.'

Gus Venable smiled. 'Thank you, your honor.' He strolled over to the wheelchair. 'We won't keep you very long, doctor, and the court deeply appreciates your coming in to testify under these trying circumstances. Are you familiar with any of the testimony that has been given here over the past month?'

Dr Barker nodded. 'I've been following it on television and in the newspapers, and it made me sick to my stomach.'

Paige buried her head in her hands.

It was all Gus Venable could do to hide his feeling of triumph. 'I'm sure a lot of us feel the same way, doctor,' the prosecutor said piously.

'I came here because I want to see justice done.'

Venable smiled. 'Exactly. So do we.'

Lawrence Barker took a deep breath, and when he spoke, his voice was filled with outrage. 'Then how the hell could you bring Dr Taylor to trial?'

Venable thought he had misunderstood him. 'I beg your pardon?'

'This trial is a farce!'

Paige and Alan Penn exchanged a stunned look.

Gus Venable turned pale. 'Dr Barker . . .'

'Don't interrupt me,' Barker snapped. 'You've used the testimony of a lot of biased, jealous people to attack a brilliant surgeon. She—'

'Just a minute!' Venable was beginning to panic. 'Isn't it true that you criticized Dr Taylor's ability so severely that she was finally ready to quit Embarcadero Hospital?'

'Yes.'

Gus Venable was starting to feel better. 'Well, then,' he said patronizingly, 'how can you say that Paige Taylor is a brilliant doctor?'

'Because it happens to be the truth.' Barker turned to look at Paige, and when he spoke again, he was talking to her as though they were the only two people in the courtroom: 'Some people are born to be doctors. You were one of those rare ones. I knew from the beginning how capable you were. I was hard on you—maybe too hard—because you were good. I was tough on you because I wanted you to be tougher on yourself. I wanted you to be perfect, because in our profession, there's no room for error. None.'

Paige was staring at him, mesmerized, her mind spinning. It was all happening too fast.

The courtroom was hushed.

'I wasn't about to let you quit.'

Gus Venable could feel his victory slipping away. His prize witness had become his worst nightmare. 'Dr Barker—it has been testified that you accused Dr Taylor of killing your patient Lance Kelly. How . . . ?'

'I told her that because she was the surgeon in charge. It was her ultimate responsibility. In fact, the anesthetist caused Mr Kelly's death.'

By now the court was in an uproar.

Paige sat there stunned.

Dr Barker went on speaking slowly, with an effort. 'And as for John Cronin leaving her that money, Dr Taylor knew nothing about it. I talked to Mr Cronin myself. He told me that he was going to leave Dr Taylor that money because he hated his family, and he said he was going to ask Dr Taylor to release him from his misery. I agreed.'

There was an uproar from the spectators. Gus Venable was standing there, a look of total bewilderment on his face.

Alan Penn leaped to his feet. 'Your honor, I move for a dismissal!'

Judge Young was slamming her gavel down. 'Quiet!' she yelled. She looked at the two attorneys. 'Into my chambers.'

Judge Young, Alan Penn, and Gus Venable were seated in Judge Young's chambers.

Gus Venable was in a state of shock. 'I . . . I don't know what to say. He's obviously a sick man, your honor. He's confused. I want a battery of psychiatrists to examine him and—'

366

'You can't have it both ways, Gus. It looks like your case just went up in smoke. Let's save you any further embarrassment, shall we? I'm going to grant a dismissal on the murder charge. Any objection?'

There was a long silence. Finally, Venable nodded. 'I guess not.'

Judge Young said, 'Good decision. I'm going to give you some advice. Never, *never* call a witness unless you know what he's going to say.'

The court was in session again. Judge Young said, 'Ladies and gentlemen of the jury, thank you for your time and your patience. The court is going to grant a dismissal on all charges. The defendant is free.'

Paige turned to blow Jason a kiss, then hurried over to where Dr Barker was seated. She slid down to her knees and hugged him.

'I don't know how to thank you,' she whispered.

'You never should have gotten into this mess in the first place,' he growled. 'Damned fool thing to do. Let's get out of here and go somewhere where we can talk.'

Judge Young heard. She stood up and said, 'You may use my chambers if you like. That's the least we can do for you.'

Paige, Jason, and Dr Barker were in the judge's chambers, alone.

Dr Barker said, 'Sorry they wouldn't let me come here to help you sooner. You know what goddam doctors are like.'

367

Paige was near tears. 'I can't tell you how much I . . .'

'Then don't!' he said gruffly.

Paige was studying him, suddenly remembering something. 'When did you speak to John Cronin?'

'*What?*'

'You heard me. When did you speak to John Cronin?'

'*When?*'

She said slowly, 'You never even *met* John Cronin. You didn't know him.'

There was the trace of a smile on Barker's lips. 'No. But I know you.'

Paige leaned over and threw her arms around him.

'Don't get sloppy,' he growled. He looked over at Jason. 'She gets sloppy sometimes. You'd better take good care of her, or you'll have to answer to me.'

Jason said, 'Don't worry, sir. I will.'

Paige and Jason were married the following day. Dr Barker was their best man.

EPILOGUE

Paige Curtis went into private practice and is affiliated with the prestigious North Shore Hospital. Paige used the million dollars John Cronin left her to set up a medical foundation in her father's name in Africa.

Lawrence Barker shares an office with Paige, as a surgical consultant.

Arthur Kane had his license revoked by the Medical Board of California.

Jimmy Ford fully recovered and married Betsy. They named their first daughter Paige.

Honey Taft moved to Ireland with Sean Reilly, and works as a nurse in Dublin.

Sean Reilly is a successful artist, and shows no symptoms of AIDS, as yet.

Mike Hunter was sentenced to state prison for armed robbery and is still serving time.

Alfred Turner joined a practice on Park Avenue and is enormously successful.

Benjamin Wallace was fired as administrator of Embarcadero County Hospital.

Lauren Harrison married her tennis pro.

Lou Dinetto was sentenced to fifteen years in the penitentiary for tax evasion.

Ken Mallory was sentenced to life imprisonment.

One week after Dinetto arrived at the penitentiary, Mallory was found stabbed to death in his cell.

The Embarcadero Hospital is still there, awaiting the next earthquake.

SIDNEY SHELDON

MORNING, NOON AND NIGHT

To Kimberly
with love

Allow the morning sun to warm
Your heart when you are young
And let the soft winds of noon
Cool your passion,
But beware the night
For death lurks there,
Waiting, waiting, waiting.

ARTHUR RIMBAUD

MORNING

Chapter One

Dmitri asked, 'Do you know we're being followed, Mr Stanford?'

'Yes.' He had been aware of them for the past twenty-four hours.

The two men and the woman were dressed casually, attempting to blend in with the summer tourists strolling along the cobbled streets in the early morning, but it was difficult to remain inconspicuous in a place as small as the fortified village of St-Paul-de-Vence.

Harry Stanford had first noticed them because they were *too* casual, trying *too* hard not to look at him. Wherever he turned, one of them was in the background.

Harry Stanford was an easy target to follow. He was six feet tall, with white hair lapping over his collar and an aristocratic, almost imperious face. He was accompanied by a strikingly lovely young brunette, a pure-white German shepherd, and Dmitri Kaminsky, a six-foot four-inch bodyguard with a bulging neck and sloping forehead. *Hard to lose us*, Stanford thought.

He knew who had sent them and why, and he was filled with a sense of imminent danger. He had learned long ago to trust his instincts. Instinct and intuition had helped make him one of the wealthiest men in the world. *Forbes* magazine estimated the value of Stanford Enterprises at six billion dollars, while the *Fortune* 500 appraised it at seven billion. The *Wall Street Journal*, *Barron's*, and the *Financial Times* had all done profiles on Harry Stanford, trying to explain his mystique, his amazing sense of timing, the ineffable acumen that had created the giant Stanford Enterprises. None had fully succeeded.

What they all agreed on was that he had an almost palpable, manic energy. He was inexhaustible. His philosophy was simple: A day without making a deal was a day wasted. He wore out his competitors, his staff, and everyone else who came in contact with him. He was a phenomenon, larger than life. He thought of himself as a religious man. He believed in God, and the God he believed in wanted him to be rich and successful, and his enemies dead.

Harry Stanford was a public figure, and the press knew everything about him. Harry Stanford was a private figure, and the press knew nothing about him. They had written about his charisma, his lavish life-style, his private plane and his yacht, and his legendary homes in Hobe Sound, Morocco, Long Island, London, the South of France, and of course his magnificent estate, Rose Hill, in the Back Bay area of Boston. But the real Harry Stanford remained an enigma.

'Where are we going?' the woman asked.

He was too preoccupied to answer. The couple on the other side of the street was using the cross-switch technique, and they had just changed partners again. Along with his sense of danger, Stanford felt a deep anger that they were invading his privacy. They had dared come to him in this place, his secret haven from the rest of the world.

St-Paul-de-Vence is a picturesque, medieval village, weaving its ancient magic on a hilltop in the Alps Maritimes, situated inland between Cannes and Nice. It is surrounded by a spectacular and enchanting landscape of hills and valleys covered with flowers, orchards, and pine forests. The village itself, a cornucopia of artists' studios, galleries and wonderful antique shops, is a magnet for tourists from all over the world.

Harry Stanford and his group turned onto the Rue Grande.

Stanford turned to the woman Sophia, 'Do you like museums?'

'Yes, *caro.*' She was eager to please him. She had never met anyone like Harry Stanford. *Wait until I tell my girlfriends about him. I didn't think there was anything left for me to learn about sex, but my God, he's so creative! He's wearing me out!*

They went up the hill to the Fondation Maeght art museum, and browsed through its renowned collection of paintings by Bonnard and Chagall and many other contemporary artists. When Harry

4

Stanford casually glanced around, he observed the woman at the other end of the gallery, earnestly studying a Miró.

Stanford turned to Sophia. 'Hungry?'

'Yes. If you are.' *Must not be pushy.*

'Good. We'll have lunch at La Colombe D'Or.'

La Colombe D'Or was one of Stanford's favorite restaurants, a sixteenth-century house at the entrance to the old village, converted into a hotel and restaurant. Stanford and Sophia sat at a table in the garden, by the pool, where Stanford could admire the Braque and Calder.

Prince, the white German shepherd, lay at his feet, ever watchful. The dog was Harry Stanford's trademark. Where Stanford went, Prince went. It was rumored that at Harry Stanford's command, the animal would tear out a person's throat. No one wanted to test that rumor.

Dmitri sat by himself at a table near the hotel entrance, carefully observing the other patrons as they came and went.

Stanford turned to Sophia. 'Shall I order for you, my dear?'

'Please.'

Harry Stanford prided himself on being a gourmet. He ordered a green salad and *fricasée de lotte* for both of them.

As they were being served their main course, Daniele Roux, who ran the hotel with her husband, François, approached the table and smiled. '*Bonjour.* Is everything all right, Monsieur Stanford?'

'Wonderful, Madame Roux.'

And it was going to be. *They are pygmies, trying to fell a giant. They're in for a big disappointment.*

Sophia said, 'I've never been here before. It's such a lovely village.'

Stanford turned his attention to her. Dmitri had picked her up for him in Nice a day earlier.

'Mr Stanford, I brought someone for you.'

'Any problem?' Stanford had asked.

Dmitri had grinned. 'None.' He had seen her in the lobby of the Hotel Negresco, and had approached her.

'Excuse me, do you speak English?'

'Yes.' She had a lilting Italian accent.

5

'The man I work for would like you to have dinner with him.'

She had been indignant. 'I'm not a *puttana*! I'm an actress,' she had said haughtily. In fact, she had had a walk-on part in Pupi Avati's last film, and a role with two lines of dialogue in a Giuseppe Tornatore film. 'Why would I have dinner with a stranger?'

Dmitri had taken out a wad of hundred-dollar bills. He pushed five into her hand. 'My friend is very generous. He has a yacht, and he is lonely.' He had watched her expression go through a series of changes from indignation, to curiosity, to interest.

'As it happens, I'm between pictures.' She smiled. 'It would probably do no harm to have dinner with your friend.'

'Good. He will be pleased.'

'Where is he?'

'St-Paul-de-Vence.'

Dmitri had chosen well. Italian. In her late twenties. A sensuous, catlike face. Full-breasted figure. Now, looking at her across the table, Harry Stanford made a decision.

'Do you like to travel, Sophia?'

'I adore it.'

'Good. We'll go on a little trip. Excuse me a moment.'

Sophia watched as he walked into the restaurant and to a public telephone outside the men's room.

Stanford put a *jeton* in the slot and dialed.

'Marine operator, please.'

Seconds later, a voice said, '*C'est l'opératrice maritime.*'

'I want to put in a call to the yacht *Blue Skies*. Whiskey bravo lima nine eight zero . . .'

The conversation lasted five minutes, and when Stanford was finished, he dialed the airport at Nice. The conversation was shorter this time.

When Stanford was through talking, he spoke to Dmitri, who rapidly left the restaurant. Then he returned to Sophia. 'Are you ready?'

'Yes.'

'Let's take a walk.' He needed time to work out a plan.

* * *

6

It was a perfect day. The sun had splashed pink clouds across the horizon and rivers of silver light ran through the streets.

They strolled along the Rue Grande, past the Église, the beautiful twelfth-century church, and stopped at the *boulangerie* in front of the Arch to buy some fresh baked bread. When they came out, one of the three watchers was standing outside, busily studying the church. Dmitri was also waiting for them.

Harry Stanford handed the bread to Sophia. 'Why don't you take this up to the house? I'll be along in a few minutes.'

'All right.' She smiled and said softly, 'Hurry, *caro*.'

Stanford watched her leave, then motioned to Dmitri.

'What did you find out?'

'The woman and one of the men are staying at Le Hameau, on the road to La Colle.'

Harry Stanford knew the place. It was a whitewashed farm-house with an orchard a mile west of St-Paul-de-Vence. 'And the other one?'

'At Le Mas d'Artigny.'

Le Mas d'Artigny was a Provençal mansion on a hillside two miles west of St-Paul-de-Vence.

'What do you want me to do with them, sir?'

'Nothing. I'll take care of them.'

Harry Stanford's villa was on the Rue de Casette, next to the *mairie*, in an area of narrow cobblestone streets and very old houses. The villa was a five-level house made of old stone and plaster. Two levels below the main house were a garage and an old *cave* used as a wine cellar. A stone staircase led to upstairs bedrooms, an office, and a tiled-roof terrace. The entire house was furnished in French antiques and filled with flowers.

When Stanford returned to the villa, Sophia was in his bedroom, waiting for him. She was naked.

'What took you so long?' she whispered.

In order to survive, Sophia Matteo often picked up money between film assignments as a call girl, and she was used to faking orgasms to please her clients, but with this man, there was no need to pretend. He was insatiable, and she found herself climaxing again and again.

When they were finally exhausted, Sophia put her arms around him and murmured happily, 'I could stay here forever, *caro*.'

I wish I could, Stanford thought, grimly.

They had dinner at Le Café de la Place in Plaza du General-de-Gaulle, near the entrance to the village. The dinner was delicious, and for Stanford the danger added spice to the meal.

When they were finished, they made their way back to the villa. Stanford walked slowly, to make certain his pursuers followed.

At one A.M., a man standing across the street watched the lights in the villa being turned off, one by one, until the building was in total darkness.

At four-thirty in the morning, Harry Stanford went into the guest bedroom where Sophia slept. He shook her gently. 'Sophia . . . ?'

She opened her eyes and looked up at him, a smile of anticipation on her face, then frowned. He was fully dressed. She sat up. 'Is something wrong?'

'No, my dear. Everything is fine. You said you liked to travel. Well, we're going to take a little trip.'

She was wide awake now. 'At this hour?'

'Yes. We must be very quiet.'

'But . . .'

'Hurry.'

Fifteen minutes later, Harry Stanford, Sophia, Dmitri, and Prince were moving down the stone staircase to the basement garage where a brown Renault was parked. Dmitri quietly opened the garage door and looked out onto the street. Except for Stanford's white Corniche, parked in front, it seemed deserted. 'All clear.'

Stanford turned to Sophia. 'We're going to play a little game. You and I are going to get in the back of the Renault and lie down on the floor.'

Her eyes widened. 'Why?'

'Some business competitors have been following me,' he said earnestly. 'I'm about to close a very large deal, and they're trying to find out about it. If they do, it could cost me a lot of money.'

'I understand,' Sophia said. She had no idea what he was talking about.

Five minutes later, they were driving past the gates of the village on the road to Nice. A man seated on a bench watched the brown Renault as it sped through the gates. At the wheel was Dmitri Kaminsky and beside him was Prince. The man hastily took out a cellular telephone and began dialing.

'We may have a problem,' he told the woman.

'What kind of problem?'

'A brown Renault just drove out of the gates. Dmitri Kaminsky was driving, and the dog was in the car, too.'

'And Stanford wasn't in the car?'

'No.'

'I don't believe it. His bodyguard never leaves him at night, and that dog never leaves him, ever.'

'Is his Corniche still parked in front of the villa?' asked the other man sent to follow Harry Stanford.

'Yes, but maybe he switched cars.'

'Or it could be a trick! Call the airport.'

Within minutes, they were talking to the tower.

'Monsieur Stanford's plane? *Oui*. It arrived an hour ago and has already refueled.'

Five minutes later, two members of the surveillance team were on their way to the airport, while the third kept watch on the sleeping villa.

As the brown Renault passed through La Coalle-sur-Loup, Stanford moved onto the seat. 'It's all right to sit up, now,' he told Sophia. He turned to Dmitri, 'Nice airport. Hurry.'

Chapter Two

Half an hour later, at the Nice airport, a converted Boeing 727 was slowly taxiing down the runway to the takeoff point. Up in the tower, the flight controller said, 'They certainly are in a hurry to get that plane off the ground. The pilot has asked for a clearance three times.'

'Whose plane is it?'

'Harry Stanford. King Midas himself.'

'He's probably on his way to make another billion or two.'

The controller turned to monitor a Learjet taking off, then picked up the microphone. 'Boeing eight nine five Papa, this is Nice departure control. You are cleared for takeoff. Five left. After departure, turn right to a heading of one four zero.'

Harry Stanford's pilot and copilot exchanged a relieved look. The pilot pressed the microphone button. 'Roger. Boeing eight nine five Papa is cleared for takeoff. Will turn right to one four zero.'

A moment later, the huge plane thundered down the runway and knifed into the gray dawn sky.

The copilot spoke into the microphone again. 'Departure, Boeing eight nine five Papa is climbing out of three thousand for flight level seven zero.'

The copilot turned to the pilot. 'Whew! Old Man Stanford was sure anxious for us to get off the ground, wasn't he?'

The pilot shrugged. 'Ours not to reason why, ours but to do and die. How's he doing back there?'

The copilot rose and stepped to the door of the cockpit, and looked into the cabin. 'He's resting.'

* * *

They telephoned the airport tower from the car.

'Mr Stanford's plane . . . Is it still on the ground?'

'*Non*, monsieur. It has departed.'

'Did the pilot file a flight plan?'

'Of course, monsieur.'

'To where?'

'The plane is headed for JKF.'

'Thank you.' He turned to his companion. 'Kennedy. We'll have people there to meet him.'

When the Renault passed the outskirts of Monte Carlo, speeding toward the Italian border, Harry Stanford said, 'There's no chance that we were followed, Dmitri?'

'No, sir. We've lost them.'

'Good.' Harry Stanford leaned back in his seat and relaxed. There was nothing to worry about. They would be tracking the plane. He reviewed the situation in his mind. It was really a question of what they knew and when they knew it. They were jackals following the trail of a lion, hoping to bring him down. Harry Stanford smiled to himself. They had underestimated the man they were dealing with. Others who had made that mistake had paid dearly for it. Someone would also pay this time. He was Harry Stanford, the confidant of presidents and kings, powerful and rich enough to make or break the economies of a dozen countries.

The 727 was in the skies over Marseilles. The pilot spoke into the microphone. 'Marseilles, Boeing eight nine five Papa is with you, climbing out of flight level one nine zero for flight level two three zero.'

'Roger.'

The Renault reached San Remo shortly after dawn. Harry Stanford had fond memories of the city, but it had changed drastically. He remembered a time when it had been an elegant town with first-class hotels and restaurants, and a casino where black tie was required and where fortunes could be lost or won in an

11

evening. Now it had succumbed to tourism, with loud-mouthed patrons gambling in their shirtsleeves.

The Renault was approaching the harbor, twelve miles from the French-Italian border. There were two marinas at the harbor, Marina Porto Sole to the east, and Porto Communale to the west. In Porto Sole, a marine attendant directed the berthing. In Porto Communale, there was no attendant.

'Which one?' Dmitri asked.

'Porto Communale,' Stanford directed. *The fewer people around, the better.*

'Yes, sir.'

A few minutes later, the Renault pulled up next to the *Blue Skies*, a sleek hundred-and-eighty-foot motor yacht. Captain Vacarro and the crew of twelve were lined up on deck. The captain hurried down the gangplank to greet the new arrivals.

'Good morning, Signor Stanford,' Captain Vacarro said. 'We'll take your luggage, and . . .'

'No luggage. Let's shove off.'

'Yes, sir.'

'Wait a minute.' Stanford was studying the crew. He frowned. 'The man on the end. He's new, isn't he?'

'Yes, sir. Our cabin boy got sick in Capri, and we took on this one. He's highly –'

'Get rid of him,' Stanford ordered.

The captain looked at him, puzzled. 'Get . . . ?'

'Pay him off. Let's get out of here.'

Captain Vacarro nodded. 'Right, sir.'

Looking around, Harry Stanford was filled with an increasing sense of foreboding. He could almost reach out and touch it. He did not want any strangers near him. Captain Vacarro and his crew had been with him for years. He could trust them. He turned to look at the girl. Since Dmitri had picked her up at random, there was no danger there. And as for Dmitri, his faithful bodyguard had saved his life more than once. Stanford turned to Dmitri. 'Stay close to me.'

'Yes, sir.'

Stanford took Sophia's arm. 'Let's go aboard, my dear.'

*   *   *

12

Dmitri Kaminsky stood on deck, watching the crew prepare to cast off. He scanned the harbor, but he saw nothing to be alarmed about. At this time of the morning, there was very little activity. The yacht's huge generators burst into life, and the vessel got under weigh.

The captain approached Harry Stanford. 'You didn't say where we were heading, Signor Stanford.'

'No, I didn't, did I, Captain?' He thought for a moment. 'Portofino.'

'Yes, sir.'

'By the way, I want you to maintain strict radio silence.'

Captain Vacarro frowned. 'Radio silence? Yes, sir, but what if . . . ?'

Harry Stanford said, 'Don't worry about it. Just do it. And I don't want anyone using the satellite phones.'

'Right, sir. Will we be laying over in Portofino?'

'I'll let you know, Captain.'

Harry Stanford took Sophia on a tour of the yacht. It was one of his prized possessions, and he enjoyed showing it off. It was a breathtaking vessel. It had a luxuriously appointed master suite with a sitting room and an office. The office was spacious and comfortably furnished with a couch, several easy chairs, and a desk, behind which was enough equipment to run a small town. On the wall was a large electronic map with a small moving boat showing the current position of the yacht. Sliding glass doors opened from the master suite onto an outside veranda deck furnished with a chaise longue and a table with four chairs. A teak railing ran along the outside. On balmy days, it was Stanford's custom to have breakfast on the veranda.

There were six guest staterooms, each with handpainted silk panels, picture windows, and a bath with a Jacuzzi. The large library was done in koa wood.

The dining room could seat sixteen guests. A fully equipped fitness salon was on the lower deck. The yacht also contained a wine cellar and a theater that was ideal for running films. Harry Stanford had one of the world's greatest libraries of pornographic movies. The furnishings throughout the vessel were exquisite, and the paintings would have made any museum proud.

'Well, now you've seen most of it,' Stanford told Sophia at the end of the tour. 'I'll show you the rest tomorrow.'

She was awed. 'I've never seen anything like it! It's . . . it's like a city!'

Harry Stanford smiled at her enthusiasm. 'The steward will show you to your cabin. Make yourself comfortable. I have some work to do.'

Harry Stanford returned to his office and checked the electronic map on the wall for the location of the yacht. *Blue Skies* was in the Ligurian Sea, heading northeast. *They won't know where I've gone*, Stanford thought. *They'll be waiting for me at JFK. When we get to Portofino, I'll straighten everything out.*

Thirty-five thousand feet in the air, the pilot of the 727 was getting new instructions. 'Boeing eight nine five Papa, you are cleared directly to Delta India November upper route forty as filed.'

'Roger. Boeing eight nine five Papa is cleared direct Dinard upper route forty as filed.' He turned to the copilot. 'All clear.'

The pilot stretched, got up, and walked to the cockpit door. He looked into the cabin.

'How's our passenger doing?' the copilot asked.

'He looks hungry to me.'

Chapter Three

The Ligurian coast is the Italian Riviera, sweeping in a semicircle from the French-Italian border around to Genoa, and then continuing down to the Gulf of La Spezia. The beautiful long ribbon of coast and its sparkling waters contain the storied ports of Portofino, Vernazza, and beyond them Elba, Sardinia, and Corsica.

Blue Skies was approaching Portofino, which even from a distance was an impressive sight, its hillsides covered with olive trees, pines, cypresses and palms. Harry Stanford, Sophia, and Dmitri were on deck, studying the approaching coastline.

'Have you been to Portofino often?' Sophia asked.

'A few times.'

'Where is your main home?'

Too personal. 'You'll enjoy Portofino, Sophia. It's really quite beautiful.'

Captain Vacarro approached them. 'Will you be having lunch aboard, Signor Stanford?'

'No, we'll have lunch at the Splendido.'

'Very good. And shall I be prepared to weigh anchor right after lunch?'

'I think not. Let's enjoy the beauty of the place.'

Captain Vacarro studied him, puzzled. One moment Harry Stanford was in a terrible hurry, and the next moment he seemed to have all the time in the world. And the radio shut down? Unheard of! *Pazzo.*

When *Blue Skies* dropped anchor in the outer harbor, Stanford, Sophia and Dmitri took the yacht's launch ashore. The small seaport was charming, with a variety of amusing shops and outdoor *trattorie* lining the single road that led up to the hills. A dozen or so small fishing boats were pulled up onto the pebbled beach.

Stanford turned to Sophia. 'We'll be lunching at the hotel on top of the hill. There's a lovely view from there.' He nodded toward a taxi stopped beyond the docks. 'Take a taxi up there, and I'll meet you in a few minutes.' He handed her some *lire*.

'Very well, *caro*.'

His eyes followed her as she walked away; then he turned to Dmitri. 'I have to make a call.'

But not from the ship, Dmitri thought.

The men went to the two phone booths at the side of the dock. Dmitri watched as Stanford stepped inside one of them, picked up the receiver, and inserted a token.

'Operator, I would like to place a call to someone at the Union Bank of Switzerland in Geneva.'

A woman was approaching the second phone booth. Dmitri stepped in front of it, blocking her way.

'Excuse me,' she said. 'I . . .'

'I'm waiting for a call.'

She looked at him in surprise. 'Oh.' She glanced hopefully at the phone booth Stanford was in.

'I wouldn't wait,' Dmitri grunted. 'He's going to be on the telephone for a long time.'

The woman shrugged and walked away.

'Hello?'

Dmitri was watching Stanford speaking into the mouthpiece.

'Peter? We have a little problem.' Stanford closed the door to the booth. He was speaking very fast, and Dmitri could not hear what he was saying. At the end of the conversation, Stanford replaced the receiver and opened the door.

'Is everything all right, Mr Stanford?' Dmitri asked.

'Let's get some lunch.'

The Splendido is the crown jewel of Portofino, a hotel with a magnificent panoramic view of the emerald bay below. The hotel

16

caters to the very rich, and jealously guards its reputation. Harry Stanford and Sophia had lunch out on the terrace.

'Shall I order for you?' Stanford asked. 'They have some specialties here that I think you might enjoy.'

'Please,' Sophia said.

Stanford ordered the *trenette al pesto*, the local pasta, veal, and *focaccia*, the salted bread of the region.

'And bring us a bottle of Schram Eighty-eight.' He turned to Sophia. 'It received a gold medal in the International Wine Challenge in London. I own the vineyard.'

She smiled. 'You're lucky.'

Luck had nothing to do with it. 'I believe that man was meant to enjoy the gustatory delights that have been put on the earth.' He took her hand in his. 'And other delights, too.'

'You're an amazing man.'

'Thank you.'

It excited Stanford to have beautiful women admiring him. This one was young enough to be his daughter and that excited him even more.

When they had finished lunch, Stanford looked at Sophia and grinned. 'Let's get back to the yacht.'

'Oh, yes!'

Harry Stanford was a protean lover, passionate and skilled. His enormous ego made him more concerned about satisfying a woman than about satisfying himself. He knew how to excite a woman's erotic zones, and he orchestrated his lovemaking in a sensuous symphony that brought his lovers to heights they had never achieved before.

They spent the afternoon in Stanford's suite, and when they were finished making love, Sophia was exhausted. Harry Stanford dressed and went to the bridge to see Captain Vacarro.

'Would you like to go on to Sardinia, Signor Stanford?' the captain asked.

'Let's stop off at Elba first.'

'Very good, sir. Is everything satisfactory?'

17

'Yes,' Stanford said. 'Everything is satisfactory.' He was feeling aroused again. He went back to Sophia's stateroom.

They reached Elba the following afternoon and anchored at Portoferraio.

As the Boeing 727 entered North American airspace, the pilot checked in with ground control.

'New York Center, Boeing eight nine five Papa is with you, passing flight level two six zero for flight level two four zero.'

The voice of New York Center came on. 'Roger, you are cleared to one two thousand, direct JFK. Call approach on one two seven point four.'

From the back of the plane came a low growl.

'Easy, Prince. That's a good boy. Let's get this seat belt around you.'

There were four men waiting when the 727 landed. They stood at different vantage points so they could watch the passengers descend from the plane. They waited for half an hour. The only passenger to come out was a white German shepherd.

Portoferraio is the main shopping center of Elba. The streets are lined with elegant, sophisticated shops, and behind the harbor, the eighteenth-century buildings are tucked under the craggy sixteenth-century citadel built by the Duke of Florence.

Harry Stanford had visited the island many times, and in a strange way, he felt at home here. This was where Napoleon Bonaparte had been sent into exile.

'We're going to look at Napoleon's house,' he told Sophia. 'I'll meet you there.' He turned to Dmitri. 'Take her to the Villa dei Mulini.'

'Yes, sir.'

Stanford watched Dmitri and Sophia leave. He looked at his watch. Time was running out. His plane would already have landed at Kennedy. When they learned that he was not aboard, the manhunt would begin again. *It will take them a while to pick*

18

up the trail, Stanford thought. *By then, everything will have been settled.*

He stepped into a phone booth at the end of the dock. 'I want to place a call to London,' Stanford told the operator. 'Barclays Bank. One seven one . . .'

Half an hour later, he picked up Sophia and brought her back to the harbor.

'You go aboard,' Stanford told her. 'I have another call to make.'

She watched him stride over to the telephone booth beside the dock. *Why doesn't he use the telephones on the yacht?* Sophia wondered.

Inside the telephone booth, Harry Stanford was saying, 'The Sumitomo Bank in Tokyo . . .'

Fifteen minutes later, when he returned to the yacht, he was in a fury.

'Are we going to be anchoring here for the night?' Captain Vacarro asked.

'Yes,' Stanford snapped. 'No! Let's head for Sardinia. Now!'

The Costa Smeralda in Sardinia is one of the most exquisite places along the Mediterranean coast. The little town of Porto Cervo is a haven for the wealthy, with a large part of the area dotted with villas built by Aly Khan.

The first thing Harry Stanford did when they docked was to head for a telephone booth.

Dmitri followed him, standing guard outside the booth.

'I want to place a call to Banca d'Italia in Rome . . .' The phone booth door closed.

The conversation lasted for almost half an hour. When Stanford came out of the phone booth, he was grim. Dmitri wondered what was going on.

Stanford and Sophia had lunch at the beach of Liscia di Vacca. Stanford ordered for them. 'We'll start with *malloreddus*.' Flakes of dough made of hard-grain wheat. 'Then the *porceddu*.' Little

19

suckling pig, cooked with myrtle and bay leaves. 'For a wine, we'll have the Vernaccia, and for dessert, we'll have *sebadas*.' Fried fritters filled with fresh cheese and grated lemon rind, dusted with bitter honey and sugar.

'*Bene, signor*.' The waiter walked away, impressed.

As Stanford turned to talk to Sophia, his heart suddenly skipped a beat. Near the entrance to the restaurant two men were seated at a table, studying him. Dressed in dark suits in the summer sun, they were not even bothering to pretend they were tourists. *Are they after me or are they innocent strangers? I mustn't let my imagination run away with me*, Stanford thought.

Sophia was speaking. 'I've never asked you before. What business are you in?'

Stanford studied her. It was refreshing to be with someone who knew nothing about him. 'I'm retired,' he told her. 'I just travel around, enjoying the world.'

'And you're all by yourself?' Her voice was filled with sympathy. 'You must be very lonely.'

It was all he could do not to laugh aloud. 'Yes, I am. I'm glad you're here with me.'

She put her hand over his. 'I, too, *caro*.'

Out of the corner of his eye, Stanford saw the two men leave.

When luncheon was over, Stanford and Sophia and Dmitri returned to town.

Stanford headed for a telephone booth. 'I want the Crédit Lyonnais in Paris . . .'

Watching him, Sophia spoke to Dmitri. 'He's a wonderful man, isn't he?'

'There's no one like him.'

'Have you been with him long?'

'Two years,' Dmitri said.

'You're lucky.'

'I know.' Dmitri walked over and stood guard right outside the telephone booth. He heard Stanford saying, 'René? You know why I'm calling . . . Yes . . . Yes . . . You will? . . . That's wonderful!' His voice was filled with relief. 'No . . . not there.

20

Let's meet in Corsica. That's perfect. After our meeting, I can return directly home. Thank you, René.'

Stanford put down the receiver. He stood there a moment, smiling, then dialed a number in Boston.

A secretary answered. 'Mr Fitzgerald's office.'

'This is Harry Stanford. Let me talk to him.'

'Oh, Mr Stanford! I'm sorry, Mr Fitzgerald is on vacation. Can someone else . . . ?'

'No. I'm on my way back to the States. You tell him I want him in Boston at Rose Hill at nine o'clock Monday morning. Tell him to bring a copy of my will and a notary.'

'I'll try to –'

'Don't try. Do it, my dear.' He put down the receiver and stood there, his mind racing. When he stepped out of the telephone booth, his voice was calm. 'I have a little business to take care of, Sophia. Go to the Hotel Pitrizza and wait for me.'

'All right,' she said flirtatiously. 'Don't be too long.'

'I won't.'

The two men watched her walk away.

'Let's get back to the yacht,' Stanford told Dmitri. 'We're leaving.'

Dmitri looked at him in surprise. 'What about . . . ?'

'She can screw her way back home.'

When they returned to the *Blue Skies*, Harry Stanford went to see Captain Vacarro. 'We're heading for Corsica,' he said. 'Let's shove off.'

'I just received an updated weather report, Signor Stanford. I'm afraid there's a bad storm. It would be better if we waited it out and –'

'I want to leave now, captain.'

Captain Vacarro hesitated. 'It will be a rough voyage, sir. It's a *libeccio* – the southwest wind. We'll have heavy seas and squalls.'

'I don't care about that.' The meeting in Corsica was going to solve all his problems. He turned to Dmitri. 'I want you to arrange for a helicopter to pick us up in Corsica and take us to Naples. Use the public telephone on the dock.'

'Yes, sir.'

Dmitri Kaminsky walked back to the dock and entered the telephone booth.

Twenty minutes later, *Blue Skies* was under weigh.

Chapter Four

His idol was Dan Quayle, and he often used the name as his touchstone.

'I don't care what you say about Quayle, he's the only politician with real values. Family – that's what it's all about. Without family values, this country would be up the creek even worse than it is. All these young kids are living together without being married, and having babies. It's shocking. No wonder there's so much crime. If Dan Quayle ever runs for president, he's sure got my vote.' It was a shame, he thought, that he couldn't vote because of a stupid law, but, regardless, he was behind Quayle all the way.

He had four children: Billy, eight, and the girls – Amy, Clarissa, and Susan, ten, twelve, and fourteen. They were wonderful children, and his greatest joy was spending what he liked to call quality time with them. His weekends were totally devoted to the children. He barbecued for them, played with them, took them to movies and ball games, and helped them with their homework. All the youngsters in the neighborhood adored him. He repaired their bikes and toys, and invited them on picnics with his family. They gave him the nickname of Papa.

On a sunny Saturday morning, he was seated in the bleachers, watching the baseball game. It was a picture-perfect day, with warm sunshine and fluffy cumulus clouds dappling the sky. His eight-year-old son, Billy, was at bat, looking very professional and grown up in his Little League uniform. Papa's three girls and his wife were at his side. *It doesn't get any better than this*, he thought happily. *Why can't all families be like ours?*

It was the bottom of the eighth inning, the score was tied, with two outs and the bases loaded. Billy was at the plate, three balls and two strikes against him.

Papa called out, encouragingly, 'Get 'em, Billy! Over the fence!'

Billy waited for the pitch. It was fast and low, and Billy swung wildly and missed.

The umpire yelled, 'Strike three!'

The inning was over.

There were groans and cheers from the crowd of parents and family friends. Billy stood there disheartened, watching the teams change sides.

Papa called out, 'It's all right, son. You'll do it next time!'

Billy tried to force a smile.

John Cotton, the team manager, was waiting for Billy. 'You're outta the game!' he said.

'But, Mr Cotton . . .'

'Go on. Get off the field.'

Billy's father watched in hurt amazement as his son left the field. *He can't do that*, he thought. *He has to give Billy another chance. I'll have to speak to Mr Cotton and explain.* At that instant, the cellular phone he carried rang. He let it ring four times before he answered it. Only one person had the number. *He knows I hate to be disturbed on weekends*, he thought angrily.

Reluctantly, he lifted the antenna, pressed a button, and spoke into the mouthpiece. 'Hello?'

The voice at the other end spoke quietly for several minutes. Papa listened, nodding from time to time Finally he said, 'Yes. I understand. I'll take care of it.' He put the phone away.

'Is everything all right, darling?' his wife asked.

'No. I'm afraid it isn't. They want me to work over the week-end. I was planning a nice barbecue for us tomorrow.'

His wife took his hand and said lovingly, 'Don't worry about it. Your work is more important.'

Not as important as my family, he thought stubbornly. *Dan Quayle would understand.*

His hand began to itch fiercely and he scratched it. *Why does it do that?* he wondered. *I'll have to see a dermatologist one of these days.*

John Cotton was the assistant manager at the local supermarket. A burly man in his fifties, he had agreed to manage the Little League team because his son was a ballplayer. His team had lost that afternoon because of young Billy.

The supermarket had closed, and John Cotton was in the parking lot, walking toward his car, when a stranger approached him, carrying a package.

'Excuse me, Mr Cotton.'

'Yes?'

'I wonder if I could talk to you for a moment?'

'The store is closed.'

'Oh, it's not that. I wanted to talk to you about my son. Billy is very upset that you took him out of the game and told him he couldn't play again.'

'Billy is your son? I'm sorry he was even *in* the game. He'll never be a ballplayer.'

Billy's father said earnestly, 'You're not being fair, Mr Cotton. I know Billy. He's really a fine ballplayer. You'll see. When he plays next Saturday –'

'He isn't *going* to play next Saturday. He's out.'

'But . . .'

'No buts. That's it. Now, if there's nothing else . . .'

'Oh, there is.' Billy's father had unwrapped the package in his hand, revealing a baseball bat. He said pleadingly, 'This is the bat that Billy used. You can see that it's chipped, so it isn't fair to punish him because –'

'Look, mister, I don't give a damn about the bat. Your son is out!'

Billy's father sighed unhappily. 'You're sure you won't change your mind?'

'No chance.'

As Cotton reached for the door handle of his car, Billy's father swung the bat against the rear window, smashing it.

25

Cotton stared at him in shock. 'What . . . what the hell are you doing?'

'Warming up,' Papa explained. He raised the bat and swung it again, smashing it against Cotton's kneecap.

John Cotton screamed and fell to the ground, writhing in pain. 'You're crazy!' he yelled. 'Help!'

Billy's father knelt beside him and said softly, 'Make one more sound, and I'll break your other kneecap.'

Cotton stared up at him in agony, terrified.

'If my son isn't in the game next Saturday, I'll kill you and I'll kill your son. Do I make myself clear?'

Cotton looked into the man's eyes and nodded, fighting to keep from screaming with pain.

'Good. Oh, and I wouldn't want this to get out. I've got friends.' He looked at his watch. He had just enough time to catch the next flight to Boston.

His hand began to itch again.

At seven o'clock Sunday morning, dressed in a vested suit and carrying an expensive leather briefcase, he walked past Vendome, through Copley Square, and on to Stuart Street. A half block past the Park Plaza Castle, he entered the Boston Trust Building and approached the guard. With dozens of tenants in the huge building, there would be no way the guard at the reception desk could identify him.

'Good morning,' the man said.

'Good morning, sir. May I help you?'

He sighed. 'Even God can't help me. They think I have nothing to do but spend my Sundays doing the work that someone else should have done.'

The guard said, sympathetically, 'I know the feeling.' He pushed a log book forward. 'Would you sign in, please?'

He signed in and walked over to the bank of elevators. The office he was looking for was on the fifth floor. He took the elevator to the sixth floor, walked down a flight, and moved down the corridor. The legend on the door read, RENQUIST, RENQUIST & FITZGERALD, ATTORNEYS AT LAW. He looked around to make certain the corridor was deserted, then opened his briefcase and took out a small pick and a tension tool. It took him five seconds to open the locked door. He stepped inside and closed the door behind him.

The reception room was furnished in old-fashioned, conservative taste, as befitted one of Boston's top law firms. The man stood there a moment, orienting himself, then moved toward the back, to a filing room where records were kept. Inside the room was a bank of steel cabinets with alphabetical labels on the front. He tried the cabinet marked *R-S*. It was locked.

From his briefcase, he removed a blank key, a file, and a pair of pliers. He pushed the blank key inside the small cabinet lock, gently turning it from side to side. After a moment, he withdrew it and examined the black markings on it. Holding the key with the pair of pliers, he carefully filed off the black spots. He put the key into the lock again, and repeated the procedure. He was humming quietly to himself as he picked the lock, and he smiled as he suddenly realized what he was humming: 'Far Away Places'. I'll take my family on vacation, he thought happily. *A real vacation. I'll bet the kids would love Hawaii.*

The cabinet drawer came open, and he pulled it toward him. It took only a moment to find the folder he wanted. He removed a small Pentax camera from his briefcase and went to work. Ten minutes later he was finished. He took several pieces of Kleenex from the briefcase, walked over to the water cooler, and wet them. He returned to the filing room and wiped up the steel shavings on the floor. He locked the file cabinet, made his way out to the corridor, locked the front door to the offices, and left the building.

Chapter Five

At sea, later that evening, Captain Vacarro came to Harry Stanford's stateroom.

'Signor Stanford . . .'

'Yes?'

The captain pointed to the electronic map on the wall. 'I'm afraid the winds are getting worse. The *libeccio* is centered in the Strait of Bonifacio. I would suggest that we take shelter in a harbor until –'

Stanford cut him short. 'This is a good ship, and you're a good captain. I'm sure you can handle it.'

Captain Vacarro hesitated. 'As you say, signor. I will do my best.'

'I'm sure you will, captain.'

Harry Stanford sat in the office of his suite, planning his strategy. He would meet René in Corsica and get everything straightened out. After that, the helicopter would fly him to Naples, and from there he would charter a plane to take him to Boston. *Everything is going to be fine*, he decided. *All I need is forty-eight hours. Just forty-eight hours.*

He was awakened at 2 A.M. by the wild pitching of the yacht and a howling gale outside. Stanford had been in storms before, but this was one of the worst. Captain Vacarro had been right. Harry Stanford got out of bed, holding on to the nightstand to steady himself, and made his way to the wall map. The ship was in the Strait of Bonifacio. *We should be in Ajaccio in the next few hours*, he thought. *Once we're there, we'll be safe.*

*   *   *

The events that occurred later that night were a matter of speculation. The papers strewn around the veranda suggested that the strong wind had blown some of the others away, and that Harry Stanford had tried to retrieve them, but because of the pitching yacht he had lost his balance and fallen overboard. Dmitri Kaminsky saw him fall into the water and immediately grabbed the intercom.

'Man overboard!'

Chapter Six

Capitaine François Durer, *chef de police* in Corsica, was in a foul mood. The island was overcrowded with stupid summer tourists who were incapable of holding onto their passports, their wallets, or their children. Complaints had come streaming in all day long to the tiny police headquarters at 2 Cours Napoléon off Rue Sergent Casalonga.

'A man snatched my purse.'

'My ship sailed without me. My wife is on board.'

'I bought this watch from someone on the street. It has nothing inside.'

'The drugstores here don't carry the pills I need.'

The problems were endless, endless, endless.

And now it seemed that the capitaine had a body on his hands.

'I have no time for this now,' he snapped.

'But they're waiting outside,' his assistant informed him. 'What shall I tell them?'

Capitaine Durer was impatient to get to his mistress. His impulse was to say, 'Take the body to some other island,' but he was, after all, the chief police official on the island.

'Very well.' He sighed. 'I'll see them briefly.'

A moment later, Captain Vacarro and Dmitri Kaminsky were ushered into the office.

'Sit down,' Capitaine Durer said, ungraciously.

The two men took chairs.

'Tell me, please, exactly what occurred.'

Captain Vacarro said, 'I'm not sure exactly. I didn't see it happen.' He turned to Dmitri Kaminsky. 'He was an eyewitness. Perhaps he should explain it.'

30

Dmitri took a deep breath. 'It was terrible. I work . . . worked for the man.'

'Doing what, monsieur?'

'Bodyguard, masseur, chauffeur. Our yacht was caught in the storm last night. It was very bad. He asked me to give him a massage to relax him. Afterward, he asked me to get him a sleeping pill. They were in the bathroom. When I returned, he was standing out on the veranda, at the railing. The storm was tossing the yacht around. He had been holding some papers in his hand. One of them flew away, and he reached out to grab for it, lost his balance, and fell over the side. I raced to save him, but there was nothing I could do. I called for help. Captain Vacarro immediately stopped the yacht, and through the captain's heroic efforts, we found him. But it was too late. He had drowned.'

'I am very sorry.' He could not have cared less.

Captain Vacarro spoke up. 'The wind and the sea carried the body back to the yacht. It was pure luck, but now we would like permission to take the body home.'

'That should be no problem.' He would still have time to have a drink with his mistress before he went home to his wife. 'I will have a death certificate and an exit visa for the body prepared at once.' He picked up a yellow pad. 'The name of the victim?'

'Harry Stanford.'

Capitaine Durer was suddenly very still. He looked up. 'Harry Stanford?'

'Yes.'

'*The* Harry Stanford?'

'Yes.'

And Capitaine Durer's future suddenly became much brighter. The gods had dropped manna in his lap. Harry Stanford was an international legend! The news of his death would reverberate around the world, and he, Capitaine Durer, was in control of the situation. The immediate question was how to manipulate it for the maximum benefit to himself. Durer sat there, staring into space, thinking.

'How soon can you release the body?' Captain Vacarro asked.

He looked up. 'Ah. That's a good question.' *How much time*

31

will it take for the press to arrive? Should I ask the yacht's captain to participate in the interview? No. Why share the glory with him? I will handle this alone. 'There is much to be done,' he said regretfully. 'Papers to prepare . . .' He sighed. 'It could well be a week or more.'

Captain Vacarro was appalled. 'A week or more? But you said –'

'There are certain formalities to be observed,' Durer said sternly. 'These matters can't be rushed.' He picked up the yellow pad again. 'Who is the next of kin?'

Captain Vacarro looked at Dmitri for help.

'I guess you'd better check with his attorneys in Boston.'

'The names?'

'Renquist, Renquist and Fitzgerald.'

Chapter Seven

Although the legend on the door read RENQUIST, RENQUIST & FITZGERALD, the two Renquists had been long deceased. Simon Fitzgerald was still very much alive, and at seventy-six, he was the dynamo that powered the office, with sixty attorneys working under him. He was perilously thin, with a full mane of white hair, and he walked with the sternly straight carriage of a military man. At the moment, he was pacing back and forth, his mind in a turmoil.

He stopped in front of his secretary. 'When Mr Stanford telephoned, didn't he give any indication of what he wanted to see me about so urgently?'

'No, sir. He just said he wanted you to be at his house at nine o'clock Monday morning, and to bring his will and a notary.'

'Thank you. Ask Mr Sloane to come in.'

Steve Sloane was one of the bright, innovative attorneys in the office. A Harvard Law School graduate in his forties, he was tall and lean, with blond hair, amusedly inquisitive blue eyes, and an easy, graceful presence. He was the troubleshooter for the firm, and Simon Fitzgerald's choice to take over one day. *If I had had a son*, Fitzgerald thought, *I would have wanted him to be like Steve*. He watched as Steve Sloane walked in.

'You're supposed to be salmon fishing up in Newfoundland,' Steve said.

'Something came up. Sit down, Steve. We have a problem.'

Steve sighed. 'What else is new?'

'It's about Harry Stanford.'

Harry Stanford was one of their most prestigious clients. Half

33

a dozen other law firms handled various Stanford Enterprises subsidiaries, but Renquist, Renquist & Fitzgerald handled his personal affairs. Except for Fitzgerald, none of the members of the firm had ever met him, but he was a legend around the office.

'What's Stanford done now?' Steve asked.

'He's gotten himself dead.'

Steve looked at him, shocked. 'He's *what*?'

'I just received a fax from the French police in Corsica. Apparently Stanford fell off his yacht and drowned yesterday.'

'My God!'

'I know you've never met him, but I've represented him for more than thirty years. He was a difficult man.' Fitzgerald leaned back in his chair, thinking about the past. 'There were really two Harry Stanfords – the public one who could coax the birds off the money tree, and the sonofabitch who took pleasure in destroying people. He was a charmer, but he could turn on you like a cobra. He had a split personality – he was both the snake charmer and the snake.'

'Sounds fascinating.'

'It was about thirty years ago – thirty-one, to be exact – when I joined this law firm. Old Man Renquist handled Stanford then. You know how people use the phrase "larger than life"? Well, Harry Stanford was really larger than life. If he didn't exist, you couldn't have invented him. He was a colossus. He had an amazing energy and ambition. He was a great athlete. He boxed in college and was a ten-goal polo player. But even when he was young, Harry Stanford was impossible. He was the only man I've ever known who was totally without compassion. He was sadistic and vindictive, and he had the instincts of a vulture. He loved forcing his competitors into bankruptcy. It was rumored that there was more than one suicide because of him.'

'He sounds like a monster.'

'On the one hand, yes. On the other hand, he founded an orphanage in New Guinea and a hospital in Bombay, and he gave millions to charity – anonymously. No one ever knew what to expect next.'

'How did he become so wealthy?'

'How's your Greek mythology?'

'I'm a little rusty.'

'You know the story of Oedipus?'

Steve nodded. 'He killed his father to get his mother.'

'Right. Well, that was Harry Stanford. Only he killed his father to get his mother's *vote*.'

Steve was staring at him. 'What?'

Fitzgerald leaned forward. 'In the early thirties, Harry's father had a grocery store here in Boston. It did so well that he opened a second one, and pretty soon he had a small chain of grocery stores. When Harry finished college, his father brought him into the business as a partner and put him on the board of directors. As I said, Harry was ambitious. He had big dreams. Instead of buying meat from packing houses, he wanted the chain to raise its own livestock. He wanted it to buy land and grow its own vegetables, can its own goods. His father disagreed, and they fought a lot.

'Then Harry had his biggest brainstorm of all. He told his father he wanted the company to build a chain of supermarkets that sold everything from automobiles to furniture to life insurance, at a discount, and charge customers a membership fee. Harry's father thought he was crazy, and he turned down the idea. But Harry didn't intend to let anything get in his way. He decided he had to get rid of the old man. He persuaded his father to take a long vacation, and while he was away, Harry went to work charming the board of directors.

'He was a brilliant salesman and he sold them on his concept. He persuaded his aunt and uncle, who were on the board, to vote for him. He romanced the other members of the board. He took them to lunch, went fox hunting with one, golfing with another. He slept with a board member's wife who had influence over her husband. But it was his mother who held the largest block of stock and had the final vote. Harry persuaded her to give it to him and to vote against her husband.'

'That's unbelievable!'

'When Harry's father returned, he learned that his family had voted him out of the company.'

'My God!'

'There's more. Harry wasn't satisfied with that. When his father tried to get into his own office, he found that he was barred from the building. And, remember, Harry was only in his thirties then. His nickname around the company was the Iceman. But credit where credit is due, Steve. He single-handedly built Stanford Enterprises into one of the biggest privately held conglomerates in the world. He expanded the company to include timber, chemicals, communications, electronics, and a staggering amount of real estate. And he wound up with all the stock.'

'He must have been an incredible man,' Steve said.

'He was. To men – and to women.'

'Was he married?'

Simon Fitzgerald sat there for a long time, remembering. When he finally spoke he said, 'Harry Stanford was married to one of the most beautiful women I've ever seen. Emily Temple. They had three children, two boys and a girl. Emily came from a very social family in Hobe Sound, Florida. She adored Harry, and she tried to close her eyes to his cheating, but one day it got to be too much for her. She had a governess for the children, a woman named Rosemary Nelson. Young and attractive. What made her even more attractive to Harry Stanford was the fact that she refused to go to bed with him. It drove him crazy. He wasn't used to rejection. Well, when Harry Stanford turned on the charm, he was irresistible. He finally got Rosemary into bed. He got her pregnant, and she went to see a doctor. Unfortunately, the doctor's son-in-law was a columnist, and he got hold of the story and printed it. There was one hell of a scandal. You know Boston. It was all over the newspapers. I still have clippings about it somewhere.'

'Did she get an abortion?'

Fitzgerald shook his head. 'No. Harry wanted her to have one, but she refused. They had a terrible scene. He told her he loved her and wanted to marry her. Of course, he had told that to dozens of women. But Emily overheard their conversation, and in the middle of that same night she committed suicide.'

'That's awful. What happened to the governess?'

'Rosemary Nelson disappeared. We know that she had a

36

daughter she named Julia, at St Joseph's Hospital in Milwaukee. She sent a note to Stanford, but I don't believe he even bothered to reply. By then, he was involved with someone new. He wasn't interested in Rosemary anymore.'

'Charming . . .'

'The real tragedy is what happened later. The children rightfully blamed their father for their mother's suicide. They were ten, twelve, and fourteen at the time. Old enough to feel the pain, but too young to fight their father. They hated him. And Harry's greatest fear was that one day they would do to him what he had done to his own father. So he did everything he could to make sure that never happened. He sent them away to different boarding schools and summer camps, and arranged for his children to see as little of one another as possible. They received no money from him. They lived on the small trust that their mother had left them. All their lives he used the carrot-and-stick approach with them. He held out his fortune as the carrot, then withdrew it if they displeased him.'

'What's happened to the children?'

'Tyler is a judge in the circuit court in Chicago. Woodrow doesn't do anything. He's a playboy. He lives in Hobe Sound and gambles on golf and polo. A few years ago, he picked up a waitress in a diner, got her pregnant, and to everyone's surprise, married her. Kendall is a successful fashion designer, married to a Frenchman. They live in New York.' He stood up. 'Steve, have you ever been to Corsica?'

'No.'

'I'd like you to fly there. They're holding Harry Stanford's body, and the police refuse to release it. I want you to straighten out the matter.'

'All right.'

'If there's a chance of your leaving today . . .'

'Right. I'll work it out.'

'Thanks. I appreciate it.'

On the Air France commuter flight from Paris to Corsica, Steve Sloane read a travel book about Corsica. He learned that the

37

island was largely mountainous, that its principal port city was Ajaccio, and that it was the birthplace of Napoleon Bonaparte. The book was filled with interesting statistics, but Steve was totally unprepared for the beauty of the island. As the plane approached Corsica, far below he saw a high solid wall of white rock that resembled the White Cliffs of Dover. It was breathtaking.

The plane landed at Ajaccio airport and a taxi took Steve down the Cours Napoléon, the main street that stretched from Place General de Gaulle northward to the train station. He had made arrangements for a plane to stand by to fly Harry Stanford's body back to Paris, where the coffin would be transferred to a plane to Boston. All he needed was to get a release for the body.

Steve had the taxi drop him off at the Préfecture building on Cours Napoléon. He went up one flight of stairs and walked into the reception office. A uniformed sergeant was seated at the desk.

'*Bonjour. Puis-je vous aider?*'

'Who is in charge here?'

'Capitaine Durer.'

'I would like to see him, please.'

'And what is it of concern in relationship to?' The sergeant was proud of his English.

Steve took out his business card. 'I'm the attorney for Harry Stanford. I've come to take his body back to the States.'

The sergeant frowned. 'Remain, please.' He disappeared into Capitaine Durer's office, carefully closing the door behind him. The office was crowded, filled with reporters from television and news services from all over the globe. Everyone seemed to be speaking at the same time.

'Capitaine, why was he out in a storm when . . . ?'

'How could he fall off a yacht in the middle of . . . ?'

'Was there any sign of foul play?'

'Have you done an autopsy?'

'Who else was on the ship with . . . ?'

'Please, gentlemen.' Capitaine Durer held up his hand. 'Please, gentlemen. Please.' He looked around the room at all the reporters hanging on his every word, and he was ecstatic. He had dreamed of moments like this. *If I handle this properly, it will mean a big promotion and –*

The sergeant interrupted his thoughts. 'Capitaine . . .' He whispered in Durer's ear and handed him Steve Sloane's card.

Capitaine Durer studied it and frowned. 'I can't see him now,' he snapped. 'Tell him to come back tomorrow at ten o'clock.'

'Yes, sir.'

Capitaine Durer watched thoughtfully as the sergeant left the room. He had no intention of letting anyone take away his moment of glory. He turned back to the reporters and smiled. 'Now, what were you asking . . . ?'

In the outer office, the sergeant was saying to Sloane, 'I am sorry, but Capitaine Durer is very busy immediately. He would like you to expose yourself here tomorrow morning at ten o'clock.'

Steve Sloane looked at him in dismay. 'Tomorrow morning? That's ridiculous – I don't want to wait that long.'

The sergeant shrugged. 'That is of your chosen, monsieur.'

Steve frowned. 'Very well. I don't have a hotel reservation. Can you recommend a hotel?'

'*Mais oui.* I am pleased to have recommended the Colomba, eight Avenue de Paris.'

Steve hesitated. 'Isn't there some way . . . ?'

'Ten o'clock tomorrow morning.'

Steve turned and walked out of the office.

In Durer's office, the capitaine was happily coping with the barrage of reporters' questions.

A television reporter asked, 'How can you be sure it was an accident?'

Durer looked into the lens of the camera. 'Fortunately, there was an eyewitness to this terrible event. Monsieur Stanford's cabin has an open veranda. Apparently some important papers flew out of his hand, onto the terrace, and he ran to retrieve them. When he reached out, he lost his balance and fell into the water. His bodyguard saw it happen and immediately called for help. The ship stopped, and they were able to retrieve the body.'

'What did the autopsy show?'

'Corsica is a small island, gentlemen. We are not properly equipped to do a full autopsy. However, our medical examiner reports that the cause of death was drowning. We found seawater in his lungs. There were no bruises or any signs of foul play.'

'Where is the body now?'

'We are keeping it in the cold storage room until authorization is given for it to be taken away.'

One of the photographers said, 'Do you mind if we take a picture of you, capitaine?'

Capitaine Durer hesitated for a dramatic moment. 'No. Please, gentlemen, do what you must.'

And the cameras began to flash.

He had lunch at La Fontana on Rue Nôtre Dame, and with the rest of the day to kill, started exploring the town.

Ajaccio was a colorful Mediterranean town that still basked in the glory of having been Napoleon Bonaparte's birthplace. *I think Harry Stanford would have identified with this place*, Steve thought.

It was the tourist season in Corsica, and the streets were crowded with visitors chatting away in French, Italian, German and Japanese.

That evening Steve had an Italian dinner at Le Boccaccio and returned to his hotel.

'Any messages?' he asked the room clerk, optimistically.

'No, monsieur.'

He lay in bed haunted by what Simon Fitzgerald had told him about Harry Stanford.

Did she get an abortion?

No. Harry wanted her to have one, but she refused. They had a terrible scene. He told her he loved her and wanted to marry her. Of course, he had told that to dozens of women. But Emily overheard their conversation, and in the middle of that same night she committed suicide.

Steve wondered how she had done it.

He finally fell asleep.

*   *   .   *

40

At ten o'clock the following morning, Steve Sloane appeared again at the Préfecture. The same sergeant was seated behind the desk.

'Good morning,' Steve said.

'*Bonjour*, monsieur. Can I help to assist you?'

Steve handed the sergeant another business card. 'I'm here to see Capitaine Durer.'

'A moment.' The sergeant got up, walked into the inner office, and closed the door behind him.

Capitaine Durer, dressed in an impressive new uniform, was being interviewed by an RAI television crew from Italy. He was looking into the camera. 'When I took charge of the case, the first thing I did was to make certain that there was no foul play involved in Monsieur Stanford's death.'

The interviewer asked, 'And you were satisfied that there was none, capitaine?'

'Completely satisfied. There is no question but that it was an unfortunate accident.'

The director said, '*Bene*. Let us cut to another angle and a closer shot.'

The sergeant took the opportunity to hand Capitaine Durer Sloane's business card. 'He is outside.'

'What is the matter with you?' Durer growled. 'Can't you see I'm busy? Have him come back tomorrow.' He had just received word that there were a dozen more reporters on their way, some from as far away as Russia and South Africa. '*Demain*.'

'*Oui*.'

'Are you ready, capitaine?' the director asked.

Capitaine Durer smiled. 'I'm ready.'

The sergeant returned to the outer office. 'I am sorry, monsieur. Capitaine Durer is out of business today.'

'So am I,' Steve snapped. 'Tell him that all he has to do is sign a paper authorizing the release of Mr Stanford's body, and I'll be on my way. That's not too much to ask, is it?'

'I am afraid, yes. The capitaine has many responsibilities, and –'

'Can't someone else give me the authorization?'

41

'Oh, no, monsieur. Only the capitaine can do the authority.'

Steve Sloane stood there, seething. 'When can I see him?'

'I suggest if you try again tomorrow morning.'

The phrase 'try again' grated on Steve's ears.

'I'll do that,' he said. 'By the way, I understand there was an eyewitness to the accident – Mr Stanford's bodyguard, a Dmitri Kaminsky.'

'Yes.'

'I would like to talk to him. Could you tell me where he's staying?'

'Australia.'

'Is that a hotel?'

'No, monsieur.' There was pity in his voice. 'It is a country.'

Steve's voice rose an octave. 'Are you telling me that the only witness to Stanford's death was allowed by the police to leave here before anyone could interrogate him?'

'Capitaine Durer interrogated him.'

Steve took a deep breath. 'Thank you.'

'No problems, monsieur.'

When Steve returned to his hotel, he reported back to Simon Fitzgerald.

'It looks like I'm going to have to stay another night here.'

'What's going on, Steve?'

'The man in charge seems to be very busy. It's the tourist season. He's probably looking for some lost purses. I should be out of here by tomorrow.'

'Stay in touch.'

In spite of his irritation, Steve found the island of Corsica enchanting. It had almost a thousand miles of coastline, with soaring, granite mountains that stayed snow-topped until July. The island had been ruled by the Italians until France took it over, and the combination of the two cultures was fascinating.

During his dinner at the Crêperie U San Carlu, he remembered how Simon Fitzgerald had described Harry Stanford. *He was the only man I've ever known who was totally without compassion . . . a sadistic and vindictive man.*

Well, Harry Stanford is causing a hell of a lot of trouble even in death, Steve thought.

On the way to his hotel, Steve stopped at a newsstand to pick up a copy of the *International Herald Tribune*. The headline read: WHAT WILL HAPPEN TO THE STANFORD EMPIRE? He paid for the newspaper, and as he turned to leave, his eye was caught by the headlines in some of the foreign papers on the stand. He picked them up and looked through them, stunned. Every single newspaper had front-page stories about the death of Harry Stanford, and in each one of them, Capitaine Durer was prominently featured, his photograph beaming from the pages. *So that's what's keeping him so busy! We'll see about that.*

At nine forty-five the following morning, Steve returned to Capitaine Durer's reception office. The sergeant was not at his desk, and the door to the inner office was ajar. Steve pushed it open and stepped inside. The capitaine was changing into a new uniform, preparing for his morning press interviews. He looked up as Steve entered.

'*Qu'est-ce que vous faites ici? C'est un bureau privé! Allez-vous-en!*'

'I'm with the *New York Times*,' Steve Sloane said.

Instantly, Durer brightened. 'Ah, come in, come in. You said your name is . . . ?'

'Jones. John Jones.'

'Can I offer you something, perhaps? Coffee? Cognac?'

'Nothing, thanks,' Steve said.

'Please, please, sit down.' Durer's voice became somber. 'You are here, of course, about the terrible tragedy that has happened on our little island. Poor Monsieur Stanford.'

'When do you plan to release the body?' Steve asked. Capitaine Durer sighed. 'Ah, I am afraid not for many, many days. There are a great number of forms to fill out in the case of a man as important as Monsieur Stanford. There are protocols to be followed, you understand.'

'I think I do,' Steve said.

'Perhaps ten days. Perhaps, two weeks.' *By then the interest of the press will have cooled down.*

'Here's my card,' Steve said. He handed Capitaine Durer a card.

The capitaine glanced at it, then took a closer look. 'You are an attorney. You are not a reporter?'

'No. I'm Harry Stanford's attorney.' Steve Sloane rose. 'I want your authorization to release his body.'

'Ah, I wish I could give it to you,' Capitaine Durer said, regretfully. 'Unfortunately, my hands are tied. I do not see how –'

'Tomorrow.'

'That is impossible! There is no way . . .'

'I suggest that you get in touch with your superiors in Paris. Stanford Enterprises has several very large factories in France. It would be a shame if our board of directors decided to close all of them down and build in other countries.'

Capitaine Durer was staring at him. 'I . . . I have no control over such matters, monsieur.'

'But *I* do,' Steve assured him. 'You will see that Mr Stanford's body is released to me tomorrow, or you're going to find yourself in more trouble than you can possibly imagine.' Steve turned to leave.

'Wait! Monsieur! Perhaps in a few days, I can –'

'Tomorrow.' And Steve was gone.

Three hours later, Steve Sloane received a telephone call at his hotel.

'Monsieur Sloane? Ah, I have wonderful news for you! I have managed to arrange for Mr Stanford's body to be released to you immediately. I hope you appreciate the trouble . . .'

'Thank you. A private plane will leave here at eight o'clock tomorrow morning to take us back. I assume all the proper papers will be in order by then.'

'Yes, of course. Do not worry. I will see to –'

'Good.' Steve replaced the receiver.

Capitaine Durer sat there for a long time. *Merde! What bad luck! I could have been a celebrity for at least another week.*

*   *   *

44

When the plane carrying Harry Stanford's body landed at Logan International Airport in Boston, there was a hearse waiting to meet it. Funeral services were to be held three days later.

Steve Sloane reported back to Simon Fitzgerald.

'So the old man is finally home,' Fitzgerald said. 'It's going to be quite a reunion.'

'A reunion?'

'Yes. It should be interesting,' he said. 'Harry Stanford's children are coming here to celebrate their father's death. Tyler, Woody and Kendall.'

Chapter Eight

Judge Tyler Stanford had first seen the story on Chicago's station WBBM. He had stared at the television set, mesmerized, his heart pounding. There was a picture of the yacht *Blue Skies*, and a news commentator was saying, '. . . in a storm, in Corsican waters, when the tragedy occurred. Dmitri Kaminsky, Harry Stanford's bodyguard, was a witness to the accident, but was unable to save his employer. Harry Stanford was known in financial circles as one of the shrewdest . . .'

Tyler sat there, watching the shifting images, remembering, remembering . . .

It was the loud voices that had awakened him in the middle of the night. He was fourteen years old. He had listened to the angry voices for a few minutes, then crept down the upstairs hall to the staircase. In the foyer below, his mother and father were having a fight. His mother was screaming, and he watched his father slap her across the face.

The picture on the television set shifted. There was a scene of Harry Stanford in the Oval Office of the White House, shaking hands with President Ronald Reagan. 'One of the cornerstones of the president's new financial task force, Harry Stanford has been an important adviser to . . .'

They were playing football in back of the house, and his brother, Woody, threw the ball toward the house. Tyler chased it, and as he picked it up he heard his father, on the other side of the hedge. 'I'm in love with you. You know that!'

He stopped, thrilled that his mother and father were not fighting, and then he heard the voice of their governess, Rosemary. 'You're married. I want you to leave me alone.'

And he suddenly felt sick to his stomach. He loved his mother and he loved Rosemary. His father was a terrifying stranger.

The picture on the screen flashed to a series of shots of Harry Stanford posing with Margaret Thatcher . . . President Mitterrand . . . Mikhail Gorbachev . . . The announcer was saying, 'The legendary tycoon was equally at home with factory workers and world leaders.'

He was passing the door to his father's office when he heard Rosemary's voice. 'I'm leaving.' And then his father's voice, 'I won't let you leave. You've got to be reasonable, Rosemary! This is the only way that you and I can . . .'

'I won't listen to you. And I'm keeping the baby!'

Then Rosemary had disappeared.

The scene on the television set shifted again. There were old clips of the Stanford family in front of a church, watching a coffin being lifted into a hearse. The commentator was saying, '. . . Harry Stanford and the children beside the coffin . . . Mrs Stanford's suicide was attributed to her failing health. According to police investigators, Harry Stanford . . .'

In the middle of the night, he had been shaken awake by his father. 'Get up, son. I have some bad news for you.'

The fourteen-year-old boy began to tremble.

'Your mother had an accident, Tyler.'

It was a lie. His father had killed her. She had committed suicide because of his father and his affair with Rosemary.

The newspapers had been filled with the story. It was a scandal that rocked Boston, and the tabloids took full advantage of it. There was no way to keep the news from the Stanford children. Their classmates made their lives hell. In just twenty-four hours,

47

the three young children had lost the two people they loved most. And it was their father who was to blame.

'I don't care if he is our father.' Kendall sobbed. 'I hate him.'

'Me, too!'

'Me, too!'

They thought about running away, but they had nowhere to go. They decided to rebel.

Tyler was delegated to talk to him. 'We want a different father. We don't want you.'

Harry Stanford had looked at him and said, coldly, 'I think we can arrange that.'

Three weeks later, they were all shipped off to different boarding schools.

As the years went by, the children saw very little of their father. They read about him in newspapers, or watched him on television, escorting beautiful women or chatting with celebrities, but the only time they were with him was on what he called 'occasions' – photo opportunities at Christmas time or other holidays – to show what a devoted father he was. After that, the children were sent back to their different schools and camps until the next 'occasion'.

Tyler sat hypnotized by what he was watching. On the television screen was a montage of factories in different parts of the world, with pictures of his father. '. . . one of the largest privately held conglomerates in the world. Harry Stanford, who created it, was a legend . . . The question in the minds of Wall Street experts is, What is going to happen to the family-owned company now that its founder is gone? Harry Stanford left three children, but it is not known who will inherit the multibillion-dollar fortune that Stanford left behind, or who will control the corporation . . .'

He was six years old. He loved roaming around the large house, exploring all the exciting rooms. The only place that was off-limits to him was his father's office. Tyler was aware that important meetings went on in there. Impressive-looking men dressed in dark suits were constantly coming and going, meeting with his father. The fact that the office was off-limits to Tyler made it irresistible.

One day when his father was away, Tyler decided to go into the office. The huge room was overpowering, awesome. Tyler stood there, looking at the large desk and at the huge leather chair that his father sat in. *One day I'm going to sit in that chair, and I'm going to be important like Father.* He moved over to the desk and examined it. There were dozens of official-looking papers on it. He moved around to the back of the desk and sat in his father's chair. It felt wonderful. *I'm important now, too!*

'*What the hell are you doing?*'

Tyler looked up, startled. His father stood in the doorway, furious.

'Who told you you could sit behind that desk?'

The young boy was trembling. 'I . . . I just wanted to see what it was like.'

His father stormed over to him. 'Well, you'll never know what it's like! *Never!* Now get the hell out of here and *stay out!*'

Tyler ran upstairs, sobbing, and his mother came to his room. She put her arms around him. 'Don't cry, darling. It's going to be all right.'

'It's . . . it's *not* going to be all right,' he sobbed. 'He . . . he hates me!'

'No. He doesn't hate you.'

'All I did was to sit in his chair.'

'It's *his* chair, darling. He doesn't want anyone to sit in it.'

He could not stop crying. She held him close and said, 'Tyler, when your father and I were married, he said he wanted me to be part of his company. He gave me one share of stock. It was kind of a family joke. I'm going to give you that share. I'll put it in a trust for you. So now you're part of the company, too. All right?'

There were one hundred shares of stock in Stanford Enterprises, and Tyler was now a proud owner of one share.

When Harry Stanford heard what his wife had done, he scoffed, 'What the hell do you think he's going to do with that one share? Take over the company?'

*   *   *

Tyler switched off the television set and sat there, adjusting to the news. He felt a deep sense of satisfaction. Traditionally, sons wanted to be successful to please their fathers. Tyler Stanford had longed to be a success so he could *destroy* his father.

As a child, he had a recurring dream that his father was charged with murdering his mother, and Tyler was the one who would pass sentence. *I sentence you to die in the electric chair!* Sometimes the dream would vary, and Tyler would sentence his father to be hanged or poisoned or shot. The dreams became almost real.

The military school he was sent to was in Mississippi, and it was four years of pure hell. Tyler hated the discipline and the rigid life-style. In his first year at school, he seriously contemplated committing suicide, and the only thing that stopped him was the determination not to give his father that satisfaction. *He killed my mother. He's not going to kill me.*

It seemed to Tyler that his instructors were particularly hard on him, and he was sure his father was responsible. Tyler refused to let the school break him. Although he was forced to go home on holidays, his visits with his father grew more and more unpleasant.

His brother and sister were also home for holidays, but there was no sense of kinship. Their father had destroyed that. They were strangers to one another, waiting for the holidays to be over so they could escape.

Tyler knew that his father was a multibillionaire but the small allowance that Tyler, Woody, and Kendall had came from their mother's estate. As he grew older, Tyler wondered whether he was entitled to the family fortune. He was sure he and his siblings were being cheated. *I need an attorney.* That, of course, was out of the question, but his next thought was, *I'm going to become an attorney.*

When Tyler's father heard about his son's plans, he said, 'So, you're going to become a lawyer, huh? I suppose you think I'll give you a job with Stanford Enterprises. Well, forget it. I wouldn't let you within a mile of it!'

*   *   *

50

When Tyler was graduated from law school he could have practised in Boston, and because of the family name he would have been welcomed on the boards of dozens of companies, but he preferred to get far away from his father.

He decided to set up a law practice in Chicago. In the beginning, it was difficult. He refused to trade on his family name, and clients were scarce. Chicago politics were run by the Machine, and Tyler very quickly learned that it would be advantageous for a young lawyer to become involved with the powerful central Cook County Lawyers Association. He was given a job with the district attorney's office. He had a keen mind and was a quick study, and it was not long before he became invaluable to them. He prosecuted felons accused of every conceivable crime, and his record of convictions was phenomenal.

He rose rapidly through the ranks, and finally the day came when he received his reward. He was appointed Cook County circuit court judge. He had thought his father finally would be proud of him. He was wrong.

'You? A circuit court judge? For God's sake, I wouldn't let you judge a baking contest!'

Judge Tyler Stanford was a short, slightly overweight man with sharp, calculating eyes and a hard mouth. He had none of his father's charisma or attractiveness. His outstanding feature was a deep, sonorous voice, perfect for pronouncing sentence.

Tyler Stanford was a private man who kept his thoughts to himself. He was forty years old, but he looked much older than his years. He prided himself on having no sense of humor. Life was too grim for levity. His only hobby was chess, and once a week he played at a local club, where he invariably won.

Tyler Stanford was a brilliant jurist, held in high esteem by his fellow judges, who often came to him for advice. Very few people were aware that he was one of *the* Stanfords. He never mentioned his father's name.

The judge's chambers were in the large Cook County Criminal Court Building at Twenty-sixth and California streets, a fourteen-storey stone edifice with steps leading up to the front entrance.

It was in a dangerous neighborhood, and a notice outside stated: BY JUDICIAL ORDER, ALL PERSONS ENTERING THIS BUILDING SHALL SUBMIT TO SEARCH.

This was where Tyler spent his days, hearing cases involving robbery, burglary, rape, shootings, drugs and murders. Ruthless in his decisions, he became known as the Hanging Judge. All day long he listened to defendants pleading poverty, child abuse, broken homes, and a hundred other excuses. He accepted none of them. A crime was a crime and had to be punished. And in the back of his mind, always, was his father.

Tyler Stanford's fellow judges knew very little about his personal life. They knew that he had had a bitter marriage and was now divorced, and that he lived alone in a small three-bedroom Georgian house on Kimbark Avenue in Hyde Park. The area was surrounded by beautiful old homes, because the great fire of 1871 that razed Chicago had whimsically spared the Hyde Park district. He made no friends in the neighborhood, and his neighbors knew nothing about him. He had a housekeeper who came in three times a week, but Tyler did the shopping himself. He was a methodical man with a fixed routine. On Saturdays, he went to Harper Court, a small shopping mall near his home, or to Mr G's Fine Foods or Medici's on Fifty-seventh Street.

From time to time, at official gatherings, Tyler would meet the wives of his fellow jurists. They sensed that he was lonely, and they offered to introduce him to women friends or invite him to dinner. He always declined.

'I'm busy that evening.'

His evenings seemed to be full, but they had no idea what he was doing with them.

'Tyler isn't interested in anything but the law,' one of the judges explained to his wife. 'And he's just not interested in meeting any women yet. I heard he had a terrible marriage.'

He was right.

After his divorce, Tyler had sworn to himself that he would never become emotionally involved again. And then he had met

52

Lee, and everything had suddenly changed. Lee was beautiful, sensitive and caring – the one Tyler wanted to spend the rest of his life with. Tyler loved Lee, but why should Lee love him? A successful model, Lee had dozens of admirers, most of them wealthy. And Lee liked expensive things.

Tyler had felt that his cause was hopeless. There was no way to compete with others for Lee's affection. But overnight, with the death of his father, everything could change. He could become wealthy beyond his wildest dreams.

He could give Lee the world.

Tyler walked into the chambers of the chief judge. 'Keith, I'm afraid I have to go to Boston for a few days. Family affairs. I wonder if you would have someone take over my caseload for me.'

'Of course. I'll arrange it,' the chief judge said.

'Thank you.'

That afternoon, Judge Tyler Stanford was on his way to Boston. On the plane, he thought again about his father's words on that terrible day: *I know your dirty little secret.*

Chapter Nine

It was raining in Paris, a warm July rain that sent pedestrians racing along the street for shelter or looking for nonexistent taxis. Inside the auditorium of a large gray building on a corner of Rue Faubourg St Honoré, there was panic. A dozen half-naked models were running around in a kind of mass hysteria, while ushers finished setting up chairs and carpenters pounded away at last-minute bits of carpentry. Everyone was screaming and gesticulating wildly, and the noise level was painful.

In the eye of the hurricane, trying to bring order out of chaos, was the *maîtresse* herself, Kendall Stanford Renaud. Four hours before the fashion show was scheduled to begin, everything was falling apart.

Catastrophe: John Fairchild of *W* was unexpectedly going to be in Paris, and there was no seat for him.

Tragedy: the speaker system was not working.

Disaster: one of the top models was ill.

Emergency: two of the make-up artists were fighting backstage and were far behind schedule.

Calamity: all the seams on the cigarette skirts were tearing.

In other words, Kendall thought wryly, *everything is normal*.

Kendall Stanford Renaud could have been mistaken for one of the models herself, and at one time she had been a model. She exuded carefully plotted elegance from her golden chignon to her Chanel pumps. Everything about her – the curve of her arm, the shade of her nail polish, the timbre of her laugh – bespoke well-mannered chic. Her face, if stripped of its careful make-up, was actually plain, but Kendall took pains to see that no one ever realized this, and no one ever did.

She was everywhere at once.

'Who lit that runway, Ray Charles?'

'I want a blue backdrop . . .'

'The lining is showing. Fix it!'

'I don't want the models doing their hair and make-up in the holding area. Have Lulu find them a dressing room!'

Kendall's venue manager came hurrying up to her. 'Kendall, thirty minutes is too long! Too long! The show should be no more than twenty-five minutes.'

She stopped what she was doing. 'What do you suggest, Scott?'

'We could cut a few of the designs and –'

'No. I'll have the models move faster.'

She heard her name called again, and turned.

'Kendall, we can't locate Pia. Do you want Tami to switch to the charcoal gray jacket with the trousers?'

'No. Give that to Dana. Give the cat suit and tunic to Tami.'

'What about the dark gray jersey?'

'Monique. And make sure she wears the dark gray stockings.'

Kendall looked at the board holding a set of Polaroid pictures of the models in a variety of gowns. When they were set, the pictures would be placed in a precise order. She ran a practiced eye over the board. 'Let's change this. I want the beige cardigan out first, then the separates, followed by the strapless silk jersey, then the taffeta evening gown, the afternoon dresses with matching jackets . . .'

Two of her assistants hurried up to her.

'Kendall, we're having an argument about the seating. Do you want the retailers together, or do you want to mix them with the celebrities?'

The other assistant spoke up. 'Or we could mix the celebrities and press together.'

Kendall was hardly listening. She had been up for two nights, checking everything to make sure nothing would go wrong. 'Work it out yourselves,' she said.

She looked around at all the activity and thought about the

55

show that was about to begin, and the famous names from all over the world who would be there to applaud what she had created. *I should thank my father for all this. He told me I would never succeed . . .*

She had always known that she wanted to be a designer. From the time she was a little girl, she had had a natural sense of style. Her dolls had the trendiest outfits in town. She would show off her latest creations for her mother's approval. Her mother would hug her and say, 'You're very talented, darling. Someday you're going to be a very important designer.'

And Kendall was sure of it.

In school, Kendall studied graphic design, structural drawing, spatial conceptions, and color coordination.

'The best way to begin,' one of her teachers had advised her, 'is to become a model yourself. That way, you will meet all the top designers, and if you keep your eyes open, you will learn from them.'

When Kendall had mentioned her dream to her father, he had looked at her and said, '*You?* A model! You must be joking!'

When Kendall finished school, she returned to Rose Hill. *Father needs me to run the house*, she thought. There were a dozen servants, but no one was really in charge. Since Harry Stanford was away a good deal of the time, the staff was left to its own devices. Kendall tried to organize things. She scheduled the household activities, served as hostess for her father's parties, and did everything she could to make him comfortable. She was longing for his approval. Instead, she suffered a barrage of criticisms.

'Who hired that damned chef? Get rid of him.'

'I don't like the new dishes you bought. Where the hell is your taste . . . ?'

'Who told you you could redecorate my bedroom? Keep the hell out of there.'

No matter what Kendall did, it was never good enough.

It was her father's domineering cruelty that finally drove her

56

out of the house. It had always been a loveless household, and her father had paid no attention to his children, except to try to control and discipline them. One night, Kendall overheard her father saying to a visitor, 'My daughter has a face like a horse. She's going to need a lot of money to hook some poor sucker.'

It was the final straw. The following day, Kendall left Boston and headed for New York.

Alone in her hotel room, Kendall thought, *All right. Here I am in New York. How do I become a designer? How do I break into the fashion industry? How do I get anyone even to notice me?* She remembered her teacher's advice. *I'll start as a model. That's the way to begin.*

The following morning, Kendall looked through the yellow pages, copied a list of modeling agencies, and began making the rounds. *I have to be honest with them*, Kendall thought. *I'll tell them that I can stay with them only temporarily, until I get started designing.*

She walked into the office of the first agency on her list. A middle-aged woman behind a desk said, 'May I help you?'

'Yes. I want to be a model.'

'So do I, dearie. Forget it.'

'What?'

'You're too tall.'

Kendall's jaw tightened. 'I'd like to see whoever is in charge here.'

'You're looking at her. I own this joint.'

The next half a dozen stops were no more successful.

'You're too short.'

'Too thin.'

'Too fat.'

'Too young.'

'Too old.'

'Wrong type.'

By the end of the week, Kendall was getting desperate. There was one more name on her list.

*   *   *

57

Paramount Models was the top modeling agency in Manhattan. There was no one at the reception desk.

A voice from one of the offices said, 'She'll be available next Monday. But you can have her for only one day. She's booked solid for the next three weeks.'

Kendall walked over to the office and peered inside. A woman in a tailored suit was talking on the phone.

'Right. I'll see what I can do.' Roxanne Marinack replaced the receiver and looked up. 'Sorry, we aren't looking for your type.'

Kendall said desperately, 'I can be any type you want me to be. I can be taller or I can be shorter. I can be younger or older, thinner –'

Roxanne held up her hand. 'Hold it.'

'All I want is a chance. I really *need* this.'

Roxanne hesitated. There was an appealing eagerness about the girl and she did have an exquisite figure. She was not beautiful, but possibly with the right make-up . . . 'Have you had any experience?'

'Yes. I've been wearing clothes all my life.'

Roxanne laughed. 'All right. Let me see your portfolio.'

Kendall looked at her blankly. 'My portfolio?'

Roxanne sighed. 'My dear girl, no self-respecting model walks around without a portfolio. It's your bible. It's what your prospective clients are going to look at.' Roxanne sighed again. 'I want you to get two head shots – one smiling and one serious. Turn around.'

'Right.' Kendall began to turn.

'Slowly.' Roxanne studied her. 'Not bad. I want a photo of you in a bathing suit or lingerie, whatever is the most flattering for your figure.'

'I'll get one of each,' she said eagerly.

Roxanne had to smile at her earnestness. 'All right. You're . . . er . . . different, but you might have a shot.'

'Thank you.'

'Don't thank me too soon. Modeling for fashion magazines isn't as simple as it looks. It's a tough business.'

'I'm ready for it.'

'We'll see. I'm going to take a chance on you. I'll send you out on some go-sees.'

'I'm sorry?'

'A go-see is where clients catch up on all the new models. There will be models from other agencies there, too. It's kind of a cattle call.'

'I can handle it.'

That had been the beginning. Kendall went on a dozen go-sees before a designer was interested in having her wear his clothes. She was so tense, she almost spoiled her chances by talking too much.

'I really love your dresses, and I think they would look good on me. I mean, they would look good on *any* woman, of course. They're wonderful! But I think they'll look especially good on me.' She was so nervous that she was stammering.

The designer nodded sympathetically. 'This is your first job, isn't it?'

'Yes, sir.'

He had smiled. 'All right. I'll try you. What did you say your name was?'

'Kendall Stanford.' She wondered if he would make the connection between her and *the* Stanfords, but of course, there was no reason for him to.

Roxanne had been right. Modeling was a tough business. Kendall had to learn to accept constant rejection, go-sees that led nowhere, and weeks without work. When she did work, she was in make-up at six A.M., finished a shoot, went on to the next, and often didn't get through until after midnight.

One evening, after a long day's shoot with half a dozen other models, Kendall looked in a mirror and groaned, 'I won't be able to work tomorrow. Look how puffy my eyes are!'

One of the models said, 'Put cucumber slices over your eyes. Or you can put some camomile tea bags in hot water, let them cool, and put them over your eyes for fifteen minutes.'

In the morning, the puffiness was gone.

*　　*　　*

Kendall envied the models who were in constant demand. She would hear Roxanne arranging their bookings: 'I originally gave Scaasi a secondary on Michelle. Call and tell them that she will be available, so I'm moving them up to a tentative.'

Kendall quickly learned never to criticize the clothes she was modeling. She became acquainted with some of the top photographers in the business, and had a photo composite made to go with her portfolio. She carried a model's bag filled with necessities – clothes, make-up, a nail-care bag, and jewelry. She learned to blow-dry her hair upside down to give it more body, and to add curl to her hair with heated rollers.

There was a lot more to learn. She was a favorite of the photographers, and one of them pulled her aside to give her some advice. 'Kendall, always save your smiling shots for the end of the shoot. That way, your mouth will have less creasing.'

Kendall was becoming more and more popular. She was not the conventional drop-dead beauty that was the hallmark of most models, but she had something more, a graceful elegance.

'She's got class,' one of the advertising agents said.

And that summed it up.

She was also lonely. From time to time she went out on dates, but they were meaningless. She was working steadily, but she felt she was no nearer to her goal than she was when she had first arrived in New York. *I have to find a way to make contact with the top designers*, Kendall thought.

'I have you booked for the next four weeks,' Roxanne told her. 'Everybody loves you.'

'Roxanne . . .'

'Yes, Kendall?'

'I don't want to do this anymore.'

Roxanne stared at her disbelievingly. 'What?'

'I want to do runway modeling.'

Runway modeling was what most models aspired to. It was the most exciting and the most lucrative form of modeling.

Roxanne was dubious. 'That's almost impossible to break into and –'

'I'm going to.'

Roxanne studied her. 'You really mean it, don't you?'

'Yes.'

Roxanne nodded. 'All right. If you're serious about this, the first thing you have to do is learn to walk the beam.'

'What?'

Roxanne explained.

That afternoon, Kendall bought a six-foot narrow wooden beam, sandpapered it to avoid splinters, and placed it on her floor. The first few times she tried to walk on it, she fell off. *This is not going to be easy*, Kendall decided. *But I'm going to do it*.

Each morning she got up early and practiced walking the beam on the balls of her feet. *Lead with the pelvis. Feel with the toes. Lower the heel.* Day by day her balance improved.

She strode up and back in front of a full-length mirror, with music playing. She learned to walk with a book on her head. She practiced changing rapidly from sneakers and shorts to high heels and an evening gown.

When Kendall felt that she was ready, she went back to Roxanne.

'I'm sticking my neck out for you,' Roxanne told her. 'Ungaro is looking for a runway model. I recommended you. He's going to give you a chance.'

Kendall was thrilled. Ungaro was one of the most brilliant designers in the business.

The following week, Kendall arrived at the show. She tried to seem as casual as the other models.

Ungaro handed Kendall the first outfit she was to wear and smiled. 'Good luck.'

'Thanks.'

When Kendall went out on the runway, it was as though she had been doing it all her life. Even the other models were impressed. The show was a big success, and from that time on

Kendall was a member of the elite. She started working with the giants of the fashion industry – Yves Saint Laurent, Halston, Christian Dior, Donna Karan, Calvin Klein, Ralph Lauren, St John. Kendall was in constant demand, traveling to shows all over the world. In Paris, the haute couture shows took place in January and July. In Milan, the peak months were March, April, May and June, while in Tokyo, shows peaked in April and October. It was a hectic, busy life, and she loved every minute of it.

Kendall kept working and she kept learning. She modeled the clothes of famous designers and thought about the changes she would make if *she* were the designer. She learned how clothes were supposed to fit, and how fabric was supposed to move and swing around the body. She learned about cuts and drapes and tailoring, and what body parts women wanted to hide, and what parts they wanted to show. She made sketches at home, and the ideas seemed to flow. One day, she took a portfolio of her sketches to the head buyer at I Magnin's. The buyer was impressed. 'Who designed these?' she asked.

'I did.'

'They're good. They're very good.'

Two weeks later, Kendall went to work for Donna Karan as an assistant and began to learn the business side of the garment trade. At home, she kept designing clothes. One year later, she had her first fashion show. It was a disaster.

The designs were ordinary and nobody cared. She gave a second show, and no one came.

I'm in the wrong profession, Kendall thought.

One day you're going to be a very famous designer.

What am I doing wrong? Kendall wondered.

The epiphany came in the middle of the night. Kendall awakened and lay in bed, thinking, *I'm designing dresses for models to wear. I should be designing for real women with real jobs and real families. Smart, but comfortable. Chic, but practical.*

It took Kendall about a year to get her next show on, but it was an instant success.

*   *   *

Kendall rarely returned to Rose Hill, and when she did, the visits were dreadful. Her father had not changed. If anything, he had gotten worse.

'Haven't hooked anybody yet, eh? Probably never will.'

It was at a charity ball that Kendall met Marc Renaud. He worked at the international desk of a New York brokerage house, where he dealt with foreign currencies. Five years younger than Kendall, he was an attractive Frenchman, tall and lean. He was charming and attentive, and Kendall was immediately attracted to him. He asked her to dine the next evening, and that night Kendall went to bed with him. They were together every night after that.

One evening, Marc said, 'Kendall, I'm madly in love with you, you know.'

She said softly, 'I've been looking for you all my life, Marc.'

'There is a serious problem. You are a big success. I don't make anywhere near as much money as you. Perhaps one day –'

Kendall had put her finger to his lips. 'Stop it. You've given me more than I could ever have hoped for.'

On Christmas Day, Kendall took Marc to Rose Hill to meet her father.

'You're going to marry *him*?' Harry Stanford exploded. 'He's a nobody! He's marrying you for the money he thinks you're going to get.'

If Kendall had needed any further reason to marry Marc, that would have been it. They got married in Connecticut the following day. And Kendall's marriage to Marc gave her happiness she had never known before.

'You mustn't let your father bully you,' he had told Kendall. 'All his life, he has used his money as a weapon. We don't need his money.'

And Kendall had loved him for that.

Marc was a wonderful husband – kind, considerate, and caring. *I have everything*, Kendall thought happily. *The past is dead*. She had succeeded in spite of her father. In a few hours, the fashion world was going to be focused on her talent.

The rain had stopped. It was a good omen.

The show was stunning. At its end, with music playing and flash bulbs popping, Kendall walked out onto the runway, took a bow and received an ovation. Kendall wished that Marc could have been in Paris with her to share her triumph, but his brokerage house had refused to give him the time off.

When the crowd had left, Kendall went back to her office, feeling euphoric. Her assistant said, 'A letter came for you. It was hand-delivered.'

Kendall looked at the brown envelope her assistant handed her, and she felt a sudden chill. She knew what it was about before she opened it. The letter read:

> *Dear Mrs Renaud,*
>   *I regret to inform you that the Wild Animal Protection Association is short of funds again. We will need $100,000 immediately to cover our expenses. The money should be wired to account number 804072-A at the Crédit Suisse bank in Zurich.*

There was no signature.

Kendall sat there, staring at it, numb. *It's never going to stop. The blackmail is never going to stop.*

Another assistant came hurrying into the office. 'Kendall! I'm so sorry. I just heard some terrible news.'

I can't bear any more terrible news, Kendall thought. 'What . . . what is it?'

'There was an announcement on Radio-Télé Luxembourg. Your father is . . . dead. He drowned.'

It took Kendall a moment for it to sink in. Her first thought was, *I wonder what would have made him prouder? My success or the fact that I'm a murderer?*

Chapter Ten

Peggy Malkovich had been married to Woodrow 'Woody' Stanford for two years, but to the residents of Hobe Sound, she was still referred to as 'that waitress'.

Peggy had been waiting on tables at the Rain Forest Grille when Woody first met her. Woody Stanford was the golden boy of Hobe Sound. He lived in the family villa, had classical good looks, was charming and gregarious, and a target for all the eager debutantes in Hobe Sound, Philadelphia, and Long Island. It was therefore a seismic shock when he suddenly eloped with a twenty-five-year-old waitress who was plain-looking, a high-school dropout, and the daughter of a day laborer and a housewife.

It was even more of a shock because everyone had been expecting Woody to marry Mimi Carson, a beautiful, intelligent young heiress to a timber fortune who was madly in love with Woody.

As a rule, the residents of Hobe Sound preferred to gossip about the affairs of their servants rather than their peers, but in Woody's case, his marriage was so outrageous that they made an exception. The information quickly spread that he had gotten Peggy Malkovich pregnant and then married her. They were quite sure which was the greater sin.

'For God's sake, I can understand the boy getting her pregnant, but you don't marry a waitress!'

The whole affair was a classic case of *déjà vu*. Twenty-four years earlier, Hobe Sound had been rocked by a similar scandal involving the Stanfords. Emily Temple, the daughter of one of the founding families, had committed suicide because her husband had gotten the children's governess pregnant.

Woody Stanford made no secret of the fact that he hated his father, and the general feeling was that he had married the waitress out of spite, to show that he was a more honorable man than his father.

The only person invited to the wedding was Peggy's brother, Hoop, who flew in from New York. Hoop was two years older than Peggy and worked in a bakery in the Bronx. He was tall and emaciated, with a pock-marked face and a heavy Brooklyn accent.

'You're gettin' a great girl,' he told Woody after the ceremony.

'I know,' Woody said tonelessly.

'You take good care of my sister, huh?'

'I'll do my best.'

'Yeah. Cool.'

An unmemorable conversation between a baker and the son of one of the wealthiest men in the world.

Four weeks after the wedding, Peggy lost the baby.

Hobe Sound is a very exclusive community, and Jupiter Island is the most exclusive part of Hobe Sound. The island is bordered on the west by the Intercoastal Waterway and on the east by the Atlantic Ocean. It is a haven of privacy – wealthy, self-contained and protective, with more police per capita than in almost any other place in the world. Its residents pride themselves on being understated. They drive Tauruses or station wagons, and own small sailboats, an eighteen-foot Lightning or a twenty-four-foot Quickstep.

If one was not born to it, one had to earn the right to be a member of this Hobe Sound community. After the marriage between Woodrow Stanford and 'that waitress', the burning question was, what were the residents going to do about accepting the bride into their society?

Mrs Anthony Pelletier, the doyen of Hobe Sound, was the arbiter of all social disputes, and her devout mission in life was to protect her community against parvenus and the nouveau riche. When newcomers arrived at Hobe Sound and were unfortunate enough to displease Mrs Pelletier, it was her custom to have delivered to them, by her chauffeur, a leather traveling case. It was her way of informing them that they were not welcome in the community.

Her friends delighted in telling the story of the garage mechanic and his wife who had bought a house in Hobe Sound. Mrs Pelletier had sent them her ritual traveling bag, and when the wife learned its significance, she laughed. She said, 'If that old harridan thinks she can drive me out of this place, she's crazy!'

But strange things began to happen. Workmen and repairmen were suddenly unavailable, the grocer was always out of items that she ordered, and it was impossible to become a member of the Jupiter Island Club or even to get a reservation at any of the good local restaurants. And no one spoke to them. Three months after receiving the suitcase, the couple sold their home and moved away.

So it was that when word of Woody's marriage got out, the community held its collective breath. Excommunicating Peggy Malkovich would also mean excommunicating her popular husband. There were bets being quietly made.

For the first few weeks, there were no invitations to dinners or to any of the usual community functions. But the residents liked Woody and, after all, his grandmother on his mother's side had been one of the founders of Hobe Sound. Gradually, people started inviting him and Peggy to their homes. They were eager to see what his bride was like.

'The old girl must have something special or Woody never would have married her.'

They were in for a big disappointment. Peggy was dull and graceless, she had no personality, and she dressed badly. *Dowdy* was the word that came to people's minds.

Woody's friends were baffled. 'What on earth does he see in her? He could have married *anyone*.'

One of the first invitations was from Mimi Carson. She had been devastated by the news of Woody's marriage, but she was too proud to reveal it.

When her closest friend had tried to console her by saying, 'Forget it, Mimi! You'll get over him,' Mimi had replied, 'I'll live with it, but I'll never get over him.'

Woody tried hard to make a success of the marriage. He knew he had made a mistake, and he did not want to punish Peggy for it. He tried desperately to be a good husband. The problem was that Peggy had nothing in common with him or with any of his friends.

The only person Peggy seemed comfortable with was her brother, and she and Hoop spoke on the telephone every day.

'I miss him,' Peggy complained to Woody.

'Would you like to have him come down and stay with us for a few days?'

'He can't.' And she looked at her husband and said spitefully, 'He's got a job.'

At parties, Woody attempted to bring Peggy into the conversations, but it was quickly apparent that she had nothing to contribute. She sat in corners, tongue-tied, nervously licking her lips, obviously uncomfortable.

Woody's friends were aware that even though he was staying at the Stanford villa, he was estranged from his father and that he was living off the small annuity that his mother had left him. His passion was polo and he rode the ponies owned by friends. In the world of polo, players are ranked by goals, with ten goals being the best. Woody was nine goals, and he had ridden with Mariano Aguerre from Buenos Aires, Wicky el Effendi from Texas, Andres Diniz from Brazil, and dozens of other top goals. There were only about twelve ten-goal players in the world, and Woody's driving ambition was to be the thirteenth.

'You know why, don't you?' one of his friends remarked. 'His father was ten goals.'

Because Mimi Carson knew that Woody could not afford to buy his own polo ponies, she purchased a string for him to play. When friends asked why, she said, 'I want to make him happy in any way I can.'

When newcomers asked what Woody did for a living, people just shrugged. In reality, he was living a secondhand life, making money playing skins at golf, betting on polo matches, borrowing other people's polo ponies and racing yachts, and on occasion, other people's wives.

The marriage with Peggy was deteriorating rapidly, but Woody refused to admit it.

'Peggy,' he would say, 'when we go to parties, please try to join in the conversation.'

'Why should I? Your friends all think they're too good for me.'

'Well, they're not,' Woody assured her.

Once a week, the Hobe Sound Literary Circle met at the country club for a discussion of the latest books, followed by a luncheon.

On this particular day, as the ladies were dining, the steward approached Mrs Pelletier. 'Mrs Woodrow Stanford is outside. She would like to join you.'

A hush fell over the table.

'Show her in,' Mrs Pelletier said.

A moment later, Peggy walked into the dining room. She had washed her hair and pressed her best dress. She stood there, nervously looking at the group.

Mrs Pelletier gave her a nod, then said pleasantly, 'Mrs Stanford.'

Peggy smiled eagerly, 'Yes, ma'am.'

'We won't need you. We already have a waitress.' And Mrs Pelletier turned back to her lunch.

When Woody heard the story, he was furious. 'How dare she do that to you!' He took her in his arms. 'Next time, ask me before you do a thing like that, Peggy. You have to be *invited* to that luncheon.'

'I didn't know,' she said sullenly.

'It's all right. Tonight we're having dinner at the Blakes', and I want –'

'I won't go!'

'But we've accepted their invitation.'

'You go.'

'I don't want to go without you.'

'I'm not going.'

Woody went alone, and after that, he began going to every party without Peggy.

He would come home at all hours, and Peggy was sure he had been with other women.

The accident changed everything.

It happened during a polo match. Woody was playing the Number One position, and a member of the opposing team, trying to stroke the ball in close quarters, accidently hit the legs of the pony that Woody was riding. The pony went down and rolled on top of him. In the pile-up that followed, a second pony kicked Woody. At the emergency room of the hospital, the doctors diagnosed a broken leg, three fractured ribs, and a punctured lung.

Over the next two weeks, there were three separate operations, and Woody was in excruciating pain. The doctors gave him morphine to ease it. Peggy came to visit him every day. Hoop flew in from New York to console his sister.

His physical pain was unbearable, and the only relief Woody had was from the drugs the doctors kept prescribing for him. It was shortly after Woody got home that he seemed to change. He began to have violent mood swings. One minute he was his usual ebullient self, and the next minute he would go into a sudden rage or a deep depression. At dinner, laughing and telling jokes, Woody would suddenly become angry and abusive toward Peggy and storm out. In the middle of a sentence he would drift off into a deep reverie. He became forgetful. He would make dates and not show up; he would invite people to his home and not be there when they arrived. Everyone was concerned about him.

Soon, he became abusive to Peggy in public. Bringing a cup of coffee to a friend one morning, Peggy spilled some and Woody sneered, 'Once a waitress, always a waitress.'

Peggy also began to show signs of physical abuse, and when people asked her what happened, she would make excuses.

'I bumped into a door' or 'I fell down,' and she would make

light of it. The community was outraged. Now it was Peggy they were feeling sorry for. But when Woody's erratic behavior offended someone, Peggy would defend her husband.

'Woody is under a lot of stress,' Peggy would insist. 'He isn't himself.' She would not allow anyone to say anything against him.

It was Dr Tichner who finally brought it out into the open. He asked Peggy to come see him in his office one day.

She was nervous. 'Is something wrong, doctor?'

He studied her a moment. She had a bruise on her cheek, and her eye was swollen.

'Peggy, are you aware that Woody is doing drugs?'

Her eyes flashed with indignation. 'No! I don't believe it!' She stood up. 'I won't listen to this!'

'Sit down, Peggy. It's about time you faced the truth. It's becoming obvious to everyone else. Surely you've noticed his behavior. One minute he's on top of the world, talking about how wonderful everything is, and the next minute he's suicidal.'

Peggy sat there, watching him, her face pale.

'He's addicted.'

Her lips tightened. 'No,' she said stubbornly. 'He's not.'

'He is. You've got to be realistic. Don't you want to help him?'

'Of course, I do!' She was wringing her hands. 'I'd do anything to help him. *Anything*.'

'All right. Then let's start. I want you to help me get Woody into a rehabilitation center. I've asked him to come in and see me.'

Peggy looked at him for a long time, then nodded. 'I'll talk to him,' she said quietly.

That afternoon, when Woody walked into Dr Tichner's office, he was in a euphoric mood. 'You wanted to see me, doc? It's about Peggy, isn't it?'

'No. It's about you, Woody.'

Woody looked at him in surprise. 'Me? What's my problem?'

'I think you know what your problem is.'

'What are you talking about?'

71

'If you go on like this, you're going to destroy your life and Peggy's life. What are you taking, Woody?'

'Taking?'

'You heard me.'

There was a long silence.

'I want to help you.'

Woody sat there, staring at the floor. When he finally spoke, his voice was hoarse. 'You're right. I've . . . I've tried to kid myself, but I can't any longer.'

'What are you on?'

'Heroin.'

'My God!'

'Believe me, I've tried to stop, but I . . . I can't.'

'You need help, and there are places where you can get it.'

Woody said wearily, 'I hope to God you're right.'

'I want you to go to the Harbor Group Clinic in Jupiter. Will you try it?'

There was a brief hesitation. 'Yes.'

'Who's supplying you with the heroin?' Dr Tichner asked.

Woody shook his head. 'I can't tell you that.'

'Very well. I'll make arrangements for you at the clinic.'

The following morning, Dr Tichner was seated in the office of the chief of police.

'Someone is supplying him with heroin,' Dr Tichner said, 'but he won't tell me who.'

Chief of Police Murphy looked at Dr Tichner and nodded. 'I think I know who.'

There were several possible suspects. Hobe Sound was a small enclave, and everyone knew everyone else's business.

A liquor store had opened recently on Bridge Road that made deliveries to their Hobe Sound customers at all hours of the day and night.

A doctor at a local clinic had been fined for overprescribing drugs.

A gymnasium had opened a year earlier, on the other side of

the waterway, and it was rumored that the trainer took steroids and had other drugs available for his good customers.

But Chief of Police Murphy had another suspect in mind.

Tony Benedotti had served as a gardener for many of the homes in Hobe Sound for years. He had studied horticulture and loved spending his days creating beautiful gardens. The gardens and lawns he tended were the loveliest in Hobe Sound. He was a quiet man who kept to himself, and the people he worked for knew very little about him. He seemed to be too well educated to be a gardener, and people were curious about his past.

Murphy sent for him.

'If this is about my driver's license, I renewed it,' Benedotti said.

'Sit down,' Murphy ordered.

'Is there some kind of problem?'

'Yeah. You're an educated man, right?'

'Yes.'

The chief of police leaned back in his chair. 'So how come you're a gardener?'

'I happen to love nature.'

'What else do you happen to love?'

'I don't understand.'

'How long have you been gardening?'

Benedotti looked at him, puzzled. 'Have any of my customers been complaining?'

'Just answer the question.'

'About fifteen years.'

'You have a nice house and a boat?'

'Yes.'

'How can you afford all that on what you make as a gardener?'

Benedotti said, 'It's not that big a house, and it's not that big a boat.'

'Maybe you make a little money on the side.'

'What do you . . . ?'

'You work for some people in Miami, don't you?'

'Yes.'

73

'There's a lot of Italians there. Do you ever do them some little favors?'

'What kind of favors?'

'Like pushing drugs.'

Benedotti looked at him, horrified. 'My God! Of course not.'

Murphy leaned forward. 'Let me tell you something, Benedotti. I've been keeping an eye on you. I've had a talk with a few of the people you work for. They don't want you or your Mafia friends here anymore. Is that clear?'

Benedotti squeezed his eyes shut for a second, then opened them. 'Very clear.'

'Good. I'll expect you out of here by tomorrow. I don't want to see your face again.'

Woody Stanford went into the Harbor Group Clinic for three weeks, and when he came out, he was the old Woody – charming, gracious, and delightful to be with. He went back to playing polo, riding Mimi Carson's ponies.

Sunday was the Palm Beach Polo & Country Club's eighteenth anniversary, and South Shore Boulevard was heavy with traffic as three thousand fans converged on the polo grounds. They rushed to fill the box seats on the west side of the field and the bleachers at the opposite end. Some of the finest players in the world were going to be in the day's game.

Peggy was in a box seat next to Mimi Carson, as Mimi's guest.

'Woody told me that this is your first polo match, Peggy. Why haven't you been to one before?'

Peggy licked her lips. 'I . . . I guess I've always been too nervous to watch Woody play. I don't want him to get hurt again. It's a very dangerous sport, isn't it?'

Mimi said thoughtfully, 'When you get eight players, each weighing about one hundred and seventy-five pounds, and their nine-hundred-pound ponies racing at each other over three hundred yards at forty miles an hour – yes, accidents can happen.'

Peggy shuddered. 'I couldn't stand it if anything happened to Woody again. I really couldn't. I go crazy worrying about him.'

74

Mimi Carson said gently, 'Don't worry. He's one of the best. He studied under Hector Barrantas, you know.'

Peggy was looking at her blankly. 'Who?'

'He's a ten-goal player. One of the legends of polo.'

'Oh.'

There was a murmur from the crowd as the ponies moved across the field.

'What's happening?' Peggy asked.

'They just finished a practice session before the game. They're ready to begin now.'

On the field, the two teams were starting to line up under the hot Florida sun, getting ready for the umpire's throw-in.

Woody looked wonderful, tan and fit and lithe – ready to do battle. Peggy waved and blew him a kiss.

Both teams were lined up now, side by side. The players held their mallets down for the throw-in.

'There are usually six periods of play, called chukkers,' Mimi Carson explained to Peggy. 'Each chukker lasts seven minutes. The chukker ends when the bell rings. Then there's a short rest. They change ponies every period. The team that scores the most goals wins.'

'Right.'

Mimi wondered just how much Peggy understood.

On the field, the players' eyes were fixed on the umpire, anticipating when the ball would be tossed. The umpire looked around at the crowd, then suddenly bowled the white plastic ball between the two rows of players. The game had begun.

The action was swift. Woody made the first play, getting possession of the ball and hitting an offside forehand. The ball sped toward a player on the opposing team. The player galloped down the field after it. Woody rode up to him and hooked his mallet to spoil his shot.

'Why did Woody do that?' Peggy asked.

Mimi Carson explained. 'When your opponent gets the ball, it's legal to hook his mallet so he can't score or pass. Woody will use an offside stroke next to control the ball.'

The action was happening so fast that it was almost impossible to follow.

There were cries of, 'Center.'

'Boards.'

'Leave it . . .'

And the players were racing down the field at full speed. The ponies – usually pure or three-quarter thoroughbred – were responsible for 75 percent of their riders' successes. The ponies had to be fast, and have what players call polo sense, being able to anticipate their rider's every move.

Woody was brilliant during the first three chukkers, scoring two goals in each one and being cheered on by the roaring crowd. His mallet seemed to be everywhere. It was the old Woody Stanford, riding like the wind, fearless. By the end of the fifth chukker, Woody's team was well ahead. The players went off the field for the break.

As Woody passed Peggy and Mimi, sitting in the front row, he smiled at both of them.

Peggy turned to Mimi Carson, excitedly. 'Isn't he wonderful?' She looked over at Peggy. 'Yes. In every way.'

Woody's teammates were congratulating him.

'Right on the mark, old boy! You were fabulous!'

'Great plays!'

'Thanks.'

'We're going out there and rub their noses in it some more. They haven't got a chance!'

Woody grinned. 'No problem.'

He watched his teammates move out to the field, and he suddenly felt exhausted. *I pushed myself too hard*, he thought. *I wasn't really ready to go back to the game yet. I'm not going to be able to keep this up. If I go out there, I'll make a fool of myself.* He began to panic, and his heart started to pound. *What I need is a little pick-me-up. No! I won't do that. I can't. I promised. But the team is waiting for me. I'll do it just this once, and never again. I swear to God, this is the last time.* He went to his car and reached into the glove compartment.

*   *   *

When Woody returned to the field, he was humming to himself, and his eyes were unnaturally bright. He waved to the crowd, and joined his waiting team. *I don't even need a team*, he thought. *I could beat those bastards single-handedly. I'm the best damned player in the world.* He was giggling to himself.

The accident occurred during the sixth chukker, although some of the spectators were to insist later that it was no accident.

The ponies were bunched together, racing toward the goal, and Woody had control of the ball. Out of the corner of his eye he saw one of the opposing players closing in on him. Using a tail shot, he sent the ball to the rear of the pony. It was picked up by Rick Hamilton, the best player on the opposing team, who began racing toward the goal. Woody was after him at full speed. He tried to hook Hamilton's mallet and missed. The ponies were getting closer to the goal. Woody kept desperately trying to get possession of the ball, and failed each time.

As Hamilton neared the goal, Woody deliberately swerved his pony to crash into Hamilton and ride him off the ball. Hamilton and his pony went tumbling to the ground. The crowd rose to its feet, screaming. The umpire angrily blew the whistle and held up a hand.

The first rule in polo is that when a player has possession of the ball and is heading toward the goal, it is illegal to cut across the line in which the player is traveling. Any player who crosses that line creates a dangerous situation and commits a foul.

Play stopped.

The umpire approached Woody, anger in his voice. 'That was a deliberate foul, Mr Stanford!'

Woody grinned. 'It wasn't my fault! His damned pony –'

'The opponents will receive a penalty goal.'

The chukker turned into a disaster. Woody committed two more blatant violations within three minutes of each other. The penalties resulted in two more goals for the other team. In each case the opponents were awarded a free penalty shot on an unguarded goal. In the last thirty seconds of the game, the opposing team scored the winning goal. What had been an assured victory, had turned into a rout.

In the box, Mimi Carson was stunned by the sudden turn of events.

Peggy said timidly, 'It didn't go well, did it?'

Mimi turned to her. 'No, Peggy. I'm afraid it didn't.'

A steward approached the box. 'Miss Carson, may I have a word with you?'

Mimi Carson turned to Peggy. 'Excuse me a moment.'

Peggy watched them walk away.

After the game, Woody's team was very quiet.

Woody was too ashamed to look at the others. Mimi Carson hurried over to Woody.

'Woody, I'm afraid I have some terrible, terrible news.' She put a hand on his shoulder. 'Your father is dead.'

Woody looked up at her and shook his head from side to side. He began to sob. 'I'm . . . I'm responsible. It's m . . . my fault.'

'No. You mustn't blame yourself. It isn't your fault.'

'Yes, it is,' Woody cried. 'If it weren't for my penalties, we would have won the game.'

Chapter Eleven

Julia Stanford had never known her father, and now he was dead, reduced to a black headline in the *Kansas City Star*: TYCOON HARRY STANFORD DROWNS AT SEA! She sat there, staring at his photograph on the front page of the newspaper, filled with conflicting emotions. *Do I hate him because of the way he treated my mother, or do I love him because he's my father? Do I feel guilty because I never tried to get in touch with him, or do I feel angry because he never tried to find me? It doesn't matter anymore*, she thought. *He's gone.*

Her father had been dead to her all her life, and now he had died again, cheating her out of something she had no words for. Inexplicably, she felt an overwhelming sense of loss. *Stupid!* Julia thought. *How can I miss someone I never knew?* She looked at the newspaper photograph again. *Do I have anything of him in me?* Julia stared into the mirror on the wall. *The eyes. I have the same deep gray eyes.*

Julia went into her bedroom closet, removed a battered cardboard box, and from it lifted a leather-bound scrapbook. She sat on the edge of her bed and opened the box. For the next two hours, she pored over its familiar contents. There were countless photographs of her mother in her governess's uniform, with Harry Stanford and Mrs Stanford and their three young children. Most of the pictures had been taken on their yacht, at Rose Hill, or at the Hobe Sound villa.

Julia picked up the yellowed newspaper clippings recounting the scandal that had happened so many years before in Boston. The faded headlines were lurid:

LOVE NEST ON BEACON HILL

BILLIONAIRE HARRY STANFORD IN SCANDAL

TYCOON'S WIFE COMMITS SUICIDE

GOVERNESS ROSEMARY NELSON DISAPPEARS

There were dozens of gossip columns filled with innuendos. Julia sat there for a long time, lost in the past.

She had been born at St Joseph's Hospital in Milwaukee. Her earliest memories were of living in dreary walk-up apartments and constantly moving from city to city. There were times when there was no money at all, and little to eat. Her mother was continually ill, and it had been difficult for her to find steady work. The young girl quickly learned never to ask for toys or new dresses.

Julia started school when she was five, and her classmates would mock her because she wore the same dress and scruffy shoes every day. When the other children teased her, Julia fought them. She was a rebel, and she was always being brought up before the principal. Her teachers didn't know what to do with her. She was in constant trouble. She might have been expelled except for one thing: she was the brightest student in her class.

Her mother had told Julia that her father was dead, and she had accepted that. But when Julia was twelve years old, she stumbled across a picture album filled with photographs of her mother with a group of strangers.

'Who are these people?' Julia asked.

And Julia's mother decided that the time had come.

'Sit down, my darling.' She took Julia's hand and held it tightly. There was no way to break the news tactfully. 'That is your father, and your half sister, and your two half brothers.'

Julia was looking at her, puzzled. 'I don't understand.'

The truth had finally come out, shattering Julia's peace of mind. Her father was alive! And she had a half sister and two half brothers. It was too much to comprehend. 'Why . . . why did you lie to me?'

'You were too young to understand. Your father and I . . .

had an affair. He was married, and I . . . I had to leave, to have you.'

'I hate him!' Julia said.

'You mustn't hate him.'

'How could he have done this to you?' she demanded.

'What happened was my fault as much as his.' Each word was agony. 'Your father was a very attractive man, and I was young and foolish. I knew that nothing could ever come of our affair. He told me he loved me . . . but he was married and had a family. And . . . and then I became pregnant.' It was difficult for her to go on. 'A reporter got hold of the story and it was in all the newspapers. I ran away. I intended for you and me to go back to him, but his wife killed herself, and I . . . I could never face him or the children again. It was my fault you see. So don't blame him.'

But there was a part of the story Rosemary never revealed to her daughter. When the baby was born, the clerk at the hospital said, 'We're filling out the birth certificate. The baby's name is Julia Nelson?'

Rosemary had started to say yes, and then she thought fiercely, *No! She's Harry Stanford's daughter. She's entitled to his name, and his support.*

'My daughter's name is Julia Stanford.'

She had written to Harry Stanford, telling him about Julia, but she had never had a reply.

Julia was fascinated by the idea that she had a family she had not known about, and also by the fact that they were famous enough to be written about in the press. She went to the public library and looked up everything she could about Harry Stanford. There were dozens of articles about him. He was a billionaire, and he lived in another world, a world that Julia and her mother were totally excluded from.

One day, when one of Julia's classmates teased her about being poor, Julia said defiantly, 'I'm not poor! My father is one of the richest men in the world. We have a yacht and an airplane, and a dozen beautiful homes.'

Her teacher heard her. 'Julia, come up here.'

Julia approached the teacher's desk. 'You must not tell a lie like that.'

'It's not a lie,' Julia retorted. 'My father is a billionaire! He knows presidents and kings!'

The teacher looked at the young girl standing before her in her shabby cotton dress and said, 'Julia, that's not true.'

'It is!' Julia said stubbornly.

She was sent to the principal's office. She never mentioned her father at school again.

Julia learned that the reason she and her mother kept moving from city to city was because of the news media. Harry Stanford was constantly in the press, and the gossip newspapers and magazines kept digging up the old scandal. Investigative reporters would eventually discover who Rosemary Nelson was and where she lived, and she would have to take Julia and flee.

Julia read every newspaper story that appeared about Harry Stanford, and each time, she was tempted to telephone him. She wanted to believe that during all those years he had been desperately searching for her mother. *I'll call and say, 'This is your daughter. If you want to see us . . .'*

And he would come to them and fall in love all over again, and marry her mother, and they would all live happily together.

Julia Stanford grew into a beautiful young woman. She had lustrous dark hair, a laughing, generous mouth, the luminous grey eyes of her father, and a gently curved figure. But when she smiled, people forgot about everything else but that smile.

Because they were forced to move so often, Julia went to schools in five different states. During the summers she worked as a clerk in a department store, behind the counter in a drugstore, and as a receptionist. She was always fiercely independent.

They were living in Kansas City, Kansas, when Julia finished college on a scholarship. She was not sure what she wanted to do with her life. Friends, impressed by her beauty, suggested that she become a movie actress.

'You'd be a star overnight!'

Julia had dismissed the idea with a casual, 'Who wants to get up that early every morning?'

But the real reason she was not interested was because she wanted, above all, her privacy. It seemed to Julia that all their lives, she and her mother had been hounded by the press because of what had happened so many years earlier.

Julia's dream of one day uniting her mother and father ended the day her mother died. Julia felt an overpowering sense of loss. *My father has to know*, Julia thought. *Mother was a part of his life*. She looked up the telephone number of his business headquarters in Boston. A receptionist answered.

'Good morning, Stanford Enterprises.'

Julia hesitated.

'Stanford Enterprises. Hello? May I help you?'

Slowly Julia replaced the receiver. *Mother wouldn't have wanted me to make that call*.

She was alone now. She had no one.

Julia buried her mother at Memorial Park Cemetery in Kansas City. There were no mourners. Julia stood at the graveside and thought, *It isn't fair, Mama. You made one mistake and paid for it the rest of your life. I wish I could have taken some of your pain away. I love you very much, Mama. I'll always love you*. All she had left of her mother's years on earth was a collection of old photographs and clippings.

With her mother gone, Julia's thoughts turned to the Stanford family. They were rich. She could go to them for help. *Never*, she decided. *Not after the way Harry Stanford treated my mother*.

But she had to earn a living. She was faced with a career decision. She thought wryly, *Maybe I'll become a brain surgeon*.

Or a painter?

Opera singer?

Physicist?

Astronaut?

83

She settled for a secretarial course at night school at Kansas City Kansas Community College.

The day after Julia finished the course, she visited an employment agency. There were a dozen applicants waiting to see the employment counselor. Sitting next to Julia was an attractive woman her age.

'Hi! I'm Sally Connors.'

'Julia Stanford.'

'I've got to get a job today,' Sally moaned. 'I've been kicked out of my apartment.'

Julia heard her name called.

'Good luck!' Sally said.

'Thanks.'

Julia walked into the office of the employment counselor.

'Sit down, please.'

'Thank you.'

'I see from your application that you have a college education and summer work experience. And you have a high recommendation from the secretarial school.' She looked at the dossier on her desk. 'You take shorthand at ninety words per minute, and type at sixty words per minute?'

'Yes, ma'am.'

'I might have just the thing for you. There's a small firm of architects that's looking for a secretary. The salary isn't very large, I'm afraid.'

'That's okay,' Julia said quickly.

'Very well. I'm going to send you over there.' She handed Julia a slip of paper with a typed name and address on it. 'They'll interview you at noon tomorrow.'

Julia smiled happily. 'Thank you.' She was filled with a sense of excitement.

When Julia came out of the office, Sally's name was being called.

'I hope you get something,' Julia said.

'Thanks!'

On an impulse, Julia decided to stay and wait. Ten minutes later, when Sally came out of the inner office, she was grinning.

'I got an interview! She telephoned, and I'm going to the American Mutual Insurance Company tomorrow for a receptionist job. How did you do?'

'I'll know tomorrow, too.'

'I'm sure we'll make it. Why don't we have lunch together and celebrate?'

'Fine.'

At lunch they talked, and their friendship clicked instantly.

'I looked at an apartment in Overland Park,' Sally said. 'It's a two-bedroom and bath, with a kitchen and living room. It's really nice. I can't afford it alone, but if the two of us . . .'

Julia smiled. 'I'd like that.' She crossed her fingers. 'If I get the job.'

'You'll get it!' Sally assured her.

On the way to the offices of Peters, Eastman & Tolkin, Julia thought, *This could be my big opportunity. This could lead anywhere. I mean, this isn't just a job. I'll be working for architects. Dreamers who build and shape the city's skyline, who create beauty and magic out of stone. Maybe I'll study architecture myself, so that I can help them and be a part of that dream.*

The office was in a dingy old commercial building on Amour Boulevard. Julia took the elevator to the third floor, got off and stopped at a scarred door marked PETERS, EASTMAN & TOLKIN, ARCHITECTS. She took a deep breath to calm herself and entered.

Three men were waiting for her in the reception room, examining her as she walked in the door.

'You're here for the secretarial job?'

'Yes, sir.'

'I'm Al Peters.' The bald one.

'Bob Eastman.' The ponytail.

'Max Tolkin.' The potbelly.

They all appeared to be somewhere in their forties.

'We understand this is your first secretarial job,' Al Peters said.

85

'Yes, it is,' Julia replied. Then quickly she added, 'But I'm a fast learner. I'll work very hard.' She decided not to mention her idea about going to school to study architecture yet. She would wait until they got to know her better.

'All right, we'll try you out,' Bob Eastman said, 'and see how it goes.'

Julia felt a sense of exhilaration. 'Oh, thank you! You won't be –'

'About the salary,' Max Tolkin said. 'I'm afraid we can't pay very much at the beginning.'

'That's all right,' Julia said. 'I . . .'

'Three hundred a week,' Al Peters told her.

They were right. It was not much money. Julia made a quick decision. 'I'll take it.'

They looked at one another and exchanged smiles.

'Great!' Al Peters said. 'Let me show you around.'

The tour took only a few seconds. There was the little reception room and three small offices that looked as though they had been furnished by the Salvation Army. The lavatory was down the hall. They were all architects, but Al Peters was the businessman, Bob Eastman was the salesman, and Max Tolkin handled construction.

'You'll be working for all of us,' Peters told her.

'Fine.' Julia knew she was going to make herself indispensable to them.

Al Peters looked at his watch. 'It's twelve thirty. How about some lunch?'

Julia felt a little thrill. She was part of the team now. *They're inviting me to lunch.*

He turned to Julia. 'There's a delicatessen down the block. I'll have a corned beef sandwich on rye with mustard, potato salad, and a Danish.'

'Oh.' *So much for 'They're inviting me to lunch.'*

Tolkin said, 'I'll have a pastrami and some chicken soup.'

'Yes, sir.'

Bob Eastman spoke up. 'I'll have the pot roast platter and a soft drink.'

'Oh, make sure the corned beef is lean,' Al Peters told her.

'Lean corned beef.'

Max Tolkin said, 'Make sure that the soup is hot.'

'Right. Soup hot.'

Bob Eastman said, 'Make my soft drink a diet cola.'

'Diet cola.'

'Here's some money.' Al Peters handed her a twenty dollar bill.

Ten minutes later, Julia was in the delicatessen, talking to the man behind the counter. 'I want one lean corned beef sandwich on rye with mustard, potato salad, and a Danish. A pastrami sandwich and very hot chicken soup. And a pot roast platter and diet cola.'

The man nodded. 'You work for Peters, Eastman, and Tolkin, huh?'

Julia and Sally moved into the apartment in Overland Park the following week. The apartment consisted of two small bedrooms, a living room with furniture that had seen too many tenants, a kitchenette, dinette, and a bathroom. *They'll never confuse this place with the Ritz*, Julia thought.

'We'll take turns at cooking,' Sally suggested.

'Fine.'

Sally prepared the first meal, and it was delicious.

The next night was Julia's turn. Sally took one bite of the dish that Julia had made and said, 'Julia, I don't have a lot of life insurance. Why don't I do the cooking and you do the cleaning?'

The two roommates got along well. On weekends they would go to see movies at the Glenwood 4, and shop at the Bannister Mall. They bought their clothes at the Super Flea Discount House. One night a week they went out to an inexpensive restaurant for dinner – Stephenson's Old Apple Farm or the Café Max for Mediterranean specialties. When they could afford it, they would drop in at Charlie Charlies to hear jazz.

*   *   *

Julia enjoyed working for Peters, Eastman & Tolkin. To say that the firm was not doing well was an understatement. Clients were scarce. Julia felt that she wasn't doing much to help build the skyline of the city, but she enjoyed being around her three bosses. They were like a surrogate family, and each one confided his problems to Julia. She was capable and efficient, and she very quickly reorganized the office.

Julia decided to do something about the lack of clients. But what? She soon had the answer. There was an item in the *Kansas City Star* about a luncheon for a new executive secretary organization. The chairperson was Susan Bandy.

The following day, at noon, Julia said to Al Peters, 'I may be a little late coming back from lunch.'

He smiled. 'No problem, Julia.' He thought how lucky they were to have her.

Julia arrived at the Plaza Inn and went to the room where the luncheon was being given. The woman seated at the table near the door said, 'May I help you?'

'Yes. I'm here for the Executive Women's luncheon.'

'Your name?'

'Julia Stanford.'

The woman looked at the list in front of her. 'I'm afraid I don't see your –'

Julia smiled. 'Isn't that just like Susan? I'll have to have a talk with her. I'm the executive secretary with Peters, Eastman, and Tolkin.'

The woman looked uncertain. 'Well . . .'

'Don't worry about it. I'll just go in and find Susan.'

In the banquet room was a group of well-dressed women chatting among themselves. Julia approached one of them. 'Which one is Susan Bandy?'

'She's over there.' She indicated a tall, striking-looking woman in her forties.

Julia went up to her. 'Hi. I'm Julia Stanford.'

'Hello.'

'I'm with Peters, Eastman, and Tolkin. I'm sure you've heard of them.'

'Well, I . . .'

'They're the fastest growing architectural firm in Kansas City.'

'I see.'

'I don't have a lot of time to spare, but I would like to contribute whatever I can to the organization.'

'Well, that's very kind of you, Miss . . . ?'

'Stanford.'

That was the beginning.

The Executive Women's organization represented most of the top firms in Kansas City, and in no time at all, Julia was networking with them. She had lunch with one or more of the individual members at least once a week.

'Our company is going to put up a new building in Olathe.'

And Julia would immediately report back to her bosses.

'Mr Hanley wants to build a summer home in Tonganoxie.'

And before anyone else found out about it, Peters, Eastman & Tolkin had the jobs.

Bob Eastman called Julia in one day and said, 'You deserve a raise, Julia. You're doing a great job. You're one hell of a secretary!'

'Would you do me a favor?' Julia asked.

'Sure.'

'Call me an executive secretary. It will help my credibility.'

From time to time, Julia would read newspaper articles about her father, or watch him being interviewed on television. She never mentioned him to Sally or to her employers.

When Julia was younger, one of her daydreams had been that, like Dorothy, she would one day be whisked away from Kansas to some beautiful, magical place. It would be a place filled with yachts and private planes and palaces. But now, with the news of her father's death, that dream was ended forever. *Well, I got the Kansas part right*, she thought wryly.

I have no family left. But I do, Julia corrected herself. *I have two half brothers and a half sister. They're family. Should I go visit them? Good idea? Bad idea? I wonder how we would feel about one another?*

Her decision turned out to be a matter of life or death.

Chapter Twelve

It was the gathering of a clan of strangers. It had been years since they had seen or communicated with one another.

Judge Tyler Stanford arrived in Boston by plane.

Kendall Stanford Renaud flew in from Paris. Marc Renaud took the train from New York.

Woody Stanford and Peggy drove up from Hobe Sound.

The heirs had been notified that the funeral services would take place at King's Chapel. The street outside the church was barricaded, and there were policemen to hold back the crowd that had gathered to watch the dignitaries arrive. The vice president of the United States was there, as well as senators and ambassadors and statesmen from as far away as Turkey and Saudi Arabia. During his lifetime, Harry Stanford had cast a large shadow, and all seven hundred seats in the chapel would be occupied.

Tyler and Woody and Kendall, with their spouses, met inside the vestry. It was an awkward meeting. They were alien to one another, and the only thing they had in common was the body of the man in the hearse outside the church.

'This is my husband, Marc,' Kendall said.

'This is my wife, Peggy. Peggy, my sister, Kendall, and my brother, Tyler.'

There were polite exchanges of hellos. They stood there, uncomfortably studying one another, until an usher came up to the group.

'Excuse me,' he said in a hushed voice. 'The services are about to begin. Would you follow me, please?'

He led them to a reserved pew at the front of the chapel. They took their seats and waited, each preoccupied with his or her own thoughts.

To Tyler, it felt strange to be back in Boston. The only good memories he had of it were when his mother and Rosemary were alive. When he was eleven, Tyler had seen a print of the famous Goya painting *Saturn Devouring His Son*, and he had always identified it with his father.

And now, Tyler, looking over at his father's coffin as it was carried into the church by the pallbearers, thought, *Saturn is dead.*

'*I know your dirty little secret.*'

The minister stepped into the chapel's historic wine-glass shaped pulpit.

'"Jesus said unto her, I am the resurrection and the life: he that believeth in me, though he were dead, yet shall he live: and whosoever liveth and believeth in me shall never die."'

Woody was feeling exhilarated. He had taken a hit of heroin before coming to the church, and it had not worn off yet. He glanced over at his brother and sister. *Tyler has put on weight. He looks like a judge. Kendall has turned into a beauty, but she seems to be under a strain. I wonder if it's because Father died? No. She hated him as much as I did.* He looked at his wife, seated next to him. *I'm sorry I didn't get to show her off to the old man. He would have died of a heart attack.*

The minister was speaking.

'"Like as a father pitieth *his* children, *so* the Lord pitieth them that fear him. For he knoweth our frame; he remembereth that we are dust."'

Kendall was not listening to the service. She was thinking about the red dress. Her father had telephoned her in New York one afternoon.

'*So you've become a big-shot designer, have you? Well, let's see how good you are. I'm taking my new girlfriend to a charity ball Saturday night. She's your size. I want you to design a dress for her.'*

'Saturday? I can't, Father. I . . .'

'You'll do it.'

And she had designed the ugliest dress she could conceive of. It had a large black bow in front and yards of ribbons and lace. It was a monstrosity. She had sent it to her father, and he had telephoned her again.

'I got the dress. By the way, my girlfriend can't make it Saturday, so you're going to be my date, and you're going to wear that dress.'

'No!'

And then the terrible phrase: *'You don't want to disappoint me, do you?'*

And she had gone, not daring to change the dress, and had spent the most humiliating evening of her life.

'"For we brought nothing into this world, and it is certain we can carry nothing out. The Lord gave, and the Lord hath taken away; blessed be the name of the Lord!"'

Peggy Stanford was uncomfortable. She was awed by the splendor of the huge church and the elegant-looking people in it. She had never been to Boston before, and to her it meant the world of Stanfords, with all its pomp and glory. These people were so much better than she was. She took her husband's hand.

'"All flesh is grass, and all the goodliness thereof is as the flower of the field . . . The grass withereth, the flower fadeth; but the word of our God shall stand forever."'

Marc was thinking about the blackmail letter that his wife had received. It had been worded very carefully, very cleverly. It would be impossible to find out who was behind it. He looked at Kendall, seated next to him, pale and tense. *How much more can she take?* he wondered. He moved closer to her.

*   *   *

93

'"Unto God's gracious mercy and protection we commit you. The Lord bless you and keep you. The Lord make his face to shine upon you and be gracious unto you. The Lord lift up the light of his countenance upon you and give you peace, now and forever. Amen."'

With the service finished, the minister announced, 'The burial services will be private – family members only.'

Tyler looked at the coffin and thought about the body inside. Last night, before the casket was secured, he had gone straight from Boston's Logan International Airport to the viewing at the funeral home.

He wanted to see his father dead.

Woody watched as the coffin was carried out of the church past the staring mourners, and he smiled: *Give the people what they want.*

The graveside ceremony at the old Mount Auburn Cemetery in Cambridge was brief. The family watched Harry Stanford's body being lowered to its final resting place, and as the dirt was being thrown onto the casket the minister said, 'There's no need for you to stay any longer if you don't wish to.'

Woody nodded. 'Right.' The effect of the heroin was beginning to wear off, and he was starting to feel jittery. 'Let's get the hell out of here.'

Marc said, 'Where are we going?'

Tyler turned to the group. 'We're staying at Rose Hill. It's all been arranged. We'll stay there until the estate is settled.'

A few minutes later, they were in limousines on their way to the house.

Boston had a strict social hierarchy. The nouveau riche lived on Commonwealth Avenue, and the social climbers on Newbury Street. Less affluent old families lived on Marlborough Street. Back Bay was the city's newest and most prestigious address, but Beacon Hill was still the citadel for Boston's oldest and wealthiest families. It was a rich mixture of Victorian townhouses and brownstones, old churches and chic shopping areas.

Rose Hill, the Stanford estate, was a beautiful old Victorian house that stood amid three acres of land on Beacon Hill. The house that the Stanford children had grown up in was filled with unpleasant memories. When the limousines arrived in front of the house, the passengers got out and stared up at the old mansion.

'I can't believe Father isn't going to be inside, waiting for us,' Kendall said.

Woody grinned. 'He's too busy trying to run things in hell.'

Tyler took a deep breath. 'Let's go.'

As they approached the front door it opened, and Clark, the butler, stood there. He was in his seventies, a dignified, capable servant who had worked at Rose Hill for more than thirty years. He had watched the children grow up, and had lived through all the scandals.

Clark's face lit up as he saw the group. 'Good afternoon!'

Kendall gave him a warm hug. 'Clark, it's so good to see you again.'

'It's been a long time, Miss Kendall.'

'It's Mrs Renaud now. This is my husband, Marc.'

'How do you do, sir?'

'My wife has told me a great deal about you.'

'Nothing too terrible I hope, sir.'

'On the contrary. She has only fond memories of you.'

'Thank you, sir.' Clark turned to Tyler. 'Good afternoon, Judge Stanford.'

'Hello, Clark.'

'It's a pleasure to see you, sir.'

'Thank you. You're looking very well.'

'So are you, sir. I'm so sorry about what has happened.'

'Thank you. Are you set up here to take care of all of us?'

'Oh, yes. I think we can make everyone comfortable.'

'Am I in my old room?'

Clark smiled. 'That's right.' He turned to Woody. 'I'm pleased to see you, Mr Woodrow. I want to –'

Woody grabbed Peggy's arm. 'Come on,' he said curtly. 'I want to get freshened up.'

The others watched as Woody pushed past them and took Peggy upstairs.

The rest of the group walked into the huge drawing room. The room was dominated by a pair of massive Louis XIV armoires. Scattered around the room were a giltwood console table with a molded marble top, and an array of exquisite period chairs and couches. An ormolu chandelier hung from the high ceiling. On the walls were dark medieval paintings.

Clark turned to Tyler. 'Judge Stanford, I have a message for you. Mr Simon Fitzgerald would like you to telephone him to tell him when it would be convenient to arrange a meeting with the family.'

'Who is Simon Fitzgerald?' Marc asked.

Kendall replied. 'He's the family attorney. Father has been with him forever but we've never met him.'

'I presume he wants to discuss the disposition of the estate,' Tyler said. He turned to the others. 'If it's all right with all of you, I'll arrange for him to meet us here tomorrow morning.'

'That will be fine,' Kendall said.

'The chef is preparing dinner,' Clark told them. 'Will eight o'clock be satisfactory?'

'Yes,' Tyler said. 'Thank you.'

'Eva and Millie will show you to your rooms.'

Tyler turned to his sister and her husband. 'We'll meet down here at eight, shall we?'

As Woody and Peggy entered their bedroom upstairs, Peggy asked, 'Are you all right?'

'I'm fine,' Woody snapped. 'Leave me alone.'

She watched him go into the bathroom and slam the door shut. She stood there, waiting.

Ten minutes later, Woody came out. He was smiling. 'Hi, baby.'

'Hi.'

'Well, how do you like the old house?'

'It's . . . it's enormous.'

'It's a monstrosity.' He walked over to the bed and put his arms around Peggy. 'This is my old room. These walls were covered with sports posters – the Bruins, the Celtics, the Red Sox. I wanted to be an athlete. I had big dreams. In my senior year in boarding school, I was captain of the football team. I got offers of admission from half a dozen college coaches.'

'Which one did you take?'

He shook his head. 'None of them. My father said they were only interested in the Stanford name, that they just wanted money from him. He sent me to an engineering school where they didn't play football.' He was silent for a moment. Then he mumbled, 'I could'a been a contenda . . .'

She looked at him puzzled. 'What?'

He looked up. 'Didn't you ever see *On the Waterfront*?'

'No.'

'It was a line that Marlon Brando said. It means we both got screwed.'

'Your father must have been tough.'

Woody gave a short, derisive laugh. 'That's the nicest thing anyone has ever said about him. I remember when I was just a kid, I fell off a horse. I wanted to get back on and ride again. My father wouldn't let me. "You'll never be a rider," he said. "You're too clumsy."' Woody looked up at her. 'That's why I became a nine-goal polo player.'

They came together at the dinner table, strangers to one another, seated in an uncomfortable silence, their only connection childhood traumas.

Kendall looked around the room. Terrible memories mingled with an appreciation for its beauty. The dining table was classical French, an early Louis XV, surrounded by Directoire walnut chairs. In one corner was a blue-and-cream painted French provincial corner armoire. On the walls were drawings by Watteau and Fragonard.

Kendall turned to Tyler. 'I read about your decision in the *Fiorello* case. He deserved what you gave him.'

'It must be exciting being a judge,' Peggy said.

'Sometimes it is.'

'What kind of cases do you handle?' Marc inquired.

'Criminal cases – rapes, drugs, murder.'

Kendall turned pale and started to say something, and Marc grabbed her hand and squeezed it as a warning.

Tyler said politely to Kendall, 'You've become a successful designer.'

Kendall was finding it hard to breathe. 'Yes.'

'She's fantastic,' Marc said.

'And Marc, what do you do?'

'I'm with a brokerage house.'

'Oh, you're one of those young Wall Street millionaires.'

'Well, not exactly, judge. I'm really just getting started.'

Tyler gave Marc a patronizing look. 'I guess it's lucky you have a successful wife.'

Kendall blushed and whispered in Marc's ear, 'Pay no attention. Remember I love you.'

Woody was beginning to feel the effect of the drug. He turned to look at his wife. 'Peggy could use some decent clothes,' he said. 'But she doesn't care how she looks. Do you, angel?'

Peggy sat there, embarrassed, not knowing what to say.

'Maybe a little waitress costume?' Woody suggested.

Peggy said, 'Excuse me.' She got up from the table and fled upstairs.

They were all staring at Woody.

He grinned. 'She's oversensitive. So, we're having a discussion about the will tomorrow, eh?'

'That's right,' Tyler said.

'I'll make you a bet the old man didn't leave us one dime.'

Marc said, 'But there's so much money in the estate . . .'

Woody snorted. 'You didn't know our father. He probably left us his old jackets and a box of cigars. He liked to use his money to control us. His favorite line was "*You don't want to disappoint*

98

me, do you?" And we all behaved like good little children because, as you said, there was so much money. Well, I'll bet the old man found a way to take it with him.'

Tyler said, 'We'll know tomorrow, won't we?'

Early the following morning, Simon Fitzgerald and Steve Sloane arrived. Clark escorted them into the library. 'I'll inform the family that you're here,' he said.

'Thank you.' They watched him leave.

The library was huge and opened onto a garden through two large French doors. The room was paneled in dark-stained oak, and the walls were lined with bookcases filled with handsome leather-bound volumes. There was a scattering of comfortable chairs and Italian reading lamps. In one corner stood a customized beveled-glass and ormolu-mounted mahogany cabinet that displayed Harry Stanford's enviable gun collection. Special drawers had been designed beneath the display case to house the ammunition.

'It's going to be an interesting morning,' Steve said. 'I wonder how they're going to react.'

'We'll find out soon enough.'

Kendall and Marc came into the room first.

Simon Fitzgerald said, 'Good morning. I'm Simon Fitzgerald. This is my associate, Steve Sloane.'

'I'm Kendall Renaud, and this is my husband, Marc.'

The men shook hands.

Woody and Peggy entered the room.

Kendall said, 'Woody, this is Mr Fitzgerald and Mr Sloane.'

Woody nodded. 'Hi. Did you bring the cash with you?'

'Well, we really . . .'

'I'm only kidding! This is my wife, Peggy.' Woody looked at Steve. 'Did the old man leave me anything or . . . ?'

Tyler entered the room. 'Good morning.'

'Judge Stanford?'

'Yes.'

'I'm Simon Fitzgerald, and this is Steve Sloane, my associate. It was Steve who arranged to have your father's body brought back from Corsica.'

Tyler turned to Steve. 'I appreciate that. We're not sure what happened exactly. The press has had so many different versions of the story. Was there foul play involved?'

'No. It seems to have been an accident. Your father's yacht was caught in a terrible storm off the coast of Corsica. According to a deposition from Dmitri Kaminsky, his bodyguard, your father was standing on the outside veranda of his cabin and the wind blew some papers out of his hand. He reached for them, lost his balance, and fell overboard. By the time they recovered his body, it was too late.'

'What a horrible way to die.' Kendall shuddered.

'Did you talk to this Kaminsky person?' Tyler asked.

'Unfortunately, no. By the time I arrived in Corsica, he had left.'

Fitzgerald said, 'The captain of the yacht had advised your father not to sail into that storm, but for some reason, he was in a hurry to return here. He had arranged for a helicopter to bring him back. There was some kind of urgent problem.'

Tyler asked, 'Do you know what the problem was?'

'No. I cut short my vacation to meet him back here. I don't know what –'

Woody interrupted. 'That's all very interesting, but it's ancient history, isn't it? Let's talk about the will. Did he leave us anything or not?' His hands were twitching.

'Why don't we sit down?' Tyler suggested.

They took chairs. Simon Fitzgerald sat at the desk, facing them. He opened a briefcase and started to take out some papers.

Woody was ready to explode. '*Well?* For God's sake, did he or didn't he?'

Kendall said, 'Woody . . .'

'I know the answer,' Woody said angrily. 'He didn't leave us a damn cent.'

Fitzgerald looked into the faces of the children of Harry Stanford. 'As a matter of fact,' he said, 'each of you will share equally in the estate.'

Steve could feel the sudden euphoria that swept through the room.

Woody was staring at Fitzgerald, openmouthed. '*What? Are you serious?*' He jumped to his feet. 'That's fantastic!' He turned to the others. 'Did you hear that? The old bastard finally came through!' He looked at Simon Fitzgerald. 'How much money are we talking about?'

'I don't have the exact figure. According to the latest issue of *Forbes* magazine, Stanford Enterprises is worth six billion dollars. Most of it is invested in various corporations, but there is roughly four hundred million dollars available in liquid assets.'

Kendall was listening, stunned. 'That's more than a hundred million dollars for each of us. I can't believe it!' *I'm free,* she thought. *I can pay them off and be rid of them forever.* She looked at Marc, her face shining, and squeezed his hand.

'Congratulations,' Marc said. He knew more than the others what the money would mean.

Simon Fitzgerald spoke up. 'As you know, ninety-nine percent of the shares in Stanford Enterprises was held by your father. So those shares will be divided equally among you. Also, now that his father is deceased, Judge Stanford owns outright that other one percent that had been held in trust. Of course, there will be certain formalities. Furthermore, I should inform you that there is a possibility of another heir being involved.'

'Another heir?' Tyler asked.

'Your father's will specifically provides that the estate is to be divided equally among his issue.'

Peggy looked puzzled. 'What . . . what do you mean by *issue*?'

Tyler spoke up. 'Natural-born descendants and legally adopted descendants.'

Fitzgerald nodded. 'That is correct. Any descendant born out of wedlock is deemed a descendant of the mother and the father, whose protection is established under the law of the jurisdiction.'

'What are you saying?' Woody asked impatiently.

'I'm saying that there may be another claimant.'

Kendall looked at him. 'Who?'

Simon Fitzgerald hesitated. There was no way to be tactful. 'I'm sure that you are all aware of the fact that a number of years ago, your father sired a child by a governess who worked here.'

'Rosemary Nelson,' Tyler said.

'Yes. Her daughter was born at St Joseph's Hospital in Milwaukee. She named her Julia.'

The room was thick with silence.

'Hey!' Woody exclaimed. 'That was twenty-five years ago.'

'Twenty-six, to be exact.'

Kendall asked, 'Does anyone know where she is?'

Simon Fitzgerald could hear Harry Stanford's voice: '*She wrote to tell me that it was a girl. Well, if she thinks she's going to get a dime out of me, she can go to hell.*' 'No,' Fitzgerald said slowly. 'No one knows where she is.'

'Then what the hell are we talking about?' Woody demanded.

'I just wanted all of you to be aware that if she does appear, she will be entitled to an equal share of the estate.'

'I don't think we have anything to worry about,' Woody said confidently. 'She probably never even knew who her father was.'

Tyler turned to Simon Fitzgerald. 'You say you don't know the exact amount of the estate. May I ask why not?'

'Because our firm handles only your father's personal affairs. His corporate affairs are represented by two other law firms. I've been in touch with them and have asked them to prepare financial statements as soon as possible.'

'What kind of timeframe are we talking about?' Kendall asked anxiously. *We will need $100,000 immediately to cover our expenses.*

'Probably two to three months.'

Marc saw the consternation on his wife's face. He turned to Fitzgerald. 'Isn't there some way to hurry things along?'

Steve Sloane answered. 'I'm afraid not. The will has to go through probate court, and their calendar is rather heavy right now.'

'What is a probate court?' Peggy asked.

'*Probate* is from the past participle of *probare* – to prove. It's the act of –'

'She didn't ask you for a damned English lesson!' Woody exploded. 'Why can't we just wrap things up now?'

Tyler turned to his brother. 'The law doesn't work that way.

102

When there's a death, the will has to be filed in the probate court. There has to be an appraisal of all assets – real estate, closely held corporations, cash, jewelry – then an inventory has to be prepared and filed in the court. Taxes have to be taken care of, and specific bequests paid. After that, a petition is filed for permission to distribute the balance of the estate to the beneficiaries.'

Woody grinned, 'What the hell. I've waited almost forty years to be a millionaire. I guess I can wait another month or two.'

Simon Fitzgerald stood up. 'Aside from your father's bequests to you, there are some minor gifts, but they don't affect the bulk of the estate.' Fitzgerald looked around the room. 'Well, if there's nothing else . . .'

Tyler rose. 'I think not. Thank you, Mr Fitzgerald, Mr Sloane. If there are any problems, we'll be in touch.'

Fitzgerald nodded to the group. 'Ladies and gentlemen.' He turned and went toward the door, Steve Sloane following him.

Outside, in the driveway, Simon Fitzgerald turned to Steve. 'Well, now you've met the family. What do you think?'

'It was more like a celebration than a mourning. I'm puzzled by something, Simon. If their father hated them as much as they seem to hate him, why did he leave them all that money?'

Simon Fitzgerald shrugged. 'That's something we'll never know. Maybe that's why he was coming to see me, to leave the money to someone else.'

None of the group was able to sleep that night, each lost in his or her own thoughts.

Tyler was thinking, *It's happened. It's really happened! I can afford to give Lee the world. Anything! Everything!*

Kendall was thinking, *As soon as I get the money, I'll find a way to buy them off permanently, and I'll make sure they never bother me again.*

Woody was thinking, *I'm going to have the best string of polo ponies in the world. No more borrowing other people's ponies. I'm going to be ten goals!* He glanced over at Peggy, sleeping at his side. *The first thing I'll do is get rid of this stupid bitch.* Then

103

he thought, *No, I can't do that* . . . He got out of bed and went into the bathroom. When he came out, he was feeling wonderful.

The atmosphere at breakfast the next morning was exuberant.

'Well,' Woody said happily, 'I suppose all of you have been making plans.'

Marc shrugged. 'How does one plan for something like this? It is an unbelievable amount of money.'

Tyler looked up. 'It's certainly going to change all our lives.'

Woody nodded. 'The bastard should have given it to us while he was alive, so we could have enjoyed it then. If it's not impolite to hate the dead, I have to tell you something . . .'

Kendall said reproachfully, 'Woody . . .'

'Well, let's not be hypocrites. We all despised him, and he deserved it. Just look what he tried to –'

Clark came into the room. He stood there, apologetically. 'Excuse me,' he said. 'There is a Miss Julia Stanford at the door.'

NOON

Chapter Thirteen

'*Julia Stanford?*'

They stared at one another, frozen.

'The hell she is!' Woody exploded.

Tyler said quickly, 'I suggest we adjourn to the library.' He turned to Clark. 'Would you send the young lady in there, please?'

'Yes, sir.'

She stood in the doorway, looking at each of them, obviously ill at ease. 'I . . . I probably shouldn't have come,' she said.

'You're damn right!' Woody said. 'Who the hell are you?'

'I'm Julia Stanford.' She was almost stammering in her nervousness.

'No. I mean who are you *really*?'

She started to say something, then shook her head. 'I . . . My mother was Rosemary Nelson. Harry Stanford was my father.'

The group looked at one another.

'Do you have any proof of that?' Tyler asked.

She swallowed. 'I don't think I have any *real* proof.'

'Of course you don't,' Woody snapped. 'How do you have the nerve to – ?'

Kendall interrupted. 'This is rather a shock to all of us, as you can imagine. If what you're saying is true, then you're . . . you're our half sister.'

Julia nodded. 'You're Kendall.' She turned to Tyler. 'You're Tyler.' She turned to Woody. 'And you're Woodrow. They call you Woody.'

'As *People* Magazine could have told you,' Woody said sarcastically.

Tyler spoke up. 'I'm sure you can understand our position, Miss . . . er . . . Without some positive proof, there's no way we could possibly accept . . .'

'I understand.' She looked around nervously. 'I don't know why I came here.'

'Oh, I think you do,' Woody said. 'It's called money.'

'I'm not interested in the money,' she said indignantly. 'The truth is that I . . . I came here hoping to meet my family.'

Kendall was studying her. 'Where is your mother?'

'She passed away. When I read that our father died . . .'

'You decided to look us up,' Woody said mockingly.

Tyler spoke. 'You say you have no legal proof of who you are.'

'Legal? I . . . I suppose not. I didn't even think about that. But there are things I couldn't possibly know about unless I had heard them from my mother.'

'For example?' Marc said.

She stopped to think. 'I remember my mother used to talk about a greenhouse in back. She loved plants and flowers, and she would spend hours there.'

Woody spoke up. 'Photographs of that greenhouse were in a lot of magazines.'

'What else did your mother tell you?' Tyler asked.

'Oh, there were so many things! She loved to talk about all of you and the good times you used to have.' She thought for a moment. 'There was the day she took you on the swan boats when you were very young. One of you almost fell overboard. I don't remember which one.'

Woody and Kendall looked over at Tyler.

'I was the one,' he said.

'She took you shopping at Filene's. One of you got lost, and everyone was in a panic.'

Kendall said slowly, 'I got lost that day.'

'Yes? What else?' Tyler asked.

'She took you to the Union Oyster House and you tasted your first oyster and got sick.'

'I remember that.'

They stared at each other, silent.

She looked at Woody. 'You and Mother went to the Charlestown Navy Yard to see the USS *Constitution*, and you wouldn't leave. She had to drag you away.' She turned to Kendall. 'And in the Public Garden one day, you picked some flowers and were almost arrested.'

Kendall swallowed. 'That's right.'

They were all listening to her intently now, fascinated.

'One day, Mother took all of you to the natural history museum, and you were terrified of the mastadon and sea serpent skeleton.'

Kendall said slowly, 'None of us slept that night.'

Julia turned to Woody. 'One Christmas, she took you skating. You fell down and broke a tooth. When you were seven years old, you fell out of a tree and had to have your leg stitched up. You had a scar.'

Woody said reluctantly, 'I still do.'

She turned to the others. 'One of you was bitten by a dog. I forgot which one. My mother rushed you to the emergency room at Massachusetts General.'

Tyler nodded. 'I had to have shots against rabies.'

Her words were coming out in a torrent now. 'Woody, when you were eight years old, you ran away. You were going to Hollywood to become an actor. Your father was furious with you. He made you go to your room without dinner. Mother sneaked some food up to your room.'

Woody nodded, silent.

'I . . . I don't know what else I can tell you. I . . .' She suddenly remembered something. 'I have a photograph in my purse.' She opened her purse and took it out. She handed the picture to Kendall.

They all gathered around to look at it. It was a picture of the three of them when they were children, standing next to an attractive young woman in a governess's uniform.

'Mother gave me that.'

Tyler asked, 'Did she leave you anything else?'

She shook her head. 'No. I'm sorry. She didn't want anything around that reminded her of Harry Stanford.'

'Except you, of course,' Woody said.

She turned to him, defiantly. 'I don't care whether you believe me or not. You don't understand . . . I . . . I was so hoping –' She broke off.

Tyler spoke. 'As my sister said, your sudden appearance is rather a shock for us. I mean . . . someone appearing out of nowhere and claiming to be a member of the family . . . you can see our problem. I think we need a little time to discuss this.'

'Of course, I understand.'

'Where are you staying?'

'At the Tremont House.'

'Why don't you go back there? We'll have a car take you. And we'll be in touch shortly.'

She nodded. 'All right.' She looked at each of them for a moment, and then said softly, 'No matter what you think – you're my family.'

'I'll walk you to the door,' Kendall said.

She smiled. 'That's all right. I can find my own way. I feel as if I know every inch of this house.'

They watched her turn and walk out of the room.

Kendall said, 'Well! It . . . it looks as though we have a sister.'

'I don't believe it,' Woody retorted.

'It seems to me . . . ,' Marc began.

They were all talking at once. Tyler raised a hand. 'This isn't getting us anywhere. Let's look at this logically. In a sense, this person is on trial here and we're her jurors. It's up to us to determine her innocence or guilt. In a jury trial, the decision must be unanimous. We must all agree.'

Woody nodded. 'Right.'

Tyler said, 'Then I would like to cast the first vote. I think the lady is a fraud.'

'A fraud? How can she be?' Kendall demanded. 'She couldn't possibly know all those intimate details about us if she weren't real.'

Tyler turned to her. 'Kendall, how many servants worked in this house when we were children?'

Kendall looked at him, puzzled. 'Why?'

'Dozens, right? And some of them would have known everything this young lady told us. Over the years, there have been maids, chauffeurs, butlers, chefs. Any one of them could have given her that photograph as well.'

'You mean . . . she could be in league with someone?'

'One or more,' Tyler said. 'Let's not forget that there's an enormous amount of money involved.'

'She says she doesn't want the money.' Marc reminded them.

Woody nodded. 'Sure, that's what she *says*.' He looked at Tyler. 'But how do we prove she's a fake? There's no way that –'

'There *is* a way,' Tyler said thoughtfully.

They all turned to him.

'How?' Marc asked.

'I'll have the answer for you tomorrow.'

Simon Fitzgerald said slowly, 'Are you saying that Julia Stanford has appeared after all these years?'

'A woman who *claims* she's Julia Stanford has appeared.' Tyler corrected him.

'And you don't believe her?' Steve asked.

'Absolutely not. The only so-called proof of her identity that she offered were some incidents from our childhood that at least a dozen former employees could have been aware of and an old photograph that really doesn't prove a thing. She could be in league with any one of them. I intend to prove she's a fraud.'

Steve frowned. 'How do you propose to do that?'

'It's very simple. I want a DNA test done.'

Steve Sloane was surprised. 'That would mean exhuming your father's body.'

'Yes.' Tyler turned to Simon Fitzgerald. 'Will that be a problem?'

'Under the circumstances, I could probably obtain an exhumation order. Has she agreed to this test?'

111

'I haven't asked her yet. If she refuses, it's an affirmation that she's afraid of the results.' He hesitated. 'I have to confess that I don't like doing this. But I think it's the only way we can determine the truth.'

Fitzgerald was thoughtful for a moment. 'Very well.' He turned to Steve. 'Will you handle this?'

'Of course.' He looked at Tyler. 'You're probably familiar with the procedure. The next of kin – in this case, any of the deceased's children – has to apply to the coroner's office for an exhumation permit. You'll have to tell them the reason for the request. If it's approved, the coroner's office will contact the funeral home and give them permission to go ahead. Someone from the coroner's office has to be present at the exhumation.'

'How long will this take?' Tyler asked.

'I'd say three or four days to get an approval. Today is Wednesday. We should be able to exhume the body on Monday.'

'Good.' Tyler hesitated. 'We're going to need a DNA expert, someone who will be convincing in a courtroom, if it ever goes that far. I was hoping you might know someone.'

Steve said, 'I know just the man. His name is Perry Winger. He's here in Boston. He's given expert testimony in trials all over the country. I'll call him.'

'I'd appreciate it. The sooner we get this over with, the better it will be for all of us.'

At ten o'clock the following morning, Tyler walked into the Rose Hill library, where Woody, Peggy, Kendall and Marc were waiting. At Tyler's side was a stranger.

'I want you to meet Perry Winger,' Tyler said.

'Who is he?' Woody asked.

'He's our DNA expert.'

Kendall looked at Tyler. 'What in the world do we need a DNA expert for?'

Tyler said, 'To prove that this stranger, who so conveniently appeared out of nowhere, is an impostor. I have no intention of letting her get away with this.'

'You're going to dig the old man up?' Woody asked.

'That's right. I have our attorneys working on the exhumation order now. If the woman is our half sister, the DNA will prove it. If she's not – it will prove that, too.'

Marc said, 'I'm afraid I don't understand about this DNA.'

Perry Winger cleared his throat. 'Simply put, deoxyribonucleic acid – or DNA – is the molecule of heredity. It contains each individual's unique genetic code. It can be extracted from traces of blood, semen, saliva, hair roots, and even bone. Traces of it can last in a corpse for more than fifty years.'

'I see. So it is really quite simple,' Marc said.

Perry Winger frowned. 'Believe me, it is not. There are two types of DNA testing. A PCR test, which takes three days to get results, and the more complex RFLP test, which takes six to eight weeks. For our purposes, the simpler test will be sufficient.'

'How do you do the test?' Kendall asked.

'There are several steps. First, the sample is collected and the DNA is cut into fragments. The fragments are sorted by length by placing them on a bed of gel and applying an electric current. The DNA, which is negatively charged, moves toward the positive and, several hours later, the fragments have arranged themselves by length.' He was just getting warmed up. 'Alkaline chemicals are used to split the DNA fragments apart, then the fragments are transferred to a nylon sheet, which is immersed in a bath, and radioactive probes –'

The eyes of his listeners were beginning to glaze over.

'How accurate is this test?' Woody interrupted.

'It's one hundred percent accurate in determining if the man is *not* the father. If the test is positive, it's ninety-nine point nine percent accurate.'

Woody turned to his brother. 'Tyler, you're a judge. Let's say for the sake of argument that she really is Harry Stanford's child. Her mother and our father were never married. Why should she be entitled to anything?'

'Under the law,' Tyler explained, 'if our father's paternity is established, she would be entitled to an equal share with the rest of us.'

'Then I say let's go ahead with the damned DNA test and expose her!'

Tyler, Woody, Kendall, Marc and Julia were seated at a table in the dining-room restaurant at the Tremont House.

Peggy remained behind at Rose Hill. 'All this talk about digging up a body gives me the creeps,' she said.

Now the group was facing the woman claiming to be Julia Stanford.

'I don't understand what you're asking me to do.'

'It's really very simple,' Tyler informed her. 'A doctor will take a skin sample from you to compare with our father's. If the DNA molecules match, it's positive proof that you're really his daughter. On the other hand, if you're not willing to take the test . . .'

'I . . . I don't like it.'

Woody closed in. 'Why not?'

'I don't know.' She shuddered. 'The idea of digging up my father's body to . . . to . . .'

'To prove who you are.'

She looked into each of their faces. 'I wish all of you would –'

'Yes?'

'There's no way I can convince you, is there?'

'Yes,' Tyler said. 'Agree to take this test.'

There was a long silence.

'All right. I'll do it.'

The exhumation order had been more difficult to obtain than anyone had anticipated. Simon Fitzgerald had spoken to the coroner personally.

'No! For God's sake, Simon! I can't do that! Do you know what a stink that would cause? I mean, we aren't dealing with John Doe here; we're dealing with Harry Stanford. If this ever leaked out, the media would have a field day!'

'Marvin, this is important. Billions of dollars are at stake here. So you make sure it doesn't leak out.'

'Isn't there some other way you can . . . ?'

'I'm afraid not. The woman is very convincing.'

'But the family is not convinced.'

'No.'

'Do you think she's a fraud, Simon?'

'Frankly, I don't know. But my opinion doesn't matter. In fact, none of our opinions matters. A court will demand proof, and the DNA test will provide that.'

The coroner shook his head. 'I knew old Harry Stanford. He would have hated this. I really shouldn't let . . .'

'But you will.'

The coroner sighed. 'I suppose so. Would you do me a favor?'

'Of course.'

'Keep this quiet. Let's not have a media circus.'

'You have my word. Top secret. I'll have just the family there.'

'When do you want to do this?'

'We would like to do it on Monday.'

The coroner sighed again. 'All right. I'll call the funeral home. You owe me one, Simon.'

'I won't forget this.'

At nine o'clock Monday morning, the entrance to the section of Mount Auburn Cemetery where Harry Stanford's body was buried was temporarily closed off 'for maintenance repairs'. No strangers were allowed into the grounds. Woody, Peggy, Tyler, Kendall, Marc, Julia, Simon Fitzgerald, Steve Sloane, and Dr Collins, a representative from the coroner's office, stood at the site of Harry Stanford's grave, watching four employees of the cemetery raise his coffin. Perry Winger waited off to the side.

When the coffin reached ground level, the foreman turned to the group. 'What do you want us to do now?'

'Open it, please,' Fitzgerald said. He turned to Perry Winger. 'How long will this take?'

'No more than a minute. I'll just get a quick skin sample.'

'All right,' Fitzgerald said. He nodded to the foreman. 'Go ahead.'

The foreman and his assistants began to unseal the coffin.

'I don't want to see this,' Kendall said. 'Do we have to?'

'Yes!' Woody told her. 'We really do.'

They all watched, fascinated, as the lid of the coffin was slowly removed and pushed to one side. They stood there, staring down.

'Oh, my God!' Kendall exclaimed.

The coffin was empty.

Chapter Fourteen

Back at Rose Hill, Tyler had just gotten off the phone. 'Fitzgerald says there won't be any media leaks. The cemetery certainly doesn't want that kind of bad publicity. The coroner has ordered Dr Collins to keep his mouth shut, and Perry Winger can be trusted not to talk.'

Woody wasn't paying any attention. 'I don't know how the bitch did it!' he said. 'But she isn't going to get away with it!' He glared at the others. 'I suppose you don't think she arranged it?'

Tyler said slowly, 'I'm afraid I have to agree with you, Woody. No one else possibly could have had a reason for doing this. The woman is clever and resourceful, and she's obviously not working alone. I'm not sure exactly what we're up against.'

'What are we going to do now?' Kendall asked.

Tyler shrugged. 'Frankly, I don't know. I wish I did. I'm sure she plans to go to court to contest the will.'

'Does she have a chance of winning?' Peggy asked timidly.

'I'm afraid she does. She's very persuasive. She had some of us convinced.'

'There must be *something* we can do,' Marc exclaimed. 'What about bringing the police in on this?'

'Fitzgerald says they're already looking into the disappearance of the body, and they've come to a dead end. No pun intended,' Tyler said. 'What's more, the police want this kept quiet, or they'll have every weirdo in town turning up a body.'

'We can ask them to investigate this phony!'

Tyler shook his head. 'This is not a police matter. It's a private –' He stopped for a moment, then said thoughtfully, 'You know . . .'

117

'What?'

'We *could* hire a private investigator to try to expose her.'

'That's not a bad idea. Do you know one?'

'No, not locally. But we could ask Fitzgerald to find someone. Or . . .' He hesitated. 'I've never met him, but I've heard about a private detective the district attorney in Chicago uses a great deal. He has an excellent reputation.'

Marc spoke up. 'Why don't we find out if we can hire him?'

Tyler looked around. 'That's up to the rest of you.'

'What can we lose?' Kendall asked.

'He could be expensive,' Tyler warned.

Woody snorted. 'Expensive? We're talking about billions of dollars.'

Tyler nodded. 'Of course. You're right.'

'What's his name?'

Tyler frowned. 'I can't remember. Simpson . . . Simmons . . . No, that's not it. It sounds something like that. I can call the district attorney's office in Chicago.'

The group watched as Tyler picked up the telephone on the console and dialed a number. Two minutes later, he was speaking to an assistant district attorney. 'This is Judge Tyler Stanford. I understand that your office retains a private detective from time to time who does excellent work for you. His name is something like Simmons or –'

The voice on the other end said, 'Oh, you must mean Frank Timmons.'

'Timmons! Yes, that's it.' Tyler looked at the others and smiled. 'I wonder if you could give me his telephone number so I can contact him directly?'

After he wrote down the telephone number, Tyler replaced the receiver.

He turned to the group, and said, 'Well, then, if we all agree, I'll try to reach him.'

Everyone nodded.

The following afternoon, Clark came into the drawing room, where the group was waiting. 'Mr Timmons is here.'

118

He was a man in his forties, with a pale complexion and the solid build of a boxer. He had a broken nose and bright, inquisitive eyes. He looked from Tyler to Marc and Woody, questioningly. 'Judge Stanford?'

Tyler nodded. 'I'm Judge Stanford.'

'Frank Timmons,' he said.

'Please have a seat, Mr Timmons.'

'Thank you.' He sat down. 'You're the one who telephoned, right?'

'Yes.'

'To be honest, I don't know what I can do for you. I don't have any official connections here.'

'This is purely unofficial,' Tyler assured him. 'We merely want to trace the background of a young woman.'

'You told me on the phone she claims to be your half sister, and there's no way of running a DNA test.'

'That's right,' Woody said.

He looked at the group. 'And you don't believe she's your half sister?'

There was a moment's hesitation.

'We don't,' Tyler told him. 'On the other hand, it's just possible that she is telling the truth. What we want to hire you to do is provide irrefutable evidence that she is either genuine or a fraud.'

'Fair enough. It will cost you a thousand dollars a day and expenses.'

Tyler said, 'A *thousand* . . . ?'

'We'll pay it.' Woody cut in.

'I'll need all the information you have on this woman.'

Kendall said, 'There doesn't seem to be very much.'

Tyler spoke up. 'She has no proof of any kind. She came in with a lot of stories that she says her mother told her about our childhood, and –'

He held up a hand. 'Hold it. Who was her mother?'

'Her *purported* mother was a governess we had as children named Rosemary Nelson.'

'What happened to her?'

They looked at one another uncomfortably.

Woody spoke up. 'She had an affair with our father and got pregnant. She ran away and had a baby girl.' He shrugged. 'She disappeared.'

'I see. And this woman claims to be her child?'

'That's right.'

'That's not a lot to go on.' He sat there, thinking. Finally he looked up. 'All right. I'll see what I can do.'

'That's all we ask,' Tyler said.

The first move he made was to go to the Boston Public Library and read all the micro-*fiche* about the twenty-six-year-old scandal involving Harry Stanford, the governess, and Mrs Stanford's suicide. There was enough material for a novel.

His next step was to visit Simon Fitzgerald.

'My name is Frank Timmons. I'm –'

'I know who you are, Mr Timmons. Judge Stanford asked me to cooperate with you. What can I do for you?'

'I want to trace Harry Stanford's illegitimate daughter. She'd be about twenty-eight, right?'

'Yes. She was born August ninth, 1969, at St Joseph's Hospital in Milwaukee, Wisconsin. Her mother named her Julia.' He shrugged. 'They disappeared. I'm afraid that's all the information we have.'

'It's a beginning,' he said. 'It's a beginning.'

Mrs Dougherty, the superintendent at St Joseph's Hospital in Milwaukee, was a gray-haired woman in her sixties.

'Yes, of course, I remember,' she said. 'How could I ever forget it? There was a terrible scandal. There were stories in all the newspapers. The reporters here found out who she was, and they wouldn't leave the poor girl alone.'

'Where did she go when she and the baby left here?'

'I don't know. She left no forwarding address.'

'Did she pay her bill in full before she left, Mrs Dougherty?'

'As a matter of fact . . . she didn't.'

'How do you happen to remember that?'

'Because it was so sad. I remember she sat in that very chair

120

you're sitting in, and she told me that she could pay only part of her bill, but she promised to send me the money for the rest of it. Well, that was against hospital rules, of course, but I felt so sorry for her, she was so ill when she left here, and I said yes.'

'And did she send you the rest of the money?'

'She certainly did. About two months later. Now I recall she had gotten a job at some secretarial service.'

'You wouldn't happen to remember where that was, would you?'

'No. Goodness, that was about twenty-five years ago, Mr Timmons.'

'Mrs Dougherty, do you keep all your patients' records on file?'

'Of course.' She looked up at him. 'Do you want me to go through the records?'

He smiled pleasantly. 'If you wouldn't mind.'

'Will it help Rosemary?'

'It could mean a great deal to her.'

'If you'll excuse me.' Mrs Dougherty left the office.

She returned fifteen minutes later, holding a paper in her hand. 'Here it is. Rosemary Nelson. The return address is, The Elite Typing Service. Omaha, Nebraska.'

The Elite Typing Service was run by a Mr Otto Broderick, a man in his sixties.

'We hire so many temporary employees.' He protested. 'How do you expect me to remember someone who worked here that long ago?'

'This was a rather special case. She was a single woman in her late twenties, in poor health. She had just had a baby and –'

'Rosemary!'

'That's right. Why do you remember her?'

'Well, I like to associate things, Mr Timmons. Do you know what mnemonics is?'

'Yes.'

'Well, that's what I use. I associate words. There was a movie out called *Rosemary's Baby*. So when Rosemary came in and told me she had a baby, I put the two things together and . . .'

121

'How long was Rosemary Nelson with you?'

'Oh, about a year, I guess. Then the press found out who she was, somehow, and they wouldn't leave her alone. She left town in the middle of the night to get away from them.'

'Mr Broderick, do you have any idea where Rosemary Nelson went when she left here?'

'Florida, I think. She wanted a warmer climate. I recommended her to an agency I knew there.'

'May I have the name of that agency?'

'Certainly. It's the Gale Agency. I can remember it because I associated it with the big storms they have down in Florida every year.'

Ten days after his meeting with the Stanford family, he returned to Boston. He had telephoned ahead, and the family was waiting for him. They were seated in a semi-circle, facing him as he entered the drawing room at Rose Hill.

'You said you had some news for us, Mr Timmons,' Tyler said.

'That's right.' He opened a briefcase and pulled out some papers. 'This has been a most interesting case,' he said. 'When I began –'

'Cut to the chase,' Woody said impatiently. 'Is she a fraud or not?'

He looked up. 'If you don't mind, Mr Stanford, I would like to present this in my own way.'

Tyler gave Woody a warning look. 'That's fair enough. Please go ahead.'

They watched him consult his notes. 'The Stanford governess, Rosemary Nelson, had a female child sired by Harry Stanford. She and the child went to Omaha, Nebraska, where she went to work for The Elite Typing Service. Her employer told me that she had difficulty with the weather.'

'Next, I traced her and her daughter to Florida, where she worked for the Gale Agency. They moved around a great deal. I followed the trail to San Francisco, where they were living up to ten years ago. That was the end of the trail. After that, they disappeared.' He looked up.

'That's *it*, Timmons?' Woody demanded. 'You lost the trail ten years ago?'

'No, that is *not* it.' He reached into his briefcase and took out another paper. 'The daughter, Julia, applied for a driver's license when she was seventeen.'

'What good is that?' Marc asked.

'In the state of California drivers are required to have their fingerprints taken.' He held up a card. 'These are the real Julia Stanford's fingerprints.'

Tyler said, excitedly, 'I see! If they match –'

'Then she would really be our sister.' Woody interrupted.

He nodded. 'That's right. I brought a portable fingerprint kit with me, in case you want to check her out now. Is she here?'

Tyler said, 'She's at a local hotel. I've been talking to her every morning, trying to persuade her to stay here until we get this resolved.'

'We've got her!' Woody said. 'Let's get over there!'

Half an hour later, the group was entering a hotel room at the Tremont House. As they walked in, she was packing a suitcase.

'Where are you going?' Kendall asked.

She turned to face them. 'Home. It was a mistake for me to come here in the first place.'

Tyler said, 'You can't blame us for . . . ?'

She turned on him, furious. 'Ever since I arrived, I've been met with nothing but suspicion. You think I came here to take some money away from you. Well, I didn't. I came because I wanted to find my family. I . . . never mind.' She returned to her packing.

Tyler said, 'This is Frank Timmons. He's a private detective.'

She looked up. 'Now what? Am I being arrested?'

'No, ma'am. Julia Stanford obtained a driver's license in San Francisco when she was seventeen years old.'

She stopped. 'That's right. Is that against the law?'

'No, ma'am. The point is –'

'The point is' – Tyler interrupted – 'that Julia Stanford's fingerprints are on that license.'

She looked at them. 'I don't understand. What . . . ?'

Woody spoke up. 'We want to check them against your finger-prints.'

Her lips tightened. 'No! I won't allow it!'

'Are you saying that you won't let us take your fingerprints?'

'That's right.'

'Why not?' Marc asked.

Her body was rigid. 'Because all of you make me feel like I'm some kind of criminal. Well, I've had enough! I want you to leave me alone.'

Kendall said gently, 'This is your chance to prove who you really are. We've been as upset by all this as you have. We would like to settle it.'

She stood there, looking into their faces, one by one. Finally she said wearily, 'All right. Let's get this over with.'

'Good.'

'Mr Timmons . . . ,' Tyler said.

'Right.' He took out a small fingerprint kit and set it up on the table. He opened the ink pad. 'Now, if you'll just step over here, please.'

The others watched as she walked over to the table. He picked up her hand and, one by one, pressed her fingertips onto the pad. Next, he pressed them onto a piece of white paper. 'There. That wasn't so bad, was it?' He placed the driver's license next to the fresh fingerprints.

The group walked over to the table and looked down at the two sets of prints.

They were identical.

Woody was the first to speak.

'They're . . . the . . . same.'

Kendall was looking at her with a mixture of feelings. 'You really are our sister, aren't you?'

She was smiling through her tears. 'That's what I've been trying to tell you.'

Everybody was suddenly talking at once.

'It's incredible . . . !'

'After all these years . . .'

'Why didn't your mother ever come back . . . ?'

'I'm sorry we gave you such a bad time.'

Her smile lit up the room. 'It's all right. Everything's all right now.'

Woody picked up the fingerprint card and looked at it in awe. 'My, God! This is a billion-dollar card.' He put the card in his pocket. 'I'm going to have it bronzed.'

Tyler turned to the group. 'This calls for a real celebration! I suggest we all go back to Rose Hill.' He turned to her and smiled. 'We'll give you a welcome home party. Let's get you checked out of here.'

She looked around at them, and her eyes were shining. 'It's like a dream come true. I finally have a family!'

Half an hour later they were back at Rose Hill, and she was settling into her new room. The others were downstairs, talking excitedly.

'She must feel as though she's just been through the Inquisition,' Tyler mused.

'She has,' Peggy replied. 'I don't know how she stood it.'

Kendall said, 'I wonder how she's going to adjust to her new life.'

'The same way we're all going to adjust,' Woody said dryly. 'With a lot of champagne and caviar.'

Tyler rose. 'I, for one, am glad it's finally settled. Let me go up and see if she needs any help.'

He went upstairs and walked along the corridor to her room. He knocked at her door and called loudly, 'Julia?'

'It's open. Come in.'

He stood in the doorway, and they stared silently at each other. And then Tyler carefully closed the door, held out his hands, and broke into a slow grin.

When he spoke, he said, 'We did it, Margo! We did it!'

NIGHT

Chapter Fifteen

He had plotted it with the ineffable skill of a chess master. Only this had been the most lucrative chess game in history, with stakes of billions of dollars – and he had won! He was filled with a sense of invincible power. *Is this how you felt when you closed a big deal, Father? Well, this is a bigger deal than you ever made. I've planned the crime of the century, and I've gotten away with it.*

In a sense, it had all started with Lee. *Beautiful, wonderful Lee.* The person he loved most in the world. They had met in the Berlin, the gay bar on West Belmont Avenue. Lee was tall and muscular and blond, and he was the most beautiful man Tyler had ever seen.

Their meeting had started with, 'May I buy you a drink?'

Lee had looked him over and nodded. 'That would be nice.'

After the second drink, Tyler had said, 'Why don't we have a drink over at my place?'

Lee had smiled. 'I'm expensive.'

'How expensive?'

'Five hundred dollars for the night.'

Tyler had not hesitated. 'Let's go.'

They spent the night at Tyler's home.

Lee was warm and sensitive and caring, and Tyler felt a closeness to him that he had never had with any other human being. He was flooded with emotions he had not known existed. By morning, Tyler was madly in love.

In the past, he had picked up young men at the Cairo and the

Bijou Theater and several other gay hangouts in Chicago, but now he knew that all that was going to change. From now on, he wanted only Lee.

In the morning, while Tyler was preparing breakfast, he said, 'What would you like to do tonight?'

Lee looked at him in surprise. 'Sorry. I have a date tonight.'

Tyler felt as though he had been hit in the stomach.

'But, Lee, I thought that you and I . . .'

'Tyler, dear, I'm a very valuable piece of merchandise. I go to the highest bidder. I like you, but I'm afraid you really can't afford me.'

'I can give you anything you want,' Tyler said.

Lee smiled lazily. 'Really? Well, what I want is a trip to St Tropez on a beautiful white yacht. Can you afford that?'

'Lee, I'm richer than all your friends put together.'

'Oh? I thought you said you are a judge.'

'Well, I am, yes, but I'm *going* to be rich. I mean . . . very rich.'

Lee put his arm around him. 'Don't fret, Tyler. I'm free a week from Thursday. Those eggs look delicious.'

That was the beginning. Money had been important to Tyler before, but now it became an obsession. He needed it for Lee. He could not get him out of his mind. The thought of him making love with other men was unbearable. *I've got to have him for my own.*

From the age of twelve, Tyler had known that he was homosexual. One day, his father had caught him fondling and kissing a boy from his school, and Tyler had borne the full brunt of his father's fury. 'I can't believe I have a son who's a faggot! Now that I know your dirty little secret, I'm going to keep a close eye on you, sister.'

Tyler's marriage was a cosmic joke, perpetrated by a god with a macabre sense of humor.

'There's someone I want you to meet,' Harry Stanford said.

It was Christmas and Tyler was at Rose Hill for the holidays.

Kendall and Woody had already made their departures and Tyler was planning his when the bombshell dropped.

'You're going to get married.'

'Married? That's out of the question! I don't . . .'

'Listen to me, sister. People are beginning to talk about you, and I can't have that. It's bad for my reputation. If you get married, that will shut them up.'

Tyler was defiant. 'I don't care what people say. This is my life.'

'And I want it to be a rich life for you, Tyler. I'm getting older. Pretty soon . . .' He shrugged.

The carrot and the stick.

Naomi Schuyler was a plain-looking woman, from a middle-class family, whose flaming desire in life was to 'better' herself. She was so impressed by Harry Stanford's name that she would probably have married his son if he were pumping gas instead of being a judge.

Harry Stanford had taken Naomi to bed once. When someone asked him why, Stanford replied, 'Because she was there.'

She quickly bored him, and he decided she would be perfect for Tyler.

What Harry Stanford wanted, Harry Stanford got.

The wedding took place two months later. It was a small wedding – one hundred and fifty people – and the bride and groom went to Jamaica for their honeymoon. It was a fiasco.

On their wedding night Naomi said, 'What kind of man have I married, for God's sake? What have you got a dick for?'

Tyler tried to reason with her. 'We don't need sex. We can live separate lives. We'll stay together, but we'll each have our own . . . friends.'

'You're damned right, we will!'

Naomi took out her vengeance on him by becoming a black-belt shopper. She bought everything at the most expensive stores in the city, and took shopping trips to New York.

'I can't afford your extravagances on my income,' Tyler protested.

'Then get a raise. I'm your wife. I'm entitled to be supported.'

Tyler went to his father and explained the situation.

Harry Stanford grinned. 'Women can be damned expensive, can't they? You'll just have to handle it.'

'But, Father, I need some –'

'Someday you'll have all the money in the world.'

Tyler tried to explain it to Naomi, but she had no intentions of waiting until 'someday'. She sensed that that 'someday' might never come. When Naomi had squeezed what she could out of Tyler, she sued for divorce, settled for what was left of his bank account, and disappeared.

When Harry Stanford heard the news, he said, 'Once a faggot, always a faggot.'

And that was the end of that.

His father went out of his way to demean Tyler. One day, when Tyler was on the bench, in the middle of a trial, his bailiff came up to him and whispered, 'Excuse me, Your Honor . . .'

Tyler had turned to him, impatiently. 'Yes?'

'There's a telephone call for you.'

'*What?* What's the matter with you? I'm in the middle of –'

'It's your father, Your Honor. He says it's very urgent and he must talk to you immediately.'

Tyler was furious. His father had no right to interrupt him. He was tempted to ignore the call. But on the other hand, if it was that urgent . . .

Tyler stood up. 'Court is recessed for fifteen minutes.'

Tyler hurried into his chambers and picked up the telephone. 'Father?'

'I hope I'm not disturbing you, Tyler.' There was malice in his voice.

'As a matter of fact, you are. I'm in the middle of a trial and –'

'Well, give him a traffic ticket and forget it.'

'Father . . .'

'I need your help with a serious problem.'

'What kind of problem?'

'My chef is stealing from me.'

132

Tyler could not believe what he was hearing. He was so angry he could hardly speak. 'You called me off the bench because . . . ?'

'You're the law, aren't you? Well, he's breaking the law. I want you to come back to Boston and check out my whole staff. They're robbing me blind!'

It was all Tyler could do to keep from exploding. 'Father . . .'

'You just can't trust those damn employment agencies.'

'I'm in the middle of a trial. I can't possibly go to Boston now.'

There was a moment of ominous silence. 'What did you say?'

'I said . . .'

'You aren't going to disappoint me again, are you, Tyler? Maybe I should talk to Fitzgerald about some changes in my will.'

And there was the carrot again. The money. His share of the billions of dollars waiting for him when his father died.

Tyler cleared his throat. 'If you could send your plane for me . . .'

'Hell, no! If you play your cards right, judge, that plane will belong to you one day. Just think about that. Meanwhile, fly commercial like everyone else. But I want you to get your ass back here!' The line went dead.

Tyler sat there, filled with humiliation. *My father has done this to me all my life. To hell with him! I won't go. I won't go.*

Tyler flew to Boston that evening.

Harry Stanford employed a staff of twenty-two. There was a phalanx of secretaries, butlers, housekeepers, maids, chefs, chauffeurs, gardeners, and a bodyguard.

'Thieves, every damned one of them,' Harry Stanford complained to Tyler.

'If you're so worried, why don't you hire a private detective or go to the police?'

'Because I have you,' Harry Stanford said. 'You're a judge, right? Well, you judge them for me.'

It was pure malevolence.

Tyler looked around the huge house with its exquisite furniture

133

and paintings, and he thought of the dreary little house he lived in. *This is what I deserve to have,* he thought. *And one day, I'll have it.'*

Tyler talked to the butler, Clark, and other senior members of the staff. He interviewed the servants, one by one, and checked their résumés. Most of the employees were fairly new because Harry Stanford was an impossible man to work for. The staff turnover at the house was extraordinary. Some of them lasted only a day or two. A few new employees were guilty of petty pilfering, and one was an alcoholic, but other than that, Tyler could see no problem.

Except for Dmitri Kaminsky.

Dmitri Kaminsky had been hired by his father as a bodyguard and masseur. Sitting on the bench had made Tyler a good judge of character, and there was something about Dmitri that Tyler instantly mistrusted. He was the most recent employee. Harry Stanford's former bodyguard had quit – Tyler could imagine why – and he had recommended Kaminsky.

The man was huge, with a barrel chest and large, muscular arms. He spoke English with a thick Russian accent. 'You want to see me?'

'Yes.' Tyler gestured to a chair. 'Sit down.' He had looked at the man's employment record, and it had told him very little, except that Dmitri had come from Russia recently. 'You were born in Russia?'

'Yes.' He was watching Tyler warily.

'What part?'

'Smolensk.'

'Why did you leave Russia to come to America?'

Kaminsky shrugged. 'There is more opportunity here.'

Opportunity for what? Tyler wondered. There was something evasive about the man's manner. They spoke for twenty minutes, and at the end of that time Tyler was convinced that Dmitri Kaminsky was concealing something.

*   *   *

Tyler telephoned Fred Masterson, an acquaintance of his with the FBI.

'Fred, I want you to do me a favor.'

'Sure. If I'm ever in Chicago, will you fix my traffic tickets?'

'I'm serious.'

'Shoot.'

'I want you to check on a Russian who came over here six months ago.'

'Wait a minute. You're talking CIA, aren't you?'

'Maybe, but I don't know anyone at CIA.'

'Neither do I.'

'Fred, if you could do this for me, I would really be grateful.'

Tyler heard a sigh.

'Okay. What's his name?',

'Dmitri Kaminsky.'

'I'll tell you what I'll do. I know someone at the Russian Embassy in D.C. I'll see if he has any information on Kaminsky. If not, I'm afraid I can't help you.'

'I'd appreciate it.'

That evening, Tyler had dinner with his father. Subconsciously, Tyler had hoped that his father would have aged, would have become more fragile, more vulnerable with time. Instead, Harry Stanford looked hale and hearty, in his prime. *He's going to live forever.* Tyler thought despairingly. *He'll outlive all of us.*

The conversation at dinner was completely one-sided.

'I just closed a deal to buy the power company in Hawaii . . .'

'I'm flying over to Amsterdam next week to straighten out some GATT complication . . .'

'The secretary of state has invited me to accompany him to China . . .'

Tyler scarcely got in a word. At the end of the meal, his father rose. 'How are you coming along with the servant problem?'

'I'm still checking them out, Father.'

'Well, don't take forever,' his father growled, and walked out of the room.

* * *

135

The following morning, Tyler received a call from Fred Masterson at the FBI.

'Tyler?'

'Yes.'

'You picked a real beauty.'

'Oh?'

'Dmitri Kaminsky was a hit man for *polgoprudnenskaya*.'

'What the hell is that?'

'I'll explain. There are eight criminal groups that have taken over in Moscow. They all fight among themselves, but the two most powerful groups are the *chechens* and the *polgoprudnenskaya*. Your friend Kaminsky worked for the second group. Three months ago, they handed him a contract on one of the leaders of the *chechens*. Instead of carrying out the contract, Kaminsky went to him to make a better deal. The *polgoprudnenskaya* found out about it and put out a contract on Kaminsky. Gangs have a quaint custom over there. First they chop off your fingers, then they let you bleed for a while, and then they shoot you.'

'My God!'

'Kaminsky got himself smuggled out of Russia, but they're still looking for him. And looking hard.'

'That's incredible,' Tyler said.

'That's not all. He's also wanted by the state police for a few murders. If you know where he is, they'd love to have that information.'

Tyler was thoughtful for a moment. He could not afford to get involved in this. *It could mean giving testimony and wasting a lot of time.*

'I have no idea. I was just checking him out for a Russian friend. Thanks, Fred.'

Tyler found Dmitri Kaminsky in his room, reading a hardcore porno magazine. Dmitri rose as Tyler walked into the room.

'I want you to pack your things and get out of here.'

Dmitri stared at him. 'What's the matter?'

'I'm giving you a choice. You're either out of here by this afternoon, or I'll tell the Russian police where you are.'

Dmitri's face turned pale.

'Do you understand?'

'*Da*. I understand.'

Tyler went to see his father. *He's going to be pleased*, he thought. *I've done him a real favor*. He found him in the study.

'I checked on all the staff,' Tyler said, 'and . . .'

'I'm impressed. Did you find any little boys to take to bed with you?'

Tyler's face turned red. 'Father . . .'

'You're a queer, Tyler, and you'll always be a queer. I don't know how the hell anything like you came from my loins. Go on back to Chicago with your gutter friends.'

Tyler stood there, fighting to control himself. 'Right,' he said stiffly. He started to leave.

'Is there anything about the staff you found out that I should know?'

Tyler turned and studied his father a moment. 'No,' he said slowly. 'Nothing.'

When Tyler went to Kaminsky's room, he was packing.

'I'm going,' Kaminsky said sullenly.

'Don't. I've changed my mind.'

Dmitri looked up, puzzled. 'What?'

'I don't want you to leave. I want you to stay on as my father's bodyguard.'

'What about . . . you know, the other thing?'

'We're going to forget about that.'

Dmitri was watching him, warily. 'Why? What do you want me to do?'

'I'd like you to be my eyes and ears here. I need someone to keep an eye on my father, and let me know what goes on.'

'Why should I?'

'Because if you do as I say, I'm not going to turn you over to the Russians. And because I'm going to make you a rich man.'

Dmitri Kaminsky studied him a moment. A slow grin lit his face. 'I'll stay.'

It was the opening gambit. The first pawn had been moved.

That had been two years earlier. From time to time, Dmitri had passed on information to Tyler. It was mostly unimportant gossip about Harry Stanford's latest romance or bits of business that Dmitri had overheard. Tyler had begun to think he had made a mistake, that he should have turned Dmitri in to the police. And then the fateful telephone call had come from Sardinia, and the gamble had paid off.

'I'm with your father on his yacht. He just called his attorney. He's meeting him in Boston Monday to change his will.'

Tyler thought of all the humiliations his father had heaped on him through the years, and he was filled with a terrible rage. *If he changes his will, I've taken all those years of abuse for nothing. I'm not going to let him get away with this! There is only one way to stop him.*

'Dmitri, I want you to call me again on Saturday.'

'Right.'

Tyler replaced the receiver and sat there, thinking. It was time to bring in the knight.

Chapter Sixteen

In the Circuit Court of Cook County, there was a constant ebb and flow of defendants accused of arson, rape, drug dealing, murder, and a variety of other illegal and unsavory activities. In the course of a month, Judge Tyler Stanford dealt with at least half a dozen murder cases. The majority never went to trial since the attorneys for the defendant would offer to plea bargain, and because the court calendars and prisons were so overcrowded, the State would usually agree. The two sides would then strike a deal and go to Judge Stanford for his approval.

The case of Hal Baker was an exception.

Hal Baker was a man with good intentions and bad luck. When he was fifteen, his older brother had talked him into helping him rob a grocery store. Hal had tried to dissuade him, and when he couldn't, he went along with him. Hal was caught, and his brother escaped. Two years later, when Hal Baker got out of reform school, he was determined never to get in trouble with the law again. One month later, he accompanied a friend to a jewelry store.

'I want to pick out a ring for my girlfriend.'

Once inside the store, his friend pulled out a gun and yelled, 'This is a holdup!'

In the ensuing excitement, a clerk was shot to death. Hal Baker was caught and arrested for armed robbery. His friend escaped.

While Baker was in prison, Helen Gowan, a social worker who had read about his case and felt sorry for him, went to visit him. It was love at first sight, and when Baker was released from prison, he and Helen were married. Over the next eight years, they had four lovely children.

Hal Baker adored his family. Because of his prison record, he had a difficult time finding jobs, and to support his family he reluctantly went to work for his brother, carrying out various acts of arson, robbery and assault. Unfortunately for Baker, he was caught flagrante delicto in the commission of a burglary. He was arrested, held in jail, and tried in Judge Tyler Stanford's court.

It was time for sentencing. Baker was a second offender with a bad juvenile record, and it was such a clear-cut case that the assistant district attorneys were making bets on how many years Judge Stanford would give Baker. 'He'll throw the book at him!' one of them said. 'I'll bet he gives him twenty years. Stanford's not called the Hanging Judge for nothing.'

Hal Baker, who felt deep in his heart that he was innocent, was acting as his own attorney. He stood before the bench, dressed in his best suit, and said, 'Your Honor, I know I made a mistake, but we're all human, aren't we? I have a wonderful wife and four children. I wish you could meet them, Your Honor – they're great. What I did, I did for them.'

Tyler Stanford sat on the bench, listening, his face impassive. He was waiting for Hal Baker to finish so he could pass sentence. *Does this fool really think he's going to get off with that stupid sob story?*

Hal Baker was finishing, '. . . and so you see, Your Honor, even though I did the wrong thing, I did it for the right reason: family. I don't have to tell you how important that is. If I go to prison, my wife and children will starve. I know I made a mistake, but I'm willing to make up for it. I'll do anything you want me to do, Your Honor . . .'

And that was the phrase that caught Tyler Stanford's attention. He looked at the defendant before him with a new interest. '*Anything you want me to do.*' Tyler suddenly had the same instinct he had had about Dmitri Kaminsky. Here was a man who might be very useful one day.

To the prosecutor's utter astonishment, Tyler said, 'Mr Baker, there are extenuating circumstances in this case. Because of them and because of your family, I am going to put you on probation for five years. I will expect you to perform six hundred hours of public service. Come into my chambers, and we will discuss it.'

In the privacy of his chambers, Tyler said, 'You know, I could still send you to prison for a long, long time.'

Hal Baker turned pale. 'But, Your Honor! You said . . .'

Tyler leaned forward. 'Do you know the most impressive thing about you?'

Hal Baker sat there, trying to think what was impressive about himself. 'No, Your Honor.'

'Your feelings about your family,' Tyler said piously. 'I really admire that.'

Hal Baker brightened. 'Thank you, sir. They're the most important thing in the world to me. I –'

'Then you wouldn't want to lose them, would you? If I sent you to prison, your children would grow up without you; your wife would probably find another man. Do you see what I'm getting at?'

Hal Baker was baffled. 'N . . . no, Your Honor. Not exactly.'

'I'm saving your family for you, Baker. I would think you'd be grateful.'

Hal Baker said fervently, 'Oh, I *am*, Your Honor! I can't tell you how grateful I am.'

'Perhaps you can prove it to me in the future. I may be calling on you to do some little errands for me.'

'*Anything!*'

'Good. I'm placing you on probation, and if I should find any-thing in your behavior that displeases me . . .'

'You just tell me what you want,' Baker begged.

'I'll let you know when the time comes. Meanwhile, this will be strictly confidential between the two of us.'

Hal Baker put his hand over his heart. 'I would die before I'd tell anyone.'

'You're right,' Tyler assured him.

*   *   *

141

It was a short time after that when Tyler received the phone call from Dmitri Kaminsky. '*Your father just called his attorney. He's meeting him in Boston on Monday to change his will.*'

Tyler knew that he had to see that will. It was time to call Hal Baker.

'. . . the name of the firm is Renquist, Renquist, and Fitzgerald. Make a copy of the will and bring it to me.'

'No problem. I'll take care of it, Your Honor.'

Twelve hours later, Tyler had a copy of the will in his hands. He read it and was filled with a sense of elation. He and Woody and Kendall were the sole heirs. *And on Monday Father is planning to change the will. The bastard is going to take it away from us!* Tyler thought bitterly. *After all we've gone through . . . those billions belong to us. He's made us earn them!* There was only one way to stop him.

When Dmitri's second telephone call came, Tyler said, 'I want you to kill him. Tonight.'

There was a long silence. 'But if I'm caught . . .'

'Don't get caught. You'll be at sea. A lot of things can happen there.'

'All right. When it's over . . . ?'

'The money and a plane ticket to Australia will be waiting for you.'

And then later, the last wonderful phone call.

'I did it. It was easy.'

'No! No! No! I want to hear the details. Tell me everything. Don't leave anything out . . .'

And as Tyler listened, he could visualize the scene unfolding before his eyes.

'We were in a bad storm on our way to Corsica. He called and asked me to come to his cabin and give him a massage . . .'

Tyler found himself gripping the phone. 'Yes. Go on . . .'

Dmitri had fought to keep his balance against the wild pitching of the yacht as he headed for Harry Stanford's stateroom. He knocked at the cabin door and, after a moment, he heard Stanford's voice.

'Come in!' Stanford yelled. He was stretched out on the massage table. 'It's my lower back.'

'I'll take care of it. Just relax, Mr Stanford.'

Dmitri went over to the massage table and spread oil on Stanford's back. His strong fingers went to work, skillfully kneading the tight muscles. He could feel Stanford begin to relax.

'That feels good.' Stanford sighed.

'Thank you.'

The massage lasted an hour, and when Dmitri was through, Stanford was almost asleep.

'I'm going to run a warm bath for you,' Dmitri said. He went into the bathroom, stumbling with the motion of the ship. He turned on the warm seawater tap in the black onyx tub and returned to the bedroom. Stanford was still lying on the table, his eyes closed.

'Mr Stanford . . .'

Stanford opened his eyes.

'Your bath is ready.'

'I don't think I need . . .'

'It will really make sure you get a good night's sleep.' He helped Stanford off the table and steered him toward the bathroom.

Dmitri watched Harry Stanford lower himself into the tub.

Stanford looked up into Dmitri's cold eyes, and in that instant, his instinct told him what was about to happen. 'No!' he cried. He started to get up.

Dmitri put his huge hands on top of Harry Stanford's head and pushed him under the water. Stanford struggled violently, trying to come up for air, but he was no match for the giant. Dmitri held him under while the seawater got into his victim's lungs, and finally all movement stopped. He stood there, breathing hard, then staggered into the other room.

Dmitri went over to the desk, fighting the rolling motion of the ship, picked up some papers and slid open the glass door to the outside veranda, letting in the howling wind. He scattered some of the papers on the veranda and threw some overboard.

Satisfied, he returned to the bathroom once more and pulled Stanford's body out of the tub. He dressed him in his pajamas, robe and slippers, and carried the body out onto the veranda. Dmitri stood at the railing a moment, then heaved the body overboard. He counted to five seconds, then picked up the telephone and shouted, 'Man overboard!'

Listening to Dmitri recount the story of the murder, Tyler felt a sexual thrill. He could taste the seawater filling his father's lungs and feel the gasping for breath, the terror. And then nothingness.

It's over, Tyler thought. Then he corrected himself. *No. The game is just beginning. It's time to play the queen.*

Chapter Seventeen

The last chess piece fell into place by accident.

Tyler had been thinking about his father's will, and he felt outraged that Woody and Kendall were getting an equal share of the estate with him. *They don't deserve it. If it had not been for me, they both would have been cut out of the will completely. They would have had nothing. It's not fair, but what can I do about it?*

He had the one share of stock that his mother had given him long ago, and he remembered his father's words: *'What do you think he's going to do with that share? Take over the company?'*

Together, Tyler thought, *Woody and Kendall have two-thirds of Father's Stanford Enterprises stock. How can I get control with only my one extra share?* And then the answer came to him, and it was so ingenious that it stunned him.

'I should inform you that there is a possibility of another heir being involved . . . Your father's will specifically provides that the estate is to be divided equally among his issue. Your father sired a child by a governess who worked here . . .'

If Julia showed up, there would be four of us, Tyler thought. *And if I could control her share, I would then have fifty percent of Father's stock plus the one percent I already own. I could take over Stanford Enterprises. I could sit in my father's chair.* His next thought was, *Rosemary is dead, and she probably never told her daughter who her father was. Why does it have to be the real Julia Stanford?*

The answer was Margo Posner.

*　　*　　*

145

He had first encountered her two months earlier, as court was called into session. The bailiff had turned to the spectators in the courtroom. 'Oyez, oyez. The Circuit Court of Cook County is now in session, the Honorable Judge Tyler Stanford presiding. All rise.'

Tyler walked in from his chambers and sat down at the bench. He looked down at the docket. The first case was *State of Illinois v Margo Posner*. The charges were assault and attempted murder.

The prosecuting attorney rose. 'Your Honor, the defendant is a dangerous person who should be kept off the streets of Chicago. The State will prove that the defendant has a long criminal history. She has been convicted of shoplifting, larceny, and is a known prostitute. She was one of a stable of women working for a notorious pimp named Rafael. In January of this year, they got into an altercation and the defendant willfully and cold-bloodedly shot him and his companion.'

'Did either victim die?' Tyler asked.

'No, Your Honor. They were hospitalized with serious injuries. The gun in Margo Posner's possession was an illegal weapon.'

Tyler turned to look at the defendant, and he felt a sense of surprise. She did not fit the image of what he had just heard about her. She was a well-dressed, attractive young woman in her late twenties, and there was a quiet elegance about her that completely belied the charges against her. *That just goes to prove*, Tyler thought wryly, *you never know*.

He listened to the arguments from both sides, but his eyes were drawn to the defendant. There was something about her that reminded him of his sister.

When the summations were finished the case went to the jury, and in less than four hours they returned with a verdict of guilty on all counts.

Tyler looked down at the defendant and said, 'The court cannot find any extenuating circumstances in this case. You are herewith sentenced to five years at Dwight Correctional Center. Next case.'

And it was not until Margo Posner was being led away that Tyler realized what it was about her that reminded him so much of Kendall. She had the same dark gray eyes. The Stanford eyes.

* * *

146

Tyler did not think about Margo Posner again until the telephone call from Dmitri.

The beginning chess game had been successfully completed. Tyler had planned each move carefully in his mind. He'd used the classical queen's gambit: Decline opening, moving the queen pawn two squares. It was time to move into the middle game.

Tyler went to visit Margo Posner at the women's prison.

'Do you remember me?' Tyler asked.

She stared at him. 'How could I forget you? You're the one who sent me to this place.'

'How are you getting along?' Tyler asked.

She grimaced. 'You must be kidding! It's a hellhole here.'

'How would you like to get out?'

'How would I . . .? Are you serious?'

'I'm very serious. I can arrange it.'

'Well, that . . . that's great! Thanks. But what do I have to do for it?'

Well, there *is* something I want you to do for me.'

She looked at him, flirtatiously. 'Sure. That's no problem.'

'That's not what I had in mind.'

She said, warily, 'What *did* you have in mind, judge?'

'I want you to help me play a little joke on someone.'

'What kind of joke?'

'I want you to impersonate someone.'

'Impersonate someone? I wouldn't know how to –'

'There's twenty-five thousand dollars in it for you.'

Her expression changed. 'Sure,' she said quickly. 'I can impersonate anyone. Who did you have in mind?'

Tyler leaned forward and began to talk.

Tyler had Margo Posner released into his custody.

As he explained to Keith Percy, the chief judge, 'I learned that she's a very talented artist, and she's eager to live a normal, decent life. I think it's important that we rehabilitate that type of person whenever we can, don't you?'

Keith was impressed and surprised. 'Absolutely, Tyler. That's a wonderful thing you're doing.'

Tyler moved Margo into his home and spent five full days briefing her on the Stanford family.

'What are the names of your brothers?'

'Tyler and Woodruff.'

'Woodrow.'

'That's right – Woodrow.'

'What do we call him?'

'Woody.'

'Do you have a sister?'

'Yes. Kendall. She's a designer.'

'Is she married?'

'She's married to a Frenchman. His name is . . . Marc Renoir.'

'Renaud.'

'Renaud.'

'What was your mother's name?'

'Rosemary Nelson. She was a governess to the Stanford children.'

'Why did she leave?'

'She got knocked up by . . .'

'Margo!' Tyler admonished her.

'I mean, she became pregnant by Harry Stanford.'

'What happened to Mrs Stanford?'

'She committed suicide.'

'What did your mother tell you about the Stanford children?'

Margo stopped to think for a minute.

'Well?'

'There was the time you fell out of the swan boat.'

'I didn't fall out!' Tyler said. 'I *almost* fell out.'

'Right. Woody almost got arrested for picking flowers in the Public Garden.'

'That was Kendall . . .'

He was ruthless. They went over the scenario again and again, late into the nights, until Margo was exhausted.

148

'Kendall was bitten by a dog.'

'*I* was bitten by the dog.'

She rubbed her eyes. 'I can't think straight anymore. I'm so tired. I need some sleep.'

'You can sleep later!'

'How long is this going to go on?' she asked defiantly.

'Until I think you're ready. Now let's go through it again.'

And on it went, over and over, until Margo became letter perfect. When the day finally arrived that she knew the answer to every question Tyler asked, he was satisfied.

'You're ready,' he said. He handed her some legal documents.

'What's this?'

'It's just a technicality,' Tyler said casually.

What he had her sign was a paper giving her share of the Stanford estate to a corporation controlled by a second corporation, which in turn was controlled by an offshore subsidiary of which Tyler Stanford was the sole owner. There was no way they could trace the transaction back to Tyler.

Tyler handed Margo five thousand dollars in cash. 'You'll get the balance when the job is done,' he told her. '*If* you convince them that you're Julia Stanford.'

From the moment Margo had appeared at Rose Hill, Tyler had played the devil's advocate. It was the classic antipositional chess move.

'I'm sure you can understand our position, Miss . . . er . . . Without some positive proof, there's no way . . .

'. . . I think the lady is a fraud . . .

'How many servants worked in this house when we were children? . . . Dozens, right? And some of them would have known everything this young lady told us . . . Any one of them could have given her that photograph . . . Let's not forget that there's an enormous amount of money involved.'

His crowning move had been when he had demanded a DNA test. He had called Hal Baker and given him his new instructions: *'Dig up Harry Stanford's body and dispose of it.'*

And then his inspiration of calling in a private detective. With

149

the family present, he had telephoned the district attorney's office in Chicago.

'This is Judge Tyler Stanford. I understand that your office retains a private detective from time to time who does excellent work for you. His name is something like Simmons or –'

'Oh, you must mean Frank Timmons.'

'Timmons! Yes, that's it. I wonder if you could give me his telephone number so I can contact him directly?'

Instead, he had summoned Hal Baker and introduced him as Frank Timmons.

At first Tyler had planned for Hal Baker merely to pretend to go through the motions of checking on Julia Stanford, but then he decided it would make a more impressive report if Baker really pursued it. The family had accepted Baker's findings without question.

Tyler's plan had gone off without a hitch. Margo Posner had played her part perfectly, and the fingerprints had been the crowning touch. Everyone was convinced that she was the real Julia Stanford.

'I, for one, am glad it's finally settled. Let me go up and see if she needs any help.'

He went upstairs and walked along the corridor to Julia's room. He knocked at her door and called loudly, 'Julia?'

'It's open. Come in.'

He stood in the doorway and they stared silently at each other. And then Tyler carefully closed the door, held out his hands, and broke into a slow grin.

When he spoke, he said, 'We did it, Margo! We did it!'

Chapter Eighteen

In the offices of Renquist, Renquist & Fitzgerald, Steve Sloane and Simon Fitzgerald were having coffee.

'As the great bard once said, "Something is rotten in the state of Denmark."'

'What's bothering you?' Fitzgerald asked.

Steve sighed. 'I'm not sure. It's the Stanford family. They puzzle me.'

Simon Fitzgerald snorted. 'Join the club.'

'I keep coming back to the same question, Simon, but I can't find the answer to it.'

'What's the question?'

'The family was anxious to exhume Harry Stanford's body so they could check his DNA against the woman's. So I think we have to assume that the only possible motive for getting rid of the body would be to ensure that the woman's DNA could *not* be checked against Harry Stanford's. The only one who could have anything to gain from that would be the woman herself, if she were a fraud.'

'Yes.'

'And yet this private detective, Frank Timmons – I checked with the district attorney's office in Chicago, and he has a great reputation – came up with fingerprints that prove she *is* the real Julia Stanford. My question is, who the hell dug up Harry Stanford's body and why?'

'That's a billion-dollar question. If . . .'

The intercom buzzed. A secretary's voice came over the box. 'Mr Sloane, there's a call for you on two.'

Steve Sloane picked up the telephone on the desk. 'Hello . . .'

151

The voice on the other end of the line said, 'Mr Sloane, this is Judge Stanford. I would appreciate it if you could drop by Rose Hill this morning.'

Steve Sloane glanced at Fitzgerald. 'Right. In about an hour?'

'That will be fine. Thank you.'

Steve replaced the receiver. 'My presence is requested at the Stanford house.'

'I wonder what they want.'

'Ten to one they want to speed up the probate so they can get their hands on all that beautiful money.'

'Lee? It's Tyler. How are you?'

'Fine, thanks.'

'I really miss you.'

There was a slight pause. 'I miss you too, Tyler.'

The words thrilled him. 'Lee, I have some really exciting news. I can't discuss it over the phone, but it's something that's going to make you very happy. When you and I –'

'Tyler, I have to go. Someone's waiting for me.'

'But . . .'

The line went dead.

Tyler sat there a moment. Then he thought, *He wouldn't have said he missed me if he didn't mean it.*

With the exception of Woody and Peggy, the family was gathered in the drawing room at Rose Hill. Steve studied their faces.

Judge Stanford seemed very relaxed.

Steve glanced at Kendall. She seemed unnaturally tense. Her husband had come up from New York the day before for the meeting. Steve looked over at Marc. The Frenchman was good-looking, a few years younger than his wife.

And then there was Julia. She seemed to be taking her acceptance into the family very calmly. *I would have expected someone who had just inherited a billion dollars or so to be a little more excited*, Steve thought.

He glanced at their faces again, wondering if one of them was

152

responsible for having Harry Stanford's body stolen, and if so, which one? And why?

Tyler was speaking. 'Mr Sloane, I'm familiar with the probate laws in Illinois, but I don't know how much they differ from the laws in Massachusetts. We were wondering whether there wasn't some way to expedite the procedure.'

Steve smiled to himself. *I should have made Simon take that bet.* He turned to Tyler. 'We're already working on it, Judge Stanford.'

Tyler said pointedly, 'The Stanford name might be useful in speeding things up.'

He's right about that, Steve thought. He nodded. 'I'll do everything I can. If it's at all possible to –'

There were voices from the staircase.

'Just shut up, you stupid bitch! I don't want to hear another word. Do you understand?'

Woody and Peggy came down the stairs and into the room. Peggy's face was badly swollen, and she had a black eye. Woody was grinning, and his eyes were bright.

'Hello, everybody. I hope the party's not over.'

The group was looking at Peggy in shock.

Kendall rose. 'What happened to you?'

'Nothing. I . . . I bumped into a door.'

Woody took a seat. Peggy sat next to him. Woody patted her hand and asked solicitously, 'Are you all right, my dear?'

Peggy nodded, not trusting herself to speak.

'Good.' Woody turned to the others. 'Now, what did I miss?'

Tyler looked at him disapprovingly. 'I just asked Mr Sloane if he could expedite the probating of the will.'

Woody grinned. 'That would be nice.' He turned to Peggy. 'You'd like some new clothes, wouldn't you, darling?'

'I don't need any new clothes,' she said timidly.

'That's right. You don't go anywhere, do you?' He turned to the others. 'Peggy is very shy. She doesn't have anything to talk about, do you?'

Peggy got up and ran out of the room.

153

'I'll see if she's all right,' Kendall said. She rose and hurried after her.

My God! Steve thought. *If Woody behaves like this in front of others, what must it be like when he and his wife are alone?*

Woody turned to Steve. 'How long have you been with Fitzgerald's law firm?'

'Five years.'

'How they could stand working for my father, I'll never know.'

Steve said carefully, 'I understand your father was . . . could be difficult.'

Woody snorted. 'Difficult? He was a two-legged monster. Did you know he had nicknames for all of us? Mine was Charlie. He named me after Charlie McCarthy, a dummy that a ventriloquist named Edgar Bergen had. He called my sister Pony, because he said she had a face like a horse. Tyler was called . . .'

Steve said, uncomfortably, 'I really don't think you should –'

Woody grinned. 'It's all right. A billion dollars heals a lot of wounds.'

Steve rose. 'Well, if there's nothing else, I think I had better be going.' He could not wait to get outside, into the fresh air.

Kendall found Peggy in the bathroom, putting a cold cloth to her swollen cheek.

'Peggy? Are you all right?'

Peggy turned. 'I'm fine. Thank you. I . . . I'm sorry about what happened down there.'

'You're apologizing? You should be furious. How long has he been beating you?'

'He doesn't beat me,' Peggy said obstinately. 'I bumped into a door.'

Kendall moved closer to her. 'Peggy, why do you put up with this? You don't have to, you know.'

There was a pause. 'Yes, I do.'

Kendall looked at her, puzzled. 'Why?'

She turned. 'Because I love him.' She went on, the words pouring out. 'He loves me, too. Believe me, he doesn't always act like this. The thing is, he – sometimes he's not himself.'

154

'You mean, when he's on drugs.'

'No!'

'Peggy . . .'

'No!'

'Peggy . . .'

Peggy hesitated. 'I suppose so.'

'When did it start?'

'Right . . . right after we got married.' Peggy's voice was ragged. 'It started because of a polo game. Woody fell off his pony and was badly hurt. While he was in the hospital, they gave him drugs to help with the pain. *They* got him started.' She looked at Kendall, pleadingly. 'So you see, it wasn't his fault, was it? After Woody got out of the hospital, he . . . he kept on using drugs. Whenever I tried to get him to quit, he would . . . beat me.'

'Peggy, for God's sake! He needs help! Don't you see that? You can't do this alone. He's a drug addict. What does he take? Cocaine?'

'No.' There was a small silence. 'Heroin.'

'My God! Can't you make him get some help?'

'I've tried.' Her voice was a whisper. 'You don't know how I've tried! He's gone to three rehabilitation hospitals.' She shook her head. 'He's all right for a while, and then . . . he starts again. He . . . he can't help it.'

Kendall put her arms around Peggy. 'I'm so sorry,' she said.

Peggy forced a smile. 'I'm sure Woody will be all right. He's trying hard. He really is.' Her face lit up. 'When we were first married, he was so much fun to be with. We used to laugh all the time. He would bring me little presents and –' Her eyes filled with tears. 'I love him so much!'

'If there's anything I can do . . .'

'Thank you,' Peggy whispered. 'I appreciate that.'

Kendall squeezed her hand. 'We'll talk again.'

Kendall started down the stairs to join the others. She was thinking, *When we were children, before Mother died, we made such wonderful plans. 'You're going to be a famous designer, Sis, and I'm going to be the world's greatest athlete!' And the sad part*

155

of it, Kendall thought, *is that he could have been. And now this.*

Kendall was not sure if she felt more sorry for Woody or for Peggy.

As Kendall reached the bottom of the stairs, Clark approached her, carrying a tray with a letter on it. 'Excuse me, Miss Kendall. A messenger just delivered this for you.' He handed her the envelope.

Kendall looked at it in surprise. 'Who . . . ?' She nodded. 'Thank you, Clark.'

Kendall opened the envelope, and as she began to read the letter, she turned pale. 'No!' she said, under her breath. Her heart was pounding, and she felt a wave of dizziness. She stood there, bracing herself against a table, trying to catch her breath.

After a moment, she turned and walked into the drawing room, her face pale. The meeting was breaking up.

'Marc . . .' Kendall forced herself to appear calm. 'May I see you for a moment?'

He looked at her, concerned. 'Yes, certainly.'

Tyler asked Kendall, 'Are you all right?'

She forced a smile. 'I'm fine, thank you.'

She took Marc's hand and led him upstairs. When they entered the bedroom, Kendall closed the door.

Marc said, 'What is it?'

Kendall handed him the envelope. The letter read:

> *Dear Mrs Renaud,*
> *Congratulations! Our Wild Animal Protection Association was delighted to read of your good fortune. We know how interested you are in the work we are doing, and we are counting on your further support. Therefore, we would appreciate it if you would deposit 1 million US dollars in our numbered bank account in Zurich within the next ten days. We look forward to hearing from you shortly.*

As in the other letters, all the Es were broken.

'The bastards!' Marc exploded.

'How did they know I was here?' Kendall asked.

Marc said bitterly, 'All they had to do was pick up a news-paper.' He read the letter again and shook his head. 'They aren't going to quit. We *have* to go to the police.'

'No!' Kendall cried. 'We can't! It's too late! Don't you see? It would be the end of everything. *Everything!*'

Marc took her in his arms and held her tightly. 'All right. We'll find a way.'

But Kendall knew that there was no way.

It had happened a few months earlier, on what had started out to be a glorious spring day. Kendall had gone to a friend's birth-day party in Ridgefield, Connecticut. It had been a wonderful party, and Kendall had chatted with old friends. She had had a glass of champagne. In the middle of a conversation, she had suddenly looked at her watch. 'Oh, no! I had no idea it was so late. Marc is waiting for me.'

There were hasty good-byes, and Kendall had gotten into her car and driven off. Driving back to New York, she had decided to take a winding country road over to I684. She was traveling at almost fifty miles per hour as she rounded a sharp curve and spotted a car parked on the right side of the road. Kendall auto-matically swerved to the left. At that moment, a woman carrying a handful of freshly picked flowers started to cross the narrow road. Kendall tried frantically to avoid her, but it was too late. Everything seemed to happen in a blur. She heard a sickening thud as she hit the woman with her left front fender. Kendall brought the car to a screeching stop, her whole body trembling violently. She ran back to where the woman was lying in the road, covered with blood.

Kendall stood there, frozen. Finally she bent down and turned the woman over, and looked into her sightless eyes. 'Oh, my God!' Kendall whispered. She felt the bile rising in her throat. She looked up, desperate, not knowing what to do. She swung around in a panic. There were no cars in sight. *She's dead,* Kend-all thought. *I can't help her. This was not my fault, but they'll accuse me of reckless drunk driving. My blood will show alcohol. I'll go to prison!*

She took one last look at the body of the woman, then hurried back to her car. The left front fender was dented, and there were blood spots on it. *I've got to put the car away in a garage,* Kendall thought. *The police will be searching for it.* She got into the car and drove off.

For the rest of the drive into New York, she kept looking into the rearview mirror, expecting to see flashing red lights and to hear the sound of a siren. She drove into the garage on Ninety-sixth Street where she kept her car. Sam, the owner of the garage, was talking to Red, his mechanic. Kendall got out of the car.

'Evenin', Mrs Renaud,' Sam said.

'Go . . . Good evening.' She was fighting to keep her teeth from chattering.

'Put it away for the night?'

'Yes . . . yes, please.'

Red was looking at the fender. 'You got a bad dent here, Mrs Renaud. Looks like there's blood on it.'

The two men were looking at her.

Kendall took a deep breath. 'Yes. I . . . I hit a deer on the highway.'

'You're lucky it didn't do more damage,' Sam said. 'A friend of mine hit a deer and it ruined his car.' He grinned. 'Didn't do much for the deer either.'

'If you'll just put it away,' Kendall said tightly.

'Sure.'

Kendall walked over to the garage door, then looked back. The two men were staring at the fender.

When Kendall got home and told Marc about the terrible thing that had happened, he took her in his arms and said, 'Oh, my God! Darling, how could . . . ?'

Kendall was sobbing. 'I . . . I couldn't help it. She started across the road right in front of me. She . . . she had been picking flowers and –'

'Ssh! I'm sure it wasn't your fault. It was an accident. We've got to report this to the police.'

'I know. You're right. I . . . I should have stayed there and waited for them to come. I just . . . panicked, Marc. Now it's a hit-and-run. But there wasn't anything I could do for her. She was dead. You should have seen her face. It was awful.'

He held her for a long time, until she quieted down.

When Kendall spoke, she said tentatively, 'Marc . . . do we have to go to the police?'

He frowned. 'What do you mean?'

She was fighting hysteria. 'Well, it's over, isn't it? Nothing can bring her back. What good would it do for them to punish me? I didn't mean to do it. Why couldn't we just pretend it never happened?'

'Kendall, if they ever traced –'

'How can they? There was no one around.'

'What about your car? Was it damaged?'

'There's a dent. I told the garage attendant I hit a deer.' She was fighting for control. 'Marc, no one saw the accident. Do you know what would happen to me if they arrested me and sent me to prison? I'd lose my business, everything I've built up all these years, and for what? For something that's already done! It's over!' She began to sob again.

He held her close. 'Ssh! We'll see. We'll see.'

The morning papers gave the story a big play. What gave it added drama was the fact that the dead woman had been on her way to Manhattan to be married. The *New York Times* covered it as a straight news story, but the *Daily News* and *Newsday* played it up as a heart-tugging drama.

Kendall bought a copy of each newspaper, and she became more and more horrified at what she had done. Her mind was filled with all the terrible ifs.

If I hadn't gone to Connecticut for my friend's birthday . . .

If I had stayed home that day . . .

If I hadn't had anything to drink . . .

If the woman had picked the flowers a few seconds earlier or a few seconds later . . .

I'm responsible for murdering another human being!

Kendall thought of the terrible grief she had caused the

woman's family, and her fiancé's family, and she felt sick to her stomach again.

According to the newspapers, the police were asking for information from anyone who might have a clue about the hit-and-run.

They have no way of finding me, Kendall thought. *All I have to do is act as if nothing happened.*

When Kendall went to the garage to pick up her car the next morning, Red was there.

'I wiped the blood off the car,' he said. 'Do you want me to fix the dent?'

Of course! She should have thought of it sooner. 'Yes, please.'

Red was looking at her strangely. Or was it her imagination?

'Sam and I talked about it last night,' he said. 'It's funny, you know. A deer should have done a lot more damage.'

Kendall's heart began to beat wildly. Her mouth was suddenly so dry she could hardly speak. 'It was . . . a small deer.'

Red nodded laconically. 'Must have been real small.'

Kendall could feel his eyes on her as she drove out of the garage.

When Kendall walked into her office her secretary, Nadine, took one look at her and said, 'What happened to you?'

Kendall froze. 'What . . . what do you mean?'

'You look shaky. Let me get you some coffee.'

'Thanks.'

Kendall walked over to the mirror. Her face looked pale and drawn. *They're going to know just by looking at me!*

Nadine came into the office with a cup of hot coffee. 'Here. This will make you feel better.' She looked at Kendall curiously. 'Is everything all right?'

'I . . . I had a little accident yesterday,' Kendall said.

'Oh? Was anyone hurt?'

In her mind, she could see the face of the dead woman. 'No. I . . . I hit a deer.'

'What about your car?'

'It's being repaired.'

160

'I'll call your insurance company.'

'Oh, no, Nadine, please don't.'

Kendall saw the surprised look in Nadine's eyes.

It was two days later that the first letter came:

> *Dear Mrs Renaud,*
>
> *I'm the chairman of the Wild Animal Protection Association, which is in desperate need. I'm sure that you would like to help us out. The organization needs money to preserve wild animals. We are especially interested in deer. You can wire $50,000 to account number 804072-A at the Crédit Suisse bank in Zurich. I would strongly suggest that the money be there within the next five days.*

It was unsigned. All the Es in the letter were broken. Enclosed in the envelope was a newspaper clipping about the accident.

Kendall read the letter twice. The threat was unmistakable. She agonized over what to do. *Marc was right,* she thought. *I should have gone to the police.* But now everything was worse. She was a fugitive. If they found her now, it would mean prison and disgrace, as well as the end of her business.

At lunchtime, she went to her bank. 'I want to wire fifty thousand dollars to Switzerland.'

When Kendall got home that evening, she showed the letter to Marc.

He was stunned. 'My God!' he said. 'Who could have sent this?'

'Nobody . . . nobody knows.' She was trembling.

'Kendall, *someone* knows.'

Her body was twitching. 'There was no one around, Marc! I –'

'Wait a minute. Let's try to figure this out. Exactly what happened when you returned to town?'

'Nothing. I . . . I put the car in the garage, and –' She stopped. *'You got a bad dent here, Mrs Renaud. Looks like there's blood on it.'*

161

Marc saw the expression on her face. 'What?'

She said slowly, 'The owner of the garage and his mechanic were there. They saw the blood on the fender. I told them I hit a deer, and they said there should have been a lot more damage.' She remembered something else. 'Marc . . .'

'Yes?'

'Nadine, my secretary. I told her the same thing. I could see that she didn't believe me either. So it had to be one of the three of them.'

'No,' Marc said slowly.

She stared at him. 'What do you mean?'

'Sit down, Kendall, and listen to me. If any of them was suspicious of you, they could have told your story to a dozen people. The report of the accident has been in all the newspapers. Someone has put two and two together. I think the letter was a bluff, testing you. It was a terrible mistake to send that money.'

'But why?'

'Because now they *know* you're guilty, don't you see? You've given them the proof they needed.'

'Oh, God! What should I do?' Kendall asked.

Marc Renaud was thoughtful for a moment. 'I have an idea how we can find out who these bastards are.'

At ten o'clock the following morning, Kendall and Marc were seated in the office of Russell Gibbons, vice president of the Manhattan First Security Bank.

'And what can I do for you, today?' Mr Gibbons asked.

Marc said, 'We would like to check on a numbered bank account in Zurich.'

'Yes?'

'We want to know whose account it is.'

Gibbons rubbed his hands across his chin. 'Is there a crime involved?'

Marc said quickly, 'No! Why do you ask?'

'Well, unless there's some kind of criminal activity, such as laundering money or breaking the laws of Switzerland or the United States, Switzerland will not violate the secrecy of its numbered bank accounts. Their reputation is built on confidentiality.'

'Surely, there's some way to . . . ?'

'I'm sorry. I'm afraid not.'

Kendall and Marc looked at each other. Kendall's face was filled with despair.

Marc rose. 'Thank you for your time.'

'I'm sorry I couldn't help you.' He ushered them out of his office.

When Kendall drove into the garage that evening, neither Sam nor Red was around. Kendall parked her car, and as she passed the little office, through the window she saw a typewriter on a stand. She stopped, staring at it, wondering if it had a broken letter E. *I have to find out*, she thought.

She walked over to the office, hesitated a moment, then opened the door and stepped inside. As she moved toward the typewriter, Sam suddenly appeared out of nowhere.

'Evenin', Mrs Renaud,' he said. 'Can I help you?'

She spun around, startled. 'No. I . . . I just left my car. Good night.' She hurried toward the door.

'Good night, Mrs Renaud.'

In the morning, when Kendall passed the garage office, the typewriter was gone. In its place was a personal computer.

Sam saw her staring at it. 'Nice, huh? I decided to bring this place into the twentieth century.'

Now that he could afford it?

When Kendall told Marc about it that evening, he said thoughtfully, 'It's a possibility, but we need proof.'

Monday morning, when Kendall went to her office, Nadine was waiting for her.

'Are you feeling better, Mrs Renaud?'

'Yes. Thank you.'

'Yesterday was my birthday. Look what my husband got me!' She walked over to a closet and pulled out a luxurious mink coat. 'Isn't it beautiful?'

163

Chapter Nineteen

Julia Stanford enjoyed having Sally as a roommate. She was always upbeat and fun and cheerful. She had had a bad marriage and had sworn never to get involved with a man again. Julia wasn't sure what Sally's definition of *never* was, because she seemed to be out with a different man every week.

'Married men are the best,' Sally philosophized. 'They feel guilty, so they're always buying you presents. With a single man, you have to ask yourself, why is he still single?'

She said to Julia, 'You aren't dating anyone, are you?'

'No.' Julia thought of the men who had wanted to take her out. 'I don't want to go out just for the sake of going out, Sally. I have to be with someone I really care about.'

'Well, have I got a man for you!' Sally said. 'You're going to love him! His name is Tony Vinetti. I told him all about you, and he's dying to meet you.'

'I really don't think –'

'He'll pick you up tomorrow night at eight o'clock.'

Tony Vinetti was tall, very tall, in an appealing, ungainly way. His hair was thick and dark, and his smile exploded disarmingly as he looked at Julia.

'Sally wasn't exaggerating. You're a knockout!'

'Thank you,' Julia said. She felt a little shiver of pleasure.

'Have you ever been to Houston's?'

It was one of the finest restaurants in Kansas City.

'No.' The truth was that she could not afford to eat at Houston's. Not even with the raise she had been given.

'Well, that's where we have a reservation.'

*   *   *

164

At dinner, Tony talked mostly about himself, but Julia did not mind. He was entertaining and charming. '*He's drop-dead gorgeous*,' Sally had said. And he was.

The dinner was delicious. For dessert, Julia had ordered chocolate soufflé and Tony had ice cream. As they were lingering over coffee, Julia thought, *Is he going to ask me to his apartment, and if he does, will I go? No. I can't do that. Not on the first date. He'll think I'm cheap. When we go out the next time . . .*

The check arrived. Tony scanned it and said, 'It looks right.' He ticked off the items on the check. 'You had the pâté and the lobster . . .'

'Yes.'

'And you had the French fries and salad, and the soufflé, right?'

She looked at him, puzzled. 'That's right . . .'

'Okay.' He did some quick addition. 'Your share of the bill is fifty dollars and forty cents.'

Julia sat there in shock. 'I beg your pardon?'

Tony grinned. 'I know how independent you women are today. You won't let guys do anything for you, will you? There,' he said magnanimously, 'I'll take care of your share of the tip.'

'I'm sorry it didn't work out,' Sally apologized. 'He's really a honey. Are you going to see him again?'

'I can't afford him,' Julia said bitterly.

'Well, I have someone else for you. You'll love –'

'No. Sally, I really don't want . . .'

'Trust me.'

Ted Riddle was a man in his late thirties and, Julia had to admit, quite attractive. He took her to Jennie's Restaurant on Historic Strawberry Hill, famous for its authentic Croatian food.

'Sally really did me a favor,' Riddle said. 'You're very lovely.'

'Thank you.'

'Did Sally tell you I have an advertising agency?'

'No. She didn't.'

'Oh, yes. I have one of the biggest firms in Kansas City. Everybody knows me.'

'That's nice. I –'

'We handle some of the biggest clients in the country.'

'You do? I'm not –'

'Oh, yes. We handle celebrities, banks, big businesses, chain stores . . .'

'Well, I –'

'. . . supermarkets. You name it, we represent them all.'

'That's –'

'Let me tell you how I got started.'

He never stopped talking during dinner, and the only subject was Ted Riddle.

'He was probably just nervous,' Sally apologized.

'Well, I can tell you, he made *me* nervous. If there's anything you want to know about the life of Ted Riddle since the day he was born, just ask me!'

'Jerry McKinley.'

'What?'

'Jerry McKinley. I just remembered. He used to date a girlfriend of mine. She was absolutely crazy about him.'

'Thanks, Sally, but no.'

'I'm going to call him.'

The following night, Jerry McKinley appeared. He was nice-looking, and he had a sweet and engaging personality. When he walked in the door and looked at Julia he said, 'I know blind dates are always difficult. I'm rather shy myself, so I know how you must feel, Julia.'

She liked him immediately.

They went to the Evergreen Chinese Restaurant on State Avenue for dinner.

'You work for an architectural firm. That must be exciting. I don't think people realize how important architects are.'

He's sensitive, Julia thought happily. She smiled. 'I couldn't agree with you more.'

The evening was delightful, and the more they talked, the more Julia liked him. She decided to be bold.

'Would you like to come back to the apartment for a nightcap?' she asked.

'No. Let's go back to my place.'

'Your place?'

He leaned forward and squeezed her hand. 'That's where I keep the whips and chains.'

Henry Wesson owned an accounting firm in the building where Peters, Eastman & Tolkin was quartered. Two or three mornings a week, Julia would find herself in the elevator with him. He seemed a pleasant enough man. He was in his thirties, quietly intelligent-looking, sandy haired, and he wore black rimmed glasses.

The acquaintance began with polite nods, then, 'Good morning,' then, 'You're looking very well today,' and after a few months, 'I wonder if you'd like to have dinner with me some evening?' He was watching her eagerly, waiting for an answer.

Julia smiled. 'All right.'

It was instant love on Henry's part. On their first date, he took Julia to EBT, one of the top restaurants in Kansas City. He was obviously thrilled to be out with her.

He told her a little about himself. 'I was born right here in good old KC. My father was born here, too. The acorn doesn't fall far from the oak. You know what I mean?'

Julia knew what he meant.

'I always knew I wanted to be an accountant. When I got out of school, I went to work for the Bigelow & Benson Financial Corporation. Now I have my own firm.'

'That's nice,' Julia said.

'That's about all there is to tell about me. Tell me about you.'

Julia was silent for a moment. *I'm the illegitimate daughter of one of the richest men in the world. You've probably heard of him. He just drowned. I'm an heiress to his estate.* She looked around the elegant room. *I could buy this restaurant, if I wanted to. I could probably buy this whole town, if I wanted to.*

Henry was staring at her. 'Julia?'

'Oh! I . . . I'm sorry. I was born in Milwaukee. My . . . my father died when I was young. My mother and I traveled around the country a great deal. When she passed away, I decided to stay here and get a job.' *I hope my nose isn't growing.*

Henry Wesson put a hand over hers. 'So you've never had a man to take care of you.' He leaned forward and said earnestly, 'I would like to take care of you for the rest of your life.'

Julia looked at him in surprise. 'I don't mean to sound like Doris Day, but we hardly know each other.'

'I want to change that.'

When Julia got home, Sally was waiting for her. 'Well?' she asked. 'How did your date go?'

Julia said, thoughtfully, 'He's very sweet, and . . .'

'He's crazy about you!'

Julia smiled. 'I think he proposed.'

Sally's eyes widened. 'You *think* he proposed? My, God! Don't you know if the man proposed or not?'

'Well, he said he wanted to take care of me for the rest of my life.'

'That's a proposal!' Sally exclaimed. 'That's a proposal! Marry him! Quick! Marry him before he changes his mind!'

Julia laughed. 'What's the hurry?'

'Listen to me. Invite him over here for dinner. I'll cook it, and you tell him you made it.'

Julia laughed. 'Thank you. No. When I find the man I want to marry, we may be eating Chinese food out of cartons, but believe me, the dinner table will be beautifully set with flowers and candlelight.'

On their next date, Henry said, 'You know, Kansas City is a great place to bring up kids.'

'Yes, it is.' Julia's only problem was that she wasn't sure that she wanted to bring up *his* children. He was reliable, sober, decent, but . . .

She discussed it with Sally.

168

'He keeps asking me to marry him,' Julia said.

'What's he like?'

She thought for a moment, trying to think of the most romantic and exciting things she could say about Henry Wesson. 'He's reliable, sober, decent . . .'

Sally looked at her a moment. 'In other words, he's dull.'

Julia said defensively, 'He isn't exactly dull.'

Sally nodded, knowingly. 'He's dull. Marry him.'

'What?'

'Marry him. Good dull husbands are hard to find.'

Getting from one payday to the next was a financial minefield. There were paycheck deductions, and rent, and automobile expenses, and groceries, and clothes to buy. Julia owned a Toyota Tercel, and it seemed to her that she spent more on it than she did on herself. She was constantly borrowing money from Sally.

One evening, when Julia was getting dressed, Sally said, 'It's another big Henry night, huh? Where's he taking you tonight?'

'We're going to Symphony Hall. Cleo Laine is performing.'

'Has old Henry proposed again?'

Julia hesitated. The truth was that Henry proposed every time they were together. She felt pressured, but she could not bring herself to say yes.

'Don't lose him,' Sally warned.

Sally is probably right. Julia thought. *Henry Wesson would make a good husband. He's . . .* She hesitated. *He's sober, reliable, decent . . . Is that enough?*

As Julia was going out the door, Sally called, 'Can I borrow your black shoes?'

'Sure.' And Julia was gone.

Sally went into Julia's bedroom and opened the closet door. The pair of shoes she wanted was on the top shelf. As she reached for them, a cardboard box that was sitting precariously on the shelf fell down, and its contents spilled out all over the floor.

'Damn!' Sally bent down to gather up the papers. They

169

consisted of dozens of newspaper clippings, photographs, and articles, and they were all about the Harry Stanford family. There seemed to be hundreds of them.

Suddenly, Julia came hurrying back into the room. 'I forgot my –' She stopped as she saw the papers on the floor. 'What are you doing?'

'I'm sorry,' Sally apologized. 'The box fell down.'

Blushing, Julia bent down and started putting the papers back in the box.

'I had no idea you were so interested in the rich and famous,' Sally said.

Silently, Julia kept shoving the papers into the box. As she gathered a handful of photographs, she came across a small gold heart-shaped locket that her mother had given her before she died. Julia put the locket aside.

Sally was studying her, puzzled. 'Julia?'

'Yes.'

'Why are you so interested in Harry Stanford?'

'I'm not. I . . . This was my mother's.'

Sally shrugged. 'Okay.' She reached for a paper. It was from a scandal magazine, and the headline caught her eye: TYCOON GETS CHILDREN'S GOVERNESS PREGNANT – BABY BORN OUT-OF-WEDLOCK – MOTHER AND BABY DISAPPEAR!

Sally was staring at Julia, openmouthed. 'My God! You're Harry Stanford's daughter!'

Julia's mouth tightened. She shook her head and continued putting the papers back.

'Aren't you?'

Julia stopped. 'Please, I'd rather not talk about it, if you don't mind.'

Sally jumped to her feet. '*You'd rather not talk about it? You're the daughter of one of the richest men in the world, and you'd rather not talk about it? Are you insane?*'

'Sally . . .'

'Do you know how much he was worth? Billions.'

'That has nothing to do with me.'

'If you're his daughter, it has *everything* to do with you. You're an heiress! All you have to do is tell the family who you are, and –'

'No.'

'No . . . what?'

'You don't understand.' Julia rose and then sank down on the bed. 'Harry Stanford was an awful man. He abandoned my mother. She hated him, and I hate him.'

'You don't *hate* anyone with that much money. You *understand* them.'

Julia shook her head. 'I don't want any part of them.'

'Julia, heiresses don't live in crummy apartments and buy clothes at flea markets, and borrow to pay the rent. Your family would *hate* knowing you live like this. They'd be humiliated.'

'They don't even know I'm alive.'

'Then you've got to tell them.'

'Sally . . .'

'Yes?'

'Drop the subject.'

Sally looked at her for a long time. 'Sure. By the way, you couldn't loan me a million or two till payday, could you?'

Chapter Twenty

Tyler was becoming frantic. For the past twenty-four hours he had been dialing Lee's home number, and there had been no answer. *Who is he with?* Tyler agonized. *What is he doing?*

He picked up the telephone and dialed once again. The phone rang for a long time, and just as Tyler was about to hang up, he heard Lee's voice. 'Hello.'

'Lee! How are you?'

'Who the hell is this?'

'It's Tyler.'

'Tyler?' There was a pause. 'Oh, yes.'

Tyler felt a twinge of disappointment. 'How are you?'

'Fine,' Lee said.

'I told you I was going to have a wonderful surprise for you.'

'Yes?' He sounded bored.

'Do you remember what you said to me about going to St Tropez on a beautiful white yacht?'

'What about it?'

'How would you like to leave next month?'

'Are you serious?'

'You bet I am.'

'Well, I don't know. You've got a friend with a yacht?'

'I'm about to *buy* a yacht.'

'You're not on something, are you, judge?'

'On . . . ? No, no! I've just come into some money. A lot of money.'

'St Tropez, huh? Yeah, that sounds great. Sure, I'd love to go with you.'

Tyler felt a deep sense of relief. 'Wonderful! Meanwhile, don't . . .' He couldn't bring himself even to think about it. 'I'll be in touch with you, Lee.' He replaced the receiver and sat on the edge of his bed. *'I'd love to go with you.'* He could visualize the two of them on a beautiful yacht, cruising around the world together. *Together.*

Tyler picked up the telephone book and turned to the yellow pages.

The offices of John Alden Yachts Inc are located on Boston's Commercial Wharf. The sales manager came up to Tyler as he entered.

'What can I do for you today, sir?'

Tyler looked at him and said casually, 'I'd like to buy a yacht.' The words rolled off his tongue.

His father's yacht would probably be part of the estate, but Tyler had no intention of sharing a ship with his brother and sister.

'Motor or sail?'

'I . . . er . . . I'm not sure. I want to be able to go around the world in it.'

'We're probably talking motor.'

'It must be white.'

The sales manager looked at him strangely. 'Yes, of course. How large a boat did you have in mind?'

Blue Skies is one hundred and eighty feet.

'Two hundred feet.'

The sales manager blinked. 'Ah. I see. Of course, a yacht like that would be very expensive, Mr – . . .'

'Judge Stanford. My father was Harry Stanford.'

The man's face lit up.

'Money is no object,' Tyler said.

'Certainly not! Well, Judge Stanford, we're going to find you a yacht that everyone will envy. White, of course. Meanwhile, here is a portfolio of some available yachts. Call me when you decide which ones you're interested in.'

*   *   *

173

Woody Stanford was thinking about polo ponies. All his life he had had to ride his friends' ponies, but now he could afford to buy the finest string in the world.

He was on the telephone, talking to Mimi Carson. 'I want to buy your ponies,' Woody said. His voice was filled with excitement. He listened a moment. 'That's right, the whole stable. I'm very serious. Right.'

The conversation lasted half an hour, and when Woody replaced the receiver, he was grinning. He went to find Peggy.

She was seated alone on the veranda. Woody could still see the bruises on her face where he had hit her.

'Peggy . . .'

She looked up, warily. 'Yes?'

'I have to talk to you. I . . . I don't know where to begin.'

She sat there, waiting.

He took a deep breath. 'I know I've been a rotten husband. Some of the things I've done are inexcusable. But, darling, all that is going to change now. Don't you see? We're rich. Really rich. I want to make everything up to you.' He took her hand. 'I'm going to get off drugs this time. I really am. We're going to have a whole different life.'

She looked into his eyes, and said tonelessly, 'Are we, Woody?'

'Yes. I promise. I know I've said it before, but this time it's really going to work. I've made up my mind. I'm going to a clinic somewhere where they can cure me. I want to get out of this hell I've been in. Peggy . . .' There was desperation in his voice. 'I can't do it without you. You know I can't.'

She looked at him a long time, then cradled him in her arms. 'Poor baby. I know,' she whispered. 'I know. I'll help you . . .'

It was time for Margo Posner to leave.

Tyler found her in the study. He closed the door. 'I just wanted to thank you again, Margo.'

She smiled. 'It's been fun. I really had a good time.' She looked up at him archly. 'Maybe I should become an actress.'

He smiled. 'You'd be good at it. You certainly fooled this audience.'

'I did, didn't I?'

'Here's the rest of your money.' He took an envelope out of his pocket. 'And your plane ticket back to Chicago.'

'Thank you.'

He looked at his watch. 'You'd better get going.'

'Right. I just want you to know that I appreciate everything. I mean, your getting me out of prison and all.'

He smiled. 'That's all right. Have a good trip.'

'Thanks.'

He watched her go upstairs to pack. The game was over. *Check and check mate.*

Margo Posner was in her bedroom finishing packing when Kendall walked in.

'Hi, Julia. I just wanted to –' She stopped. 'What are you doing?'

'I'm going home.'

Kendall looked at her in surprise. 'So soon? Why? I was hoping we might spend some time together and get acquainted. We have so many years to catch up on.'

'Sure. Well, some other time.'

Kendall sat on the edge of the bed. 'It's like a miracle, isn't it? Finding each other after all these years?'

Margo went on with her packing. 'Yeah. It's a miracle, all right.'

'You must feel like Cinderella. I mean, one minute you're living a perfectly average life and the next minute someone hands you a billion dollars.'

Margo stopped her packing. 'What?'

'I said . . .'

'A *billion* dollars?'

'Yes. According to Father's will, that's what we each inherit.'

Margo was looking at Kendall, stunned. 'We each get a billion dollars?'

'Didn't they tell you?'

'No,' Margo said slowly. 'They didn't tell me.' There was a thoughtful expression on her face. 'You know, Kendall, you're right. Maybe we should get better acquainted.'

*   *   *

Tyler was in the solarium, looking at photographs of yachts, when Clark approached him.

'Excuse me, Judge Stanford. There's a telephone call for you.'

'I'll take it in here.'

It was Keith Percy in Chicago.

'Tyler?'

'Yes.'

'I have some really great news for you!'

'Oh?'

'Now that I'm retiring, how would you like to be appointed chief judge?'

It was all Tyler could do to keep from giggling. 'That would be wonderful, Keith.'

'Well, it's yours!'

'I . . . I don't know what to say.' *What should I say?* '*Billionaires don't sit on the bench in a dirty little courtroom in Chicago, handing out sentences to the misfits of the world?*' *Or* '*I'll be too busy sailing around the world on my yacht?*'

'How soon can you get back to Chicago?'

'It will be a while,' Tyler said. 'I have a lot to do here.'

'Well, we'll all be waiting for you.'

Don't hold your breath. 'Good-bye.' He replaced the receiver and glanced at his watch. It was time for Margo to be leaving for the airport. Tyler went upstairs to see if she was ready.

When he walked into Margo's bedroom, she was unpacking her suitcase.

He looked at her in surprise. 'You're not ready.'

She looked up at him and smiled. 'No. I'm unpacking. I've been thinking. I like it here. Maybe I should stay awhile.'

He frowned. 'What are you talking about? You're catching a plane to Chicago.'

'There'll be another plane along, Judge.' She grinned. 'Maybe I'll even buy my own.'

'What are you saying?'

'You told me you wanted me to help you play a little joke on someone.'

'Yes?'

176

'Well, the joke seems to be on me. I'm worth a billion dollars.'

Tyler's expression hardened. 'I want you to get out of here. Now.'

'Do you? I think I'll go when I'm ready,' Margo said. 'And I'm not ready.'

Tyler stood there, studying her. 'What . . . what is it you want?'

She nodded. 'That's better. The billion dollars I'm supposed to get. You were planning to keep it for yourself, right? I figured you were pulling a little scam to pick up some extra money, but a billion dollars! That's a different ball game. I think I deserve a share of that.'

There was a knock at the bedroom door.

'Excuse me,' Clark said. 'Luncheon is served.'

Margo turned to Tyler. 'You go along. I won't be joining you. I have some important errands to run.'

Later that afternoon, packages began to arrive at Rose Hill. There were boxes of dresses from Armani, sportswear from Scaasi Boutique, lingerie from Jordan Marsh, a sable coat from Neiman Marcus, and a diamond bracelet from Cartier. All the packages were addressed to Miss Julia Stanford.

When Margo walked in the door at four thirty, Tyler was waiting to confront her, furious.

'What do you think you're doing?' he demanded.

She smiled. 'I needed a few things. After all, your sister has to be well dressed, doesn't she? It's amazing how much credit a store will give you when you're a Stanford. You will take care of the bills, won't you?'

'Julia . . .'

'Margo.' She reminded him. 'By the way, I saw the pictures of yachts on the table. Are you planning to buy one?'

'That's none of your business.'

'Don't be too sure. Maybe you and I will take a cruise. We'll name the yacht *Margo*. Or should we name it *Julia*? We can go around the world together. I don't like being alone.'

Tyler took a deep breath. 'It seems that I underestimated you. You're a very clever young woman.'

'Coming from you, that's a big compliment.'

'I hope that you're also a reasonable young woman.'

'That depends. What do you call reasonable?'

'One million dollars. Cash.'

Her heart began to beat faster. 'And I can keep the things I bought today?'

'All of them.'

She took a deep breath. 'You have a deal.'

'Good. I'll get the money to you as quickly as I can. I'll be going back to Chicago in the next few days.' He took a key from his pocket and handed it to her. 'Here's the key to my house. I want you to stay there and wait for me. And don't talk to anyone.'

'All right.' She tried to hide her excitement. *Maybe I should have asked for more,* she thought.

'I'll book you on the next plane out of here.'

'What about the things I bought . . . ?'

'I'll have them sent on to you.'

'Good. Hey, we both came out of this great, didn't we?'

He nodded. 'Yes. We did.'

Tyler took Margo to Logan International Airport to see her off.

At the airport she said, 'What are you going to tell the others? About my leaving, I mean.'

'I'll tell them that you had to go visit a very good friend who became ill, a friend in South America.'

She looked at him wistfully. 'Do you want to know something, judge? That yachting trip would have been fun.'

Over the loudspeaker, her flight was being called.

'That's me, I guess.'

'Have a nice flight.'

'Thanks. I'll see you in Chicago.'

Tyler watched her go into the departures terminal and stood there, waiting until the plane took off. Then he went back to the limousine and said to the driver, 'Rose Hill.'

When Tyler arrived back at the house, he went directly to his room and telephoned Chief Judge Keith Percy.

'We're all waiting for you, Tyler. When are you coming back? We're planning a little celebration in your honor.'

'Very soon, Keith,' Tyler said. 'Meanwhile, I could use your help with a problem I've run into.'

'Certainly. What can I do for you?'

'It's about a felon I tried to help. Margo Posner. I believe I told you about her.'

'I remember. What's the problem?'

'The poor woman has deluded herself into believing she's my sister. She followed me to Boston and tried to murder me.'

'My God! That's terrible!'

'She's on her way back to Chicago now, Keith. She stole the key to my house, and I don't know what she plans to do next. The woman is a dangerous lunatic. She's threatened to kill my whole family. I want her committed to the Reed Mental Health Facility. If you'll fax me the commitment papers, I'll sign them. I'll arrange for her psychiatric examinations myself.'

'Of course. I'll take care of it immediately, Tyler.'

'I'd appreciate it. She's on United Airlines Flight 307. It arrives at eight fifteen tonight. I suggest that you have people there at the airport to pick her up. Tell them to be careful. She should be put in maximum security at Reed, and not allowed any visitors.'

'I'll see to it. I'm sorry you had to go through this, Tyler.'

There was a shrug in Tyler's voice. 'You know what they say, Keith: "No good deed, no matter how small, goes unpunished."'

At dinner that evening Kendall asked, 'Isn't Julia joining us tonight?'

Tyler said regretfully, 'Unfortunately, no. She asked me to say good-bye to all of you. She's gone to take care of a friend in South America who's had a stroke. It was rather sudden.'

'But the will has not been . . .'

'Julia has given me her power of attorney and wants me to arrange for her share to go into a trust fund.'

A servant placed a bowl of Boston clam chowder in front of Tyler.

'Ah,' he said. 'That looks delicious! I'm hungry tonight.'

* * *

United Airlines Flight 307 was making its final approach to O'Hare International Airport on schedule. A metallic voice came over the loudspeaker. 'Ladies and gentlemen, would you fasten your seat belts, please?'

Margo Posner had enjoyed the flight tremendously. She had spent most of the time dreaming about what she was going to do with the million dollars and all the clothes and jewelry she had bought. *And all because I was busted! Isn't that a kick!*

When the plane landed, Margo gathered the things she had carried on board and started to walk down the ramp. A flight attendant stayed directly behind her. Near the plane was an ambulance, flanked by two paramedics in white jackets, and a doctor. The flight attendant saw them and pointed to Margo.

As Margo stepped off the ramp, one of the men approached her. 'Excuse me,' he said.

Margo looked up at him. 'Yes?'

'Are you Margo Posner?'

'Why, yes. What's . . . ?'

'I'm Dr Zimmerman.' He took her arm. 'We'd like you to come with us, please.' He started leading her toward the ambulance.

Margo tried to jerk away. 'Wait a minute! What are you doing?' she demanded.

The other two men had moved to either side of her to hold her arms.

'Just come along quietly, Miss Posner,' the doctor said.

'Help!' Margo screamed. 'Help me!'

The other passengers were standing there, gaping.

'What's the matter with all of you?' Margo yelled. 'Are you blind? I'm being kidnapped! I'm Julia Stanford! I'm Harry Stanford's daughter!'

'Of course, you are,' Dr Zimmerman said soothingly. 'Just calm down.'

The observers watched in astonishment as Margo was carried into the back of the ambulance, kicking and screaming.

Inside the ambulance, the doctor took out a syringe and pressed the needle into Margo's arm. 'Relax,' he said. 'Everything is going to be all right.'

'You must be crazy!' Margo said. 'You must be . . .' Her eyes began to droop.

The ambulance doors closed, and the ambulance sped away.

When Tyler got the report, he laughed out loud. He could visualize the greedy bitch being carried off. He would arrange for her to be kept in a mental health facility for the rest of her life.

Now the game is really over, he thought. *I've done it! The old man would turn over in his grave – if he still had one – if he knew that I was getting control of Stanford Enterprises. I'll give Lee everything he's ever dreamed of.*

Perfect. Everything was perfect.

The events of the day had filled Tyler with a sexual excitement. *I need some relief.* He opened his suitcase and from the back of it took out a copy of *Damron's Guide*. There were several gay bars listed in Boston. He chose the Quest on Boylston Street. *I'll skip dinner. I'll go straight to the club.* And then he thought, *What an oxymoron!*

Julia and Sally were getting dressed to go to work. Sally asked, 'How was your date with Henry last night?'

'The same.'

'That bad, huh? Have the marriage banns been posted yet?'

'God, forbid!' Julia said. 'Henry is sweet, but . . .' She sighed. 'He isn't for me.'

'*He* might not be,' Sally said, 'but *these* are for you.' She handed Julia five envelopes.

They were all bills. Julia opened them. Three of them were marked OVERDUE and another was marked THIRD NOTICE. Julia studied them a moment.

'Sally, I wonder if you could lend me . . . ?'

Sally looked at her in amazement. 'I don't understand you.'

'What do you mean?'

'You're working like a galley slave, you can't pay your bills, and all you have to do is lift your little finger and you could come up with a few million dollars, give or take some change.'

'It's not my money.'

'Of course, it's your money!' Sally snapped. 'Harry Stanford was your father, wasn't he? Ergo, you're entitled to a share of his estate. And I don't use the word *ergo* very often.'

'Forget it. I told you how he treated my mother. He wouldn't have left me a dime.'

Sally sighed. 'Damn! And I was looking forward to living with a millionaire!'

They walked down to the parking lot where they kept their cars. Julia's space was empty. She stared at it in shock. 'It's gone!'

'Are you sure you parked your car here last night?' Sally asked. 'Yes.'

'Someone stole it!'

Julia shook her head. 'No,' she said slowly.

'What do you mean?'

She turned to look at Sally. 'They must have repossessed it. I'm three payments behind.'

'Wonderful,' Sally said tonelessly. 'That's just wonderful.'

Sally was unable to get her roommate's situation out of her mind. *It's like a fairy tale,* Sally thought. *A princess who doesn't know she's a princess. Only in this case, she knows it, but she's too proud to do anything about it. It's not fair! The family has all that money, and she has nothing. Well, if she won't do something about it, I damn well will. She'll thank me for it.*

That evening, after Julia went out, Sally examined the box of clippings again. She took out a recent newspaper article mentioning that the Stanford heirs had gone back to Rose Hill for the funeral services.

If the princess won't go to them, Sally thought, *they're going to come to the princess.*

She sat down and began to write a letter. It was addressed to Judge Tyler Stanford.

Chapter Twenty-one

Tyler Stanford signed the commitment papers putting Margo Posner in Reed Mental Health Facility. Three psychiatrists were required to agree to the commitment, but Tyler knew that that would be easy for him to handle.

He reviewed everything he had done from the very beginning, and decided that there had been no flaws in his game plan. Dmitri had disappeared in Australia, and Margo Posner had been disposed of. That left Hal Baker, but he would be no problem. Everyone had an Achilles' heel, and his was his stupid family. *No, Baker will never talk because he couldn't bear the thought of spending his life in prison, away from his dear ones.*

Everything was perfect.

The minute the will is probated, I'll return to Chicago and pick up Lee. Maybe we'll even buy a house in St Tropez. He began to get aroused at the thought. *We'll sail around the world in my yacht. I've always wanted to see Venice . . . and Positano . . . and Capri . . . We'll go on safari in Kenya, and see the Taj Mahal together in the moonlight. And who do I owe all this to? To Daddy. Dear old Daddy. 'You're a queer, Tyler, and you'll always be a queer. I don't know how the hell anything like you came from my loins.'*

Well, who has the last laugh now, Father?

Tyler went downstairs to join his brother and sister for lunch. He was hungry again.

'It's really a pity that Julia had to leave so quickly,' Kendall said. 'I would have liked to have gotten to know her better.'

'I'm sure she plans to return as soon as she can,' Marc said.

That's certainly true, Tyler thought. He would make sure she never got out.

The talk turned to the future.

Peggy said, shyly, 'Woody is going to buy a group of polo ponies.'

'It's not a group!' Woody snapped. 'It's a string. A *string* of polo ponies.'

'I'm sorry, darling. I just –'

'Forget it!'

Tyler said to Kendall, 'What are your plans?'

'. . . *We are counting on your further support . . . We would appreciate it if you would deposit 1 million US dollars . . . within the next ten days.*'

'Kendall?'

'Oh. I'm going to . . . to expand the business. I'll open shops in London and in Paris.'

'That sounds exciting,' Peggy said.

'I have a show in New York in two weeks. I have to run down there and get it ready.'

Rendall looked over at Tyler. 'What are you going to do with your share of the estate?'

Tyler said piously, 'Charity, mostly. There are so many worthy organizations that need help.'

He was only half listening to the conversation at the table. He looked around the table at his brother and sister. *If it weren't for me, you'd be getting nothing. Nothing!*

He turned to look at Woody. His brother had become a dope addict, throwing his life away. *Money won't help him,* Tyler thought. *It will only buy him more dope.* He wondered where Woody was getting the stuff.

Tyler turned to his sister. Kendall was bright and successful, and she had made the most of her talents.

Marc was seated next to her, telling an amusing anecdote to Peggy. *He's attractive and charming. Too bad he's married.*

And then there was Peggy. He thought of her as Poorpeggy. Why she put up with Woody was beyond him. *She must love him very much. She certainly hasn't gotten anything out of her marriage.*

He wondered what the expressions on their faces would be if he stood up and said, '*I control Stanford Enterprises. I had our father murdered, his body dug up, and I hired someone to impersonate our half sister.*' He smiled at the thought. It was difficult holding a secret as delicious as the one he had.

After lunch, Tyler went to his room to telephone Lee again. There was no answer. *He's out with someone,* Tyler thought, despairingly. *He doesn't believe me about the yacht. Well, I'll prove it to him! When is that damn will going to be probated? I'll have to call Fitzgerald, or that young lawyer, Steve Sloane.*

There was a knock at the door. Clark stood there. 'Excuse me, Judge Stanford. A letter arrived for you.'

Probably from Keith Percy, congratulating me. 'Thank you, Clark.' He took the envelope. It had a Kansas City return address. He stared at it a moment, puzzled, then opened it and began to read the letter.

> *Dear Judge Stanford:*
> *I think you should know that you have a half sister named Julia. She is the daughter of Rosemary Nelson and your father. She lives here in Kansas City. Her address is 1425 Metcalf Avenue, Apartment 3B, Kansas City, Kansas.*
> *I'm sure Julia would be most happy to hear from you.*
> *Sincerely,*
> *A Friend*

Tyler stared at the letter disbelievingly, and he felt a cold chill. 'No!' he cried aloud. 'No!' *I won't have it! Not now! Maybe she's a fake.* But he had a terrible feeling that this Julia was genuine. *And now the bitch is coming forward to claim her share of the estate! My share,* Tyler corrected himself. *It doesn't belong to her. I can't let her come here. It would ruin everything. I would have to explain the other Julia, and. . . He shuddered. 'No!' I have to have her taken care of. Fast.*

He reached for the telephone and dialed Hal Baker's number.

Chapter Twenty-two

The dermatologist shook his head. 'I've seen cases similar to yours, but never one this bad.'

Hal Baker scratched his hand and nodded.

'You see, Mr Baker, we were confronted with three possibilities. Your itching could have been caused by a fungus, an allergy, or it could be neurodermatitis. The skin scraping I took from your hand and put under the microscope showed me that it wasn't a fungus. And you said you didn't handle chemicals on the job . . .'

'That's right.'

'So, we've narrowed it down. What you have is lichen simplex chronicus or localized neurodermatitis.'

'That sounds awful. Is there something you can do about it?'

'Fortunately, there is.' The doctor took a tube from a cabinet in a corner of the office and opened it. 'Is your hand itching now?'

Hal Baker scratched again. 'Yes. It feels like it's on fire.'

'I want you to rub some of this cream on your hand.'

Hal Baker squeezed out some of the cream and began to rub it into his hand. It was like a miracle.

'The itching has stopped!' Baker said.

'Good. Use that, and you won't have any more problem.'

'Thank you, doctor. I can't tell you what a relief this is.'

'I'll give you a prescription. You can take the tube with you.'

'Thank you.'

Driving home, Hal Baker was singing aloud. It was the first time since he had met Judge Tyler Stanford that his hand had not itched. It was a wonderful feeling of freedom. Still whistling, he pulled into the garage, and walked into the kitchen. Helen was waiting for him.

'You had a telephone call,' she said. 'A Mr Jones. He said it was urgent.'

His hand began itching.

He had hurt some people, but he had done it for the love of his kids. He had committed some crimes, but it was for the family. Hal Baker did not believe he really had been at fault. This was different. This was a cold-blooded murder.

When he had returned the phone call, he had protested. 'I can't do that, judge. You'll have to find someone else.'

There had been a silence. And then, 'How's the family?'

The flight to Kansas City was uneventful. Judge Stanford had given him detailed instructions. '*Her name is Julia Stanford. You have her address and apartment number. She won't be expecting you. All you have to do is go there and handle her.*'

He took a taxi from the Kansas City Downtown Airport to downtown Kansas City.

'Beautiful day,' the taxi driver said.

'Yep.'

'Where did you come in from?'

'New York. I live here.'

'Nice place to live.'

'Sure is. I have a little repair work to do around the house. Would you drop me off at a hardware store?'

'Right.'

Five minutes later, Hal Baker was saying to a clerk in the store, 'I need a hunting knife.'

'We have just the thing, sir. Would you come this way, please?'

The knife was a thing of beauty, about six inches long, with a sharp pointed end and serrated edges.

'Will this do?'

'I'm sure it will,' Hal Baker said.

'Will that be cash or charge?'

'Cash.'

His next stop was at a stationery store.

Hal Baker studied the apartment building at 1425 Metcalf Avenue for five minutes, examining exits and entrances. He left and returned at 8 P.M., when it began to get dark. He wanted to make sure that if Julia Stanford had a job, she would be home from work. He had noted that the apartment building had no doorman. There was an elevator, but he took the stairs. It was not smart to be in small enclosed places. They were traps. He reached the third floor. Apartment 3B was down the hall on the left. The knife was taped to the inside pocket of his jacket. He rang the doorbell. A moment later, the door opened, and he found himself facing an attractive woman.

'Hello.' She had a nice smile. 'Can I help you?'

She was younger than he had expected, and he wondered fleetingly why Judge Stanford wanted her killed. *Well, that's none of my business.* He took out a card and handed it to her.

'I'm with the A. C. Nielsen Company,' he said smoothly. 'We don't have any of the Nielsen family in this area, and we're looking for people who might be interested.'

She shook her head. 'No, thanks.' She started to close the door.

'We pay one hundred dollars a week.'

The door stayed half open.

'A hundred dollars a week?'

'Yes, ma'am.'

The door was wide open now.

'All you have to do is record the names of the programs you watch. We'll give you a contract for one year.'

Five thousand dollars! 'Come in,' she said.

He walked into the apartment.

'Sit down, Mr –'

'Allen. Jim Allen.'

'Mr Allen. How did you happen to select me?'

'Our company does random checking. We have to make sure that none of the people is involved in television in any way, so

189

we can keep our survey accurate. You don't have any connection with any television production programs or networks, do you?'

She laughed. 'Gosh, no. What would I have to do exactly?'

'It's really very simple. We'll give you a chart with all the television programs listed on it, and all you have to do is make a check mark every time you watch a program. That way our computer can figure out how many viewers each program has. The Nielsen family is scattered around the United States, so we get a clear picture of which shows are popular in which areas and with whom. Would you be interested?'

'Oh, yes.'

He took out some printed forms and a pen. 'How many hours a day do you watch television?'

'Not very many. I work all day.'

'But you do watch some television?'

'Oh, certainly. I watch the news at night, and sometimes an old movie. I like Larry King.'

He made a note. 'Do you watch much educational television?'

'I watch PBS on Sundays.'

'By the way, do you live alone here?'

'I have a roommate, but she's not here.'

So they were alone.

His hand began to itch. He started to reach into his inside pocket to untape the knife. He heard footsteps in the hall outside. He stopped.

'Did you say I get five thousand dollars a year just for doing this?'

'That's right. Oh, I forgot to mention. We also give you a new color TV set.'

'That's fantastic!'

The footsteps were gone. He reached inside his pocket again, and felt the handle of the knife. 'Could I have a glass of water, please? It's been a long day.'

'Certainly.' He watched her get up and go over to the small bar in the corner. He slipped the knife out of its sheath and moved up behind her.

She was saying, 'My roommate watches PBS more than I do.'

He lifted the knife, ready to strike.

'But Julia's more intellectual than I am.'

Baker's hand froze in midair. 'Julia?'

'My roommate. Or she was. She's gone. I found a note when I got home saying she had left and didn't know when she'd be –' She turned around, holding the glass of water, and saw the upraised knife in his hand. 'What . . . ?'

She screamed.

Hal Baker turned and fled.

Hal Baker telephoned Tyler Stanford. 'I'm in Kansas City, but the girl is gone.'

'What do you mean, gone?'

'Her roommate says she left.'

He was silent for a moment. 'I have a feeling she's headed for Boston. I want you to get up here right away.'

'Yes, sir.'

Tyler Stanford slammed down the receiver and began to pace. *Everything had been going so perfectly!* The girl had to be found and disposed of. She was a loose cannon. Even after he received control of the estate, Tyler knew he would not rest easy as long as she was alive. *I've got to find her*, Tyler thought. *I've got to! But where?*

Clark came into the room. 'Excuse me, Judge Stanford. There is a Miss Julia Stanford here to see you.'

Chapter Twenty-three

It was because of Kendall that Julia decided to go to Boston. Returning from lunch one day, Julia passed an exclusive dress shop, and in the window was an original design by Kendall. Julia looked at it for a long time. *That's my sister,* Julia thought. *I can't blame her for what happened to my mother. And I can't blame my brothers.* And suddenly she was filled with an overpowering desire to see them, to meet them, to talk to them, to have a family at last.

When Julia returned to the office, she told Max Tolkin that she would be gone for a few days. Embarrassed, she said, 'I wonder if I could have an advance on my salary?'

Tolkin smiled. 'Sure. You have a vacation coming. Here. Have a good time.'

Will I have a good time? Julia wondered. *Or am I making a terrible mistake?*

When Julia returned home, Sally had not arrived yet. *I can't wait for her,* Julia decided. *If I don't go now, I'll never go.* She packed her suitcase and left a note.

On the way to the bus terminal, Julia had second thoughts. *What am I doing? Why did I make this sudden decision?* Then she thought wryly, *Sudden? It's taken me fourteen years!* She was filled with an enormous sense of excitement. What was her family going to be like? She knew that one of her brothers was a judge, the other was a famous polo player, and her sister was a famous designer. *It's a family of achievers,* Julia thought, *and who am I? I hope they don't look down on me.* Merely thinking about what lay ahead made Julia's heart skip a beat. She boarded a Grey-hound bus and was on her way.

When the bus arrived at South Station in Boston, Julia found a taxi.

'Where to, lady?' the driver asked.

And Julia completely lost her nerve. She had intended to say, 'Rose Hill.' Instead, she said, 'I don't know.'

The taxi driver turned around to look at her. 'Gee, I don't know, either.'

'Could you just drive around? I've never been to Boston before.'

He nodded. 'Sure.'

They drove west along Summer Street until they reached the Boston Common.

The driver said, 'This is the oldest public park in the United States. They used to use it for hangings.'

And Julia could hear her mother's voice. '*I used to take the children to the Common in the winter to ice-skate. Woody was a natural athlete. I wish you could have met him, Julia. He was such a handsome boy. I always thought he was going to be the successful one in the family.*' It was as though her mother were with her, sharing this moment.

They had reached Charles Street, the entrance to the Public Garden. The driver said, 'See those bronze ducklings? Believe it or not, they've all got names.'

'*We used to have picnics in the Public Garden. There are cute bronze ducklings at the entrance. They're named Jack, Kack, Lack, Mack, Nack, Ouack, Pack, and Quack.*' Julia had thought that was so funny that she had made her mother repeat the names over and over again.

Julia looked at the meter. The drive was getting expensive. 'Could you recommend an inexpensive hotel?'

'Sure. How about the Copley Square Hotel?'

'Would you take me there, please?'

'Right.'

Five minutes later, they pulled up in front of the hotel.

'Enjoy Boston, lady.'

'Thank you.' *Am I going to enjoy it, or will it be a disaster?* Julia paid the driver and went into the hotel. She approached the young clerk behind the desk.

'Hello,' he said. 'May I help you?'

'I'd like a room, please.'

'Single?'

'Yes.'

'How long will you be staying?'

She hesitated. *An hour? Ten years?* 'I don't know.'

'Right.' He checked the key rack. 'I have a nice single for you on the fourth floor.'

'Thank you.' She signed the register in a neat hand. *Julia Stanford.*

The clerk handed her a key. 'There you are. Enjoy your stay.'

The room was small, but neat and clean. As soon as Julia unpacked, she telephoned Sally.

'Julia? My God! Where are you?'

'I'm in Boston.'

'Are you all right?' She sounded hysterical.

'Yes. Why?'

'Someone came to the apartment, looking for you, and I think he wanted to kill you!'

'What are you talking about?'

'He had a knife and . . . you should have seen the look on his face . . .' She was gasping for breath. 'When he found out I wasn't you, he ran!'

'I don't believe it!'

'He said he was with A. C. Nielsen, but I called their office, and they never heard of him! Do you know anyone who would want to harm you?'

'Of course not, Sally! Don't be ridiculous! Did you call the police?'

'I did. But there wasn't much they could do except tell me to be more careful.'

'Well, I'm just fine, so don't worry.'

194

She heard Sally take a deep breath. 'All right. As long as you're okay. Julia?'

'Yes.'

'Be careful, will you?'

'Of course.' *Sally and her imagination! Who in the world would want to kill me?*

'Do you know when you're coming back?'

The same kind of question the clerk had asked her. 'No.'

'You're there to see your family, aren't you?'

'Yes.'

'Good luck.'

'Thanks, Sally.'

'Keep in touch.'

'I will.'

Julia replaced the receiver. She stood there, wondering what to do next. *If I had any brains, I would get back on the bus and go home. I've been stalling. Did I come to Boston to see the sights? No. I came here to meet my family. Am I going to meet them? No . . . Yes . . .*

She sat on the edge of the bed, her mind in a turmoil. *What if they hate me? I must not think that. They're going to love me, and I'm going to love them.* She looked at the telephone and thought, *Maybe it would be better if I called them. No. Then they might not want to see me.* She went to the closet and selected her best dress. *If I don't do it now, I'll never do it,* Julia decided.

Thirty minutes later, she was in a taxi on her way to Rose Hill to meet her family.

Chapter Twenty-four

Tyler was staring at Clark in disbelief. 'Julia Stanford . . . is here?'

'Yes, sir.' There was a puzzled tone in the butler's voice. 'But it isn't the same Miss Stanford who was here earlier.'

Tyler forced a smile. 'Of course not. I'm afraid it's an impostor.'

'An impostor, sir?'

'Yes. They'll be coming out of the woodwork, Clark, all claiming a right to the family fortune.'

'That's terrible, sir. Shall I call the police?'

'No,' Tyler said quickly. That was the last thing he wanted. 'I'll handle it. Send her into the library.'

'Yes, sir.'

Tyler's mind was racing. So the real Julia Stanford had finally showed up. It was fortunate that none of the other members of the family was home at the moment. He would have to get rid of her immediately.

Tyler walked into the library. Julia was standing in the middle of the room, looking at a portrait of Harry Stanford. Tyler stood there a moment, studying the woman. She was beautiful. It was too bad that . . .

Julia turned around and saw him. 'Hello.'

'Hello.'

'You're Tyler.'

'That's right. Who are you?'

Her smile faded. 'Didn't . . . ? I'm Julia Stanford.'

'Really? You'll forgive my asking, but do you have any proof of that?'

'Proof? Well, yes ... I ... that is ... no *proof*. I just assumed –'

He moved closer to her. 'How did you happen to come here?'

'I decided that it was time to meet my family.'

'After twenty-six years?'

'Yes.'

Looking at her, listening to her speak, there was no question in Tyler's mind. She was genuine, dangerous, and would have to be disposed of quickly.

Tyler forced a smile. 'Well, you can imagine what a shock this is to me. I mean, for you to appear here out of the blue and ...'

'I know. I'm sorry. I probably should have called first.'

Tyler asked casually, 'You came to Boston alone?'

'Yes.'

His mind was racing. 'Does anyone else know you're here?'

'No. Well, my roommate, Sally, in Kansas City.'

'Where are you staying?'

'At the Copley Square Hotel.'

'That's a nice hotel. What room are you in?'

'Four nineteen.'

'All right. Why don't you go back to your hotel and wait there for us? I want to prepare Woody and Kendall for this. They're going to be as surprised as I was.'

'I'm sorry. I should have –'

'No problem. Now that we've met, I know that everything is going to be just fine.'

'Thank you, Tyler.'

'You're welcome' – he almost choked on the word. 'Julia. Let me call a taxi for you.'

Five minutes later, she was gone.

Hal Baker had just returned to his hotel room in downtown Boston when the telephone call came. He picked it up.

'Hal?'

'I'm sorry. I have no news yet, judge. I've combed this whole town. I went to the airport and –'

'She's here, stupid!'

197

'What?'

'She's here in Boston. She's staying at the Copley Square Hotel, room four nineteen. I want her taken care of tonight. And I don't want any more bungling, do you understand?'

'What happened was not my –'

'Do you understand?'

'Yes, sir.'

'Then do it!' Tyler slammed down the receiver. He went to find Clark.

'Clark, about that young woman who was here pretending she was my sister?'

'Yes, sir?'

'I wouldn't say anything about it to the other members of the family. It would just upset them.' ·

'I understand, sir. You're very thoughtful.'

Julia walked over to the Ritz-Carlton for dinner. The hotel was beautiful, just as her mother had described it. *On Sunday, I used to take the children there for brunch.* Julia sat in the dining room and visualized her mother there at a table with young Tyler, Woody and Kendall. *I wish I could have grown up with them*, Julia thought. *But at least I'm going to meet them now.* She wondered whether her mother would have approved of what she was doing. Julia had been taken aback by Tyler's reception. He had seemed . . . cold. *But that's only natural*, Julia thought. *A stranger walks in and says, 'I'm your sister.' Of course he would be suspicious. But I'm sure I can convince them.*

When the check came, Julia stared at it in shock. *I have to be careful*, she thought. *I have to have enough money left to take the bus back to Kansas.*

As she stepped outside the Ritz-Carlton, a tour bus was getting ready to leave. On an impulse, she boarded it. She wanted to see as much of her mother's city as she could.

Hal Baker strode into the lobby of the Copley Square Hotel as though he belonged there and took the stairs to the fourth floor. This time there would be no mistake. Room 419 was in the middle of the corridor. Hal Baker scanned the hallway to make sure no one was around, and knocked on the door. There was no answer. He knocked again. 'Miss Stanford?' Still no answer.

He took a small case from his pocket and selected a pick. It took him only seconds to open the door. Hal Baker stepped inside, closing the door behind him. The room was empty.

'Miss Stanford?'

He walked into the bathroom. Empty. He went back into the bedroom. He took a knife out of his pocket, moved a chair in back of the door, and sat in the dark, waiting. It was one hour later when he heard someone approaching.

Hal Baker rose quickly and stood behind the door, the knife in his hands. He heard the key turn in the lock, and the door started to swing open. He raised the knife high over his head, ready to strike. Julia Stanford stepped in and pressed the light switch on. He heard her say, 'Very well. Come in.'

A crowd of reporters poured into the room.

Chapter Twenty-five

It was Gordon Wellman, the night manager at the Copley Square Hotel, who inadvertently saved Julia's life. He had come on duty at six o'clock that evening, and had automatically checked the hotel register. When he came across the name of Julia Stanford, he stared at it in surprise. Ever since Harry Stanford had died, the newspapers had been full of stories about the Stanford family. They had dredged up the ancient scandal of Stanford's affair with the children's governess and the suicide of Stanford's wife. Harry Stanford had an illegitimate daughter named Julia. There were rumors that she had come to Boston in secret. Shortly after going on a shopping spree, she had reportedly left for South America. Now, it seemed that she was back. *And she's staying at my hotel!* Gordon Wellman thought excitedly.

He turned to the front-desk clerk. 'Do you know how much publicity this could mean for the hotel?'

A minute later, he was on the telephone to the press.

When Julia arrived back at the hotel after her sightseeing tour, the lobby was filled with reporters, eagerly awaiting her. As soon as she walked into the lobby, they pounced.

'Miss Stanford! I'm from the *Boston Globe*. We've been looking for you, but we heard that you had left town. Could you tell us . . . ?'

A television camera was pointed at her. 'Miss Stanford, I'm with WCVB-TV. We'd like to get a statement from you . . .'

'Miss Stanford, I'm from the *Boston Phoenix*. We want to know your reaction to . . .'

'Look this way, Miss Stanford! Smile! Thank you.'

Flashes were popping.

Julia stood there, filled with confusion. *Oh, my God,* she thought. *The family is going to think that I'm some kind of publicity hound.* She turned to the reporters. 'I'm sorry. I have nothing to say.'

She fled into the elevator. They piled in after her.

'*People* magazine wants to do a story on your life, and what it feels like to be estranged from your family for over twenty-five years.'

'We heard you had gone to South America.'

'Are you planning to live in Boston . . . ?'

'Why aren't you staying at Rose Hill . . . ?'

She got out of the elevator at the fourth floor and hurried down the corridor. They were at her heels. There was no way to escape them.

Julia took out her key and opened the door to her room. She stepped inside and turned on the light. 'Very well. Come in.'

Hidden behind the door, Hal Baker was caught by surprise, the knife in his raised hand. As the reporters shoved past him, he quickly put the knife back in his pocket and mingled with the group.

Julia turned to the reporters. 'All right. One question at a time, please.'

Frustrated, Baker backed toward the door and slipped out. Judge Stanford was not going to be pleased.

For the next thirty minutes, Julia answered questions as best she could. Finally, they were gone.

Julia locked the door and went to bed.

In the morning, the television stations and newspapers featured stories about Julia Stanford.

Tyler read the papers and was furious. Woody and Kendall joined him at the breakfast table.

'What's all this nonsense about some woman calling herself Julia Stanford?' Woody asked.

'She's a phony,' Tyler said glibly. 'She came to the door yesterday, demanding money, and I sent her away. I didn't expect her to pull a cheap publicity stunt like this. Don't worry. I'll take care of her.'

He put in a call to Simon Fitzgerald. 'Have you seen the morning papers?'
'Yes.'
'This con artist is going around town claiming that she's our sister.'
Fitzgerald said, 'Do you want me to have her arrested?'
'No! That would only create more publicity. I want you to get her out of town.'
'All right. I'll take care of it, Judge Stanford.'
'Thank you.'

Simon Fitzgerald sent for Steve Sloane.
'There's a problem,' he said.
Steve nodded. 'I know. I've heard the morning news and seen the papers. Who is she?'
'Obviously someone who thinks she can horn in on the family fortune. Judge Stanford suggested we get her out of town. Will you handle her?'
'My pleasure,' Steve said grimly.

One hour later, Steve was knocking on Julia's hotel room door.
When Julia opened the door and saw him standing there she said, 'I'm sorry. I'm not talking to any more reporters. I . . .'
'I'm not a reporter. May I come in?'
'Who are you?'
'My name is Steve Sloane. I'm with the law firm representing the Harry Stanford estate.'
'Oh. I see. Yes. Come in.'
Steve walked into the room.
'Did you tell the press that you are Julia Stanford?'
'I'm afraid I was caught off guard. I didn't expect them, you see, and . . .'
'But you *did* claim to be Harry Stanford's daughter?'
'Yes. I am his daughter.'

202

He looked at her and said cynically, 'Of course, you have proof of that.'

'Well, no,' Julia said slowly. 'I don't.'

'Come on,' Steve insisted. 'You must have *some* proof.' He intended to nail her with her own lies.

'I have nothing,' she said.

He studied her, surprised. She was not what he had expected. There was a disarming frankness about her. *She seems intelligent. How could she have been stupid enough to come here claiming to be Harry Stanford's daughter without any proof?*

'That's too bad,' Steve said. 'Judge Stanford wants you to get out of town.'

Julia's eyes widened. 'What?'

'That's right.'

'But . . . I don't understand. I haven't even met my other brother or sister.'

So she's determined to keep up the bluff, Steve thought. 'Look, I don't know who you are, or what your game is, but you could go to jail for this. We're giving you a break. What you're doing is against the law. You have a choice. Either you can get out of town and stop bothering the family, or we can have you arrested.'

Julia stood there in shock. 'Arrested? I . . . I don't know what to say.'

'It's your decision.'

'They don't even want to see me?' Julia asked numbly.

'That's putting it mildly.'

She took a deep breath. 'All right. If that's what they want, I'll go back to Kansas. I promise you, they'll never hear from me again.'

Kansas. You came a long way to pull your little scam. 'That's very wise.' He stood there a moment, watching her, puzzled. 'Well, good-bye.'

She did not reply.

Steve was in Simon Fitzgerald's office.

'Did you see the woman, Steve?'

'Yes. She's going back home.' He seemed distracted.

203

'Good. I'll tell Judge Stanford. He'll be pleased.'

'Do you know what's bugging me, Simon?'

'What?'

'The dog didn't bark.'

'I beg your pardon?'

'The Sherlock Holmes story. The clue was in what *didn't* happen.'

'Steve, what does that have to do with –'

'She came here without any *proof.*'

Fitzgerald looked at him, puzzled. 'I don't understand. That should have *convinced* you.'

'On the contrary. Why would she come here, all the way from Kansas, claiming to be Harry Stanford's daughter, and not have a single thing to back it up?'

'There are a lot of weirdos out there, Steve.'

'She's not a weirdo. You should have seen her. And there are a couple of other things that bother me, Simon.'

'Yes?'

'Harry Stanford's body disappeared. When I went to talk to Dmitri Kaminsky, the only witness to Stanford's accident, *he* had disappeared . . . And no one seems to know where the first Julia Stanford suddenly disappeared to.'

Simon Fitzgerald was frowning. 'What are you saying?'

Steve said, slowly, 'There's something going on that needs to be explained. I'm going to have another talk with the lady.'

Steve Sloane walked into the lobby of the Copley Square Hotel and approached the desk clerk. 'Would you ring Miss Julia Stanford, please?'

The clerk looked up. 'Oh, I'm sorry. Miss Stanford has checked out.'

'Did she leave a forwarding address?'

'No, sir. I'm afraid not.'

Steve stood there, frustrated. There was nothing more he could do. *Well, maybe I was wrong,* he thought philosophically. *Maybe she really is an impostor. Now we'll never know.* He turned and went out into the street. The doorman was ushering a couple into a taxi.

'Excuse me,' Steve said.

The doorman turned. 'Taxi, sir?'

'No. I want to ask you a question. Did you see Miss Stanford come out of the hotel this morning?'

'I certainly did. Everybody was staring at her. She's quite a celebrity. I got a taxi for her.'

'I don't suppose you know where she went?' He found that he was holding his breath.

'Sure. I told the cab driver where to take her.'

'And where was that?' Steve asked impatiently.

'To the Greyhound bus terminal at South Station. I thought it was strange that someone as rich as that would . . .'

'I do want a taxi.'

Steve walked into the crowded Greyhound bus terminal and looked around. Julia was nowhere to be seen. *She's gone*, Steve thought despairingly. A voice on a loudspeaker was calling out the departing buses. He heard the voice say, '. . . and Kansas City,' and Steve hurried out to the loading platform.

Julia was just starting to get on the bus.

'Hold it!' he called.

She turned, startled.

Steve hurried up to her. 'I want to talk to you.'

She looked at him, angry. 'I have nothing more to say to you.' She turned to go.

He grabbed her arm. 'Wait a minute! We really have to talk.'

'My bus is leaving.'

'There'll be another one.'

'My suitcase is on it.'

Steve turned to a porter. 'This woman is about to have a baby. Get her suitcase out of there. Quick!'

The porter looked at Julia in surprise. 'Right.' He hurriedly opened the luggage compartment. 'Which is yours, lady?'

Julia turned to Steve, puzzled. 'Do you know what you're doing?'

'No,' Steve said.

She studied him a moment, then made a decision. She pointed to her suitcase. 'That one.'

The porter pulled it out. 'Do you want me to get you an ambulance or anything?'

'Thank you. I'll be fine.'

Steve picked up the suitcase, and they headed for the exit. 'Have you had breakfast?'

'I'm not hungry,' she said coldly.

'You'd better have something. You're eating for two now, you know.'

They had breakfast at Julien. Julia sat across from Steve, her body rigid with anger.

When they had ordered, Steve said, 'I'm curious about something. What made you think you could claim part of the Stanford estate without any proof at all of your identity?'

She looked at him indignantly. 'I didn't go there to claim part of the Stanford estate. My father wouldn't have left anything to me. I wanted to meet my family. Obviously they didn't want to meet me.'

'Do you have *any* documents . . . any kind of proof at all of who you are?'

She thought of all the clippings piled up in her apartment and shook her head. 'No. Nothing.'

'There's someone I want you to talk to.'

'This is Simon Fitzgerald.' Steve hesitated. 'Er . . .'

'Julia Stanford.'

Fitzgerald said skeptically, 'Sit down, miss.'

Julia sat on the edge of a chair, ready to get up and walk out.

Fitzgerald was studying her. She had the Stanford deep gray eyes, but so did lots of other people. 'You claim you're Rosemary Nelson's daughter.'

'I don't claim anything. I *am* Rosemary Nelson's daughter.'

'And where is your mother?'

'She died a number of years ago.'

'Oh, I'm sorry to hear that. Could you tell us about her?'

'No,' Julia said. 'I really would rather not.' She stood up. 'I want to get out of here.'

'Look, we're trying to help you,' Steve said.

She turned on him. 'Are you? My family doesn't want to see me. You want to turn me over to the police. I don't need that kind of help.' She started toward the door.

Steve said, 'Wait! If you are who you say you are, you must have *something* that will prove you're Harry Stanford's daughter.'

'I told you, I don't,' Julia said. 'My mother and I shut Harry Stanford out of our lives.'

'What did your mother look like?' Simon Fitzgerald asked.

'She was beautiful,' Julia said. Her voice softened. 'She was the loveliest . . .' She remembered something. 'I have a picture of her.' She took a small gold heart-shaped locket from around her neck and handed it to Fitzgerald.

He looked at her a moment, then opened the locket. On one side was a picture of Harry Stanford, and on the other side a picture of Rosemary Nelson. The inscription read TO R. N. WITH LOVE, H. S. The date was 1969.

Simon Fitzgerald stared at the locket for a long time. When he looked up, his voice was husky.

'We owe you an apology, my dear.' He turned to Steve. 'This is Julia Stanford.'

Chapter Twenty-six

Kendall had been unable to get the conversation with Peggy out of her mind. Peggy seemed incapable of coping with the situation by herself. *'Woody's trying hard. He really is . . . Oh, I love him so much!'*

He needs a lot of help, Kendall thought. *I have to do something. He's my brother. I must talk to him.*

Kendall went to find Clark.

'Is Mr Woodrow at home?'

'Yes, ma'am. I believe he's in his room.'

'Thank you.'

She thought of the scene at the table, with Peggy's bruised face. *'What happened?' 'I bumped into a door . . .' How could she have put up with it all this time?* Kendall went upstairs and knocked on the door to Woody's room. There was no answer. 'Woody?'

She opened the door and stepped inside. A bitter-almond smell permeated the room. Kendall stood there a moment, then moved toward the bathroom. She could see Woody through the open door. He was heating heroin on a piece of aluminum foil. As it began to liquify and evaporate, she watched Woody inhale the smoke from a rolled up straw he held in his mouth.

Kendall stepped into the bathroom. 'Woody . . . ?'

He looked around and grinned. 'Hi, Sis!' He turned and inhaled deeply again.

'For God's sake! Stop that!'

'Hey, relax. You know what this is called? Chasing the dragon. See the little dragon curling up in the smoke?' He was smiling happily.

'Woody, please let me talk to you.'

'Sure, Sis. What can I do for you? I know it's not a money problem. We're billionaires! What are you looking so depressed about? The sun is out, and it's a beautiful day!' His eyes were glistening.

Kendall stood there looking at him, filled with compassion. 'Woody, I had a talk with Peggy. She told me how you got started on drugs at the hospital.'

He nodded. 'Yeah. Best thing that ever happened to me.'

'No. It's the most terrible thing that ever happened to you. Do you have any idea what you're doing with your life?'

'Sure I do. It's called living it up, Sis!'

She took his hand and said, earnestly, 'You need help.'

'Me? I don't need any help. I'm fine!'

'No, you aren't. Listen to me, Woody. This is your life we're talking about, and it's not only *your* life. Think of Peggy. For years you've put her through a living hell, and she stood for it because she loves you so much. You're not only destroying your life, you're destroying hers. You've got to do something about this *now*, before it's too late. It's not important how you got started on drugs. The important thing is that you get off them.'

Woody's smile faded. He looked into Kendall's eyes and started to say something, then stopped. 'Kendall . . .'

'Yes?'

He licked his lips. 'I . . . I know you're right. I want to stop. I've tried. God, how I've tried. But I can't.'

'Of *course*, you can,' she said fiercely. 'You can do it. We're going to beat this together. Peggy and I are behind you. Who supplies you with heroin, Woody?'

He stood there, looking at her in astonishment. 'My God! You don't know?'

Kendall shook her head. 'No.'

'Peggy.'

Chapter Twenty-seven

Simon Fitzgerald looked at the gold locket for a long time. 'I knew your mother, Julia, and I liked her. She was wonderful with the Stanford children, and they adored her.'

'She adored them, too,' Julia said. 'She used to talk to me about them all the time.'

'What happened to your mother was terrible. You can't imagine what a scandal it created. Boston can be a very small town. Harry Stanford behaved very badly. Your mother had no choice but to leave.' He shook his head. 'Life must have been very difficult for the two of you.'

'Mother had a hard time. The awful thing was that I think she still loved Harry Stanford, in spite of everything.' She looked at Steve. 'I don't understand what's happening. Why doesn't my family want to see me?'

The two men exchanged a look. 'Let me explain,' Steve said. He hesitated, choosing his words carefully. 'A short time ago, a woman showed up here, claiming to be Julia Stanford.'

'But that's impossible!' Julia said. 'I'm . . .'

Steve held up a hand. 'I know. The family hired a private detective to make sure she was authentic.'

'And they found out that she wasn't.'

'No. They found out that she *was*.'

Julia looked at him, bewildered. '*What?*'

'This detective said he found fingerprints that the woman had taken when she got a driver's license in San Francisco when she was seventeen and they matched the prints of the woman calling herself Julia Stanford.'

Julia was more puzzled than ever. 'But I . . . I've never been in Indiana.'

Fitzgerald said, 'Julia, there may be an elaborate conspiracy going on to get part of the Stanford estate. I'm afraid you're caught in the middle of it.'

'I can't believe it!'

'Whoever is behind this can't afford to have two Julia Stanfords around.'

Steve added, 'The only way the plan can work successfully is to get you out of the way.'

'When you say "out of the way . . ."' She stopped, remembering something. 'Oh, no!'

'What is it?' Fitzgerald asked.

'Two nights ago I talked to my roommate, and she was hysterical. She said a man came to our apartment with a knife and tried to attack her. He thought she was me!' It was difficult for Julia to find her voice. 'Who . . . who's doing this?'

'If I had to guess, I'd say it's probably a member of the family,' Steve told her.

'But . . . *why*?'

'There's a large fortune at stake, and the will is going to be probated in a few days.'

'What does that have to do with me? My father never even acknowledged me. He wouldn't have left me anything.'

Fitzgerald said, 'As a matter of fact, if we can prove your identity, your share of the overall estate is more than a billion dollars.'

She sat there, numb. When she found her voice, she said, 'A billion dollars?'

'That's right. But someone else is after that money. That's why you're in danger.'

'I see.' She stood there looking at them, feeling a rising panic. 'What am I going to do?'

'I'll tell you what you're *not* going to do,' Steve told her. 'You're not going back to a hotel. I want you to stay out of sight until we find out what's going on.'

'I could go back to Kansas until . . .'

Fitzgerald said, 'I think it would be better if you stayed here, Julia. We'll find a place to hide you.'

'She could stay at my house,' Steve suggested. 'No one will think of looking for her there.'

The two men turned to Julia.

She hesitated. 'Well . . . yes. That will be fine.'

'Good.'

Julia said slowly, 'None of this would be happening if my father hadn't fallen off his yacht.'

'Oh, I don't think he fell,' Steve told her. 'I think he was pushed.'

They took the service elevator to the office building garage and got into Steve's car.

'I don't want anyone to see you,' Steve said. 'We have to keep you out of sight for the next few days.'

They started driving down State Street.

'How about some lunch?'

Julia looked over at him and smiled. 'You always seem to be feeding me.'

'I know a restaurant that's off the beaten path. It's an old house on Gloucester Street. I don't think anyone will see us there.'

L'Espalier was an elegant nineteenth-century townhouse with one of the finest views in Boston. As Steve and Julia walked in, they were greeted by the captain.

'Good afternoon,' he said. 'Will you come this way, please? I have a nice table for you by the window.'

'If you don't mind,' Steve said, 'we'd prefer something against the wall.'

The captain blinked. 'Against the wall?'

'Yes. We like privacy.'

'Of course.' He led them to a table in a corner. 'I'll send your waiter right over.' He was staring at Julia, and his face suddenly lit up. 'Ah! Miss Stanford. It's a pleasure to have you here. I saw your picture in the newspaper.'

Julia looked at Steve, not knowing what to say.

Steve exclaimed, 'My God! We left the children in the car! Let's go get them!' And to the captain, 'We'd like two martinis, very dry. Hold the olives. We'll be right back.'

'Yes, sir.' The captain watched the two of them hurry out of the restaurant.

'What are we doing?' Julia asked.

'Getting out of here. All he has to do is call the press, and we're in trouble. We'll go somewhere else.'

They found a little restaurant on Dalton Street and ordered lunch.

Steve sat there, studying her. 'How does it feel to be a celebrity?' he asked.

'Please don't joke about that. I feel terrible.'

'I know,' he said contritely. 'I'm sorry.' He was finding it very easy to be with her. He thought about how rude he had been when they first met.

'Do you . . . do you really think I'm in danger, Mr Sloane?' Julia asked.

'Call me Steve. Yes. I'm afraid you are. But it will be for only a little while. By the time the will is probated, we'll know who's behind this. In the meantime, I'm going to see to it that you're safe.'

'Thank you. I . . . I appreciate it.'

They were staring at each other, and when an approaching waiter saw the looks on their faces, he decided not to interrupt them.

In the car, Steve asked, 'Is this your first time in Boston?'

'Yes.'

'It's an interesting city.' They were passing the old John Hancock Building. Steve pointed to the tower. 'You see that beacon?'

'Yes.'

'It broadcasts the weather.'

'How can a beacon . . . ?'

'I'm glad you asked. When the light is a steady blue, it means the weather is clear. If it's a flashing blue, you can expect clouds

213

to be near. A steady red means rain ahead, and flashing red, snow instead.'

Julia laughed.

They reached the Harvard Bridge. Steve slowed down. 'This is the bridge that links Boston and Cambridge. It's exactly three hundred, sixty-four point four Smoots and one ear long.'

Julia turned to stare at him. 'I beg your pardon?'

Steve grinned. 'It's true.'

'What's a Smoot?'

'A Smoot is a measurement using the body of Oliver Reed Smoot, who was five feet seven inches. It started as a joke, but when the city rebuilt the bridge, they kept the marks. The Smoot became a standard of length in 1958.'

She laughed. 'That's incredible!'

As they passed the Bunker Hill Monument, Julia exclaimed, 'Oh! That's where the battle of Bunker Hill took place, isn't it?'

'No,' Steve said.

'What do you mean?'

'The battle of Bunker Hill was fought on Breed's Hill.'

Steve's home was in the Newbury Street area of Boston, a charming two-storey house with comfortable furniture and colorful prints hanging on the walls.

'Do you live here alone?' Julia asked.

'Yes. I have a housekeeper who comes in twice a week. I'm going to tell her not to come in for the next few days. I don't want anyone to know you're here.'

Julia looked at Steve and said warmly, 'I want you to know I really appreciate what you're doing for me.'

'My pleasure. Come on, I'll show you your bedroom.'

He led her upstairs to the guest room. 'This is it. I hope you'll be comfortable.'

'Oh, yes. It's lovely,' Julia said.

'I'll bring in some groceries. I usually eat out.'

'I could –' she stopped. 'On second thought, I'd better not. My roommate says my cooking is lethal.'

'I think I'm a fair hand at a stove,' Steve said. 'I'll do some cooking for us.' He looked at her and said slowly, 'I haven't had anyone to cook for for a while.' *Back off*, he told himself. *You're way off base. You couldn't keep her in handkerchiefs.*

'I want you to make yourself at home. You'll be completely safe here.'

She looked at him a long time, then smiled. 'Thank you.'

They went back downstairs.

Steve pointed out the amenities. 'Television, VCR, radio, CD player . . . you'll be comfortable.'

'It's wonderful.' She wanted to say, *'Just like I feel with you.'*

'Well, if there's nothing else,' he said awkwardly.

Julia gave him a warm smile. 'I can't think of anything.'

'Then I'll be getting back to the office. I have a lot of questions without answers.'

She watched him walk toward the door.

'Steve?'

He turned around. 'Yes?'

'Is it all right if I call my roommate? She'll be worried about me.'

He shook his head. 'Absolutely not. I don't want you to make any telephone calls or leave this house. Your life may depend on it.'

Chapter Twenty-eight

'I'm Dr Westin. Do you understand that this conversation is going to be tape-recorded?'

'Yes, doctor.'

'Are you feeling calmer now?'

'I'm calm, but I'm angry.'

'What are you angry about?'

'I shouldn't be in this place. I'm not crazy. I've been framed.'

'Oh? Who framed you?'

'Tyler Stanford.'

'*Judge* Tyler Stanford?'

'That's right.'

'Why would he want to do that?'

'For money.'

'Do you have money?'

'No. I mean, yes . . . that is . . . I could have had it. He promised me a million dollars, and a sable coat, and jewelry.'

'Why would Judge Stanford promise you that?'

'Let me start at the beginning. I'm not really Julia Stanford. My name is Margo Posner.'

'When you came in here, you insisted you were Julia Stanford.'

'Forget that. I'm really not. Look . . . here's what happened. Judge Stanford hired me to pose as his sister.'

'Why did he do that?'

'So I could get a share of the Stanford estate and turn it over to him.'

'And for doing that he promised you a million dollars, a sable coat, and some jewelry?'

'You don't believe me, do you? Well, I can prove it. He took

216

me to Rose Hill. That's where the Stanford family lives in Boston. I can describe the house to you, and I can tell you all about the family.'

'You're aware that these are very serious charges you're making?'

'You bet I am. But I suppose you won't do anything about it because he happens to be a judge.'

'You're quite wrong. I assure you that your charges will be very thoroughly investigated.'

'Good! I want the bastard locked away the same way he has me locked away. I want out of here!'

'You understand that besides my examination, two of my colleagues also will have to evaluate your mental state?'

'Let them. I'm as sane as you are.'

'Dr Gifford will be in this afternoon, and then we'll decide how we're going to proceed.'

'The sooner the better. I can't stand this damned place!'

When the matron brought Margo her lunch, the matron said, 'I just talked to Dr Gifford. He'll be here in an hour.'

'Thank you.' Margo was ready for him. She was ready for all of them. She was going to tell them everything she knew, from the very beginning. *And when I'm through,* Margo thought, *they're going to lock him up and let me go.* The thought filled her with satisfaction. *I'll be free!* And then Margo thought, *Free to do what? I'll be out on the streets again. Maybe they'll even revoke my parole and put me back in the joint!*

She threw her lunch tray against the wall. *Damn them! They can't do this to me! Yesterday I was worth a billion dollars, and today . . . Wait! Wait!* An idea flashed through Margo's mind that was so exciting that it sent a chill through her. *Holy God! What am I doing? I've already proved that I'm Julia Stanford. I have witnesses. The whole family heard Frank Timmons say that my fingerprints showed that I was Julia Stanford. Why the hell would I ever want to be Margo Posner when I can be Julia Stanford? No wonder they have me locked up in here. I must have been out of my mind!* She rang the bell for the matron.

When the matron came in, Margo said excitedly, 'I want to see the doctor right away!'

'I know. You have an appointment with him in –'

'*Now*. Right now!'

The matron took one look at Margo's expression and said, 'Calm down. I'll get him.'

Ten minutes later, Dr Franz Gifford walked into Margo's room.

'You asked to see me?'

'Yes.' She smiled apologetically. 'I'm afraid I've been playing a little game, doctor.'

'Really?'

'Yes. It's very embarrassing. You see, the truth is that I was very upset with my brother, Tyler, and I wanted to punish him. But I realize now that that was wrong. I'm not upset anymore, and I want to go home to Rose Hill.'

'I read the transcript of your interview this morning. You said that your name was Margo Posner and that you were framed.'

Margo laughed. 'That was naughty of me. I just said that to upset Tyler. No. I'm Julia Stanford.'

He looked at her. 'Can you prove that?'

This was the moment Margo had been waiting for. 'Oh, yes!' she said triumphantly. 'Tyler proved it himself. He hired a private detective named Frank Timmons, who matched my fingerprints with prints I had made for a driver's license when I was younger. They're the same. There's no question about it.'

'Detective Frank Timmons, you say?'

'That's right. He does work for the district attorney's office here in Chicago.'

He studied her a moment. 'Now, you're certain of this? You're not Margo Posner – you're Julia Stanford?'

'Absolutely.'

'And this private detective, Frank Timmons, can verify that?'

She smiled. 'He already has. All you have to do is call the district attorney's office and get hold of him.'

Dr Gifford nodded. 'All right. I'll do that.'

* * *

218

At ten o'clock the following morning, Dr Gifford, accompanied by the matron, returned to Margo's room.

'Good morning.'

'Good morning, doctor.' She looked at him eagerly. 'Did you talk to Frank Timmons?'

'Yes. I want to be sure that I understand this. Your story about Judge Stanford's involving you in some kind of conspiracy was false?'

'Completely. I said that because I wanted to punish my brother. But everything is all right now. I'm ready to go home.'

'Frank Timmons can prove that you're Julia Stanford?'

'Absolutely.'

Dr Gifford turned to the matron and nodded. She signaled to someone. A tall, lean black man walked into the room.

He looked at Margo and said, 'I'm Frank Timmons. Can I help you?'

He was a complete stranger.

Chapter Twenty-nine

The fashion show was going well. The models moved gracefully along the runway, and each new design received enthusiastic applause. The ballroom was packed. Every seat was occupied, and there were standees in the rear.

Backstage there was a stir, and Kendall turned to see what was happening. Two uniformed policemen were making their way toward her.

Kendall's heart began to race.

One of the policemen said, 'Are you Kendall Stanford Renaud?'

'Yes.'

'I'm placing you under arrest for the murder of Martha Ryan.'

'No!' she screamed. 'I didn't mean to do it! It was an accident! Please! Please! Please . . . !'

She woke up in a panic, her body trembling.

It was a recurring nightmare. *I can't go on like this*, Kendall thought. *I can't! I have to do something.*

She wanted desperately to talk to Marc. He had reluctantly returned to New York. 'I have a job to do, darling. They won't let me take any more time off.'

'I understand, Marc. I'll be back there in a few days. I have to get a show ready.'

Kendall was leaving for New York that morning, but before she went there was something she felt she had to do. The conversation with Woody had been very disturbing. *He's blaming his problems on Peggy.*

Kendall found Peggy on the veranda.

'Good morning,' Kendall said.

'Good morning.'

Kendall took a seat opposite her. 'I have to talk to you.'

'Yes?'

It was awkward. 'I had a talk with Woody. He's in bad shape. He . . . he thinks that you're the one who's been supplying him with heroin.'

'He told you that?'

'Yes.'

There was a long pause. 'Well, it's true.'

Kendall stared at her in disbelief. '*What?* I . . . I don't understand. You told me you were trying to get him *off* drugs. Why would you want to keep him addicted?'

'You really *don't* understand, do you?' Her tone was bitter. 'You live in your own little goddamned world. Well, let me tell you something, Miss Famous Designer! I was a waitress when Woody got me pregnant. I never expected Woodrow Stanford to marry me. And do you know why he did? So he could feel he was better than his father. Well, Woody married me, all right. And everybody treated me like dirt. When my brother, Hoop, came down for the wedding, they acted like he was some kind of trash.'

'Peggy . . .'

'To tell you the truth, I was dumbfounded when your brother said he wanted to marry me. I didn't even know if it was his baby. I could have been a good wife to Woody, but no one even gave me a chance. To them I was still a waitress. I didn't lose the baby, I had an abortion. I thought maybe Woody would divorce me, but he didn't. I was his token symbol of how democratic he was. Well, let me tell you something, lady. I don't need that. I'm as good as you or anyone else.'

Each word was a blow. 'Did you ever love Woody?'

Peggy shrugged. 'He was good-looking and fun, but then he had that bad fall during the polo game, and everything changed. The hospital gave him drugs, and when he got out, they expected him to stop taking them. One night, he was in pain, and I said, "I have a little treat for you." And after that, whenever he was in

221

pain, I gave him his little treat. Pretty soon he needed it, whether he was in pain or not. My brother is a pusher, and I was able to get all the heroin I needed. I made Woody beg me for it. And sometimes I'd tell him I was out of it just to watch him sweat and cry – oh, how Mr Woodrow Stanford needed me! He wasn't so high and mighty then! I goaded him into hitting me, and then he'd feel terrible about what he had done, and he'd come crawling back to me with gifts. You see, when Woody is off dope, I'm nothing. When he's on it, I'm the one who has the power. He may be a Stanford, and maybe I was only a waitress, but I control him.'

Kendall was staring at her in horror.

'Your brother's tried to quit, all right. When it got real bad, his friends would get him into a detox center, and I'd go visit him and watch the great Stanford suffer the agonies of hell. And each time he came out, I'd be waiting for him with my little treat. It was payback time.'

Kendall was finding it hard to breathe. 'You're a monster,' she said slowly. 'I want you to leave.'

'You bet! I can't wait to get out of this place.' She grinned. 'Of course, I'm not leaving for nothing. How much of a settlement will I get?'

'Whatever it is,' Kendall said, 'it will be too much. Now get out of here.'

'Right.' Then she added with an affected tone, 'I'll have my lawyer call your lawyer.'

'She's really leaving me?'

'Yes.'

'That means . . .'

'I know what it means, Woody. Can you handle it?'

He looked at his sister and smiled. 'I think so. Yes. I think I can.'

'I'm sure of it.'

He took a deep breath. 'Thanks, Kendall. I would never have had the courage to get rid of her.'

She smiled. 'What are sisters for?'

*   *   *

222

That afternoon, Kendall left for New York. The fashion showing would be in one week.

Clothing is the single biggest business in New York. A successful fashion designer can have an effect on the economy all around the world. A designer's whim has a far-flung impact on everyone from cotton pickers in India to Scottish weavers to silkworms in China and Japan. It has an effect on the wool industry and the silk industry. The Donna Karans and Calvin Kleins and Ralph Laurens are a major economic influence, and Kendall had arrived in that category. It was rumored that she was about to be named the Women's Wear Designer of the Year by the Council of Fashion Designers of America, the most prestigious award a designer could receive.

Kendall Stanford Renaud led a busy life. In September she looked at large assortments of fabrics, and in October she selected the ones she wanted for her new designs. December and January were devoted to designing the new fashions, and in February, refining them. In April, she was ready to show her fall collection.

Kendall Stanford Designs was located at 550 Seventh Avenue, sharing the building with Bill Blass and Oscar de la Renta. Her next showing was going to be at the Bryant Park tent, which could seat up to a thousand people.

When Kendall arrived at her office, Nadine said, 'I've got good news. The showing is completely booked!'

'Thank you,' Kendall said absently. Her mind was on other things.

'By the way, there's a letter marked *urgent* for you on your desk. It was just delivered by messenger.'

The words sent a jolt through Kendall's body. She walked over to her desk and looked at the envelope. The return address was *Wild Animal Protection Association, 3000 Park Avenue, New York, New York.* She stared at it for a long time. There was no 3000 Park Avenue.

Kendall opened the letter with trembling fingers.

Dear Mrs Renaud,

My Swiss banker informs me that he has not yet received the million dollars that my association requested. In view of your delinquency, I must inform you that our needs have been increased to 5 million dollars. If this payment is made, I promise we will not bother you again. You have fifteen days to deposit the money in our account. If you fail to do so, I regret that we shall have to communicate with the appropriate authorities.

It was unsigned.

Kendall stood there in a panic, reading it over and over, again and again. *Five million dollars! It's impossible,* she thought. *I can never raise that kind of money that quickly. What a fool I was!*

When Marc came home that night, Kendall showed him the letter.

'Five million dollars!' he exploded. 'That's ridiculous! Who do they think you are?'

'They know who I am,' Kendall said. 'That's the problem. I've got to get hold of some money quickly. But how?'

'I don't know . . . I suppose a bank would loan you money against your inheritance, but I don't like the idea of . . .'

'Marc, it's my life I'm talking about. *Our* lives. I'm going to see about getting that loan.'

George Meriwether was the vice president in charge of the New York Union Bank. He was in his forties and had worked his way up from a junior teller. He was an ambitious man. *One day I'll be on the board of directors,* he thought, *and after that . . . who knows?* His thoughts were interrupted by his secretary.

'Miss Kendall Stanford is here to see you.'

He felt a small *frisson* of pleasure. She had been a good customer as a successful designer, but now she was one of the wealthiest women in the world. He had tried for several years to get Harry Stanford's account, without success. And now . . .

'Show her in,' Meriwether told his secretary.

When Kendall walked into his office, Meriwether rose and greeted her with a smile and a warm handshake.

'I'm so pleased to see you,' he said. 'Do sit down. Some coffee, or something stronger?'

'No, thanks,' Kendall said.

'I want to offer my condolences on the death of your father.' His voice was suitably grave.

'Thank you.'

'What can I do for you?' He knew what she was going to say. She was going to turn her billions over to him to invest . . .

'I want to borrow some money.'

He blinked. 'I beg your pardon?'

'I need five million dollars.'

He thought rapidly. *According to the newspapers, her share of the estate should be more than a billion dollars. Even with taxes* . . . He smiled. 'Well, I don't think there will be any problem. You've always been one of our favorite customers, you know. What security would you like to put up?'

'I'm an heir in my father's will.'

He nodded. 'Yes. I read that.'

'I'd like to borrow the money against my share of the estate.'

'I see. Has your father's will been probated yet?'

'No, but it will be soon.'

'That's fine.' He leaned forward. 'Of course, we'd have to see a copy of the will.'

'Yes,' Kendall said eagerly. 'I can arrange that.'

'And we would have to have the exact amount of your share of the inheritance.'

'I don't know the exact amount,' Kendall said.

'Well, the banking laws are quite strict, you know. Probates can take some time. Why don't you come back after the probate, and I'll be happy to –'

'I need the money now,' Kendall said desperately. She wanted to scream.

'Oh, dear. Naturally, we want to do everything we can to

225

accommodate you.' He raised his hands in a helpless gesture. 'But unfortunately, our hands are tied until –'

Kendall rose to her feet. 'Thank you.'

'As soon as . . .'

She was gone.

When Kendall returned to the office, Nadine said excitedly, 'I have to talk to you.'

She was in no mood to hear Nadine's problems.

'What is it?' Kendall asked.

'My husband called me a few minutes ago. His company is transferring him to Paris. So, I'll be leaving.'

'You're go . . . going to Paris?'

Nadine beamed. 'Yes! Isn't that wonderful? I'll be sorry to leave you. But don't worry. I'll stay in touch.'

So it was Nadine. But there's no way to prove it. First the mink coat and now Paris. With five million dollars, she can afford to live anywhere in the world. How do I handle this? If I tell her that I know, she'll deny it. Maybe she'll demand more. Marc will know what to do.

'Nadine . . .'

One of Kendall's assistants came in. 'Kendall! I have to talk to you about the bridge collection. I don't think we have enough designs for –'

Kendall could bear no more. 'Excuse me. I don't feel well. I'm going home.'

Her assistant looked at her in amazement. 'But we're in the middle of . . .'

'I'm sorry . . .'

And Kendall was gone.

When Kendall walked into her apartment, it was empty. Marc was working late. Kendall looked around at all the beautiful things in the room, and thought, *They'll never stop until they take everything. They're going to bleed me dry. Marc was right. I should have gone to the police that night. Now I'm a criminal. I've got to confess. Now, while I have the courage.* She sat there, thinking

226

about what this was going to do to her, to Marc, and to her family. There would be lurid headlines, and a trial, and probably prison. It would be the end of her career. *But I can't go on like this*, Kendall thought. *I'll go crazy.*

Almost in a daze, she got up and walked into Marc's den. She remembered that he kept his typewriter on a shelf in the closet. She took it down and put it on the desk. She rolled a sheet of paper into the platen and began to type.

> *To Whom It May Concern:*
> *My name is Kendall*

She stopped. The letter E was broken.

Chapter Thirty

'Why, Marc? For God's sake, why?' Kendall's voice was filled with anguish.

'It was your fault.'

'No! I told you. It was an accident! I . . .'

'I'm not talking about the accident. I'm talking about *you*! The big successful wife who was too busy to find time for her husband.'

It was as though he had slapped her. 'That's not true. I . . .'

'All you ever thought about was yourself, Kendall. Everywhere we went, you were always the star. You let me tag along like a pet poodle.'

'That's not fair!' she said.

'Isn't it? You go off to your fashion shows all over the world so you can get your picture in the papers, and I'm sitting here alone, waiting for you to return. Do you think I liked being "Mr Kendall?" I wanted a wife. Don't worry, my darling Kendall. I consoled myself with other women while you were gone.'

Her face was ashen.

'They were real flesh-and-blood women, who had time for me. Not some damned made-up empty shell.'

'Stop it!' Kendall cried.

'When you told me about the accident, I saw a way to become free of you. Do you want to know something, my dear? I enjoyed watching you squirm when you read those letters. It paid me back a little for all the humiliation I've gone through.'

'That's enough! Pack your bags and get out of here. I never want to see you again!'

Marc grinned. 'There's very little chance of that. By the way, do you still plan to go to the police?'

'Get out!' Kendall said. *'Now!'*

'I'm leaving. I think I'll go back to Paris. And, darling, I won't tell if you won't. You're safe.'

An hour later, he was gone.

At nine o'clock in the morning, Kendall put in a call to Steve Sloane.

'Good morning, Mrs Renaud. What can I do for you?'

'I'm returning to Boston this afternoon,' Kendall said. 'I have a confession to make.'

She was seated across from Steve, looking pale and drawn. She sat there frozen, unable to begin.

Steve prompted her. 'You said you had a confession to make.'

'Yes. I . . . I killed someone.' She began to cry. 'It was an accident, but . . . I ran away.' Her face was a mask of anguish. 'I ran away . . . and left her there.'

'Take it easy,' Steve said. 'Start at the beginning.'

She began to talk.

Thirty minutes later, Steve looked out his window, thinking about what he had just heard.

'And you want to go to the police?'

'Yes. It was what I should have done in the first place. I . . . I don't care what they do to me anymore.'

Steve said thoughtfully, 'Since you're giving yourself up voluntarily and it was an accident, I think the court will be lenient.'

She was trying to control herself. 'I just want it over with.'

'What about your husband?'

She looked up. 'What about him?'

'Blackmail is against the law. You have the number of the account in Switzerland where you sent the money he stole from you. All you have to do is press charges and –'

'No!' Her tone was fierce. 'I don't want anything more to do with him. Let him go on with his life. I want to get on with mine.'

Steve nodded. 'Whatever you say. I'm going to take you down

to police headquarters. You may have to spend the night in jail, but I'll have you bailed out very quickly.'

Kendall smiled wanly. 'Now I can do something I've never done before.'

'What's that?'

'Design a dress in stripes.'

That evening, when he got home, Steve told Julia what had happened.

Julia was horrified. 'Her own husband was blackmailing her? That's terrible.' She studied him for a long moment. 'I think it's wonderful that you spend your life helping people in trouble.'

Steve looked at her and thought, *I'm the one in trouble.*

Steve Sloane was awakened by the aroma of fresh coffee and the smell of cooking bacon. He sat up in bed, startled. *Had the housekeeper come in today?* He had told her not to. Steve put on his robe and slippers, and hurried down to the kitchen.

Julia was in there, preparing breakfast. She looked up as Steve entered.

'Good morning,' she said cheerfully. 'How do you like your eggs?'

'Uh . . . scrambled.'

'Right. Scrambled eggs and bacon are my specialty. As a matter of fact, my one specialty. I told you, I'm a terrible cook.'

Steve smiled. 'You don't have to cook. If you wanted to, you could hire a few hundred chefs.'

'Am I really going to get that much money, Steve?'

'That's right. Your share of the estate will be over a billion dollars.'

She found it difficult to swallow. 'A billion . . . ? I don't believe it!'

'It's true.'

'There's not that much money in the world, Steve.'

'Well, your father had most of what there was.'

'I . . . I don't know what to say.'

'Then may I say something?'

'Of course.'

'The eggs are burning.'

'Oh! Sorry.' She quickly took them off the stove. 'I'll make another batch.'

'Don't bother. The burned bacon will be enough.'

She laughed. 'I'm sorry.'

Steve walked over to the cabinet and took out a box of cereal. 'How about a nice cold breakfast?'

'Perfect,' Julia said.

He poured some cereal into a bowl for each of them, took the milk out of the refrigerator, and they sat down at the kitchen table.

'Don't you have someone to cook for you?' Julia asked.

'You mean, am I involved with anyone?'

She blushed. 'Something like that.'

'No. I was in a relationship for two years, but it didn't work out.'

'I'm sorry.'

'What about you?' Steve asked.

She thought of Henry Wesson. 'I don't think so.'

He looked at her, curious. 'You aren't sure?'

'It's difficult to explain. One of us wants to get married,' she said tactfully, 'and one of us doesn't.'

'I see. When this is over, will you be going back to Kansas?'

'I honestly don't know. It seems so strange, being here. My mother talked to me so often about Boston. She was born here, and loved it. In a way, it's like coming home. I wish I could have known my father.'

No, you don't, Steve thought.

'Did you know him?'

'No. He dealt only with Simon Fitzgerald.'

They sat there talking for more than an hour, and there was an easy camaraderie between them. Steve filled Julia in on what had happened earlier – the arrival of the stranger who called herself Julia Stanford, the empty grave and Dmitri Kaminsky's disappearance.

'That's incredible!' Julia said. 'Who could be behind this?'

'I don't know, but I'm trying to find out,' Steve assured her. 'In the meantime, you'll be safe here. Very safe.'

She smiled, and said, 'I feel safe here. Thank you.'

He started to say something, then stopped. He looked at his watch. 'I'd better get dressed and get down to the office. I have a lot to do.'

Steve was meeting with Fitzgerald.

'Any progress yet?' Fitzgerald asked.

Steve shook his head. 'It's all smoke. Whoever planned this is a genius. I'm trying to trace Dmitri Kaminsky. He flew from Corsica to Paris to Australia. I spoke to the Sydney police. They were stunned to learn that Kaminsky is in their country. There's a circular out from Interpol, and they're looking for him. I think Harry Stanford signed his own death warrant when he called here and said he wanted to change his will. Someone decided to stop him. The only witness to what happened on the yacht that night is Dmitri Kaminsky. When we find him, we'll know a lot more.'

'I wonder if we should bring our police in on this?' Fitzgerald suggested.

Steve shook his head. 'What we know is all circumstantial, Simon. The only crime we can prove is that someone dug up a body – and we don't even know who did that.'

'What about the detective they hired, who verified the woman's fingerprints?'

'Frank Timmons. I've left three messages for him. If I don't hear back from him by six o'clock tonight, I'm going to fly to Chicago. I believe he's deeply involved.'

'What do you suppose was meant to happen to the shares of the estate that the impostor was going to get?'

'My hunch is that whoever planned this had her sign her share over to them. The person probably used some dummy trusts to hide it. I'm convinced that we're looking for a member of the family . . . I think we can eliminate Kendall as a suspect.' He told Fitzgerald about the conversation he had had with her. 'If she were behind this, she wouldn't have come forth with a

232

confession, not at this time, anyway. She would have waited until the estate was settled and she had the money. As far as her husband is concerned, I think we can eliminate Marc. He's a small-time blackmailer. He isn't capable of setting up anything like this.'

'What about the others?'

'Judge Stanford. I talked to a friend of mine with the Chicago Bar Association. My friend says everyone thinks very highly of Stanford. In fact, he's just been appointed chief judge. Another thing in his favor: Judge Stanford was the one who said that the first Julia who appeared was a fraud, and he was the one who insisted on a DNA test. I doubt he'd do something like this. Woody interests me. I'm pretty sure he's on drugs, and that's an expensive habit. I checked on his wife, Peggy. She isn't smart enough to be behind this scheme. But there's a rumor she has a brother who's bad business. I'm going to look into it.'

Steve spoke to his secretary on the intercom. 'Please get me Lieutenant Michael Kennedy of the Boston police.'

A few minutes later, she buzzed Steve. 'Lieutenant Kennedy is on line one.'

Steve picked up the phone.

'Lieutenant. Thank you for taking my call. I'm Steve Sloane with Renquist, Renquist, and Fitzgerald. We're trying to locate a relative in the matter of the Harry Stanford estate.'

'Mr Sloane, I'd be glad to help if I can.'

'Would you please check with the New York City police to see if they have any files on Mrs Woodrow Stanford's brother. His name is Hoop Malkovich. He works in a bakery in the Bronx.'

'No problem. I'll get back to you.'

'Thanks.'

After lunch, Simon Fitzgerald stopped by Steve's office.

'How's the investigation going?' he asked.

'Too slow to suit me. Whoever planned this covered his or her tracks pretty thoroughly.'

'How is Julia holding up?'

Steve smiled. 'She's wonderful.'

There was something in the tone of his voice that made Simon Fitzgerald take a closer look at him.

'She's a very attractive young lady.'

'I know,' Steve said wistfully. 'I know.'

An hour later, the call came in from Australia.

'Mr Sloane?'

'Yes.'

'Chief Inspector McPhearson here from Sydney.'

'Yes, Chief Inspector.'

'We found your man.'

Steve felt his heart jump. 'That's wonderful! I'd like to arrange immediate extradition to bring him . . .'

'Oh, I don't think there's any hurry. Dmitri Kaminsky is dead.'

Steve felt his heart sink. '*What?*'

'We found his body a little while ago. His fingers had been chopped off, and he had been shot several times.'

'*The Russian gangs have a quaint custom. First they chop off your fingers, then they let you bleed, and then they shoot you.*'

'I see. Thank you, inspector.'

Dead end. Steve sat there, staring at the wall. All his leads were disappearing. He realized how heavily he had been counting on Dmitri Kaminsky's testimony.

Steve's secretary interrupted his thoughts. 'There's a Mr Timmons for you on line three.'

Steve looked at his watch. It was 5:55 P.M. He picked up the telephone. 'Mr Timmons?'

'Yes . . . I'm sorry I couldn't return your calls earlier. I've been out of town for the past two days. What can I do for you?'

A lot, Steve thought. *You can tell me how you faked those fingerprints*. Steve chose his words carefully. 'I'm calling about Julia Stanford. When you were in Boston recently, you checked out her fingerprints and . . .'

'Mr Sloane . . .'

'Yes?'

'I've never been in Boston.'

234

Steve took a deep breath. 'Mr Timmons, according to the register at the Holiday Inn, you were here on . . .'

'Someone has been using my name.'

Steve listened, stunned. It was the final dead end, the last lead. 'I don't suppose you have any idea who it is?'

'Well, it's very strange, Mr Sloane. A woman claimed that I was in Boston and that I could identify her as Julia Stanford. I'd never seen her before in my life.'

Steve felt a surge of hope. 'Do you know who she is?'

'Yes. Her name is Posner. Margo Posner.'

Steve picked up a pen. 'Where can I reach her?'

'She's at the Reed Mental Health Facility in Chicago.'

'Thanks a lot. I really appreciate this.'

'Let's keep in touch. I'd like to know what's going on myself. I don't like people going around impersonating me.'

'Right.' Steve replaced the receiver. Margo Posner.

When Steve got home that evening, Julia was waiting to greet him.

'I fixed dinner,' she told him. 'Well, I didn't exactly fix it. Do you like Chinese food?'

He smiled. 'Love it!'

'Good. We have eight cartons of it.'

When Steve walked into the dining room, the table was set with flowers and candles,

'Is there any news?' Julia asked.

Steve said cautiously, 'We may have gotten our first break. I have the name of a woman who seems to be involved in this. I'm flying to Chicago in the morning to talk with her. I have a feeling we may have all the answers tomorrow.'

'That would be wonderful!' Julia said excitedly. 'I'll be so glad when this is over.'

'So will I,' Steve told her. *Or will I? She'll be a real part of the Stanford family – way out of my reach.*

Dinner lasted two hours, and they were not even aware of what they were eating. They talked about everything and they talked

235

about nothing, and it was as though they had known each other forever. They discussed the past and the present, and they carefully avoided talking about the future. *There is no future for us*, Steve thought unhappily.

Finally, reluctantly, Steve said, 'Well, we'd better go to bed.'

She looked at him with raised eyebrows, and they both burst out laughing.

'What I meant . . .'

'I know what you meant. Good night, Steve.'

'Good night, Julia.'

Chapter Thirty-one

Early the following morning, Steve boarded a United flight for Chicago. From Chicago's O'Hare Airport he took a taxi.

'Where to?' the driver asked.

'The Reed Mental Health Facility.'

The drive turned around looked at Steve. 'Are you okay?'

'Yes. Why?'

'Just asking.'

At Reed, Steve approached the uniformed security guard at the front desk.

The guard looked up. 'Can I help you?'

'Yes. I'd like to see Margo Posner.'

'Is she an employee?'

That had not occurred to Steve. 'I'm not sure.'

The guard took a closer look at him. 'You're not sure?'

'All I know is that she's here.'

The guard reached in a drawer and took out a roster with a list of names. After a moment, he said, 'She doesn't work here. Could she be a patient?'

'I . . . I don't know. It's possible.'

The guard gave Steve another look, then reached into a different drawer and pulled out a computer printout. He scanned it, and in the middle, he stopped. 'Posner. Margo.'

'That's right.' He was surprised. 'Is she a patient here?'

'Uh-huh. Are you a relative?'

'No . . .'

'Then I'm afraid you can't see her.'

'I *have* to see her,' Steve said. 'It's very important.'

'Sorry. I have my orders. Unless you've been cleared beforehand, you can't visit any of the patients.'

'Who's in charge here?' Steve asked.

'I am.'

'I mean, in charge of the hospital.'

'Dr Kingsley.'

'I want to see him.'

'Right.' The guard picked up the telephone and dialed a number. 'Dr Kingsley, this is Joe at the front desk. There's a gentleman here who wants to see you.' He looked up at Steve. 'Your name?'

'Steve Sloane. I'm an attorney.'

'Steve Sloane. He's an attorney . . . right.' He replaced the receiver and turned to Steve. 'Someone will be along to take you to his office.'

Five minutes later, Steve was ushered into the office of Dr Gary Kingsley. Kingsley was a man in his fifties, but he looked older and careworn.

'What can I do for you, Mr Sloane?'

'I need to see a patient you have here. Margo Posner.'

'Ah, yes. Interesting case. Are you related to her?'

'No, but I'm investigating a possible murder, and it's very important that I talk to her. I think she may be a key to it.'

'I'm sorry. I can't help you.'

'You *have* to,' Steve said. 'It's . . .'

'Mr Sloane, I couldn't help you even if I wanted to.'

'Why not?'

'Because Margo Posner is in a padded cell. She attacks everyone who goes near her. This morning, she tried to kill a matron and two doctors.'

'*What?*'

'She keeps changing her identity and screaming for her brother, Tyler, and the crew of her yacht. The only way we can quiet her is to keep her heavily sedated.'

'Oh, my God,' Steve said. 'Do you have any idea when she might come out of it?'

Dr Kingsley shook his head. 'She's under close observation. Perhaps in time she'll calm down, and we can reevaluate her condition. Until then . . .'

Chapter Thirty-two

At six A.M., a harbor patrol boat was cruising along the Charles River, when one of the policemen aboard spotted an object floating in the water ahead.

'Off the starboard bow!' he called. 'It looks like a log. Let's pick it up before it sinks something.'

The log turned out to be a body, and even more startling, a body that had been embalmed.

The policemen stared down at it and said, 'How the hell did an embalmed body get into the Charles River?'

Lieutenant Michael Kennedy was talking to the coroner. 'Are you sure of that?'

The coroner replied, 'Absolutely. It's Harry Stanford. I embalmed him myself. Later, we had an exhumation order, and when we dug up the coffin . . . Well, you know, we reported it to the police.'

'Who asked to have the body exhumed?'

'The family. They handled it through their attorney, Simon Fitzgerald.'

'I think I'll have a talk with Mr Fitzgerald.'

When Steve returned to Boston from Chicago, he went directly to Simon Fitzgerald's office.

'You look beat,' Fitzgerald said.

'Not beat – beaten. The whole thing is falling apart, Simon. We had three possible leads: Dmitri Kaminsky, Frank Timmons, and Margo Posner. Well, Kaminsky is dead, it's the wrong

Timmons, and Margo Posner is locked away in an asylum. We have nothing to –'

The voice of Fitzgerald's secretary came over the intercom. 'Excuse me. There's a Lieutenant Kennedy here to see you, Mr Fitzgerald.'

'Send him in.'

Michael Kennedy was a rugged-looking man with eyes that had seen everything.

'Mr Fitzgerald?'

'Yes. This is my associate Steve Sloane. I believe you two have spoken on the phone. Sit down. What can we do for you?'

'We just found the body of Harry Stanford.'

'What? Where?'

'Swimming in the Charles. You ordered his body dug up, didn't you?'

'Yes.'

'May I ask why?'

Fitzgerald told him.

When Fitzgerald was finished, Kennedy said, 'You have no idea who it was that posed as this investigator, Timmons?'

'No. I talked to Timmons. He has no idea, either.'

Kennedy sighed. 'It gets curiouser and curiouser.'

'Where is Harry Stanford's body now?' Steve asked.

'They're keeping him at the morgue for the present. I hope he doesn't disappear again.'

'I do, too,' Steve said. 'We'll have Perry Winger run a DNA test on Julia.'

When Steve called Tyler to tell him that his father's body had been found, Tyler was genuinely shocked.

'That's terrible!' he said. 'Who could have done a thing like that?'

'That's what we're trying to find out,' Steve told him.

Tyler was furious. *That incompetent idiot, Baker! He's going to pay for this. I have to get this settled before it gets out of hand.* 'Mr Fitzgerald, as you may be aware, I've been appointed chief judge of Cook County. I have a very heavy caseload, and they're pressuring me to return. I can't delay much longer. I'd appreciate it if you could do something to get the probate finished quickly.'

'I put in a call this morning,' Steve told him. 'It should be closed within the next three days.'

'That will be fine. Keep me informed, please.'

'I'll do that, Judge.'

Steve sat in his office reviewing the events of the past few weeks. He recalled the conversation he had had with Chief Inspector McPhearson.

'We found his body a little while ago. His fingers had been chopped off and he had been shot several times.'

But wait, Steve thought. *There's something he didn't tell me.* He picked up the telephone and put in another call to Australia.

The voice on the other end of the telephone said, 'This is Chief Inspector McPhearson.'

'Yes, Inspector. This is Steve Sloane. I forgot to ask you a question. When you found Dmitri Kaminsky's body, were there any papers on him? . . . I see . . . that's fine. Thank you very much.'

When Steve hung up the phone, his secretary's voice came over the intercom. 'Lieutenant Kennedy holding on line two.'

Steve punched the phone button.

'Lieutenant. Sorry to keep you waiting. I was on an overseas call.'

'The NYPD gave me some interesting information on Hoop Malkovich. He seems to be quite a slippery character.'

Steve picked up a pen. 'Go ahead.'

'The police believe that the bakery he works for is a front for a drug ring.' The lieutenant paused, then continued. 'Malkovich is probably a drug pusher. But he's clever. They haven't been able to nail him yet.'

'Anything else?' Steve asked.

'The police believe the operation is tied into the French mafia with a connection through Marseilles. If I learn anything else, I'll call.'

'Thanks, Lieutenant. That's very helpful.'

242

Steve put down the phone and headed out the office door.

When Steve arrived home, filled with anticipation, he called, 'Julia?'

There was no answer.

He began to panic. 'Julia!' *She's been kidnapped or killed,* he thought, and he felt a sudden sense of alarm.

Julia appeared at the top of the stairs. 'Steve?'

He took a deep breath. 'I thought . . .' He was pale.

'Are you all right?'

'Yes.'

She came down the stairs. 'Did things go well in Chicago?'

He shook his head. 'I'm afraid not.' He told her what had happened. 'We're going to have a reading of the will on Thursday, Julia. That's only three days from now. Whoever is behind this has to get rid of you by then or his – or her – plan can't work.'

She swallowed. 'I see. Do you have any idea who it is?'

'As a matter of fact . . .' The telephone rang. 'Excuse me.' Steve picked up the telephone. 'Hello?'

'This is Dr Tichner in Florida. Sorry I didn't call earlier, but I've been away.'

'Dr Tichner. Thank you for returning my call. Our firm represents the Stanford estate.'

'What can I do for you?'

'I'm calling about Woodrow Stanford. I believe he's a patient of yours.'

'Yes.'

'Does he have a drug problem, doctor?'

'Mr Sloane, I'm not at liberty to discuss any of my patients.'

'I understand. I'm not asking this out of curiosity. It's very important . . .'

'I'm afraid I can't . . .'

'You *did* have him admitted to the Harbor Group Clinic in Jupiter, didn't you?'

There was a long hesitation. 'Yes. That's a matter of record.'

'Thank you, doctor. That's all I needed to know.'

Steve replaced the receiver and stood there a moment. 'It's unbelievable!'

'What?' Julia asked.

'Sit down.'

Thirty minutes later, Steve was in his car headed for Rose Hill. All the pieces had finally fallen into place. *He's brilliant. It almost worked. It could still work if anything happened to Julia,* Steve thought.

At Rose Hill, Clark answered the door. 'Good evening, Mr Sloane.'

'Good evening, Clark. Is Judge Stanford in?'

'He's in the library. I'll tell him you're here.'

'Thank you.' He watched Clark walk off.

A minute later, the butler returned. 'Judge Stanford will see you now.'

'Thank you.'

Steve walked into the library.

Tyler was sitting in front of a chess board, concentrating. He looked up as Steve walked in.

'You wanted to see me?'

'Yes. I believe the young woman who came to see you several days ago is the real Julia. The other Julia was a fake.'

'But that's not possible.'

'I'm afraid it's true, and I've found out who's behind all this.'

There was a momentary silence. Then Tyler said slowly, 'You have?'

'Yes. I'm afraid this is going to shock you. It's your brother, Woody.'

Tyler was looking up at Steve in amazement. 'Are you saying that Woody is responsible for what's been happening?'

'That's right.'

'I . . . I can't believe it.'

'Neither could I, but it all checks out. I talked to his doctor in Hobe Sound. Did you know your brother is on drugs?'

'I . . . I've suspected it.'

'Drugs are expensive. Woody isn't working. He needs money,

and he was obviously looking for a bigger share of the estate. He's the one who hired the fake Julia, but when you came to us and asked for a DNA test, he panicked and had your father's body removed from the coffin because he couldn't afford to have that test made. That's what tipped me off. And I suspect that he sent someone to Kansas City to have the real Julia killed. Did you know that Peggy has a brother who's tied into the mob? As long as Julia's alive and there are two Julias around, his plan can't work.'

'Are you sure of all this?'

'Absolutely. There's something else, Judge.'

'Yes?'

'I don't think your father fell off his yacht. I believe that Woody had your father *murdered*. Peggy's brother could have arranged that too. I'm told he has connections with the Marseilles mafia. They could easily have paid a crew member to do it. I'm flying to Italy tonight to have a talk with the captain of the yacht.'

Tyler was listening intently. When he spoke, he said approvingly, 'That's a good idea.' *Captain Vacarro knows nothing*.

'I'll try to be back by Thursday for the reading of the will.'

Tyler said, 'What about the real Julia? . . . Are you sure she's safe?'

'Oh, yes,' Steve said. 'She's staying where no one can find her. She's at my house.'

Chapter Thirty-three

The gods are on my side. He could not believe his good fortune. It was an incredible stroke of luck. Last night, Steve Sloane had delivered Julia into his hands. *Hal Baker is an incompetent fool,* Tyler thought. *I'll take care of Julia myself this time.*

He looked up as Clark came into the room.

'Excuse me, Judge Stanford. There's a telephone call for you.'

It was Keith Percy. 'Tyler?'

'Yes, Keith.'

'I just wanted to bring you up to date on the Margo Posner matter.'

'Yes?'

'Dr Gifford just called me. The woman is insane. She's carrying on so badly that they have to have her locked away in the violent ward.'

Tyler felt a sharp sense of relief. 'I'm sorry to hear that.'

'Anyway, I wanted to ease your mind and let you know that she's no longer any danger to you or your family.'

'I appreciate that,' Tyler said. And he did.

Tyler went to his room and telephoned Lee. There was a long delay before Lee answered.

'Hello?' Tyler could hear voices in the background. 'Lee?'

'Who is this?'

'It's Tyler.'

'Oh, yeah. Tyler.'

He could hear the tinkling of glasses. 'Are you having a party, Lee?'

'Uh-huh. Do you want to join us?'

Tyler wondered who was at the party. 'I wish I could. I'm calling to tell you to get ready to go on that trip we talked about.'

Lee laughed. 'You mean, on that great big white yacht to St Tropez?'

'That's right.'

'Sure. I can be ready anytime,' he said mockingly.

'Lee, I'm serious.'

'Oh, come off it, Tyler. Judges don't have yachts. I have to go now. My guests are calling me.'

'Wait a minute!' Tyler said desperately. 'Do you know who I am?'

'Sure, you're –'

'I'm Tyler Stanford. My father was Harry Stanford.'

There was a moment of silence. 'Are you kidding me?'

'No. I'm in Boston now, settling up the estate.'

'My, God! You're *that* Stanford. I didn't know. I'm sorry. I . . . I've been hearing stuff on the news, but I didn't pay much attention. I never figured it was you.'

'That's all right.'

'You really meant it about taking me to St Tropez, didn't you?'

'Of course I did. We're going to do a lot of things together,' Tyler said. 'That is, if you want to.'

'I certainly do!' Lee's voice was suddenly filled with enthusiasm. 'Gee, Tyler, this is really great news . . .'

When Tyler replaced the receiver, he was smiling. Lee was taken care of. *Now*, he thought, *it's time to take care of my half sister.*

Tyler went into the library where Harry Stanford's gun collection was kept, opened the case, and removed a mahogany box. From a drawer below the case, he took out some ammunition. He put the ammunition in his pocket and carried the wooden box upstairs to his bedroom, locked the door behind him and opened the box. Inside were two matching Ruger revolvers, Harry Stanford's favorites. Tyler removed one, carefully loaded it, and then placed the extra ammunition and the box containing the other revolver in his bureau drawer. *One shot will do it*, he thought. They had

247

taught him to shoot well at the military school his father had sent him to. *Thank you, Father.*

Next, Tyler picked up a telephone directory and looked for Steve Sloane's home address.

280 Newbury Street, Boston.

Tyler made his way to the garage, where there were half a dozen cars. He chose the black Mercedes as being the least conspicuous. He opened the garage door and listened to see if the noise had disturbed anyone. There was only silence.

On the drive to Steve Sloane's house, Tyler thought about what he was about to do. He had never physically committed a murder before. But this time he had no choice. Julia Stanford was the last obstacle between him and his dreams. With her gone, his problems would be over. *Forever,* Tyler thought.

He drove slowly, careful not to attract attention. When he reached Newbury Street, Tyler cruised past Steve's address. A few cars were parked on the street, but no pedestrians were around.

He parked the car a block away and walked back to the house. He rang the doorbell and waited.

Julia's voice came through the door. 'Who is it?'

'It's Judge Stanford.'

Julia opened the door. She looked at him in surprise. 'What are you doing here? Is anything wrong?'

'No, not at all,' he said easily. 'Steve Sloane asked me to have a talk with you. He told me you were here. May I come in?'

'Yes, of course.'

Tyler walked into the hall and watched Julia close the door behind him. She led the way into the living room.

'Steve isn't here,' she said. 'He's on his way to San Remo.'

'I know.' He looked around. 'Are you alone? Isn't there a housekeeper or someone to stay with you?'

'No. I'm safe here. May I offer you something?'

'No, thanks.'

'What did you want to talk to me about?'

'I came to talk about you, Julia. I'm disappointed in you.'

'Disappointed . . . ?'

'You should never have come here. Did you really think you could walk in and try to collect a fortune that doesn't belong to you?'

She looked at him a moment. 'But I have a right to –'

'You have a right to nothing!' Tyler snapped. 'Where were you all those years when we were being humiliated and punished by our father? He went out of his way to hurt us every chance he got. He put us through hell. You didn't have to go through any of that. Well, we did, and we deserve the money. Not you.'

'I . . . what do you want me to do?'

Tyler gave a short laugh. 'What do I want you to do? Nothing. You've done it already. You damned near spoiled everything, do you know that?'

'I don't understand.'

'It's really quite simple.' He took out the revolver. 'You're going to disappear.'

She took a step back. 'But I . . .'

'Don't say anything. Let's not waste time. You and I are going on a little trip.'

She stiffened. 'What if I won't go?'

'Oh, you'll be going. Dead or alive. Suit yourself.'

In the moment of silence that followed, Tyler heard his voice boom out from the next room. *'Oh, you'll be going. Dead or alive. Suit yourself.'* He whirled around. 'What . . . ?'

Steve Sloane, Simon Fitzgerald, Lieutenant Kennedy, and two uniformed policemen stepped into the living room. Steve was holding a tape recorder.

Lieutenant Kennedy said, 'Give me the gun, Judge.'

Tyler froze for an instant, then he forced a smile. 'Of course. I was just trying to scare this woman into getting out of here. She's a fraud, you know.' He put the gun in the detective's outstretched hand. 'She tried to claim part of the Stanford estate. Well, I wasn't about to let her get away with it. So I . . .'

'It's over, judge,' Steve said.

249

'What are you talking about? You said Woody was responsible for . . .'

'Woody wasn't up to planning anything as clever as this, and Kendall was already very successful. So I started checking up on you. Dmitri Kaminsky was killed in Australia, but the Australian police found *your* telephone number in his pocket. You used him to murder your father. You're the one who brought in Margo Posner and then insisted she was an impostor to throw suspicion off yourself. You're the one who insisted on the DNA test and arranged to have the body removed. And you're the one who put in the phony call to Timmons. You hired Margo Posner to impersonate Julia, then had her committed to a psychiatric ward.'

Tyler looked around the room, and when he spoke, his voice was dangerously calm. 'And *a phone number* on a dead man is your evidence? I can't believe this! You set up your pitiful little trap based on *that*? You don't have a shred of proof. My telephone number was in Dmitri's pocket because I thought my father might be in danger. I told Dmitri to be careful. Obviously, he wasn't careful enough. Whoever killed my father probably killed Dmitri. That's who the police should be looking for. I called Timmons because I wanted him to find out the truth. Someone impersonated him. I have no idea who. And unless you can find him and tie him to me, you have nothing. As far as Margo Posner is concerned, I really believed that she was our sister. When she suddenly went crazy, going on a buying spree and threatening to kill us all, I persuaded her to go to Chicago. Then I arranged to have her picked up and committed. I wanted to keep all this out of the press to protect the family.'

Julia said, 'But you came here to kill me.'

Tyler shook his head. 'I had no intention of killing you. You're an impostor. I just wanted to scare you away.'

'You're lying.'

He turned to the others. 'There's something else you might consider. It's possible that none of the family is involved. It could be some insider who's manipulating this, someone who put in an impostor and planned to convince the family she was genuine

250

and then split a share of the estate with her. That didn't occur to any of you, did it?'

He turned to Simon Fitzgerald. 'I'm going to sue you both for slander, and I'm going to take away everything you've got. These are my witnesses. Before I'm through with you, you'll wish you had never heard of me. I control billions, and I'm going to use them to destroy you.' He looked at Steve. 'I promise you that your last act as a lawyer will be the reading of the Stanford will. Now, unless you want to charge me with carrying an unlicensed weapon, I'll be leaving.'

The group looked at one another uncertainly.

'No? Well, good evening, then.'

They watched helplessly as he walked out the door.

Lieutenant Kennedy was the first one to find his voice. 'My, God!' he said. 'Do you believe that?'

'He's bluffing,' Steve said slowly. 'But we can't prove it. He's right. We need proof. I thought he would crack, but I underestimated him.'

Simon Fitzgerald spoke. 'It looks like our little plan backfired. Without Dmitri Kaminsky or the testimony of the Posner woman, we have nothing but suspicions.'

'What about the threat on my life?' Julia protested.

Steve said, 'You heard what he said. He was just trying to scare you because he thought you were an impostor.'

'He wasn't just trying to scare me,' Julia said. 'He intended to kill me.'

'I know. But there isn't a thing we can do. Dickens had it right: "The law is a ass . . ." We're right back where we started.'

Fitzgerald frowned. 'It's worse than that, Steve. Tyler meant what he said about suing us. Unless we can prove our charges, we're in trouble.'

When the others had left, Julia said to Steve, 'I'm so sorry about all this. I feel responsible in a way. If I hadn't come . . .'

'Don't be silly,' Steve said.

'But he said he's going to ruin you. Can he do that?'

Steve shrugged. 'We'll have to see.'

Julia hesitated. 'Steve, I'd like to help you.'

He looked at her, puzzled. 'What do you mean?'

'Well, I'm going to have a lot of money. I'd like to give you enough so you can –'

He put his hands on her shoulders. 'Thank you, Julia. I can't take your money. I'll be fine.'

'But . . .'

'Don't worry about it.'

She shuddered. 'He's an evil man.'

'It was very brave of you to do what you did.'

'You said there was no way to get him, so I thought if you sent him here, that could be the way to trap him.'

'It looks as though we're the ones who fell into the trap, doesn't it?'

That night, Julia lay in her bed, thinking about Steve and wondering how she could protect him. *I shouldn't have come,* she thought, *but if I hadn't come, I wouldn't have met him.*

In the next room, Steve lay in bed, thinking about Julia. It was frustrating to think that she was lying in her bed with only a thin wall between them. *What am I talking about? That wall is a billion dollars thick.*

Tyler was in an exuberant mood. On the way home, he thought about what had just taken place, and how he had outwitted them. *They're pygmies trying to fell a giant,* he thought. And he had no idea that these were once his father's thoughts.

When Tyler reached Rose Hill, Clark greeted him. 'Good evening, Judge Tyler. I hope you're well this evening.'

'Never better, Clark. Never better.'

'Can I get you anything?'

'Yes. I think I'd like a glass of champagne.'

'Of course, sir.'

It was a celebration, the celebration of his victory. *Tomorrow I'll be worth over two billion dollars.* He said the phrase lovingly

over and over. 'Two billion dollars . . . two billion dollars . . .'
He decided to call Lee.

This time Lee recognized his voice immediately.

'Tyler! How are you?' His voice was warm.

'Fine, Lee.'

'I've been waiting to hear from you.'

Tyler felt a little thrill. 'Have you? How would you like to come to Boston tomorrow?'

'Sure . . . but what for?'

'For the reading of the will. I'm going to inherit over two billion dollars.'

'Two . . . that's fantastic!'

'I want you here at my side. We're going to pick out that yacht together.'

'Oh, Tyler! That sounds wonderful!'

'Then you'll come?'

'Of course, I will.'

When Lee replaced the receiver, he sat there saying lovingly over and over, 'Two billion dollars . . . two billion dollars.'

Chapter Thirty-four

The day before the reading of the will, Kendall and Woody were seated in Steve's office.

'I don't understand why we're here,' Woody said. 'The reading is supposed to be tomorrow.'

'There's someone I want you to meet,' Steve told them.

'Who?'

'Your sister.'

They were both staring at him. 'We've already met her,' Kendall said.

Steve pressed a button on the intercom. 'Would you ask her to come in, please?'

Kendall and Woody looked at each other, puzzled.

The door opened, and Julia Stanford walked into the office.

Steve stood up. 'This is your sister, Julia.'

'What the hell are you talking about?' Woody exploded. 'What are you trying to pull?'

'Let me explain,' Steve said quietly. He spoke for fifteen minutes, and finished by saying, 'Penny Winger confirmed that her DNA matches your father's.'

When he was through, Woody said, 'Tyler! I can't believe it!'

'Believe it.'

'I don't understand. The other woman's fingerprints prove that *she* is Julia,' Woody said. 'I still have the fingerprint card.'

Steve felt his pulse pounding. 'You do?'

'Yeah. I kept it as kind of a joke.'

'I want you to do me a favor,' Steve said.

*   *   *

At ten o'clock the next morning, a large group was gathered in the conference room of Renquist, Renquist & Fitzgerald. Simon Fitzgerald sat at the head of a table. In the room were Kendall, Tyler, Woody, Steve, and Julia. In addition, there were several strangers present.

Fitzgerald introduced two of them.'This is William Parker and Patrick Evans. They're with the law firms that represent Stanford Enterprises. They've brought with them the financial report on the company. I'll discuss the will first, then they can take over the meeting.'

'Let's get on with it,' Tyler said impatiently. He was sitting apart from the others. *I'm not only going to get the money, but I'm going to destroy you bastards.*

Simon Fitzgerald nodded. 'Very well.'

In front of Fitzgerald was a large file marked HARRY STANFORD – LAST WILL AND TESTAMENT. 'I'm going to give each of you a copy of the will so it won't be necessary to wade through all the technicalities. I've already told you that Harry Stanford's children will equally inherit the estate.'

Julia glanced over at Steve, a look of bemusement on her face.

I'm glad for her, Steve thought. *Even though it puts her way out of my reach.*

Simon Fitzgerald was going on. 'There are a dozen or so bequests, but they're all minor.'

Tyler was thinking, *Lee will be here this afternoon. I want to be at the airport to meet him.*

'As you were told earlier, Stanford Enterprises has assets of approximately six billion dollars.' Fitzgerald nodded toward William Parker. 'I'll let Mr Parker take it from here.'

William Parker opened a briefcase and spread some papers out on the conference table. 'As Mr Fitzgerald said, there are six billion dollars in assets. However . . .' There was a pregnant pause. He looked around the room. 'Stanford Enterprises is in debt in excess of fifteen billion dollars.'

Woody was on his feet. 'What the hell are you saying?'

Tyler's face turned ashen. 'Is this some kind of macabre joke?'

'It has to be!' Kendall said hoarsely.

Mr Parker turned to one of the men in the room. 'Mr Leonard Redding is with the Securities and Exchange Commission. I'll let him explain.'

Redding nodded. 'For the last two years, Harry Stanford was convinced that interest rates were going to fall. In the past, he had made millions by betting on that. When interest rates started to rise, he was still convinced they would drop again, and he kept leveraging his bets. He did massive borrowing to buy long-term bonds, but the interest rates went up and his borrowing costs jumped, while the value of the bonds tumbled. The banks were willing to do business with him because of his reputation and his vast fortune, but when he tried to recoup his losses by starting to invest in high-risk securities, they began to get worried. He made a series of disastrous investments. Some of the money he borrowed was pledged by securities he had bought with borrowed money as collateral for further borrowing.'

'In other words,' Patrick Evans interjected, 'he was pyramiding his debts, operating illegally.'

'That is correct. Unfortunately for him, interest rates underwent one of the steepest climbs in financial history. He had to keep borrowing money to cover the money he had already borrowed. It was a vicious circle.'

They sat there, hanging on Redding's every word.

'Your father gave his personal guarantee to the company's pension plan and illegally used that money to buy more stock. When the banks began to question what he was doing, he set up decoy companies and provided false records of solvency and fake sales of his properties to drive up the value of his paper. He was committing fraud. In the end, he was counting on a consortium of banks to bail him out of trouble. They refused. When they told the Securities and Exchange Commission what was happening, Interpol was brought into the picture.'

Redding indicated the man seated next to him. 'This is Inspector Patou, with the French Sûreté. Inspector, would you explain the rest of it, please?'

Inspector Patou spoke English with a slight French accent. 'At the request of Interpol, we traced Harry Stanford to

256

St Paul-de-Vence, and I sent three detectives there to follow him. He managed to elude them. Interpol had put out a green code to all police departments that Harry Stanford was under suspicion and should be watched. If they had known the extent of his crimes, they would have circulated a red code, or top priority, and we would have apprehended him.'

Woody was in a state of shock. '*That's* why he left us his estate. Because there was nothing in it!'

William Parker said, 'You're right about that. You were all in your father's will because the banks refused to go along with him and he knew that, in essence, he was leaving you nothing. But he spoke to René Gautier at Crédit Lyonnais, who promised to help him. The moment Harry Stanford thought that he was solvent again, he planned to change his will to cut you out of it.'

'But what about the yacht, and the plane, and the houses?' Kendall asked.

'I'm sorry,' Parker said. 'Everything will be sold to pay off part of the debt.'

Tyler sat there, numb. It was a nightmare beyond imagining. He was no longer Tyler Stanford, Multibillionaire. He was merely a judge.

Tyler got up to leave, shaken. 'I . . . I don't know what to say. If there's nothing else . . .' He had to get to the airport quickly to meet Lee and try to explain what had happened.

Steve spoke up. 'There is something else.'

He turned. 'Yes?'

Steve nodded to a man standing at the door. The door opened, and Hal Baker walked in.

'Hi, judge.'

The breakthrough had come when Woody told Steve that he had the fingerprint card.

'I'd like to see it,' Steve told him.

Woody had been puzzled. 'Why? It just has the woman's two sets of fingerprints on it, and they matched. We all checked it.'

'But the man who called himself Frank Timmons took the fingerprints, right?'

'Yes.'

'Then if he touched the card, *his* fingerprints will be on it.'

Steve's hunch had proved to be right. Hal Baker's prints were all over the card, and it had taken less than thirty minutes for the computers to reveal his identity. Steve had telephoned the district attorney in Chicago. A warrant was issued, and two detectives had appeared at Hal Baker's house.

He was in the yard playing catch with Billy.

'Mr Baker?'

'Yes.'

The detectives showed their badges. 'The district attorney would like to talk to you.'

'No. I can't.' He was indignant.

'May I ask why?' one of the detectives asked.

'You can see why, can't you? I'm playing ball with my son!'

The district attorney had read the transcript of Hal Baker's trial. He looked at the man seated in front of him and said, 'I understand you're a family man.'

'That's right,' Hal Baker said proudly. 'That's what this country is all about. If every family could –'

'Mr Baker.' He leaned forward. 'You've been working with Judge Stanford.'

'I don't know any Judge Stanford.'

'Let me refresh your memory. He put you on parole. He used you to impersonate a private detective named Frank Timmons, and we have reason to believe he also asked you to kill a Julia Stanford.'

'I don't know what you're talking about.'

'What I'm talking about is a sentence of ten to twenty years. I'm going to push for the twenty.'

Hal Baker turned pale. 'You can't do that! Why, my wife and kids would . . .'

'Exactly. On the other hand,' the district attorney said, 'if you're willing to turn state's evidence, I'm prepared to arrange for you to get off very lightly.'

258

Hal Baker was beginning to perspire. 'What . . . what do I have to do?'

'Talk to me.'

Now, in the conference room of Renquist, Renquist & Fitzgerald, Hal Baker looked at Tyler, and said, 'How are you, Judge?'

Woody looked up and exclaimed, 'Hey! It's Frank Timmons!'

Steve said to Tyler, 'This is the man you ordered to break into our offices to get you a copy of your father's will, to dig up your father's body, and to kill Julia Stanford.'

It took a moment for Tyler to find his voice. 'You're crazy! He's a convicted felon. No one is going to take his word against mine!'

'No one has to take his word,' Steve said. 'Have you seen this man before?'

'Of course. He was tried in my court.'

'What's his name?'

'His name is . . .' Tyler saw the trap. 'I mean . . . he probably has a lot of aliases.'

'When you tried him in your courtroom, his name was Hal Baker.'

'That . . . that's right.'

'But when he came to Boston, you introduced him as Frank Timmons.'

Tyler was floundering. 'Well, I . . . I . . .'

'You had him released into your custody, and you used him to try to prove that Margo Posner was the real Julia.'

'No! I had nothing to do with that. I never met that woman until she showed up here.'

Steve turned to Lieutenant Kennedy. 'Did you get that, Lieutenant?'

'Yes.'

Steve turned back to Tyler. 'We checked on Margo Posner. She was also tried in your courtroom and released into your custody. The district attorney in Chicago issued a search warrant this morning for your safe-deposit box. He called a little while ago to tell me that they found a document giving you Julia

259

Stanford's share of your father's estate. The document was signed five days before the supposed Julia Stanford arrived in Boston.'

Tyler was breathing hard, trying to regain his wits. 'I . . . I . . . This is preposterous!'

Lieutenant Kennedy said, 'I'm placing you under arrest, Judge Stanford, for conspiracy to commit murder. We'll arrange for extradition papers. You'll be sent back to Chicago.'

Tyler stood there, his world collapsing around him.

'You have the right to remain silent. If you choose to give up this right anything you say can and will be used against you in a court of law. You have the right to talk to a lawyer and have him present with you while you are being questioned. If you cannot afford to hire a lawyer, one will be appointed to represent you before any questioning, if you wish one. Do you understand?' Lieutenant Kennedy asked.

'Yes.' And then a slow triumphant smile lit his face. *I know how to beat them!* he thought happily.

'Are you ready, Judge?'

He nodded and said calmly, 'Yes. I'm ready. I'd like to go back to Rose Hill to pick up my things.'

'That's fine. We'll have these two policemen accompany you.'

Tyler turned to look at Julia, and there was so much hatred in his eyes that it made her shudder.

Thirty minutes later, Tyler and the two policemen reached Rose Hill. They walked into the front hall.

'It will take me only a few minutes to pack,' Tyler said.

They watched as Tyler went up the staircase to his room. In his room, Tyler walked over to the bureau containing the revolver and loaded it.

The sound of the shot seemed to reverberate forever.

Chapter Thirty-five

Woody and Kendall were seated in the drawing room at Rose Hill. Half a dozen men in white overalls were taking down paintings from the walls and starting to dismantle the furnishings.

'It's the end of an era,' Kendall sighed.

'It's the beginning,' Woody said. He smiled. 'I wish I could see Peggy's face when she finds out what her half of my fortune is!' He took his sister's hand. 'Are you okay? About Marc, I mean.'

She nodded. 'I'll get over it. Anyhow, I'm going to be very busy. I have a preliminary hearing in two weeks. After that, I'll see what happens.'

'I'm sure everything will be all right.' He rose. 'I have an important telephone call to make,' Woody told her. He had to break the news to Mimi Carson.

'Mimi,' Woody said apologetically, 'I'm afraid I'm going to have to go back on our deal. Things haven't worked out as I had hoped they would.'

'Are you all right, Woody?'

'Yes. A lot has been going on here. Peggy and I are finished.'

There was a long pause. 'Oh? Are you coming back to Hobe Sound?'

'Frankly, I don't know what I'm going to do.'

'Woody?'

'Yes?'

Her voice was soft. 'Come back, please.'

*   *   *

261

Julia and Steve were out on the patio.

'I'm sorry about the way things turned out,' Steve said. 'About your not getting the money, I mean.'

Julia smiled at him. 'I don't really need a hundred chefs.'

'You're not disappointed that your trip here was wasted?'

She looked up at him. 'Was it wasted, Steve?'

They never knew who made the first move, but she was in his arms, and he was holding her, and they were kissing.

'I've been wanting to do this since the first time I saw you.'

Julia shook her head. 'The first time you saw me, you told me to get out of town!'

He grinned. 'I did, didn't I? I don't ever want you to leave.'

And she thought of Sally's words. *Don't you know if the man proposed?* 'Is that a proposal?' Julia asked.

He held her tighter. 'You bet it is. Will you marry me?'

'Oh, yes!'

Kendall came out to the patio. She was holding a piece of paper in her hand.

'I . . . I just got this in the mail.'

Steve looked at her, worried. 'Not another . . . ?'

'No. I've been named Women's Wear Designer of the Year.'

Woody and Kendall and Julia and Steve were seated at the dining-room table. All around them workmen were moving chairs and couches, and carrying them off.

Steve turned to Woody. 'What are you going to do now?'

'I'm going back to Hobe Sound. First, I'm going to check in with Dr Tichner. Then a friend of mine has a string of ponies that I'm going to ride.'

Kendall looked at Julia. 'Are you going back to Kansas City?'

When I was a little girl, Julia thought, *I wished that someone would take me out of Kansas and bring me to a magical place where I would find my prince.* She took Steve's hand. 'No,' Julia said. 'I'm not going back to Kansas.'

They watched two men take down the huge portrait of Harry Stanford.

'I never did like that picture,' Woody said.